THE OXFORD CHEKHOV

VOLUME IV

STORIES

1888–1889

THE OXFORD

CHEKHOV

VOLUME IV

=====

STORIES

1888–1889

=====

Translated and edited by
RONALD HINGLEY

OXFORD UNIVERSITY PRESS
OXFORD   NEW YORK   TORONTO   MELBOURNE
1980

Oxford University Press, Walton Street, Oxford OX2 6DP

OXFORD LONDON GLASGOW
NEW YORK TORONTO MELBOURNE WELLINGTON
KUALA LUMPUR SINGAPORE JAKARTA HONG KONG TOKYO
DELHI BOMBAY CALCUTTA MADRAS KARACHI
NAIROBI DAR ES SALAAM CAPE TOWN

British Library Cataloguing in Publication Data

Chekhov, Anton Pavlovich
  The Oxford Chekhov.
  Vol. 4: Stories, 1888–1889
  I. Title II. Hingley, Ronald
  891.7′2′3   PG3456.AI   79–42960

  ISBN 0–19–211389–5

Printed in Great Britain by
Ebenezer Baylis and Son Ltd.,
The Trinity Press,
Worcester, and London

To the memory of

MAX HAYWARD

1924–1979

CONTENTS

PREFACE

THIS volume completes *The Oxford Chekhov*: the nine-volume edition of his drama and stories in English translation of which publication began in 1964.

That the work has proceeded so slowly is perhaps regrettable, but at least it has taken no longer to translate the consolidated stories of 1888–1904 (vols. iv–ix), than it took their author to write them, the period being fifteen years in each case. Such delay in producing *The Oxford Chekhov* was inevitable, as is now retrospectively clear, if editing and translating a single author was not to become the exclusive concern, over a period of many years, of such time and energies as university teaching duties left available. This edition has also had to take second place, often enough, to other researches, and to original writings that have made demands far more strenuous, including as they have so un-Chekhovian an excursion as a full-scale biography of Stalin and eleven other books. But it is unlikely that the quality of *The Oxford Chekhov* has suffered through such wilful self-indulgence. One returns to translation refreshed after endeavours of a different order, and I leave the assignment with regret, having enjoyed preparing Volume Four even more than working on its predecessors.

(a) Chekhov, Immature and Mature

The Steppe, which begins the present volume, is important for two reasons. First, it is a masterpiece in its own right, representing a signal advance on any of Chekhov's previous contributions to belles-lettres. And, secondly, it also happens to be his first work ever to have attained, or to have aimed at, publication in one of the 'Thick Journals': the serious literary reviews that had long been the traditional vehicle for works of Russian literature claiming more than ephemeral significance. The story's publication accordingly marked a notable promotion for its author, making the year 1888 the most important turning-point in his life and heralding the full flowering of his genius as a short-story writer.

During the sixteen years of life remaining to him after *The Steppe* Chekhov was to write far less intensively than in the preceding eight 'immature' years, achieving an output of fiction only one quarter as

great, if measured by quantity. But as the number of his stories, together with the bulk of his output, declined, so did the average length
of individual items considerably increase. It is these mature stories,
three score in all, that form the text of *The Oxford Chekhov*, vols.
iv–ix; to them have been added such manuscript fragments of fiction,
unpublished by the author and written during the same period, as have
survived.

   Though the distinction between a pre-*Steppe* 'immature' period and
a post-*Steppe* 'mature' period is helpful, and has been generally
accepted by scholars, it should not be taken to suggest that a miraculous
overnight transformation took place in Chekhov's approach to the
craft of fiction in early 1888. Far from it, for the later phase includes
some, though not very much, writing that falls well below his highest
level. Conversely, the earlier period includes not a few minor masterpieces, together with a host of more frivolous items; and there is also
ample material occupying every possible position between those two
poles. Such is the nature of Chekhov's prose fiction and sketches of
1880–7, comprising well over five hundred items, that there has never
been any serious prospect of its being rendered into English *in toto*.
The point is mentioned because I have been asked again and again,
during the course of my work, a very natural layman's question: was
it proposed to translate Chekhov's stories in their entirety? Of that,
as has often been explained to such friendly enquirers, there could
never have been any question, given the bulk of the early material
combined with the triviality of so much of it. The drama is a different
matter; and that, as stated above, is contained in full in this edition.[1]

(b) *Sources and Conventions*

   This volume contains Chekhov's entire output of fiction first published between March 1888 and 1 January 1889 inclusive. The translations are based on the Russian text and variants as they appear in
Sochineniya, vol. vii, of the Moscow-published *A. P. Chekhov: polnoye
sobraniye sochineny i pisem v tridsati tomakh (A. P. Chekhov: Complete
Collection of the Works and Letters in Thirty Volumes)*. This new edition
of Chekhov's works began to appear in 1974, its first volumes becoming
available in April 1975—too late to assist the preparation of the pre-
viously-published eight volumes of *The Oxford Chekhov*, which are

---

[1] For these technicalities, see Appendixes I and II ('The Shape of Chekhov's Work' and
'Chekhov in English') in Ronald Hingley, *A New Life of Anton Chekhov* (1976).

based on the less comprehensive and systematic (but very far from contemptible) twenty-volume Moscow edition '*Works, 1944–51*'. Of the thirty-volume edition, vols. i–xv of *Sochineniya (Works)* and vols. i–vi of *Pisma (Letters)* are in my possession at the time of writing. The edition is scheduled for completion in 1982 and is here referred to as '*Works, 1974–82*'. The formidable scholarship of this excellent new edition has considerably eased the editorial labours expended on the present volume. It has also led to an improvement of Chekhov's text in certain minor particulars, readings superior to those of *Works, 1944–51* having been established in a few places as the result of pains-taking collation.[1]

The treatment of proper names, of colloquial and uneducated Russian speech (particularly prevalent in *The Steppe*), of institutional and administrative terms, and of dates, follows the lines laid down in detail in the prefaces to volumes previously published: in the order iii, viii, ii, i, v, vi, ix and vii. The following place names, occurring in the text, appear to have been invented by Chekhov: Bakhchi-Salakh, Bolshaya Krepkaya, Demidovo, Dymkovo, Glinovo, Gruzovo, Kalachik, Kurikovo, Libedinskoye, Mankino, Rovnoye, Vukolovka, Yefremovshchina.

(c) Titles

Though the titles of the stories in the present volume have presented no great difficulties in translation, one of them differs from that given to the same story in my *New Life of Anton Chekhov*. What is there called *The Seizure* appears here as *A Nervous Breakdown*, which has been preferred on fuller consideration. Apologies are offered for any confusion that might occur.

(d) Errata

In *The Oxford Chekhov*, vol. vi, p. 307, the entry relating to pp. 133–4 should be emended by replacing 'weekly' with 'monthly'.

In *The Oxford Chekhov*, vol. vii, p. 231, the second paragraph of 'TEXT' should read as follows.

[1] For further comments—and some reservations—on *Works, 1974–82*, see Hingley, op. cit., pp. viii ff.

There are three previous recensions:

(a) that published in the magazine *Russkaya mysl* [*The Russian Idea*] of January 1894;

(b) that published in the selection of Chekhov's stories *Tales and Stories* (Moscow, 1894);

(c) that published in self-contained form by I. D. Sytin (Moscow, 1896).

In the same volume, p. 266, the entries on 'Presnya' and 'Razgulyay Square' should be emended to place them in the west and north-east of Moscow respectively.

In *The Oxford Chekhov*, vol. ix, p. 11, 'the ogre Marx' should read 'the ogre Marks', and alludes to Chekhov's publisher A. F. Marks, not to Karl Marx. I am most grateful to Mr. Patrick Miles of Gonville and Caius College, Cambridge, for his kindness in pointing this out.

(e) Acknowledgements

It is a pleasure to acknowledge once more my wife's expert editorial and secretarial help, which has sustained me throughout the preparation of this edition as a whole. Our son Peter kindly helped to unravel the mathematical phrase from Malinin and Burenin's text-book (page 214). I am also deeply grateful once again to Jeremy Newton (now Dr. Newton) for editorial help so generously given with this volume and also with earlier volumes during the years when he was writing his D. Phil. thesis under my supervision. May I also, on taking farewell of this edition, express my great debt to other scholars in the field, and not least to those of the Soviet Union? I should further like to emphasize my debt to Chekhov studies as they have flourished in the English-speaking world during the last thirty years. When my own first contribution to the subject (*Chekhov: A Biographical and Critical Study*) appeared in 1950 it was, so far as I know, only the fifth book wholly devoted to Chekhov (the sixth if we include Oliver Elton's Taylorian Lecture) to have been published in English. There are now at least thirty (see Bibliography, pp. 284–6), not to mention the numerous learned and critical articles that have appeared only in journals.

Baffled and fearful for humanity though Anton Pavlovich would be, could he be posthumously aware of the critical and academic industry sprouting about his name, there is still useful work to be done. For myself: *feci quod potui, faciant meliora potentes.*

RONALD HINGLEY

Frilford, Abingdon
1979

POSTSCRIPT

At the time when I delivered the typescript of this book to the publishers my friend and colleague Max Hayward was abroad and, so far as I knew, in good health; but he has since died—after a few months' illness, and in what had seemed his prime. This volume is, accordingly, dedicated with great sorrow to the memory of one to whom I had confidently expected to dedicate it in life.

Max's personality, scholarship and insights have made a profound impact on Russian studies in the West, and he has also commanded no little unofficial esteem in Russia itself. I count it a special privilege to have benefited, over a period of more than thirty years, from his friendship, his wit and his wise professional counsels.

INTRODUCTION

ANTON CHEKHOV's twenty-eighth birthday occurred (on 17 January 1888) when he was in the middle of writing *The Steppe* and had already been resident in the city of Moscow, Russia's former and future capital, for eight and a half years. By birth and upbringing he was a provincial, having spent his first two decades in Taganrog, the southern Russian port on the Sea of Azov. Here his father had kept a grocery shop until he was compelled to flee to Moscow to escape his creditors. He was followed shortly afterwards by his wife and youngest children; they left behind, for the moment, the sixteen-year-old boy who was to become the most famous member of their family.

Victim or beneficiary of a rigorous classical education at the Taganrog *gimnaziya* or high school, the young Chekhov completed his course of studies there in 1879, and then joined his family in Moscow. Five years later he graduated from Moscow University's medical faculty. By then he had already become *de facto* head of the impoverished Chekhov household, for his demoralized father could not obtain satisfactory employment, while neither of his two elder brothers would assume responsibility. Anton helped to support his mother, sister and two younger brothers by free-lance literary earnings that began in his first student year, greatly increasing after he had graduated. These resources were then supplemented by such medical fees as the young doctor received; but though he was to practise over many years, this activity was to be sporadic, erratically remunerated and—except for brief intervals—subordinated to literary work.

Little disposed to entertain serious literary ambitions in his early twenties, Chekhov began his writing career in 1880 as the author of comic trifles possessing little artistic merit: written for money, and published in the numerous humorous magazines of the period. He felt obliged to maximize these earnings by churning out more and more 'balderdash' (as he himself later called it), but a more serious sense of purpose was sometimes dimly discernible even at the outset, and asserted itself increasingly. The result was that Chekhov, chiefly popular in his early twenties as a lightweight humorist, had nevertheless already begun, during the two or three years preceding the publication of *The Steppe*, to attract the attention of Russian critics and littérateurs.

These figures from the literary world, including the elderly author
D. V. Grigorovich, detected in the young man greater potentialities
than he, by nature so delightfully modest, was inclined to discern in
himself.[1] He was urged to take his art more seriously, and to abandon
his usual practice of writing too hastily. The first fruit of this advice
was *The Steppe*. Incidentally, the unassuming Chekhov's eruption,
with this work, into one of the widely respected Thick Journals
(serious literary reviews) was not due to his own initiative; it came in
response to an invitation from the journal in question—the St. Petersburg *Severny vestnik (The Northern Herald)*.

From 1888 onwards Chekhov reserved most of his longer works for
the Thick Journals, but was far from publishing in them exclusively.
Of the items in the present volume, for example, only three (*The
Steppe, The Party* and *Lights*) achieved such publication, all in *Severny
vestnik*. Four shorter contributions (*An Awkward Business, The Beauties,
The Cobbler and the Devil, The Bet*) were brought out by St. Petersburg
newspapers to which Chekhov had already been contributing for
several years, while the remaining item (*A Nervous Breakdown*) was
consigned to a symposium commemorating a recently deceased
writer, Vsevolod Garshin.

Chekhov embarked on *The Steppe* in full consciousness of the need
to avoid the over-hasty methods of the past: he remarked, as work
was in progress, that he was writing 'slowly, as gourmets eat snipe'.
But though this indeed was to prove his most considered composition
to date, it was by no means composed as unhurriedly as its author
claimed. Creating an original work of over thirty thousand words in
little more than four weeks of concentrated activity, he attained, in
January 1888, a rate of output far greater than that achieved at any other
period of his life—not excepting the year 1886, his most prolific. As
for the post-*Steppe* period, it was to contain no comparable generative
spasm.

Though *The Steppe* begins the mature period, and does so impres-
sively, we shall search the later fiction in vain for close parallels. As
one of his longest stories it belongs, in a sense, to a small, select group
of half a dozen comparatively extensive works of later fiction, all
running to several score pages; the others are *The Duel* (1891), *Ward
Number Six* (1892), *An Anonymous Story* (1892), *Three Years* (1895)
and *My Life* (1896). From these successor-stories *The Steppe* differs,
however, in offering no plot, but merely—as its author several times

---

[1] See further, p. 239, below.

disparagingly commented—a string of episodes. Absence of plot, or the reduction of plot to a subordinate position, is of course a well established feature of Chekhov's work in general, and there are noteworthy shorter stories, such as *Peasants* and *The Student*, that resemble *The Steppe* in this respect. Never, however, did Chekhov extend plotlessness, within the compass of a single work, over such a large area of fiction as in *The Steppe*, which is also exceptional among his major works in containing so full and comprehensive an account of a journey.

Yet journeys, or at least short excursions of some kind, are a staple feature in the mature stories. Some of these are framed—as are some of the plays—between an arrival and a departure. Alternatively, an expedition occurs in the middle—a device for injecting dynamism into scenes that might otherwise seem too static? In any case it is characteristic of Chekhov that each story in this volume, except *The Bet*, should contain some trip or outing. The peculiarity of *The Steppe* is only that it is all travel: the characters are on the move from the first sentence of the story until it ends with the young hero, Yegorushka, finally settled in his new lodgings.

The Steppe is also unique among the mature works in having a child as its protagonist, and in presenting the world as seen through the eyes of this nine-year-old hero. True, Chekhov does not maintain his infant's-eye-view with total consistency, and has been criticized on that account.[1] Whether the alleged anomaly seriously detracts from the story readers of the present volume can best judge for themselves.

The Steppe further differs from Chekhov's other work in presenting such long and sustained descriptions of nature. Though he called them, in effect, 'purple passages' (*stikhi v proze*), they are one of the work's glories, and include the famous thunderstorm in Chapter VII. Effective nature descriptions had occurred in earlier works, and were to recur in Chekhov's mature period—where, however, the significant difference must be noted that nature never becomes so much of an end in itself as in *The Steppe*. Sketched in more economically, the later landscapes offer less of a pyrotechnic display, being more rigorously subordinated to the creation of a specific atmospheric context, and to the exposition of the characters' moods and temperaments.

[1] See further the discussion of Nilsson's and Chudakov's views in Jerome H. Katsell, 'Čexov's Step' Revisited', *Selected Papers in Slavic Literatures and Languages* (Ann Arbor, Mich., 1973).

That Chekhov devoted his first major work to a journey is less surprising when we remember that he himself had recently returned from a memorable journey, and in the very area of the Russian Empire portrayed in *The Steppe*. In April and May 1887 a six-week holiday had taken him back to his birthplace, Taganrog, where he had spent a fortnight renewing old friendships before touring the steppes of the Don and the eastern Ukraine. This rural backcloth reactivated different boyhood memories: of such characteristic features as the archaeologically significant *kurgany* (ancient burial mounds) and *kamennyye baby* (menhirs); the *buryan* (coarse grass and weeds); the oxen, the water-towers, the windmills, the kites, the Ukrainian peasants, the Cossacks and, above all, the immense expanse of the seemingly endless plains. Such was the steppe as its chronicler well remembered it from the summer holidays of his boyhood, for the Chekhovs had frequently camped in the prairies *en famille* on their way by horse- or ox-cart to visit Anton's paternal grandfather. He had been a serf in youth, and had become the manager of a large estate after purchasing his and his family's freedom some twenty years before the general Emancipation of the Serfs took place (in 1861).

During one of his steppe journeys the seventeen-year-old (or fifteen-year-old, according to conflicting evidence) Chekhov had fallen seriously ill with peritonitis, and had been cared for at a Jewish wayside inn which, as we know from his correspondence, became a model for the establishment of 'Moses' in the story.[1] That many another detail in *The Steppe* is lifted direct from the author's boyhood reminiscences may safely be assumed.

Another important story in the present volume, *Lights*, is also set in the south of the European part of the Russian Empire. The town in which Ananyev seduces the hapless Kitty in the story-within-the-story is characteristically termed 'N.' in the text. But it was expressly intended to be recognized, if only by inhabitants of the area, as Taganrog from references to 'the Quarantine': the local name for the Yelizaveta Park on the town's outskirts. The story's railway setting is also southern. But we cannot plot the topography of *Lights* or *The Steppe* in detail. In *The Steppe*, for example, the large city (where the action terminates) may indeed be identified as Rostov, and its river as the Don; but even so several of the associated features do not fit.[2] As is Chekhov's custom, the names of smaller locations are frequently given in these stories, but

[1] *Works*, 1974–82, *Pisma*, vol. ii. p. 195; p. 241, below.
[2] *Works*, 1974–82, *Sochineniya*, vol. vii, p. 629.

most of them are invented. Nor, to be over-rigorous, can we even determine whether parts of the action are set in southern European Russia in the strict sense, or trespass into what is now officially regarded as a separate country: the Ukraine.

Taganrog itself does not fall within the boundaries of the Ukrainian Soviet Socialist Republic as set up long after Chekhov's death. But the town's hinterland is Ukrainian in its western reaches. In any case Russians of Chekhov's period could enter or leave what is now the Ukraine without any sense of crossing a national frontier, and they would emphasize their insensitivity to Ukrainian national aspirations by calling themselves 'Great Russians' and the Ukrainians 'Little Russians'. Himself a Great Russian by birth and speech, Chekhov would yet whimsically remark, when addressing Muscovites and St. Petersburgers, that he was a 'lazy Ukrainian' (*lenivy khokhol*)—a description inaccurate in both its particulars. As this habit illustrates, he shared with other Great Russians a tendency to allude condescendingly to members of the sister-nationality, as it was later to be more formally recognized. An attempt has been made to convey such occasionally patronizing nuances in translation. For instance, in *The Party* Chekhov makes his 'Peter' refer to the Ukraine as *Khokhlandiya*, a comic sobriquet similar to 'Frogland' as an English way of alluding to France. *Khokhlandiya* is here translated (p. 132) as 'the good old South'; only with great difficulty has the temptation to render it 'dear old Bumpkinshire' been resisted. We are also reminded that Chekhov's first version of *The Party* included a comic Ukrainian nationalist whom he later deleted, and who had dreamed—poor fellow!—of liberating the Ukraine from the Russian yoke.[1] We also note that Chekhov causes his characters to speak a form of Ukrainian at two points of our text: the speech of the oats-buying customer on p. 58 and the whimsical remark made by the art student on p. 175.

The Steppe and *Lights* do not exhaust excursions into the southern landscape as represented in the present volume, for *The Beauties*, too, records what were presumably recollections of boyhood travels on Chekhov's native heath. Certainly the grandfather in the story was recognized as Chekhov's own paternal grandfather—and by another of his grandsons, Anton's cousin George Chekhov, who also noted that the coachman Karpo and the elderly Armenian were drawn from life.[2] To other southern references may be added Peter's brief

---

[1] See p. 258, below.
[2] See p. 249, below.

account (in *The Party*) of his excursion to his Khokhlandian property. However, the main action of *The Party* is set, as is that of *An Awkward Business* and much of Chekhov's other fiction, in an unidentified rural area of central European Russia. As for the remaining items in this volume, *A Nervous Breakdown* is one of the very few mature stories set in Moscow, long Chekhov's adoptive home and the city he knew best of all; the most notable other descriptions of Moscow to be found in later volumes are those in *Three Years* (1895) and (though the city is not named) *A Dreary Story* (1889). *The Cobbler and the Devil* may also be Muscovite in setting, while *The Bet* hovers in a limbo of its own: lacking Russian or other national references, it is cosmopolitan—and thus untypical of its author—in such flavour as it possesses.

Perhaps Chekhov thought the air of central Russia less salubrious than that of the south, for the three main central Russian stories of this volume (*An Awkward Business, The Party* and *A Nervous Breakdown*) are each an example of what critics have long called his 'clinical studies'. They are uncannily faithful portrayals by their doctor-author of mental or physical malaise or disease. As such they call to mind such earlier works as the story *Typhus* (1887) and the play *Ivanov* (first draft, 1887) as well as the two most splendid clinical studies of all: *A Dreary Story* (1889) and *Ward Number Six* (1892).

That Chekhov's range of social contexts is no less extensive than his geographical sweep the stories of this volume also illustrate. Late Imperial Russian society may be regarded, if we over-simplify, as divided into three main classes. There was, firstly, a privileged élite, including such overlapping categories as the gentry, landowners, members of the professions, the intelligentsia, army officers and civil servants above a certain rank. Secondly, and at the opposite end of the scale, came the lowest and least privileged order, that of the peasantry: a mass of preponderantly illiterate and superstitious muzhiks, comprising nearly a hundred million souls and some four-fifths of the population. But what of those Russians of intermediate social standing, who form our third category? We cannot assign them to a middle class in any Western sense without creating confusion, since they lacked comparable social cohesion, status, ambition and educational attainments. To this intermediate area belonged the country's parish clerks, minor court officials, hospital orderlies (*feldshera*) and many others: the NCOs of society, as it were.

It is such persons that the judge in *An Awkward Business* calls 'in-betweeners'—those who belong to neither of 'the two poles of society

... professional people and peasants' (p. 111). On the following page of the same story the doctor-protagonist picks up this idea, speaking with sympathy of those who are 'neither peasant nor master, neither fish nor fowl'. As we are reminded, the story describes a clash between this same unheroic hero (himself, as a doctor, a member of the élite) and his assistant, the obstreperous hospital orderly Smirnovsky: an 'in-between' man born (as some British hospital doctors of the 1970s might ruefully reflect) before his time. How heavily the scales were loaded against the in-between category in any clash with their social betters the story vividly demonstrates, since the doctor cannot help winning his conflict with the orderly, even though he himself does his best to lose it out of a wish to be fair.

In *A Nervous Breakdown*, too, Chekhov studies members, or at least future members, of the élite (his three students) against the background of Moscow's brothels, where the 'Madames', the staff and the prostitutes constitute another array of in-betweeners. Here, by contrast with *An Awkward Business*, the two sides are not in conflict; nor are they even effectively in communication in any sense except the coarsest.

To the intermediate area between élite and muzhiks also belonged Russia's clergy and her merchants—old-fashioned in their dress and customs, in which they resembled the peasants rather than the gentry, and often speaking a sub-standard variety of Russian more earthy than that of the upper crust. Here Father Christopher (in *The Steppe*) is typical of a certain vein in Chekhov in employing comic pseudo-erudite speech that only reveals his amiable lack of sophistication, making him amusing to the reader. Both the genial priest and his merchant friend (Kuzmichov) are on easy, friendly terms with the peasants of their entourage—who, however, never question their own subordinate role in the relationship.

In *The Party* we rise higher in the social scale (with the unimportant exception of *The Bet*) than anywhere else in the present volume. This is the world of rich landowners, lavish dowries, large estates and high officials. Moreover, despite some sympathy shown by the author for both his principal characters, the milieu is disparagingly portrayed, the story containing much effective social satire; and also, surely, an unobtrusive protest against the treatment of servants by masters who take them so much for granted.

As *The Party* reminds us more than any other item of 1888, Chekhov had, for several years and to an extent difficult to determine, come to accept the teachings of Leo Tolstoy, his famous older contemporary. Tolstoy was now chiefly active as a moralist, after first becoming popular as a panoramic novelist. As a Simple Lifer and, ultimately, a disciple of Rousseau, he rejected civilization's more complex and sophisticated trappings. So too does the Chekhov of *The Party* with his devastating exposé, recognizably Tolstoyan in so many details, of hypocritical upper-class social conventions. The influence may be detected in Olga's first encounter with her maid, the simple peasant woman Barbara, whom Chekhov began to portray as the repository of innate rustic wisdom—only to modify this approach, perhaps to the discriminating reader's relief, in the childbirth scene at the end. In the story as first published Tolstoyan elements were more prevalent than they remain in the canonical text, and included additional harping on the disagreeable sensation evoked in Olga by the back of her husband's neck. Chekhov's wise decision to prune this material was influenced by criticism from his editor, A. N. Pleshcheyev.[1]

Among the social evils pilloried by Tolstoy prostitution was numbered, and considerable Tolstoyan influence is detectable in *A Nervous Breakdown*—even though the sage himself made the splendidly bluff comment, after reading it, that the hero should have gone ahead and 'partaken of' the brothels' wares before theorizing on the subject.

Advocacy of the simple life and hostility to prostitution were only two facets in Tolstoy's restatement of the Christian ethic. Man should love his neighbour; abstain from swearing oaths and from extra-marital (or all) sexual intercourse; repent his misdeeds; not resist 'evil' by force; and so on. Of this Christian teaching *à la* Tolstoy traces may be found in *Lights*. Here Chekhov moralizes by implication against the practice of callously seducing young women; for this was the last form of 'loving one's neighbour' that Tolstoy wished to encourage. In its moralistic thrust *Lights* reminds us of earlier, still clumsier—but mercifully shorter—Tolstoy-inspired tales by Chekhov published in 1886-7: *The Beggar, An Encounter* and *In Trouble*. To the failure of *Lights* the didactic element contributes; but less so, perhaps, than the untypically 'wet' characterization, the excess of hedgerow philosophy, and the lugubrious angle of vision from which some of the narrative suffers.

Such are the defects of *Lights* that there is little temptation to challenge Chekhov's own decision to exclude it from the Collected Works that he published from 1899 onwards. However, unsatisfactory though it may be, there is no reason to regret its inclusion here—and

[1] *Works*, 1972-84, *Sochineniya*, vol. iii, p. 656.

for other reasons besides editorial consistency, which would have had to be paramount in any case. Even those who deny the story all merit—an excessively harsh judgement—may concede that the very failures of a genius can be instructive: one might arguably learn more about Dostoyevsky by studying his relatively feeble novel *A Raw Youth* than by brooding on some of his greater masterpieces.

Lights is also significant as reflecting, in the discussion of 'pessimism' and elsewhere, the spiritual crisis through which Chekhov himself was passing even as he embarked on literary maturity. It is in the years 1888–91 that we find him probing most anxiously into the riddle of existence, and incidentally seeking the answer to a closely related question: precisely what role were he and his writings to play in the unfolding human tragicomedy? Temporarily and erratically prompted, by the advice of critics and the example of the great Russian novelists who had preceded him, to attempt to change life—not merely to reflect it—through his fiction, he was now discovering by trial and error how ill-suited any overtly moralistic approach was to his art. To read *Lights* or his somewhat less unsuccessful play of the following year, *The Wood Demon*, with this in mind is to gain insights into a minor but revealing aspect of his art.

Like the earlier Tolstoyan works invoked above, *Lights* and *The Wood Demon* both incorporate well-meaning 'do-gooder' elements that Chekhov the artist had to eliminate from his system before he could give of his best; the theme was to reappear, briefly and for the last time, in the disastrous final pages of what is otherwise one of the finest stories: *The Duel*. More characteristic of the fully mature Chekhov was his expressed intention, should he decide to write a sequel to *The Steppe*, of going on to portray the unfortunate Yegorushka as an adult *bound to end up badly* one day in St. Petersburg or Moscow.[1] Here—not in the mawkish ruminations of Engineer Ananyev and the miserable Kitty—is the voice of the true, the anti-sentimental, Chekhov. To this we must add that Chekhov was, in life, a man of great kindliness and even, in the educational and medical work that he so often undertook without remuneration, what is ungenerously called a 'do-gooder'; nor, to put it mildly, did he possess the instincts of the compulsive seducer. But the demands of life and art are different. To 'do good', or at least to refrain from doing harm, to abstain from seduction (except possibly in its most discriminating form) must always be laudable in life. But to make art the vehicle for

[1] See p. 240, below.

advocating these admirable practices may, as Chekhov was quickly learning, prove downright calamitous.

We have not yet exhausted the Tolstoyan vein as it is to be traced in the present volume, since two minor stories, *The Cobbler and the Devil* and *The Bet*, both purvey yet another moral—the vanity of earthly goods—that the older writer was wont to incorporate in his moralizing fiction. Yet we note with satisfaction how ambivalent a disciple Chekhov was: the original published version of *The Bet* had contained a third chapter reversing (somewhat clumsily) the Tolstoyan moral of the first two; this material was simply jettisoned by Chekhov when he prepared the canonical text.[1]

As such ambivalence emphasizes, Chekhov never seems to have been a committed Tolstoyan. Rather was Tolstoy's doctrine, during the middle and late 1880s, a subject for sympathetic experiments which by no means always failed—as the stories of the present volume illustrate—but which succeeded roughly in proportion as the Tolstoyan ingredient was diluted. By 1894 Chekhov was ready to declare himself an outright opponent of the older writer's theories, despite his continuing admiration for Tolstoy the novelist and, after the two authors had had their first meeting in 1895, for Tolstoy the man.[2]

Chekhov's views on politics form another substratum in *The Party*, and emerge more openly if we take into account the particularly important variants in Appendix IV. As these remind us, the 1880s resembled the immediately preceding and following decade in presenting a conflict between Russia's conservatives and her liberals. The former were supporters, not always uncritical, of the Imperial Russian *status quo*; while the liberals were, naturally, advocates of reform. Given Russia's political and social system, reforms could only come about if sponsored by the ruling Autocrat, and so the arguments between conservatives and liberals tended to revolve around the specific beneficent measures already instituted by the Emperor Alexander II, who had ruled from 1855 to 1881. They had included, besides the most celebrated enactment of all (the Emancipation of the Serfs in 1861), the establishment of a new judicial structure, and of a new system of local government. In the 1880s, however, under the somewhat reactionary regime of Alexander III, these new institutions were hampered and deprived of some of their powers. To reinstate and

---

[1] For the translation of the rejected Chapter III, see pp. 273-4, below.
[2] For Tolstoy's influence, see further in Hingley, *A New Life of Anton Chekhov*, as indexed under 'Tolstoy'.

develop them was the aim of the liberals among Chekhov's contemporaries, whereas conservatives were apt to deride them and to oppose their further evolution on increasingly democratic lines. Another point at issue, as *The Party* reminds us, was higher education for women—strenuously advocated by liberals and deplored or thwarted by conservatives. On all these points several characters in *The Party* are seen to be at odds, particularly if we take the variant material into account.

What part did Chekhov himself play in the conflict? As anyone familiar with his nature could guess, he stood outside the warring ranks. And yet, characteristically detached though he might seem, he was far from indifferent. Rarely expressing strong political opinions of his own, he was apt to excoriate others who did so, from whatever viewpoint. His inclination was to call down a plague on all their houses. Hostile to conservative snobbery and selfishness, he was even more incensed by the officiousness, complacency and pretensions of the liberals of his day, and especially by their intolerance of anyone who would not uncritically accept and mindlessly parrot their pre-packaged, patronizing, self-congratulatory received opinions. In thus summarizing Chekhov's views on this matter we are expressing ourselves no more intemperately than the master himself did on frequent occasions.[1]

So much for conservatives and liberals. But what of Chekhov's attitude to the Russian revolutionary movement? So quiescent and subterranean was this in his day that he rarely found occasion to comment on it at all. An exception is his observation on Dymov, a minor but significant figure in *The Steppe*. Dymov, says Chekhov, is a mischief-maker created 'expressly for revolution'. However, 'there will never be a Russian revolution, and Dymov will end up taking to the bottle, or else in gaol. He's a superfluous man.'[2]

Chekhov has pithily expressed his own philosophy of politics and literature in a letter to Pleshcheyev of 4 October 1888. 'I fear those who read between my lines looking for messages, and are determined to see me as a liberal or a conservative. I am not a liberal. I am not a conservative. I am not an advocate of moderate reform. I am not a monk. Nor am I committed to non-commitment. I should like to be a free artist, that's all.' But how typical of Chekhov to dissociate himself so strongly from the purveyal of fictional 'messages' in the very

---

[1] See further, Hingley, op. cit., pp. 97 and 179.
[2] Letter to A. N. Pleshcheyev, 9 Feb. 1888; see p. 241, below.

year when, as our previous argument shows, he was energetically engaged—however sporadically—in propagating them! As this point illustrates, his attitude was less consistent than his occasional programmatic pronouncements would suggest.[1]

Since the 1880s humanity has, alas, become increasingly politicized, and not least in Russia itself. One suspects that those who deplore this development, and who are no more able to halt it than was Chekhov, may be prominent among the innumerable readers and theatregoers on whom his works began exercising their fascination long before they were translated for the present edition.

May this bond, if it is one, help to explain why so many of Chekhov's admirers, in his own and other countries, feel that they recognize in him so close a kindred spirit?

[1] See further the extracts from his correspondence on pp. 252–3, below.

THE STEPPE

THE STORY OF A JOURNEY

*[Степь
(История одной поездки)]*

(1888)

THE STORY OF A JOURNEY

I

On an early July morning a dilapidated springless carriage—one of those antediluvian britzkas now used in Russia only by merchants' clerks, cattle-dealers and poor priests—drove out of N., a sizeable town in Z. County, and thundered along the post road. It rumbled and squeaked at the slightest movement, to the doleful accompaniment of a pail tied to the back-board. These sounds alone, and the wretched leather tatters flapping on the peeling chassis, showed just how decrepit, how fit for the scrap heap it was.

Two residents of N. occupied the britzka. One was Ivan Kuzmichov, a clean-shaven, bespectacled merchant in a straw hat, who looked more like a civil servant than a trader. The other was Father Christopher Siriysky, principal priest at St. Nicholas's Church—a short, long-haired old man wearing a grey canvas caftan, a broad-brimmed top hat and a brightly embroidered belt. The former was absorbed in his thoughts, and kept tossing his head to keep himself awake. On his face a habitual businesslike reserve was in conflict with the cheerfulness of one who has just said good-bye to his family and had a drop to drink. The other man gazed wonderingly at God's world with moist eyes and a smile so broad that it even seemed to take in his hat brim. His face was red, as if from cold. Both Kuzmichov and Father Christopher were on their way to sell wool. They had just been indulging in cream doughnuts while taking farewell of their households, and they had had a drink despite the early hour. Both were in excellent humour.

Besides the two already described, and the coachman Deniska tirelessly whipping his pair of frisky bay horses, the carriage had another occupant: a boy of nine with a sunburnt, tear-stained face. This was Kuzmichov's nephew Yegorushka. With his uncle's permission and Father Christopher's blessing he was on his way to a school of the type intended for gentlemen's sons. His mother Olga—Kuzmichov's sister and widow of a minor official—adored educated people and refined society, and she had begged her brother to take the boy on his wool-selling trip and deliver him to this institution. Understanding neither where he was going nor why, the boy sat on the box by Deniska's side, holding the man's elbow to stop himself falling, and bobbing about like a kettle on the hob. The swift pace made his red shirt balloon at the back, and his new coachman-style hat with the peacock feather kept slipping to the back of his neck. He considered himself extremely unfortunate, and was near to tears.

As they drove past the prison Yegorushka looked at the sentries slowly pacing near the high white wall, at the small barred windows, at the cross glittering on the roof, and remembered the day of Our Lady of Kazan, a week earlier, when he and his mother had attended the celebrations at the prison church. Before that he had visited the gaol at Easter with Deniska and Lyudmila the cook, taking Easter cakes, Easter eggs, pies and roast beef. The convicts had thanked them and crossed themselves, and one had given the boy some tin studs of his own manufacture.

While the boy gazed at the familiar sights the hateful carriage raced on and left them all behind. Beyond the prison black, smoke-stained forges flashed past, and then the tranquil green cemetery with the stone wall round it. From behind the wall cheerful white crosses and tombstones peeped out, nestling in the foliage of cherry trees and seen as white patches from a distance. At blossom time, Yegorushka remembered, the white patches mingled with the cherry blooms in a sea of white, and when the cherries had ripened the white tombs and crosses were crimson-spotted, as if with blood. Under the cherries behind the wall the boy's father and his grandmother Zinaida slept day and night. When Grandmother had died she had been put in a long, narrow coffin, and five-copeck pieces had been placed on her eyes, which would not stay shut. Before dying she had been alive, and she had brought him soft poppy-seed bun rings from the market, but now she just slept and slept.

Beyond the cemetery were the smoking brickyards. From long thatched roofs, huddling close to the ground, great puffs of thick black smoke rose and floated lazily upwards. The sky above the brickyards and cemetery was dark, and the great shadows of the smoke clouds crept over the fields and across the road. In the smoke near the roofs moved people and horses covered with red dust.

With the brickyards the town ended and open country began. Yegorushka took a last look back at the town, pressed his face against Deniska's elbow and wept bitterly.

'What, still howling, you old cry-baby?' asked Kuzmichov. 'Still snivelling, you mother's darling. If you don't want to come, stay behind—nobody's forcing you.'

'Never mind, Yegorushka, old son, it's all right,' Father Christopher rapidly muttered. 'Never mind, my boy. Call on God, for you seek not evil but good. Learning is light, they say, and ignorance is darkness. Verily it is so.'

'Do you want to go back?' Kuzmichov asked.

'Yes, I d-do,' sobbed the boy.

'Then you may as well. There's no point in your coming anyway— it's a complete fool's errand.'

'Never mind, son,' Father Christopher went on. 'Call on God. Lomonosov once travelled just like this with the fishermen, and he became famous throughout Europe. Learning conjoined with faith yields fruit pleasing to God. What does the prayer say? "For the glory of the Creator, for our parents' comfort, for the benefit of church and country." That's the way of it.'

'There's various kinds of benefit.' Kuzmichov lit a cheap cigar. 'There's some study for twenty years, and all to no purpose.'

'That does happen.'

'Some benefit from book-learning, others just get their brains addled. She has no sense, my sister—wants to be like gentlefolk, she does, and make a scholar of the boy. And she can't see that I could set him up for life, doing the business I do. The point is that if everyone becomes a scholar and gentleman there won't be anyone to trade and sow crops. We'll all starve.'

'But if everyone trades and sows crops there won't be anyone to master learning.'

Thinking they had each said something weighty and cogent, Kuzmichov and Father Christopher assumed a serious air and coughed simultaneously. Having heard their talk but making nothing of it, Deniska tossed his head, sat up and whipped both bays. Silence followed.

By now a plain—broad, boundless, girdled by a chain of hills—lay stretched before the travellers' eyes. Huddling together and glancing out from behind one another, the hills merged into rising ground extending to the very horizon on the right of the road, and disappearing into the lilac-hued far distance. On and on you travel, but where it all begins and where it ends you just cannot make out. Behind them the sun was already peeping out over the town and had quietly, unfussily set about its work. First, far ahead where the sky met the earth—near some ancient burial mounds and a windmill resembling from afar a tiny man waving his arms—a broad, bright yellow band crept over the ground. Then, a minute later, another bright strip appeared a little nearer, crawled to the right and clasped the hills. Something warm touched Yegorushka's back as a stripe of light stole up behind him and darted over britzka and horses, soaring to meet other bands until the whole wide prairie suddenly flung off the penumbra of dawn, smiled and sparkled with dew.

Mown rye, coarse steppe grass, milkwort, wild hemp—all that the heat had browned, everything reddish and half dead—was now drenched in dew and caressed by the sun, and was reviving to bloom again. Arctic petrels swooped over the road with happy cries, gophers called to each other in the grass, and from somewhere far to the left came the plaint of lapwings. Scared by the carriage, a covey of partridges sprang up and flew off to the hills, softly trilling. Grasshoppers, cicadas, field crickets and mole crickets fiddled their squeaking, monotonous tunes in the grass.

But time passed, the dew evaporated, the air grew still and the disillusioned steppe assumed its jaded July aspect. The grass drooped, the life went out of everything. The sunburnt hills, brown-green and—in the distance—mauvish, with their calm, pastel shades, the plain, the misty horizon, the sky arching overhead and appearing so awesomely deep and transparent here in the steppe, where there are no woods or high hills—it all seemed boundless, now, and numb with misery.

How sultry and forlorn! As the carriage raced on Yegorushka saw only the same old sky, plain, hills. The music in the grass was hushed, the petrels had flown away, the partridges had vanished. Over the faded grass rooks idly hovered—all alike, making the steppe more monotonous still.

A kite skimmed the earth with even sweep of wings, suddenly paused in mid-air, as if pondering the tedium of existence, then fluttered its wings and sped over the prairie like an arrow. Why did it fly? What did it want? No one knew, and far away the mill flapped its sails.

Now and then, to break the monotony, came the glimpse of a white skull or boulder in the tall grass. A grey menhir loomed for a moment, or a parched willow with a blue crow on its top branch. A gopher ran across the road, and once again grass, hills and rooks flitted before the eyes.

But now, thank God, a wagon approached—loaded with sheaves of corn, with a peasant girl lying on top. Sleepy, exhausted by the heat, she lifted her head to gaze at the travellers. Deniska gaped at her, the bays craned at the sheaves, the carriage screeched as it kissed the wagon, and the prickly ears of corn brushed Father Christopher's hat.

'Look where you're going, dumpling!' shouted Deniska. 'Hey, balloon-face! Stung by a bumble bee, was you?'

The girl smiled sleepily, moved her lips and lay back again. Then a lone poplar appeared on a hill. Who planted it? Why was it there? God alone knows. It was hard to tear one's eyes away from the graceful form and green drapery. Was that beautiful object happy? There is summer's heat, there are winter's frosts and blizzards, and there are terrible autumnal nights when you see nothing but blackness, and hear only the wayward, furiously howling wind. Worst of all, you are alone, alone, alone, all your life. Beyond the poplar bands of wheat stretched their bright yellow carpet from the roadside to the top of the hill. The corn had already been cut and gathered into stooks on the hill, but at the bottom they were still reaping. Six reapers swung their scythes side by side, and the scythes cheerfully glittered, shrieking in shrill unison. The movements of the women binding the sheaves, the reapers' faces, the gleaming scythes—all showed how burning and stifling the heat was. A black dog, its tongue hanging out, ran from the reapers towards the carriage, probably meaning to bark, but stopped half way and cast a bored glance at Deniska, who shook his whip at it. It was too hot for barking. A woman straightened up, clutched her tormented back with both hands and followed Yegorushka's red shirt with her eyes. Pleased by the colour or remembering her own children, she stood motionless for a while, staring after him.

But then, after the glimpse of wheat, came another expanse of scorched plain, burnt hills, sultry sky. Again a kite hovered over the ground. Far away the mill still whirled its sails, still resembling a tiny man waving his arms. What a tedious sight! It seemed that they would never reach it, that it was running away from the carriage.

Father Christopher and Kuzmichov said nothing. Deniska whipped up his horses and shouted. Yegorushka had stopped crying and gazed listlessly about him. The heat, the tedium of the prairie had exhausted him. He seemed to have been travelling and bobbing up and down with the sun baking his back for a very long time. They had not done seven miles yet, but he already felt that it was time for a rest. The cheerful expression had gradually disappeared from his uncle's face, leaving only the businesslike reserve that lends an implacably inquisitorial air to a gaunt, clean-shaven face—especially if bespectacled, and with nose and temples covered with dust. But Father Christopher still gazed admiringly at God's world and smiled. Not speaking, he was thinking some serene, cheerful thought, and a kindly, good-humoured smile was stamped on his face. It also looked as if that serene, cheerful thought had been stamped on his brain by the heat.

'Well, Deniska, shall we overtake the wagons soon?' asked Kuzmichov.

Deniska looked at the sky, rose in his seat and whipped his horses. 'By nightfall, God willing.'

Barks were heard, and half a dozen huge prairie sheepdogs suddenly pounced at the carriage with ferocious howls as if from ambush. Extremely vicious, red-eyed with malice, their shaggy muzzles resembling enormous spiders, they surrounded the britzka and set up a hoarse bellow, jealously jostling each other, imbued with utter loathing, and seeming ready to rend horses, vehicle and people asunder. Deniska, who liked teasing and whipping, and who was glad of his opportunity, bent over with an expression of unholy glee, and lashed one dog with his whip. The dogs growled more loudly than ever and the horses rushed on. Hardly able to keep his seat, Yegorushka realized, as he looked at the dogs' eyes and teeth, that he would be torn to pieces at once if he fell off. Yet he felt no fear, and looked on with malicious glee like Deniska, sorry to have no whip in his hands.

The carriage drew level with a drove of sheep.

'Stop!' shouted Kuzmichov. 'Pull up! Whoa!'

Deniska flung his whole body back and pulled the horses up. The carriage stopped.

'Come here, man!' shouted Kuzmichov to the drover. 'And call your bloody dogs off!'

The old drover, ragged and barefoot, in a warm cap with a dirty sack on his hip and a long crook—a regular Old Testament figure—called off the dogs, doffed his cap and came up to the carriage. At the other end of the flock another no less patriarchial figure stood motionless, staring unconcernedly at the travellers.

'Whose sheep are these?' Kuzmichov asked.

'Varlamov's,' the old man answered loudly.

'Varlamov's,' repeated the shepherd at the other end of the flock.

'Now, did Varlamov pass this way yesterday or didn't he?'

'No, sir. 'Twas his bailiff as came past, and that's a fact.'

'Drive on!'

The carriage rolled on and the drovers were left behind with their vicious dogs. Yegorushka looked glumly ahead at the mauve horizon, and he now began to feel that the whirling windmill was coming nearer. It grew bigger and bigger until it was quite large and its two sails were clearly distinguishable. One was old and patched, but the other had been made with new wood only recently, and shone in the sun.

The carriage drove straight on while the windmill for some reason began moving to the left. On and on they travelled, and it kept moving to the left while remaining in view.

'A fine windmill Boltva has made for his son,' remarked Deniska. 'But why can't we see his farm?'

'It's over there, beyond the dip.'

Soon Boltva's farm did indeed appear, but the windmill still failed to retreat. Keeping pace with them, it watched Yegorushka, waving its shiny sail like some wizard of the steppes.

II

Towards midday the britzka turned off the road to the right, went on a little at walking pace, then stopped. Yegorushka heard a quiet, a most delectable gurgling, and felt a different air brush his face with its cool velvety touch. From the hill, that nature had glued together out of monstrous boulders, a thin stream of water jetted through a little pipe of hemlock wood put in by some unknown benefactor. It hit the ground, and—limpid, sparkling merrily in the sun, quietly murmuring as if fancying itself a mighty, turbulent torrent—swiftly ran away to the left. Not far from the hill the little brook broadened into a pool. The hot rays and parched soil thirstily drank it in, sapping its strength. But it must have merged with another similar stream a little further on, because dense, green, lush sedge was visible along its course about a hundred yards from the hill. As the carriage approached three snipe flew up from there with a cry.

The travellers settled down by the brook to rest and feed the horses. Kuzmichov, Father Christopher and Yegorushka sat on a felt rug in the sparse shadow cast by the britzka and the unharnessed horses, and began eating. After Father Christopher had drunk some water and eaten a hard-boiled egg the serene, cheerful thought—stamped on his brain by the heat—craved utterance. He looked at Yegorushka affectionately and chewed.

'I myself have studied, son,' he began. 'From my earliest years God imbued me with sense and understanding. And so, unlike other boys, I was rejoicing my parents and teachers by my comprehension when

I was only your age. Before I was fifteen I could speak Latin, and write Latin verse, as well as Russian. I remember being crozier-bearer to Bishop Christopher. After service one day, as I recall, on the saint's day of our most pious Sovereign Alexander the First of blessed memory, he unrobed in the chancel, looked at me kindly and asked: *"Puer bone, quam appellaris?"* And I answered: *"Christophorus sum."* And he said: *"Ergo connominati sumus"*—we were namesakes, that is. Then he asked me in Latin whose son I was. I answered, also in Latin, that my father was Deacon Siriysky of Lebedinskoye village. Noting the celerity and clarity of my answers, the Bishop blessed me, saying: "Write and tell your father that I shall not forget him and shall keep you in mind." Hearing this exchange in Latin, the priests and fathers in the chancel were also no little amazed, and each expressed his pleasure by praising me. Before I had grown whiskers, my boy, I could read Latin, Greek and French. I knew philosophy, mathematics, secular history and all branches of learning. God gave me a wonderful memory. Time was, if I'd read something once or twice I could remember it by heart. My preceptors and patrons were amazed, expecting me to become a great scholar and a church luminary. I did think of going to Kiev to continue my studies, but my parents disapproved. "You'll be studying all your life," said my father. "We'll never see the end of it." Hearing these words, I gave up learning and took an appointment. Aye, I never became a scholar, of course, but at least I didn't disobey my parents. I was a comfort to them in their old age, gave them a decent funeral. Obedience is more blessed than fasting and prayer.'

'I bet you've forgotten all you ever learnt,' Kuzmichov remarked.

'Of course I have. I'm past seventy now, praise be. I can still remember a scrap or two of philosophy and rhetoric, but languages and mathematics—I've quite forgotten them.'

Father Christopher frowned and pondered. 'What is a being?' he asked in a low voice. 'A being is an integral entity sufficient unto itself.' He flexed his neck and laughed delightedly. 'Food for the soul,' said he. 'Verily, matter nourisheth the flesh and spiritual sustenance the soul.'

'Learning's all very well,' sighed Kuzmichov. 'But if we don't overtake Varlamov we'll be taught a lesson we'll never forget.'

'He's not a needle in a haystack. We'll find him—he's knocking around in the area.'

The same three snipe flew over the sedge, their squeaks betraying alarm and vexation at being driven off the brook. The horses steadily munched and whinnied. Deniska attended them, trying to demonstrate his utter indifference to the cucumbers, pies and eggs that his masters were eating by plunging into the slaughter of the flies and horse-flies clinging to the animals' bellies and backs. Uttering a peculiar, venomously exultant guttural sound, he swatted his victims with gusto, grunting with annoyance when he missed and following each lucky fly that escaped death with his eyes.

'Deniska, what are you up to? Come and eat.' Kuzmichov sighed deeply—a sign that he was replete.

Deniska approached the mat diffidently and picked out five large yellow cucumbers—what they called 'yolkies'—not venturing to choose smaller, fresher specimens. He then took two black, cracked hard-boiled eggs, and—hesitantly, as if afraid of someone slapping his outstretched hand—touched a pie with his finger.

'Go on, help yourself,' urged Kuzmichov.

Deniska seized the pie decisively, went off far to one side and sat on the ground, his back to the carriage. There ensued a chewing noise so loud that even the horses turned round and looked at Deniska suspiciously.

After his meal Kuzmichov got a bag containing something out of the carriage. 'I'm going to sleep,' he told Yegorushka. 'You mind no one takes this bag from under my head.'

Father Christopher removed his cassock, belt and caftan, seeing which Yegorushka was downright astounded. That priests wore trousers he had had no inkling, and Father Christopher was wearing real canvas trousers tucked into his high boots, and a short cotton jacket. With his long hair and beard, and in this costume so unsuited to his calling, he looked to the boy very like Robinson Crusoe. Having disrobed, Father Christopher and Kuzmichov lay in the shade under the britzka facing each other, and closed their eyes. Deniska, who had finished chewing, stretched out belly upwards in the sun's heat and also closed his eyes. 'Make sure no one steals the horses,' he told Yegorushka and fell asleep at once.

Quietness ensued. Nothing was heard but the horses' whinnying and chewing, and some snores from the sleepers. A little way off a single lapwing wailed, and there was an occasional squeak from the three snipe, which had flown up to see if the uninvited guests had left. The brook softly lisped and gurgled, but none of these sounds trespassed on the silence or stirred the sluggish air. Far from it, they only made nature drowsier still.

Panting in the heat, which was particularly oppressive after the meal, Yegorushka ran to the sedge and surveyed the locality from there. He saw exactly what he had seen that morning: plain, hills, sky, purple horizons. But the hills were nearer and there was no windmill, for that had been left far behind. From behind the rocky hill where the stream flowed another—smoother and broader—hill loomed, with a small hamlet of five or six homesteads clinging to it. Near the huts neither people, trees nor shadows could be seen—the settlement might have choked in the hot air and withered away. To pass the time the boy caught a grasshopper in the herbage, held it to his ear in his closed hand, and listened to its pizzicato for some time. Bored with that music, he chased a flock of yellow butterflies flying up to the sedge to drink, and somehow found himself near the carriage again. His uncle and Father Christopher were fast asleep—a sleep that was sure to last two or three hours, to let the horses rest. How was the boy to get through all that time? Where could he escape the heat? No easy problem, that.

Without thinking, Yegorushka put his lips under the jet running out of the pipe. His mouth felt cold, and there was a smell of hemlock. He drank thirstily at first, and then forced himself to go on till the sharp cold had spread from his mouth throughout his body and water had spilt on his shirt. Then he went to the carriage and looked at the sleepers. His uncle's face still expressed businesslike reserve. Obsessed with his business, Kuzmichov was always brooding on it—even in his sleep, and in church during the anthem 'And the Cherubims'. Not for a minute could he forget it, and at this moment he was probably dreaming of bales of wool, wagons, prices and Varlamov. But Father Christopher—gentle, light-hearted, always ready to laugh—had never in his life known anything capable of taking a stranglehold on his entire being. In the many deals he had embarked on in his time he had been less attracted by the business side than by the bustle and contact with other people that are part of any undertaking. For instance, what interested him about their present journey was less the wool, Varlamov and the prices than the long road, conversation on the way, sleeping under the carriage and eating at the wrong times. From his expression he must be dreaming of Bishop Christopher, the Latin conversation, his wife, cream doughnuts and everything that Kuzmichov could not possibly be dreaming of.

Watching their sleepy faces, the boy unexpectedly heard someone quietly singing. It was a woman's voice—not near, but just where it came from and from what direction it was hard to tell. Despondent, dirgelike, scarcely audible, the quiet song droned on. Now it came from the right, now from the left, now from above, now from under-ground, as if an invisible spirit floated, chanting, above the steppe. Looking around him, Yegorushka could not tell where the strange song originated, but as his ears became attuned he fancied that the grass must be the singer. Half dead, already perished, it was trying—wordlessly, but plaintively and earnestly—to plead that it was guilty of no crime and that it was unfair for the sun to scorch it. It asserted the passionate love of life of a creature still young and, but for the heat and drought, potentially beautiful. Guiltless, it yet begged forgiveness, swearing that it was suffering agonies of grief and self-pity.

Yegorushka listened for a while, until the lugubrious chant began to make the air seem more suffocating, hot and stagnant than ever. To drown the sound he hummed to himself and ran to the sedge, trying to bring his feet down noisily. Then he looked all around and found the singer. Near the last hut in the hamlet stood a woman in a short petti-coat, long-legged like a heron. She was sowing, and white dust floated languidly down the hillock from her sieve. That she was the singer was now patently obvious. Two paces from her a small bareheaded boy, wearing just a smock, stood stock-still. As if bewitched by the song, he remained immobile, looking downhill—probably at Yego-rushka's red shirt.

The singing ceased. Yegorushka made his way back to the carriage and, having nothing else to do, started playing with the jet of water again.

Once again the song droned out. It was the same long-legged woman in the hamlet over the hill. Suddenly Yegorushka felt bored again, left the water-pipe and cast his eyes aloft. What he saw was so unexpected that he was a little frightened. On one of the large, awkward boulders above his head stood a chubby little boy wearing just a smock. It was the same boy—with large, protruding stomach and thin legs—who had been with the woman. Open-mouthed, unblinking, with a blank stare and in some fear—as if contemplating a ghost—he inspected Yegorushka's crimson shirt and the britzka. The red colour attracted and beguiled him, while the carriage and the men asleep under it stirred his curiosity. Perhaps he himself had not been aware that the agreeable red colour and his own inquisitiveness had lured him down from the hamlet, and by now he was probably amazed at his own boldness. Yegorushka and he surveyed each other for a while, neither speaking, and both feeling slight embarrassment.

'What's your name?' Yegorushka asked, after a long silence.

The stranger's cheeks puffed out still more. He braced his back against the rock, opened his eyes wide, moved his lips and answered in a husky bass. 'Titus.'

That was all the boys said to each other. After more silence the mysterious Titus lifted one foot, found a heelhold and climbed up the boulder backwards without taking his eyes off Yegorushka. Backing away, while staring at Yegorushka as if afraid of being hit from behind, he clambered on to the next rock and so made his way up till he vanished altogether behind a crest.

Watching him out of sight, Yegorushka clasped his knees and bowed forward. The hot rays burnt the back of his head, neck and spine. The melancholy song now died away, now floated again in the still, stifling air, the stream gurgled monotonously, the horses munched, and time seemed to drag on for ever, as if it too had stagnated and congealed. A hundred years might have passed since morning. Perhaps God wanted Yegorushka, the carriage and the horses to come to a standstill, turn to stone like the hills, and stay in the same place for ever?

The boy raised his head and looked ahead with glazed eyes. The distant, lilac-coloured background, hitherto motionless, lurched and soared off, together with the sky, into the even further beyond, dragging the brown grass and sedge behind it, while Yegorushka hurtled after the retreating perspective with phenomenal speed. An unknown force silently drew him along with the heat and the wearisome song careering in his wake. He bowed his head, closing his eyes.

Deniska was the first to awake. Something must have bitten him, for he jumped up and quickly scratched his shoulder with a 'damn you, blast you and perdition take you!'

Then he went over to the brook, drank and slowly washed. His snorting and splashing roused Yegorushka from oblivion. The boy looked at the man's wet face, covered with drops and large freckles that created a mottled effect. 'Shall we be leaving soon?' he asked.

Deniska checked the sun's height. 'Soon, that's for sure.' He dried himself on his shirt tail, assumed an air of the utmost gravity and began hopping on one foot. 'Come on, hop! Race you to the sedge!'

Yegorushka was drowsy and exhausted by the heat, but hopped after him all the same. Deniska was about twenty, a working coachman, and was going to be married. But he was still a boy at heart. He was fond of flying kites, of racing pigeons, of playing knucklebones and tag, and he was always taking part in children's games and quarrels. His employers only had to go away or fall asleep for him to start hopping, throwing stones and similar antics. Noting his genuine enthusiasm when cavorting in juvenile company, adults found it hard not to remark what a 'great oaf' he was. But children saw nothing odd in their domain being invaded by a large coachman—let him play so long as he wasn't too rough. Similarly, small dogs see nothing strange in an unsophisticated big dog intruding on them and playing with them.

Deniska overtook Yegorushka, obviously delighted to do so. He winked, and—to show that he could hop any distance on one foot—proposed that the boy should hop along the road with him, and then back to the carriage without stopping. This proposal Yegorushka declined, being out of breath and exhausted.

Suddenly assuming an air even graver than that which he wore when Kuzmichov rebuked him or threatened him with his stick, Deniska cocked his ears and dropped quietly on one knee. A stern and fearful expression, as of someone hearing heretical talk, appeared on his face, and he fixed his eyes on one spot, slowly raised his hand—holding it like a scoop—and then suddenly flopped on his stomach and slapped the scoop on the grass.

'Got him!' he hoarsely gloated, rising to his feet and presenting a big grasshopper to the boy's gaze.

Thinking to please the grasshopper, Yegorushka and Deniska stroked its broad green back with their fingers and touched its whiskers. Then Deniska caught a fat, blood-gorged fly and offered it to the grasshopper. With sublime nonchalance—as if it were an old friend of Deniska's—the creature moved its large, visor-shaped jaws and bit off the fly's belly. They let the grasshopper go, and it flashed the pink lining of its wings, landed on the grass, and at once resumed trilling. They let the fly go too. It preened its wings and flew off to the horses minus a stomach.

From beneath the carriage a deep sigh proceeded—Kuzmichov had woken up. He quickly raised his head, cast a troubled look into the distance, a look that slid unconcernedly past Yegorushka and Deniska and showed that his waking thoughts had been of wool and Varlamov.

'Father Christopher, get up—time to start,' he said anxiously. 'We've slept enough, we'll have missed our deal as it is. Hitch up the horses, Deniska.'

Father Christopher woke up, smiling the smile with which he had dozed off. Sleep had so creased and wrinkled his face that it seemed half its usual size. He washed, dressed, unhurriedly took a small, greasy psalter out of his pocket, faced east and began a whispered recital, crossing himself.

'Time to be off, Father Christopher,' Kuzmichov reproached him. 'The horses are ready. Now, look here——'

'Just a minute,' muttered Father Christopher. 'Must read my doxology. Didn't do it earlier.'

'Your doxology can wait.'

'I have to do one section every day, Kuzmichov, I really do.'

'God would forgive you.'

For a full quarter of an hour Father Christopher stood stock-still, facing east and moving his lips, while Kuzmichov looked at him almost with hatred, his shoulders fidgeting impatiently. He was particularly enraged when—after each 'Glory!'—Father Christopher took a deep breath, quickly crossed himself and thrice intoned his 'Halleluja, halleluja, halleluja, glory be to Thee, O Lord!' in a deliberately loud voice so that the others had to cross themselves too.

At last he smiled, looked at the sky, put the psalter in his pocket, and said 'Finis'.

A minute later the britzka was under way. It might have been going back instead of pressing on, for the travellers saw the same scene as before noon. The hills still swam in the lilac-hued distance and there still seemed to be no end to them. High weeds and boulders flitted past and strips of stubble sailed by, while the same rooks, and the same kite with its steadily flapping wings, flew over the steppe. More and more the air seemed to congeal in heat and silence, submissive nature became petrified and soundless. There was no wind, no cheering fresh sound, no cloud.

But then at last, as the sun began setting in the west, the prairie, the hills and the air could stand the strain and torment no longer, lost patience and tried to cast off the burden. Behind the hills, a fleecy ash-grey cloud unexpectedly appeared. It exchanged glances with the steppe, as if to say 'I'm ready', and frowned. In the stagnant air something suddenly snapped, and a violent squall of wind swirled, roaring and whistling, about the area. At once the grass and last year's vegetation raised a murmur, while a dust spiral eddied over the road and sped along the prairie, sweeping straw, dragonflies and feathers behind it in a gyrating black column, soared up into the sky, and obscured the sun. Hither and thither over the heath tufts of loose herbage raced off, stumbling and bobbing. One of them was caught by the whirlwind,

pirouetted like a bird, flew aloft, turned into a black speck and vanished. After it swept another, and then a third. Yegorushka saw two
such tufts clash and grapple like wrestlers in the azure heights.

Right by the roadside a bustard flew up. Bathed in sunshine, wings
and tail gleaming, it looked like an angler's artificial fly or a pond moth
whose wings, as it darts over the water, merge with the whiskers that
seem to have sprouted in front, behind and on all sides. Vibrating in
the air like an insect, the bird soared vertically aloft with a shimmer
of bright colours, and then—probably scared by a dust cloud—
swerved aside, the glint of it remaining visible for a long time.

Then, alarmed and baffled by a whirlwind, a corncrake sprang up
from the grass. It flew with the wind, not against it like other birds, and
so its feathers were ruffled, puffing it out to a hen's size, and giving it a
furious, imposing look. Only the rooks—grown old in the steppe and
accustomed to its upsets—calmly floated over the grass, or pecked non-
chalantly and heedlessly at the hard earth with their thick beaks.

There was a dull growl of thunder from beyond the hills, and a puff
of fresh air. Deniska whistled cheerfully, belabouring his horses, while
Father Christopher and Kuzmichov held their hats and stared at the
hills. A shower would not come amiss.

With a little more effort, with one more heave, the steppe would
assert itself, it seemed. But an invisible, oppressive force gradually
immobilized wind and air, laying the dust, until stillness reigned again
as if it had never been broken. The cloud vanished, the scorched hills
frowned, and the subdued air was still, with only the troubled lapwings
somewhere weeping and bemoaning their fate.

Soon evening came on.

III

A large bungalow with a rusty iron roof and dark windows showed
up in the gloaming. It was called a posting inn, though it had no
stableyard, and it stood in the middle of the prairie with no fencing
round it. A wretched little cherry orchard and some hurdles made a
dark patch somewhat to one side, and under the windows stood sleepy
sunflowers, their heavy heads drooping. In the orchard a miniature
windmill rattled, having been put there to scare the hares. Near the
house there was nothing to see or hear but the prairie.

Barely had the britzka halted at the porch, which had an awning,
when delighted voices were heard from inside—a man's and a woman's.
The door squeaked on its counterweight, and a tall, scraggy figure

instantly loomed up by the carriage in a flurry of arms and coat-skirts. It was the innkeeper Moses. Elderly, very pale-faced, with a handsome jet-black beard, he wore a threadbare black frock-coat that dangled from his narrow shoulders as from a coat-hanger, flapping its wing-like skirts whenever he threw his hands up in joy or horror. Besides the coat he wore broad white trousers not tucked into his boots, and a velvet waistcoat with a pattern of reddish flowers like gigantic bugs.

Recognizing the new arrivals, Moses was first rooted to the spot by the onrush of emotion, then flung up his arms and uttered a groan. His frock-coat flapped its skirts, his back curved into a bow, and his pale face twisted into a smile, as if seeing the carriage was no mere pleasure but excruciating ecstasy.

'Oh, goodness me, what a happy days this is for me!' he reedily intoned, gasping, bustling and hindering the travellers from getting out of their carriage by his antics. 'Ah, what, oh what, to do next? Mr. Kuzmichov! Father Christopher! And what a pretty little gentlemans that is sitting on the box, or may God punish me! Goodness me, but why am I standing here? Why am I not asking the guests into the parlour? Come in, I beg you most humbly. Make yourselves at home. Give me all your things. Goodness gracious me!'

Ferreting in the carriage and helping the visitors out, Moses suddenly turned back. 'Solomon, Solomon!' he bellowed in a frantic, strangled voice like a drowning man calling for help.

In the house a woman's voice repeated the 'Solomon, Solomon!'

The door squeaked on its counterweight, and on the threshold appeared a young Jew—short, with a large, beaked nose and a bald patch surrounded by coarse, curly hair. All his clothes were too short —his exceedingly shabby cutaway jacket, his sleeves and the woollen trousers that made him seem as docked and skimpy as a plucked bird. This was Moses' brother Solomon. Silently, with no greeting but a rather weird smile, he approached the carriage.

'Mr. Kuzmichov and Father Christopher are here.' Moses' tone hinted at a fear of being disbelieved. 'Aye, aye, and such a wonder it is that these good peoples are paying us a visit. Well, Solomon, take their things. This way, my honoured guests.'

A little later Kuzmichov, Father Christopher and Yegorushka were sitting at an old oak table in a large, gloomy, empty room. The table was almost isolated, since there was no other furniture in the room except for a broad sofa covered with tattered oilcloth and three objects that not everyone would have ventured to call chairs. They were a pathetic simulacrum of furniture, with oilcloth that had seen better days, and with backs canted unnaturally far back so that they closely resembled children's toboggans. It was hard to see what amenity the unknown carpenter had envisaged when giving those chair backs that pitiless curve, and one might have thought that it was not his doing but the work of some itinerant Hercules who had bent the chairs to show his strength and had then offered to put them right, only to make them even worse. The room had a lugubrious air. The walls were grey, the ceiling and cornices were smoke-stained, and there were long cracks and yawning holes of mysterious provenance on the floor, as if that same strong man had kicked them in with his heel. The room looked as if it would still have been dark even with a dozen lamps hanging in it. Neither walls nor windows boasted anything resembling decoration. On one wall, though, a list of regulations under the Two-Headed Eagle hung in a grey wooden frame, and on another wall was some engraving in a similar frame. It was inscribed 'Man's Indifference'. But to what man was indifferent was not clear since the engraving had faded considerably in course of time and was profusely fly-blown. The room smelt musty and sour.

After bringing his guests in, Moses went on twisting, gesticulating, cringing and uttering ecstatic cries, believing all these antics essential to the display of supreme courtesy and affability.

'When did our wagons go by?' Kuzmichov asked.

'One lot passed this morning, Mr. Kuzmichov, and the others rested here at dinner time and left in late afternoon.'

'Aha! Has Varlamov been by or not?'

'No, he hasn't. But his bailiff Gregory drove past yesterday morning, and he reckoned Varlamov must be over at the Molokan's farm.'

'Good. So we'll first overtake the wagons, and then go on to the Molokan's.'

'Mercy on us, Mr. Kuzmichov!' Moses threw up his arms in horror. 'Where can you go so late in the days? You enjoy a bite of supper and spend the night, and tomorrow morning, God willing, you can go and catch anyone you like.'

'There's no time. I'm sorry, Moses—some other day, not now. We'll stay a quarter of an hour and then be off. We can spend the night at the Molokan's.'

'A quarter of an hour!' shrieked Moses. 'Why, have you no fear of God? You will be making me to hide your hats and lock the door. At least have a bite to eat and some tea.'

'We've no time for tea, sugar and the rest of it,' said Kuzmichov.

Moses leant his head to one side, bent his knees, and held his open hands before him as if warding off blows. 'Mr. Kuzmichov, Father Christopher, be so kind as to take tea with me,' he implored with an excruciatingly sweet smile. 'Am I really such a bad mans that Mr. Kuzmichov cannot take tea with me?'

'All right then, we'll have some tea.' Father Christopher gave a sympathetic sigh. 'It won't take long.'

'Very well then,' agreed Kuzmichov.

Moses, flustered, gave a joyful gasp, cringed as if he had just jumped out of cold water into the warm, and ran to the door. 'Rosa, Rosa! Bring the samovar,' he shouted in the frantic, strangled voice with which he had previously called Solomon.

A minute later the door opened and in came Solomon carrying a large tray. He put it on the table, gave a sarcastic sidelong look, grinned the same weird grin. Now, by the light of the lamp, it was possible to see that smile distinctly. It was highly complex, expressing a variety of feelings, but with one predominant—blatant contempt. He seemed to be brooding on something both funny and silly, to feel both repugnance and scorn, to be rejoicing at something or other, and to be waiting for a suitable moment to launch a wounding sneer and a peal of laughter. His long nose, thick lips and crafty, bulging eyes seemed tense with the urge to cachinnate. Looking at his face, Kuzmichov smiled sardonically.

'Why didn't you come over to the fair at N. and do us your Jewish impressions?' he asked.

Two years previously, as Yegorushka well remembered, Solomon had had great success performing scenes of Jewish life in a booth at the N. fair. But the allusion made no impression on him. He went out without answering and came back with the samovar a little later.

Having finished serving, Solomon stepped to one side, folded his arms on his chest, thrust one leg out in front of him and fixed Father Christopher with a derisive stare. There was something defiant, arrogant and contemptuous about his pose, yet it was also highly pathetic and comic because the more portentous it became the more vividly it threw into relief his short trousers, docked jacket, grotesque nose and his whole plucked, bird-like figure.

Moses brought a stool from another room and sat a little way from the table. 'Good appetite! Tea! Sugar!' He began to entertain his guests. 'Enjoy your meal. Such rare, oh, such rare guests, and I haven't seen Father Christopher these five years. And will no one tell me who this nice little gentlemans is?' He looked tenderly at Yegorushka.

'It's my sister Olga's son,' answered Kuzmichov.

'Where is he going then?'

'To school. We're taking him to the high school.'

Out of politeness Moses registered surprise, sagely twisting his head. 'Is very good.' He wagged his finger at the samovar. 'And such a fine gentlemans you'll be when you leave school, we'll all take our hats off to you. You'll be clever, rich, and oh so grand. Now, won't your Mummy be pleased? Is good, good.'

He was silent for a while and stroked his knee. 'Forgive me, Father Christopher.' He spoke with a deferential, jocular air. 'I'm going to report you to the Bishop for robbing the merchants of their living. I'll get an official application form, and write that Father Christopher can't have much moneys of his own if he has turned to trade and started selling wool.'

'Yes, it's a notion I've taken in my old age,' Father Christopher laughed. 'I've turned from priest to merchant, old son. I should be at home saying my prayers, but here I am galloping about in my chariot, even as a very Pharaoh. Ah, vanity!'

'Still, you will make much moneys.'

'A likely tale. I'll get more kicks than halfpence. The wool isn't mine, you know, it's my son-in-law Michael's.'

'Then why hasn't he gone himself?'

'Why, because—. He's only a young shaver. He bought the wool all right, but as for selling it—he has no idea, he's too young. He spent all his money, counted on making a packet and cutting a bit of a dash, but he's tried here and he's tried there, and no one will even give him what he paid for it. Well, the lad messes around with it for a twelve-month, and then he comes to me. "Dad," says he, "you sell the wool, be so kind. I'm no good at these things." Well, that's true enough. As soon as things go wrong he runs to his dad, but till then he could manage without his dad. Doesn't consult me when buying it, oh no, but now things have come unstuck it's daddy this and daddy that. But what can daddy do? If it wasn't for Ivan Kuzmichov daddy could have done nothing. What a nuisance they are.'

'Yes, childrens are a lot of trouble, believe me,' sighed Moses. 'I have six myself. It's teach the one, dose the other, carry the third round in your arms, and when they grow up they're even more nuisance. There ain't nothing new about it, it was the same in Holy Scripture.

When Jacob had small childrens he wept, but when they grew up he wept more than ever.'

Father Christopher agreed, looking pensively at his glass. 'H'm, yes. Now, me, I haven't really done anything to anger God. I've lived out my span as lucky as could be. I've found good husbands for my daughters, I've set my sons up in life, and now I'm free, I've done my job, I can go where I like. I live quietly with my wife, eat, drink, sleep, enjoy my grandchildren, say my prayers—and that's all I need! Live on the fat of the land I do, and I don't need any favours. There has been no grief in my life. Suppose the Tsar asked me what I needed and wanted now—there isn't anything! I have everything, thanks be to God. There's no happier man in all our town. True, I'm a great sinner, but then—only God's without sin, eh?'

'Aye, true enough.'

'I've lost my teeth of course, my poor old back aches and so on, I'm short of breath and all that. I fall ill, the flesh is weak, but I have lived, haven't I? You can see that for yourself. In my seventies, I am. You can't go on for ever—mustn't outstay your welcome.'

Struck by a sudden thought, Father Christopher snorted into his glass, and then laughed himself into a coughing fit. Moses, too, laughed and coughed out of politeness.

'It was so funny!' Father Christopher made a helpless gesture. 'My eldest son Gabriel comes to stay with me. He's in the medical line, a doctor with the rural council down Chernigov way. Well, now. "I'm short of breath and so on," I tell him. "Now, you're a doctor, so you cure your father." So he undresses me there and then, he does a bit of tapping and listening—the usual tricks—squeezes my stomach. "Compressed air treatment's what you need, Dad," says he.'

Father Christopher laughed convulsively until he cried, and stood up. ' "Confound your compressed air," says I. "Confound your air!" ' He laughed as he brought out the words and made a derisive gesture with both hands.

Moses also stood up, clutched his stomach and uttered a shrill peal of mirth like the yap of a pekinese.

'Confound your compressed air!' the chortling Father Christopher repeated.

Laughing two notes higher, Moses uttered a cackle so explosive that he almost lost his footing. 'Oh, my God,' groaned he in mid-guffaw. 'Let me get my breath back. Oh, such a scream you are—you'll be the death of me, you will.'

While laughing and speaking he cast apprehensive, suspicious glances at Solomon, who stood in his former posture, smiling. To judge from his eyes and grin his scorn and hatred were genuine, but so incompatible were they with his plucked-hen look that Yegorushka interpreted the challenging mien and air of blistering contempt as buffoonery deliberately designed to amuse the honoured guests.

After silently drinking half a dozen glasses of tea Kuzmichov cleared a space on the table in front of him, took his bag—the same one that he had kept under his head when sleeping beneath the carriage—untied the string and shook it. Bundles of banknotes tumbled out on the table.

'Let's count them while there's time, Father,' said Kuzmichov.

On seeing the money Moses showed embarrassment, stood up, and —as a sensitive man not wanting to know others' secrets—tiptoed from the room, balancing with his arms. Solomon stayed where he was.

'How much in the one-rouble packets?' began Father Christopher.

'They're in fifties, and the three-rouble notes are in ninety-rouble packets. The twenty-fives and the hundreds come in thousands. You count out seven thousand eight hundred for Varlamov and I'll count Gusevich's. And mind you get it right.'

Never in his life had Yegorushka seen such a pile of money as that on the table. It must have been a vast amount indeed, because the bundle of seven thousand eight hundred put aside for Varlamov seemed so small compared to the pile as a whole. All this money might have impressed Yegorushka at any other time, moving him to ponder how many bagels, dough rolls and poppy-seed cakes you could buy with it. But now he looked at it unconcernedly, aware only of the foul smell of rotten apples and paraffin that it gave off. Exhausted by the jolting ride in the britzka, he was worn out and sleepy. His head felt heavy, his eyes would scarcely stay open, and his thoughts were like tangled threads. Had it been possible he would have been glad to lay his head on the table and close his eyes to avoid seeing the lamp and the fingers moving above the heap of notes, and he would have allowed his listless, sleepy thoughts to become more jumbled still. As he struggled to stay awake he saw everything double—lamplight, cups, fingers. The samovar throbbed, and the smell of rotten apples seemed yet more acrid and foul.

'Money, money, money!' sighed Father Christopher, smiling. 'What a nuisance you are! Now, I bet young Michael's asleep, dreaming of me bringing him a pile like this.'

'Your Michael has no sense.' Kuzmichov spoke in an undertone.

'Right out of his depth, he is. But you *are* sensible and open to reason. You'd better let me have your wool, like I said, and go back home. Very well, then—I'd give you half a rouble a bale over and above your price, and that just out of respect——'

'No thanks,' Father Christopher sighed. 'I'm grateful for your concern, and I wouldn't think twice about it, of course, if I had the choice. But you see, it's not my wool, is it?'

In tiptoed Moses. Trying not to look at the heap of money out of delicacy, he stole up to Yegorushka and tugged the back of his shirt. 'Come on, little gentlemans,' said he in a low voice. 'I'll show you such a nice little bear. He's oh such a fierce, cross little bear, he is.'

Sleepy Yegorushka stood up and sluggishly plodded after Moses to look at the bear. He entered a small room where his breath was caught, before he saw anything, by the sour, musty smell that was much stronger than in the big room, and was probably spreading through the house from here. One half of the room was dominated by a double bed covered with a greasy quilt, and the other by a chest of drawers and piles of miscellaneous clothing, beginning with stiffly starched skirts and ending with children's trousers and braces. On the chest of drawers a tallow candle burnt, but instead of the promised bear Yegorushka saw a big fat Jewess with her hair hanging loose, wearing a red flannel dress with black dots.

She had difficulty in turning in the narrow space between bed and chest of drawers, and emitted protracted groaning sighs as if from toothache. Seeing Yegorushka, she assumed a woebegone air, heaved a lengthy sigh, and—before he had time to look round—put a slice of bread and honey to his lips. 'Eat, sonny, eat. Your Mummy's not here, and there's no one to feed you. Eat it up.'

Yegorushka did so, though after the fruit-drops and honey cakes that he had at home every day he thought little of the honey, half of which was wax and bees' wings. While he ate, Moses and the Jewess watched and sighed. 'Where are you going, sonny?' she asked.

'To school.'

'And how many childrens does your Mummy have?'

'Only me, there's no others.'

'Ah me!' sighed the Jewess, turning up her eyes. 'Your poor, poor Mummy. How she will miss you, how she will cry! In a year we shall be taking our Nahum to school too. Ah me!'

'Oh, Nahum, Nahum!' sighed Moses, the loose skin of his pale face twitching nervously. 'And he is so poorly.'

The greasy quilt moved, and from it emerged a child's curly head on a very thin neck. Two black eyes gleamed, staring quizzically at Yegorushka. Still sighing, Moses and the Jewess went up to the chest of drawers and began a discussion in Yiddish. Moses spoke in a deep undertone, and his Yiddish sounded like a non-stop boom, boom, booming, while his wife answered in a thin voice like a turkey hen's with a twitter, twitter, twitter. While they were conferring a second curly head on a thin neck peeped out from the greasy quilt, then a third, then a fourth. Had Yegorushka possessed a vivid imagination he might have thought that the hundred-headed hydra lay beneath that quilt.

'Boom, boom, boom,' went Moses.

'Twitter, twitter, twitter,' answered his wife.

The conference ended with her diving with a deep sigh into the chest of drawers, unwrapping some kind of green rag there, and taking out a big, heart-shaped honey-cake. 'Take it, sonny.' She gave Yegorushka the cake. 'You have no Mummy now, isn't it? Is no one to give you nice things.'

Yegorushka put the cake in his pocket and backed towards the door, unable to continue breathing the musty, sour air in which the innkeeper and his wife lived. Going back to the big room, he comfortably installed himself on the sofa and let his thoughts wander.

Kuzmichov had just finished counting the banknotes and was putting them back in his bag. He treated them with no particular respect, stuffing them in the dirty bag without ceremony, as unconcernedly as if they had been so much waste paper.

Father Christopher was talking to Solomon. 'Well, now, Solomon the Wise.' He yawned and made the sign of the cross over his mouth. 'How's business?'

'To what business do you allude?' Solomon stared at him as viciously as if some crime had been implied.

'Things in general. What are you up to?'

'Up to?' Solomon repeated the question with a shrug. 'Same as everyone else. I am, you see, a servant. I am my brother's servant. My brother is his visitors' servant. His visitors are Varlamov's servants. And if I had ten million Varlamov would be my servant.'

'But why should that be?'

'Why? Because there's no gentleman or millionaire who wouldn't lick the hand of a dirty Yid to make an extra copeck. As it is I'm a dirty Yid and a beggar, and everyone look at me as if I was a dog. But if I

had moneys, Varlamov would make as big a fool of himself for me as
Moses does for you.'

Father Christopher and Kuzmichov looked at each other, neither
of them understanding Solomon.

'How can you compare yourself to Varlamov, you idiot?' Kuzmichov
gave Solomon a stern, dour look.

'I'm not such an idiot as to compare myself to Varlamov.' Solomon
looked at the others scornfully. 'Varlamov may be a Russian, but he's
a dirty Yid at heart. Moneys and gain are his whole life, but I burnt
mine in the stove. I don't need moneys or land or sheep, and I don't
need people to fear me and take off their hats when I pass. So I am
wiser than your Varlamov and more of a man.'

A little later Yegorushka, half asleep, heard Solomon discussing
Jews in a hollow, lisping, rapid voice hoarse from the hatred that
choked him. Having begun by speaking correctly, he had later
lapsed into the style of a raconteur telling Jewish funny stories,
employing the same exaggerated Yiddish accent that he had used at
the fair.

Father Christopher interrupted him. 'Just one moment. If your faith
displeases you, change it. But to laugh at it is sinful. The man who
mocks his faith is the lowest of the low.'

'You don't understand,' Solomon rudely cut him short. 'That has
nothing to do with what I was saying.'

'Now, that just shows what a stupid fellow you are.' Father Christopher sighed. 'I instruct you as best I can and you become angry. I
speak to you as an old man, quietly, and you go off like a turkey—
cackle, cackle, cackle. You really are a funny chap.'

In came Moses. He looked anxiously at Solomon and his guests, and
again the loose skin on his face twitched nervously. Yegorushka shook
his head and looked around him, catching a glimpse of Solomon's
face just when it was turned three-quarters towards him and when
the shadow of his long nose bisected his whole left cheek. The scornful
smile half in shadow, the glittering, sneering eyes, the arrogant expression and the whole plucked hen's figure—doubling and dancing
before Yegorushka's eyes, they made Solomon look less like a clown
than some nightmare fantasy or evil spirit.

'What a devil of a fellow he is, Moses, God help him.' Father Christopher smiled. 'You'd better get him a job, find him a wife or something. He's not human.'

Kuzmichov frowned angrily while Moses cast another apprehensive, quizzical look at his brother and the guests. 'Leave the room, Solomon,' he said sternly. 'Go away.' And he added something in Yiddish.

With a brusque laugh Solomon went out.

'What was it?' Moses fearfully asked Father Christopher.

'He forgets himself,' Kuzmichov answered. 'He is rude and thinks too highly of himself.'

'I knew it!' Moses threw up his arms in horror. 'Oh, goodness gracious me!' he muttered in an undertone. 'Be so kind as to forgive him, don't be angry. That's what he's like, he is. Oh, goodness me! He's my own brothers, and he's been nothing but trouble to me, he has. Why, do you know, he——'

Moses tapped his forehead. 'He's out of his mind—a hopeless case, he is. I really don't know what I'm to do with him. He cares for no one, respects no one, fears no one. He laugh at everybody, you know, he say silly things, he get on people's nerves. You'll never believe it, but when Varlamov was here once, Solomon made some remark to him and he gave us both a taste of his whip! What for he whip me, eh? Was it my fault? If God has robbed my brother of his wits, it must be God's will. How is it my fault, eh?'

About ten minutes passed, but Moses still kept up a low muttering and sighing. 'He doesn't sleep of a night, he keeps thinking, thinking, thinking, but what he thinks about, God knows. If you go near him at night he get angry and he laugh. He doesn't like me either. And there's nothing he wants. When our Dad died he left us six thousand roubles apiece. I bought an inn, I married, and now I have childrens, but he burnt his moneys in the stove. Such a pity. Why he burn it? If he not need it, why he not give it me? Why he burn it?'

Suddenly the door squeaked on its counterweight, and the floor vibrated with footsteps. Yegorushka felt a draught of air and had the impression of a big black bird swooping past and beating its wings right by his face. He opened his eyes. His uncle had his bag in his hand, and stood near the sofa ready to leave. Holding his broad-brimmed top hat, Father Christopher was bowing to someone and smiling—not softly and tenderly as was his wont, but in a respectful, strained fashion that ill suited him. Meanwhile Moses was doing a sort of balancing act as if his body had been broken in three parts and he was trying his best not to disintegrate. Only Solomon seemed unaffected, and stood in a corner, his arms folded, his grin as disdainful as ever.

'Your Ladyship must forgive the untidiness,' groaned Moses with an excruciatingly sweet smile, taking no more notice of Kuzmichov or Father Christopher, but just balancing his whole body so as not to disintegrate. 'We're plain folk, my lady.'

Yegorushka rubbed his eyes. In the middle of the room stood what indeed was a ladyship—a very beautiful, buxom young woman in a black dress and straw hat. Before Yegorushka could make out her features the solitary graceful poplar he had seen on the hill that day somehow came into his mind.

'Was Varlamov here today?' a woman's voice asked.

'No, my lady,' Moses answered.

'If you see him tomorrow ask him to call at my place for a minute.'

Suddenly, quite unexpectedly, about an inch from his eyes Yegorushka saw velvety black eyebrows, big brown eyes and well-cared-for feminine cheeks with dimples from which smiles seemed to irradiate the whole face like sunbeams. There was a whiff of some splendid scent.

'What a pretty little boy,' said the lady. 'Who is he? See, Kazimir, what a charming child. Good heavens, he's asleep, the darling wee poppet!'

The lady firmly kissed Yegorushka on both cheeks. He smiled and shut his eyes, thinking he was asleep. The door squeaked and hurried footsteps were heard as someone came in and went out.

Then came a deep whisper from two voices. 'Yegorushka, Yegorushka, get up. We're leaving.'

Someone, Deniska apparently, set the boy on his feet and took his arm. On the way he half opened his eyes and once again saw the beautiful woman in the black dress who had kissed him. She stood in the middle of the room, watching him leave with a friendly smile and a nod. As he came to the door he saw a handsome, heavily built, dark man in a bowler hat and leggings. He must be the lady's escort.

From outside came a cry. 'Whoa there!'

At the front door Yegorushka saw a splendid new carriage and a pair of black horses. On the box sat a liveried groom holding a long whip.

Only Solomon came out to see the departing guests off, his face tense with the urge to guffaw, as if he was waiting impatiently for them to leave so that he could laugh at them to his heart's content.

'Countess Dranitsky,' whispered Father Christopher as he mounted the britzka.

'Yes, Countess Dranitsky,' repeated Kuzmichov, also in a whisper.

The impression made by the Countess's arrival must have been considerable, for even Deniska spoke in a whisper, not venturing to whip his bays and shout until the britzka had gone several hundred yards and nothing could be seen of the inn but a faint light.

IV

Who on earth was the elusive, mysterious Varlamov of whom so much was said, whom Solomon despised, whom even the beautiful Countess had need of? Sitting on the box by Deniska, the dozing Yegorushka thought about that personage. He had never set eyes on Varlamov, but he had often heard of him and imagined him. He knew that Varlamov owned acres by their scores of thousands, about a hundred thousand head of sheep and a lot of money. Of his life and activities the boy only knew that he was always 'knocking around' in the area, and that he was always in demand.

At home the boy had heard much of Countess Dranitsky too. She also owned acres by their scores of thousands, many sheep, a stud farm and a lot of money. Yet *she* did not 'knock around', but lived on a prosperous estate about which people he knew—including Kuzmichov, who often called there on business—told many a fabulous tale. For instance, it was said that in the Countess's drawing-room, which had the portraits of all the Kings of Poland hanging on the wall, there was a big, rock-shaped table-clock surmounted by a rampant gold horse with jewelled eyes and a gold rider who swung his sabre from side to side whenever the clock struck. The Countess was also said to give a ball twice a year. The gentry and officials of the county were invited, and even Varlamov attended. The guests all drank tea made from water boiled in silver samovars, ate the oddest dishes—for instance, raspberries and strawberries were served at Christmas—and danced to a band that played day and night.

'And how beautiful she is,' thought Yegorushka, remembering her face and smile.

Kuzmichov must have been thinking about the Countess too, because he spoke as follows when the carriage had gone about a mile and a half. 'Yes, and doesn't that Kazimir rob her! Two years ago I bought some wool from her, remember? And he picked up three thousand on that deal alone.'

'Just what you'd expect from a wretched Pole,' Father Christopher said.

'But she doesn't let it bother her. Young and foolish she is, with something missing in the top storey, as folks say.'

Somehow Yegorushka wanted to think only of Varlamov and the Countess, especially the Countess. His drowsy brain utterly rejected mundane thoughts and became fuddled, retaining only such magical and fantastic images as have the advantage of somehow springing into the mind automatically without taxing the thinker, but vanish without trace of their own accord at a mere shake of the head. In any case the surroundings did not encourage ordinary thoughts. On the right were dark hills, seeming to screen off something mysterious and terrifying, while on the left the whole sky above the horizon was steeped in a crimson glow, and it was hard to tell whether there was a fire somewhere or whether it was the moon about to rise. The distant prospect was visible, as by day, but now the delicate lilac hue had disappeared, obscured by the gloaming in which the whole steppe hid like Moses' children under the quilt.

On July evenings and nights quails and corncrakes no longer call, nightingales do not sing in wooded gullies, and there is no scent of flowers. But the steppe is still picturesque and full of life. Hardly has the sun gone down, hardly has darkness enfolded the earth when the day's misery is forgotten, all is forgiven, and the prairies breathe a faint sigh from their broad bosom. In the grass—as if it can no longer tell how old it is in the dark—a merry, youthful trilling, unknown by day, arises. The chattering, the whistling, the scratching, the bass, tenor and treble voices of the steppe—all blend in a continuous monotonous boom, a fine background to memories and melancholy. The monotonous chirring soothes like a lullaby. You drive on, feeling as if you are dozing, but the brusque alarm call of a wakeful bird comes from somewhere, or a vague noise resounds, like a human voice uttering a surprised, protracted sigh, and slumber closes your eyelids. Or you may drive past a bushy gully and hear the bird that prairie folk call a 'sleeper', with its cry of 'sleep, sleep, sleep'. Or another bird guffaws, or weeps in hysterical peals—an owl. Whom do they cry for? Who hears them in the steppe? God alone knows, but their cries are most mournful and plaintive. There is a scent of hay, dry grass and late flowers—a scent dense, sickly-sweet, voluptuous.

Everything is visible through the haze, but colours and outlines are hard to make out. All seems other than it is. As you journey onward you suddenly see a silhouette like a monk's on the roadside ahead of you. It does not move, but waits, holding something. A highwayman perhaps? The figure approaches, swells, draws level with the britzka, and you see that it is a solitary bush or boulder, not a man. Such immobile, waiting figures stand on the hills, hide behind the ancient barrows, peep out from the grass, all resembling human beings, all arousing suspicion.

When the moon rises the night grows pale and languid. It is as if the haze had never been. The air is limpid, fresh and warm, everything is clearly seen, and one can even make out individual blades of grass by the road. Stones and skulls stand out a long way off. The suspicious monk-like figures look blacker and gloomier against the night's bright background. The surprised sighing resounds more and more often amid the monotonous chatter, troubling the still air, and you hear the cry of a wakeful or delirious bird. Broad shadows move over the plain like clouds across the sky, and in the mysterious distance, if you peer into it for a while, grotesque, misty images loom and tower behind each other. It is a little eerie. And if you gaze at the pale, green, star-spangled sky, free of the smallest cloud or speck, you will know why the warm air is still, and why nature is alert, fearing to stir. It is afraid and reluctant to lose one second's life. Of the sky's unfathomable depth, of its boundlessness, you can judge only at sea and on the moon-lit steppe by night. It is frightening and picturesque, yet kindly. Its gaze is languorous and magnetic, but its embraces make you dizzy.

You drive on for an hour or two. On your way you meet a silent barrow or menhir—God knows who put them up, or when. A night bird silently skims the earth. And the prairie legends, the travellers' yarns, the folk tales told by some old nurse from the steppes, together with whatever you yourself have contrived to see and to grasp in spirit—you gradually recall all these things. And then, in the insects' twittering, in the sinister figures and ancient barrows, in the depths of the sky, in the moonlight, in the flight of the night bird, in everything you see and hear, you seem to glimpse the triumph of beauty, youth in the prime of strength, a lust for life. Your spirit responds to its magnificent, stern homeland and you long to fly above the steppe with the night bird. In this triumph of beauty, in this exuberance of happiness, you feel a tenseness and agonized regret, as if the steppe knew how lonely she is, how her wealth and inspiration are lost to the world —vainly, unsung, unneeded, and through the joyous clamour you hear her anguished, hopeless cry for a bard, a poet of her own.

'Whoa! Hallo there, Panteley. All well?'
'Thanks to God, Mr. Kuzmichov.'

'Seen Varlamov, lads?'

'No, we ain't.'

Yegorushka awoke and opened his eyes. The britzka had stopped. A long way ahead on the right extended a train of wagons, and men were scurrying about near them. The huge bales of wool made all the wagons seem very tall and bulging, and the horses small and short-legged.

'So we're to visit the Molokan's farm next,' said Kuzmichov in a loud voice. 'The Jew reckoned that Varlamov was staying the night there. Good-bye then, lads. Best of luck.'

'Good-bye, Mr. Kuzmichov,' answered several voices.

'I tell you what, lads,' said Kuzmichov briskly. 'You might take my boy with you. Why should he traipse around with us? Put him on your bales, Panteley, and let him ride a bit, and we'll catch you up. Off you go, Yegorushka. Go on, it'll be all right.'

Yegorushka climbed down from his box seat, and several hands picked him up. They raised him aloft, and he found himself on something big, soft and slightly wet with dew. He felt close to the sky and far from the ground.

'Hey, take your coat, old chap,' shouted Deniska far below.

The boy's overcoat and bundle were thrown up from below and fell near him. Quickly, wishing to keep his mind a blank, he put the bundle under his head, covered himself with his coat, stretched his legs right out, shivering a little because of the dew, and laughed with pleasure.

'Sleep, sleep, sleep,' he thought.

'Don't you do him no harm, you devils.' It was Deniska's voice from below.

'Good-bye, lads, and good luck,' shouted Kuzmichov. 'I'm relying on you.'

'Never fear, mister.'

Deniska shouted to his horses as the britzka creaked and rolled off, no longer along the road but somewhere off to one side. For a minute or two the wagons all seemed to have fallen asleep, since no sound was heard except the gradually expiring distant clatter of the pail tied to the britzka's back-board.

Then came a muffled shout from the head of the convoy. 'On our way, Kiryukha!'

The foremost wagon creaked, then the second and the third. Yegorushka felt his own vehicle jerk and creak as well—they were on the move. He took a firmer grip on the cord round his bale, gave another happy laugh, shifted the honey cake in his pocket, and fell asleep just as he did in his bed at home.

When he awoke the sun was already rising. Screened by an ancient burial mound, it was trying to sprinkle its light on the world, urgently thrusting its rays in all directions and flooding the horizon with gold. Yegorushka thought it was in the wrong place because it had risen behind his back on the previous day, and was further to the left now. But the whole landscape had changed. There were no more hills, and the bleak brown plain stretched endlessly in all directions. Here and there arose small barrows, and rooks flew about, as on the day before. Far ahead were the white belfries and huts of a village. As it was a Sunday the locals were at home cooking—witness the smoke issuing from all the chimneys and hanging over the village in a transparent blue-grey veil. In the gaps between the huts and beyond the church a blue river could be seen, and beyond that the hazy distance. But nothing was so unlike yesterday's scene as the road. Straddling the prairie was something less a highway than a lavish, immensely broad, positively heroic spread of tract—a grey band, much traversed, dusty like all roads and several score yards in width. Its sheer scale baffled the boy, conjuring up a fairy-tale world. Who drove here? Who needed all this space? It was strange and uncanny. One might suppose, indeed, that giants with seven-league boots were still among us, and that the heroic horses of folk myth were not extinct. Looking at the road, Yegorushka pictured half a dozen tall chariots racing side by side like some he had seen in drawings in books of Bible stories. Those chariots had each been drawn by a team of six wild and furious horses, their high wheels raising clouds of dust to the sky, while the horses were driven by men such as one might meet in dreams, or in reveries about the supernatural. How well they would have fitted the steppe and the road, these figures, had they existed!

Telegraph poles carrying two wires ran on the right-hand side of the road as far as eye could see. Ever dwindling, they vanished behind the huts and foliage near the village, only to reappear in the lilac-coloured background as thin little sticks resembling pencils stuck in the ground. On the wires sat hawks, merlins and crows, gazing unconcernedly at the moving wagons.

Lying on the last wagon of all, the boy had the whole convoy in view. There were about twenty wagons or carts, with one wagoner to three vehicles. Near Yegorushka's wagon, the last in line, walked an old, grey-bearded man, as short and gaunt as Father Christopher, but with a brown, sunburnt face, stern and contemplative. The old man may have been neither stern nor contemplative, but his red eye-lids and long, sharp nose gave his face the severe, reserved air of those accustomed to brood in solitude on serious matters. Like Father Christopher, he wore a broad-brimmed top hat—a brown, felt affair more like a truncated cone than a gentleman's topper. His feet were bare. He kept slapping his thighs and stamping his feet as he walked—probably a habit contracted in the cold winters, when he must often have come near to freezing beside his wagons. Noticing that Yego-rushka was awake, he looked at him.

'So you're awake, young man.' He was hunching his shoulders as if from cold. 'Mr. Kuzmichov's son, might you be?'

'No, his nephew.'

'His nephew, eh? Now, I've just taken off me boots, I'm bobbing along barefoot. There's something wrong with me legs, the frost got to them, and things is easier without boots. Easier, boy. Without boots, I mean. So you're his nephew, then? And he's a good sort, he is. May God grant him health. A good sort. Mr. Kuzmichov, I mean. He's gone to see the Molokan. O Lord, have mercy on us!'

The old man even spoke as if he was frozen, spacing out the words and not opening his mouth properly. He mispronounced his labial consonants, stuttering on them as if his lips were swollen. When addressing Yegorushka he did not smile once, and seemed severe.

Three wagons ahead of them walked a man in a long reddish-brown topcoat, carrying a whip. He wore a peaked cap and riding boots with sagging tops. He was not old—only about forty. When he turned round the boy saw a long red face with a thin goatee and a spongy swelling under the right eye. Besides this hideous swelling he had another specially striking peculiarity—while holding the whip in his left hand, he swung the right as if conducting an unseen choir. Occasionally he tucked the whip under his arm and conducted with both hands, humming to himself.

The next carter was a tall upstanding figure with noticeably sloping shoulders and a back as flat as a board. He held himself erect as if he was marching or had swallowed a ramrod, his arms not swinging but hanging straight down like sticks as he walked in a sort of clockwork fashion like a toy soldier, scarcely bending his knees and trying to take the longest stride possible. Where the old man or the owner of the spongy swelling took two steps he contrived to take only one, so that he seemed to be moving more slowly than anyone and to be falling behind. His face was bound with a piece of cloth, and on his head sprouted something resembling a monk's cap. He was dressed in a short Ukrainian coat all covered with patches and in dark blue oriental trousers over bast shoes.

Yegorushka could not make out the more distant carters. He lay on his stomach, picked a hole in his bale, and began twisting some wool into threads, having nothing better to do. The old man striding away below turned out less severe and serious than his face suggested. Having started a conversation he did not let it drop.

'Where are you going, then?' he asked, stamping his feet.

'To school,' answered Yegorushka.

'To school? Aha! Well, may Our Blessed Lady help you! Aye, one brain's good, but two is better. God gives one man one brain, and another man two brains, and another gets three, that's for sure. One's the brain you're born with, another comes from learning, and the third from living a good life. So it's a good thing for a man to have three brains, son. Living's easier for him, it is, and so is dying too. Dying—aye, we'll all of us come to it.'

After scratching his forehead the old man looked up, red-eyed, at Yegorushka, and went on. 'Maxim Nikolayevich, the squire from down Slavyanoserbsk way—he took his lad to school last year, he did. I don't know what he might be like in the book-learning line, but he's a good, decent lad, he is. And may God prosper them, the fine gentle-folk that they be. Aye, so he takes the lad to school, like you, since they don't have no establishment—not for learning proper, like—in them parts, that they don't. But it's a good, decent town. There's an ordinary school for the common folk, but for them as wants to be scholars there ain't nothing, there ain't. What's your name?'

'Yegorushka.'

'Yegorushka—"George", properly speaking. So your name-day's the twenty-third of April, seeing as how that's the day of the holy martyr St. Georgie-Porgie what killed the Dragon. Now, my name's Panteley—Panteley Kholodov. Aye, Kholodov's the name. I come from Tim in Kursk County myself, you may have heard tell of it. My brothers registered themselves as townsfolk—they're craftsmen in the town, they are. But I'm a countryman, and a countryman I've remained. Seven years ago I visited there, home that is. I've been in my village and in the town—in Tim, I've been, say I. They were all alive and well then, thank God, but I don't know about now. A few of them may have died. And time it is for them to die—they're all old, and some is older than me. Death's all right, nothing wrong with it. But you mustn't die without repenting, stands to reason. Ain't nothing worse than dying contumacious—oh, it's a joy to the devil is a contumacious death. But if you want to die penitent, so they won't forbid you to enter the mansions of the Lord like, you pray to the martyred St. Barbara. She'll intercede for you, she will, you take it from me. That's her place in heaven that God gave her so everyone should have the right to pray to her for repentance, see?'

Panteley muttered away, obviously not caring whether the boy heard him or not. He spoke listlessly, mumbling to himself, neither raising nor dropping his voice, but managing to say a great deal in a short time. His talk, all fragmentary and largely incoherent, lacked any interest for Yegorushka. Perhaps he spoke only to call the roll of his ideas—make sure that all were present and correct after the night spent in silence. Having finished talking about repentance, he went off again about this Maxim Nikolayevich from down Slavyanoserbsk way. 'Yes, he took the lad to school, he did, true enough.'

One of the carters walking far in front gave a sudden lurch, darted to one side, and began lashing the ground with his whip. He was a burly, broad-shouldered man of about thirty, with fair, curly hair and a healthy, vigorous look. From the motions of his shoulders and whip, from the eagerness of his posture, he was beating some live creature. A second carter ran up—a short, thick-set fellow with a full black beard, in a waistcoat with his shirt outside his trousers. He broke out in a deep, coughing laugh. 'Dymov has killed a snake, lads, as God's my witness.'

There are people whose intellect can be accurately gauged from their voice and laugh, and it was to this lucky category that the black-bearded man belonged, his voice and laugh betraying abysmal stupidity. The fair-haired Dymov had stopped lashing, picked his whip from the ground and laughed as he hurled something resembling a bit of rope towards the carts.

'It ain't a viper, 'tis a grass snake,' someone shouted.

The man with the clockwork stride and bandaged face quickly strode up to the dead snake, glanced at it and threw up his stick-like arms. 'You rotten scum!' he shouted in a hollow, tearful voice. 'Why kill the little grass snake? What had he done to you, damn you? Hey, he's killed a grass snake! How would you like to be treated like that?'

'Grass snakes oughtn't to be killed, that's true enough,' muttered

Panteley placidly. 'It ain't a viper. Look like a snake it may, but 'tis a quiet, innocent creature. A friend of man, it be, your grass snake——'

Dymov and the black-bearded man were probably ashamed, for they gave loud laughs and sauntered back to their wagons without answering these grumbles. When the hindmost wagon drew level with the place where the dead grass snake lay, the man with the bandaged face stood over the creature and addressed Panteley. 'Now, why did he kill the grass snake, old man?' he inquired plaintively.

Yegorushka could now see that the speaker's eyes were small and lack-lustre. His face looked grey and sickly, also seeming lustreless, while his chin was red, appearing extremely swollen.

'Now, why did he kill the grass snake?' he repeated, striding by Panteley's side.

'A fool has itchy hands, that's why,' the old man said. 'But you shouldn't kill a grass snake, true enough. He's a trouble-maker is that Dymov, see, he'll kill anything that comes his way. But Kiryukha didn't stop him when he should have, but just stood there a-chuckling and a-cackling. Don't take on, though, Vasya, don't let it anger you. They killed it, but never mind. Dymov's a mischief-maker and Kiryukha's just silly like. No matter. Folks are stupid, folks don't understand, so let them be. Now, Yemelyan won't never touch anything he shouldn't. Never, that's true enough, seeing as how he's educated and they're stupid. He won't touch anything, not Yemelyan won't.'

The carter with the reddish-brown topcoat and the spongy swelling —the one who liked conducting the unseen choir—stopped when he heard his name spoken, waited for Panteley and Vasya to catch up, and fell in beside them. 'What are you on about?' he asked in a hoarse, strangled voice.

'Well, Vasya here's angry,' said Panteley. 'So I said a few things to stop him taking on. Oh, my poor legs, they're so cold. It's because it's Sunday, the Lord's Day, that's why they're playing up.'

'It's the walking,' remarked Vasya.

'No, lad, no. It ain't the walking. When I walk it seems easier, it's when I lie down and warm meself—that's what does for me. Walking's easier like.'

Yemelyan, in his reddish-brown topcoat, took station between Panteley and Vasya, waving his hand as if that choir was about to sing. After a bit of a swing he lowered his arm and gave a grunt of despair. 'My voice has gone,' he said. 'Diabolical, it is. All night and all morning I've been haunted by the triple "Lord Have Mercy" that we sang at the Marinovsky wedding. I've got it on me brain and I've got it in me gizzard. I feel I could sing it, but I can't. I ain't got the voice.'

He brooded silently for a while and then went on. 'Fifteen years in the choir I was, and in all Lugansk no one had a better voice than me, belike. But then I have to go and bloody bathe in the Donets two year ago, and not one proper note have I sung since. A chill in the throat it was. Without me voice I'm like a workman with no hand.'

'True enough,' Panteley agreed.

'What I say is, I'm done for, and that's that.'

At that moment Vasya chanced to catch sight of Yegorushka. His eyes glittered and seemed even smaller. 'So there's a young gentleman a-driving with us,' he said, hiding his nose with his sleeve as if from shyness. 'Now, that's what I call a real 'igh-class cabbie! You stay with us riding the wagons and carting wool.'

The incongruity of one person combining the functions of young gentleman and cabbie must have struck him as most curious and witty, for he gave a loud snigger and continued to develop the idea. Yemelyan looked up at Yegorushka too, but cursorily and coldly. He was obsessed with thoughts of his own, and would not have noticed the boy, had it not been for Vasya. Not five minutes had passed before he was waving his arms again. Then, as he described to his companions the beauties of the wedding anthem 'Lord Have Mercy' that he had remembered in the night, he put his whip under his arm and started conducting with both his hands.

Nearly a mile from the village the convoy stopped by a well with a sweep. Lowering his pail into the well, black-bearded Kiryukha lay stomach down on the framework and thrust his mop of hair, his shoulders and part of his chest into the black hole so that Yegorushka could see only his short legs, which barely touched the ground. Seeing his head reflected from afar down at the well bottom, he was so pleased that he let off a cascade of stupid, deep-voiced laughter, and the well echoed it back. When he stood up his face and neck were red as a beetroot. The first to run up and drink was Dymov. He laughed as he drank, frequently lifting his head from the pail and saying something funny to Kiryukha. Then he cleared his throat and bellowed out half a dozen swear words for all the steppe to hear. What such words meant Yegorushka had no idea, but that they were bad he was well aware. He knew of the unspoken revulsion that they evoked in his friends and relations, he shared their feelings himself without knowing why, and he had come to assume that only the drunk and disorderly enjoyed the privilege of speaking these words aloud. He remembered the killing of the grass snake, listened to Dymov's laughter, and felt something like hatred for the man. At that moment, as ill luck would have it, Dymov spotted Yegorushka, who had climbed down from his cart and was on his way to the well.

'Lads, the old man gave birth in the night!' shouted Dymov with a loud laugh. ' 'Tis a baby boy.'

Kiryukha gave his deep-throated laugh till he coughed. Someone else laughed too, while Yegorushka blushed and conclusively decided that Dymov was a very bad man.

Bareheaded, with fair, curly hair and his shirt unbuttoned, Dymov seemed handsome and extremely strong, all his movements being those of the reckless bully who knows his own worth. He flexed his shoulders, put his hands on his hips, talked and laughed louder than the others, and looked ready to lift with one hand some weight so prodigious as to astound the entire world. His roving, ironical glance slid over the road, the string of wagons and the sky, never resting, and he seemed to be seeking something else to kill—as a pastime, just for a joke. He obviously feared no one, would stick at nothing, and probably cared not a rap for Yegorushka's opinion. But the boy now wholeheartedly detested his fair head, his clean-cut face, his strength, listening to his laughter with fear and loathing and trying to think of a suitable insult to pay him back with.

Panteley too went up to the pail. He took a green lamp-glass from his pocket, wiped it with a cloth, scooped water from the pail, drank it, then scooped again before wrapping the glass in the cloth and replacing it in his pocket.

Yegorushka was astonished. 'Why do you drink from a lamp?' he asked the old man.

The answer was evasive. 'Some drinks from a pail and some from a lamp. It's every man to his own taste. If you're one as drinks from a bucket, then drink away, and much good may it do you.'

Suddenly Vasya gave tongue in a tender, plaintive voice. 'Oh, the darling, oh, you beauty, oh, the lovely creature!' His eyes, glinting and smiling, stared into the distance, while his face took on the expression with which he had previously looked at Yegorushka.

'Who's that?' Kiryukha asked.

'A vixen, that be—a-lying on her back, playing like a dog.'

3

All peered into the distance, all looking for the vixen, but no one spotted her. Only Vasya—he of the lack-lustre, grey eyes—could see anything, and he was entranced. His sight, as Yegorushka later discovered, was remarkably acute—so much so that the brown wastes of the prairie were always full of life and content for him. He had only to look into the distance to see a fox, a hare, a great bustard, or some other creature that shuns humanity. To spot a hare running or a bustard in flight is not hard—anyone crossing the steppes saw those—but it is not given to everyone to detect wild creatures in their domestic habitat, when they are not running, hiding or looking about them in alarm. Now, Vasya could see the vixen at play, the hare washing himself with his paws, the great bustard preening his wings, and the little bustard doing his courtship-dance. Thanks to vision so keen, Vasya possessed, besides the world that everyone else sees, a whole world of his own—inaccessible to others and most delectable, presumably, for it was hard not to envy him when he went into raptures over what he beheld.

When the convoy resumed its journey church bells had started ringing for service.

V

The wagon line was drawn up on a river bank to one side of a village. As on the previous day the sun blazed away, and the air was stagnant and despondent. There were a few willows on the bank, their shadows not falling on the earth but on the water where they were wasted, while the shade under the wagons was stifling and oppressive. Azure from the reflected sky, the water urgently beckoned.

Styopka, a carter whom Yegorushka now noticed for the first time, was an eighteen-year-old Ukrainian lad in a long shirt without a belt and in broad trousers worn outside his boots and flapping like flags as he walked. He quickly undressed, ran down the steep bank and dived into the water. After plunging three times he floated on his back and shut his eyes in his delight. He smiled and wrinkled his face as if from a combination of being tickled, hurt and amused.

On a hot day, when there is nowhere to hide from the stifling heat, splashing water and a bather's heavy breathing are music in the ears. Looking at Styopka, Dymov and Kiryukha quickly undressed, laughed loudly with anticipated joy, and flopped into the water one after the other. The quiet, humble brook bombinated with their snorting, splashing and shouting. Kiryukha coughed, laughed and yelled as if someone was trying to drown him, while Dymov chased him and tried to grab his leg.

'Hey there!' shouted Dymov. 'Catch him, hold him!'

Kiryukha was laughing and enjoying himself, but his expression was the same as on dry land: a stupid, flabbergasted look, as if someone had sneaked up from behind and clouted him on the head with a blunt instrument. Yegorushka also undressed. He did not lower himself down the bank, but took a run and a flying leap from a ten-foot height. Describing an arc in the air, he hit the water and sank deep, yet without reaching the bottom. Some power, cold and agreeable to the touch, seized him and bore him back to the surface. Snorting and blowing bubbles, he came up and opened his eyes, only to find the sun reflected on the stream close by his face. First blinding sparks, then rainbow colours and dark patches twitched before his eyes. He hurriedly plunged again, opened his eyes under water and saw something dull green like the sky on a moonlit night. Once more the same power would not let him touch the bottom and stay in the cool, but bore him aloft. Up he popped, and heaved a sigh so deep that he had a feeling of vast space and freshness, not only in his chest but even in his stomach. Then, to make the most of the water, he indulged in every extravagance. He lay on his back and basked, he splashed, he turned somersaults, he swam on his face, on his side, on his back, standing up—just as he pleased till he grew tired. Glinting gold in the sun, the other bank was thickly grown with reeds, and the handsome tassels of their flowers drooped over the water. At one point the reeds quivered and nodded their flowers, which gave out a crackling noise—Styopka and Kiryukha were 'tickling' crayfish.

'Here's one! Look, lads, a crayfish!' shouted Kiryukha triumphantly, displaying what indeed was a crayfish.

Yegorushka swam up to the reeds, dived, and began grubbing among the roots. Burrowing in slimy liquid mud, he felt something sharp and unpleasant. Perhaps it really was a crayfish, but at that moment someone grabbed his leg and hauled him to the surface. Gulping, coughing, he opened his eyes and saw the wet, grinning face of the mischievous Dymov. The rascal was breathing heavily, seeming bent on further tomfoolery from the look in his eyes. He held the boy tightly by the leg, and was lifting the other hand to take hold of his neck when Yegorushka broke away with revulsion and panic, shrinking from his touch as if afraid of the bully drowning him.

'Idiot!' he pronounced. 'I'll bash your face in.' Then, feeling that this was inadequate to express his detestation, he paused in thought and spoke again. 'Swine! Son of a bitch!'

But this had no effect on Dymov, who ignored the boy and swam towards Kiryukha. 'Hey there!' he shouted. 'Let's catch some fish. Let's fish, lads!'

Kiryukha agreed. 'All right. There must be lots here.'

'Nip over to the village, Styopka, and ask the men for a net.'

'They won't lend us none.'

'They will, you ask them. Tell them it's their Christian duty, seeing as we're pilgrims, or as near as don't matter.'

'Aye, 'tis true.'

Styopka climbed out of the water, quickly dressed and ran—bareheaded, his wide trousers flapping—to the village. As for Yegorushka, the water had lost all charm for him after the clash with Dymov. He climbed out and dressed. Panteley and Vasya sat on the steep bank, dangling their legs, and watched the bathers. Close to the bank stood Yemelyan, naked and up to his knees in water, as he held the grass with one hand to stop himself falling over and stroked his body with the other. Bending down, obviously frightened of the water, he cut a comic figure with his bony shoulder-blades and the swelling under his eye. His face was grave and severe, and he looked angrily at the water as if about to curse it for once having given him that chill in the Donets and robbed him of his voice.

'Why don't you go in?' Yegorushka asked Vasya.

'Oh, er—I don't care to.'

'Why is your chin swollen?'

'It hurts. I used to work at a match factory, young sir. The doctor did say as how that was what made me jaw swell. The air ain't healthy there, and there were three other lads beside me had swollen jaws, and one of them had it rot right away.'

Styopka soon came back with the net. After so long in the water Dymov and Kiryukha had become mauve and hoarse, but set about fishing with gusto. They first stalked the deep part near the reeds. Here Dymov was up to his neck and the squat Kiryukha out of his depth. The latter gasped and blew bubbles, while Dymov bumped into prickly roots, kept falling, and got tangled in the net. Both thrashed about noisily, and all that came of their fishing was horseplay.

'It ain't half deep,' croaked Kiryukha. 'We won't catch nothing here.'

'Don't pull, blast you!' shouted Dymov, trying to work the net into position. 'Hold it where it is.'

'You won't catch nothing here,' shouted Panteley from the bank. 'You be only scaring the fish, you fools. Go to the left, 'tis shallower there.'

Once a huge fish gleamed above the net. Everyone gasped, and Dymov punched the spot where it had vanished, his face a picture of vexation.

Panteley grunted, stamping his feet. 'We've missed a perch—got away, he did.'

Moving off to the left, Dymov and Kiryukha gradually worked their way to the shallows, and fishing began in earnest. Having gone about three hundred yards from the wagons, they were seen hauling the net silently, scarcely moving their feet, while trying to get as deep and close to the reeds as they could. To frighten the fish and drive them into the net they flogged the water with their fists and raised a crackle in the reeds. Making for the other bank from the reeds, they trawled there, and then went back to the reeds, looking disappointed and lifting their knees high. They were discussing something, but what it was no one could hear. The sun scorched their backs, insects bit them, and their bodies had turned from mauve to crimson. Styopka followed, carrying a bucket—his shirt was tucked up under his armpits, and he held it in his teeth by the hem. After each successful catch he raised a fish aloft and let it glitter in the sun. 'How about that for a perch?' he shouted. 'And we've five like that!'

Every time Dymov, Kiryukha and Styopka pulled the net out they were seen grubbing in the mud, putting things in the bucket and throwing other things out. Sometimes they passed something that had got into the net from hand to hand, scrutinized it keenly, and then threw that out too.

'What have you got?' shouted voices from the bank.

Styopka gave some answer, but it was hard to tell what. Then he climbed out of the water, gripped the bucket with both hands and ran to the wagons, forgetting to let his shirt drop. 'This one's full,' he shouted, panting hard. 'Let's have another.'

Yegorushka looked at the full bucket. A young pike poked its ugly snout out of the water, with crayfish and small fry swarming around it. The boy put his hand down to the bottom and stirred the water. The pike disappeared beneath the crayfish, a perch and a tench floating up instead. Vasya also looked at the bucket. His eyes gleamed and his expression became as tender as it had when he had seen the vixen. He took something from the bucket, put it in his mouth and started to chew, making a crunching noise.

Styopka was amazed. 'Vasya's eating a live gudgeon, mates—ugh!'

'It ain't no gudgeon, 'tis a chub,' Vasya calmly answered, still munching.

He took the tail from his mouth, looked at it dotingly, and stuck it back again. While he chewed and crunched his teeth Yegorushka felt that what he saw was not a human being. Vasya's swollen chin, his lustreless eyes, his phenomenal eyesight, the fish tail in his mouth and the affectionate air with which he chewed the 'gudgeon'—it all made him look like an animal.

Yegorushka was beginning to find Vasya irksome, and in any case the fishing was over. The boy walked about by the carts, thought for a while and then plodded off to the village out of boredom.

A little later he was standing in the church, leaning his forehead on someone's back—it smelt of hemp—and listening to the choir. The service was nearly over. He knew nothing about church singing and did not care for it. After listening a while he yawned and began examining people's necks and backs. In one head, reddish-brown and wet from recent bathing, he recognized Yemelyan. The back of his hair had been cropped in a straight line, higher than was usual. The hair on his temples had also been cut back higher than it should have been, and Yemelyan's red ears stuck out like two burdock leaves, looking as if they felt out of place. Watching the back of his head and ears, the boy somehow felt that Yemelyan must be very unhappy. He remembered the man 'conducting' with his hands, his hoarse voice, his timid look during the bathing, and felt intensely sorry for him. He wanted to say something friendly. 'I'm here too.' He tugged Yemelyan's sleeve.

The tenors and basses of a choir, especially those who have ever chanced to conduct, are accustomed to looking at boys in a stern and forbidding way. Nor do they lose the habit even when they come to leave the choir. Turning to Yegorushka, Yemelyan looked at him rancorously and told him not to 'lark around' in church.

Yegorushka next made his way forward, closer to the icon-stand, where he saw some fascinating people. In front, on the right-hand side, a lady and gentleman stood on a carpet with a chair behind each of them. Wearing a freshly ironed tussore suit, the gentleman stood stock-still like a soldier on parade, and held his bluish, shaved chin aloft. His stiff collar, blue chin, bald patch and cane—all conveyed great dignity. From excess of dignity his neck was tensed, and his chin was pulled upward with such force that his head seemed ready to snap off and soar into the air at any moment. As for the lady, she was stout and elderly, and wore a white silk shawl. She inclined her head to one side, looking as if she had just done someone a favour and wanted to say: 'Don't trouble to thank me, please—I dislike that sort of thing.' All round the carpet stood a dense array of locals.

Yegorushka went up to the icon-stand and began kissing the local icons, slowly bowing to the ground before each one, looking back at the congregation without getting up, and then standing to apply his lips. The contact of his forehead with the cold floor was most gratifying. When the verger came out of the chancel with a pair of long snuffers to put the candles out, the boy jumped quickly up from the floor and ran to him. 'Has the communion bread been given out?' he asked.

'There is none,' muttered the verger gruffly. 'And it's no use you——'

When the service was over the boy unhurriedly left the church and strolled round the market place. He had seen a good many villages, villagers and village greens in his time, and the present scene held no interest for him. Having nothing to do, he called—just to pass the time of day—at a shop with a broad strip of red calico over the door. It consisted of two spacious, badly lit rooms. In one drapery and groceries were sold, while in the other were tubs of tar and horse-collars hanging from the ceiling. From the second room issued the rich tang of leather and tar. The shop floor had been watered—by some great visionary and original thinker, evidently, for it was sprinkled with embellishments and cabbalistic signs. Behind the counter, leaning his stomach on a sort of desk, stood a well upholstered, broad-faced shopkeeper. He had a round beard, obviously came from the north, and was drinking tea through a piece of sugar, sighing after each sip. His face was a mask of indifference, but each sigh seemed to say: 'Just you wait—. You're for it!'

Yegorushka addressed him. 'A copeckworth of sunflower seed.'

The shopkeeper raised his eyebrows, came out from the counter and poured a copeckworth of sunflower seed into the boy's pocket, using an empty pomade jar as measure. Not wanting to leave, the boy spent a long time examining the trays of cakes, thought a little, and pointed to some small Vyazma gingerbreads rusty with antiquity. 'How much are those?'

'Two a copeck.'

Yegorushka took from his pocket the honey cake given to him by the Jewess on the previous day. 'How much are cakes like this?'

The shopkeeper took the cake in his hands, examined it from all sides and raised an eyebrow. 'Like this, eh?'

Then he raised the other eyebrow and thought for a while. 'Two for three copecks.'

Silence ensued.

'Where do you come from?' The shopkeeper poured himself some tea from a copper teapot.

'I'm Uncle Ivan's nephew.'

'There's all sorts of Uncle Ivans.' The shopkeeper sighed, glanced at the door over Yegorushka's head, paused a moment, and asked if the boy would 'care for a drop of tea'.

'I might.' Yegorushka made a show of reluctance, though he was dying for his usual morning tea.

The shopkeeper poured a glass and gave it to him with a nibbled-looking piece of sugar. Yegorushka sat on a folding chair and drank. He also wanted to ask what a pound of sugared almonds cost, and had just broached the matter when in came a customer, and the shopkeeper put his glass to one side to attend to business. He took the customer into the part of the shop smelling of tar and had a long discussion with him. The customer—evidently a most obstinate man with ideas of his own—kept shaking his head in disagreement and backing towards the door, but the shopkeeper gained his point and began pouring oats into a large sack for him.

'Call them oats?' asked the customer mournfully. 'Them ain't oats, they'm chaff. 'Tis enough to make a cat laugh. I'm going to Bondarenko's, I am.'

When the boy got back to the river a small camp-fire was smoking on the bank—the carters were cooking their meal. In the smoke stood Styopka stirring the pot with a large, jagged spoon. Kiryukha and Vasya, eyes red from smoke, sat a little to one side, cleaning fish. Before them lay the net, covered with slime and water weeds, and with gleaming fish and crawling crayfish on it.

Yemelyan had just returned from church and was sitting next to Panteley, waving his arm and humming 'We sing to Thee' just audibly in a hoarse voice. Dymov pottered near the horses.

After cleaning the fish Kiryukha and Vasya put them and the live crayfish in the pail, rinsed them, and slopped the lot into boiling water.

'Shall I put in some fat?' asked Styopka, skimming off the froth with his spoon.

'No need—the fish will provide their own juice,' replied Kiryukha.

Before taking the pot off the fire Styopka put in three handfuls of millet and a spoonful of salt. Finally he tried it, smacked his lips, licked the spoon and gave a complacent grunt to signify that the stew was cooked.

All except Panteley sat round the pot plying their spoons.

'You there! Give the lad a spoon!' Panteley sternly remarked. 'He's surely hungry too, I reckon.'

' 'Tis plain country fare,' sighed Kiryukha.

'Aye, and it don't come amiss if you've the relish for it.'

Yegorushka was given a spoon. He started to eat, not sitting down but standing near the pot and looking into it as if it was a deep pit. The brew smelt of fishy wetness, with a fish-scale popping up now and again in the millet. The crayfish slid off their spoons, and so the men simply picked them out of the pot with their hands. Vasya was particularly unconstrained, wetting his sleeves as well as his hands in the stew. Yet it tasted very good to Yegorushka, reminding him of the crayfish soup that his mother cooked at home on fast-days. Panteley sat to one side chewing bread.

'Why don't you eat, old 'un?' Yemelyan asked him.

The old man turned squeamishly aside. 'I can't eat crayfish, rot 'em!'

During the meal general conversation took place. From this Yegorushka gathered that, despite differences of age and temperament, his new acquaintances all had one thing in common—each had a glorious past and a most unenviable present. To a man, they all spoke of their past enthusiastically, but their view of the present was almost contemptuous. Your Russian prefers talking about his life to living it. But the boy had yet to learn this, and before the stew was finished he firmly believed that those sitting round the pot were injured victims of fate. Panteley told how, in the old days before the railway, he had served on wagon convoys to Moscow and Nizhny Novgorod, and had earned so much that he hadn't known what to do with his money. And what merchants there had been in those days! What fish! How cheap everything was! But now the roads had shrunk, the merchants were stingier, the common folk were poorer, bread was dearer, and everything had diminished and dwindled exceedingly. Yemelyan said that he had once been in the choir at Lugansk, had possessed a remarkable voice, and had read music excellently, but had now become a bumpkin living on the charity of his brother, who sent him out with his horses and took half his earnings. Vasya had worked in his match factory. Kiryukha had been a coachman to a good family, and had been rated the best troika driver in the district. Dymov, son of a well-to-do peasant, had enjoyed himself and had a good time without a care in the world. But when he was just twenty his stern, harsh father—wanting to teach him the job and afraid of his becoming spoilt at home—had begun sending him out on carrier's work like a poor peasant or hired labourer. Only Styopka said nothing, but you could tell from his clean-shaven face that for him too the past had been far better than the present.

Recalling his father, Dymov stopped eating, frowned, looked sullenly at his mates, and then let his glance rest on Yegorushka. 'Take yer cap off, you heathen,' he said rudely. 'Eating with yer cap on—I must say! And you a gentleman's son!'

Yegorushka did take his hat off, not saying a word, but the stew had lost all relish for him. Nor did he hear Panteley and Vasya standing up for him. Anger with the bully rankled inside him, and he decided to do him some injury at all costs.

After dinner they all made for the carts and collapsed in their shade.

'Are we starting soon, Grandad?' Yegorushka asked Panteley.

'We'll start in God's good time. We can't leave now, 'tis too hot. O Lord, Thy will be done, O Holy Mother. You lie down, lad.'

Soon snoring proceeded from under the wagons. The boy meant to go back to the village, but on reflection he yawned and lay down by the old man.

VI

The wagons stayed by the river all day and left at sunset.

Once more the boy lay on the bales while his wagon quietly squeaked and swayed, and down below walked Panteley—stamping his feet, slapping his thighs, muttering. In the air, as on the day before, the prairie music trilled away.

The boy lay on his back with his hands behind his head, watching the sky. He saw the sunset blaze up and fade. Guardian angels, covering the horizon with their golden wings, had lain down to sleep—the day had passed serenely, a calm, untroubled night had come on, and they could stay peacefully at home in the sky. Yegorushka saw the heavens gradually darken. Mist descended on the earth, and the stars came out one after the other.

When you spend a long time gazing unwaveringly at the deep sky your thoughts and spirit somehow merge in a sense of loneliness. You begin to feel hopelessly isolated, and all that you once thought near and dear becomes infinitely remote and worthless. The stars that have looked down from the sky for thousands of years, the mysterious sky itself and the haze, all so unconcerned with man's brief life—when you are confronted with them, and try to grasp their meaning, they oppress your spirits with their silence, you think of that solitariness awaiting us all in the grave, and life's essence seems to be despair and horror.

The boy thought of his grandmother, now sleeping under the cherry trees in the cemetery. He remembered her lying in her coffin with copper coins on her eyes, remembered the lid being shut and her being lowered into the grave. He remembered, too, the hollow thud of earth clods against the lid. He pictured Grannie in the dark, cramped coffin—abandoned by all, helpless. Then he imagined her suddenly waking up, not knowing where she was, knocking on the lid, calling for help and—in the end, faint with horror—dying a second death. He imagined his mother, Father Christopher, Countess Dranitsky and Solomon as dead. But however hard he tried to see himself in a dark grave—far from his home, abandoned, helpless and dead—he did not succeed. For himself personally he could not admit the possibility of death, feeling that it was not for him.

Panteley, whose time to die had already come, walked by the wagon taking a roll-call of his thoughts. 'They was all right, proper gentle-folk they was,' he muttered. 'They took the little lad to school, but how he's doing—that we don't hear. At Slavyanoserbsk, as I say, they don't have no establishment—not for book-learning proper like. Nay, that they don't. But the lad's all right he is. When he grows up he'll help his dad. You're just a little lad now, son, but you'll grow up and keep your father and mother. That's how 'tis ordained of God— "Honour thy father and thy mother". I had children meself, but they died in a fire, me wife and kids too. Aye, that they did. Our hut burnt down on Twelfth Night eve. I weren't at home, having gone to Oryol. Aye, to Oryol. Marya—she jumped out in the street, but she remembered the children asleep in the hut, she ran back and she was burnt to death along with the little ones. Aye, next day all they could find were the bones.'

About midnight Yegorushka and the wagoners once more sat by a small camp-fire. While the prairie brushwood blazed up, Kiryukha and

Vasya were fetching water from a gully. They vanished in the darkness, but could be heard clanking their pails and talking all the time,
which meant that the gully must be near by. The firelight was a large,
flickering patch on the ground, and though the moon was bright,
everything beyond that red patch seemed black as the pit. The light
was in the wagoners' eyes, and they could see only a small part of the
road. In the darkness wagons, bales and horses were barely visible in
outline as vague mountainous hulks. About twenty paces from the
fire, where road and prairie met, a wooden grave cross slumped.
Before the fire had been lit, while he could still see a long distance, the
boy had spotted another such ramshackle old cross on the other side
of the road.

Coming back with the water, Kiryukha and Vasya filled the pot and
fixed it on the fire. Styopka took his place in the smoke near by,
holding the jagged spoon, looking dreamily at the water and waiting
for the scum to rise. Panteley and Yemelyan sat side by side silently
brooding, while Dymov lay on his stomach, his head propped on his
fists, and watched the fire with Styopka's shadow dancing over him
so that his handsome face darkened and lit up by turns. Kiryukha and
Vasya were wandering a little way off gathering weeds and brushwood for the fire. Yegorushka put his hands in his pockets, stood near
Panteley and watched the flame devour the fuel.

Everyone was resting, reflecting and glancing cursorily at the cross
with the red patches flickering on it. There is something poignant,
wistful and highly romantic about a lonely grave. You feel its silence,
sensing in it the soul of the unknown beneath the cross. Is his spirit at
ease in the steppe? Or does it grieve in the moonlight? The prairie
near the grave seems mournful, despondent and lost in thought, the
grass is sadder, and the crickets appear to chatter with less abandon.
Every passer-by spares a thought for the lonely spirit and turns to
look at the grave until it is behind him and veiled in mist.

'Why is the cross there, Grandad?' Yegorushka asked Panteley.

Panteley looked at the cross and then at Dymov. 'Nicholas, might
that be where the reapers murdered them merchants?'

Dymov reluctantly raised himself on an elbow and looked at the
road. 'Aye, that it be.'

Silence followed. Kiryukha bundled some dry grass together with a
crackling sound, and thrust it under the pot. The fire blazed up,
enveloping Styopka in black smoke, and the shadow of the cross
darted down the road near the wagons.

'Aye, they were killed,' said Dymov reluctantly. 'The merchants, father and son, were travelling icon-sellers. They put up near here in the inn that Ignatius Fomin now keeps. The old man had had a drop too much, and he started bragging about having a lot of cash on him —they're a boastful lot, of course, are merchants, God help us, and they needs must show off to the likes of us. Now, some reapers was staying at the inn at the time. Well, they heard the merchant's boasts and they took due note of 'em.'

'O Lord, mercy on us!' sighed Panteley.

Dymov continued. 'Next day, soon as it was light the merchants got ready to leave and the reapers tagged along. "Let's travel together, mister. It's more cheerful and less risky like, seeing as these be lonely parts." The merchants had to travel at walking pace to avoid breaking their icons, and that just suited them reapers.'

Dymov rose to a kneeling position, stretched and yawned. 'Well, everything went off all right, but no sooner had the merchants reached this spot than them reapers laid into 'em with the scythes. The son, good for him, grabbed a scythe from one of them and did a bit of reaping on 'is own account. But the reapers got the best of it of course, seeing there was about eight of 'em. They hacked at them merchants till there weren't a sound place on their bodies. They finished the job and dragged 'em both off the road, the father one side and the son the other. Opposite this cross there's another on the other side. Whether it still stands I don't know. You can't see from here.'

'It's there,' said Kiryukha.

'They do say as how they found little money on 'em.'

'Aye,' confirmed Panteley. 'About a hundred roubles it were.'

'Aye, and three of them died later on, seeing the merchant cut 'em so bad with the scythe. 'Twas by the blood they tracked 'em. The merchant cut the hand off one, and they do say he ran three miles without it, and was found on a little hummock right by Kurikovo. He was a-squatting with his head on his knees as if he was a-thinking, but when they looked at him the ghost had left him like, and he was dead.'

'They traced him by his bloody tracks,' said Panteley.

All looked at the cross and again there was a hush. From some-where, probably the gully, floated a bird's mournful cry: 'Sleep, sleep, sleep!'

'There's lots of wicked folks in the world,' said Yemelyan.

'Aye, that there is,' agreed Panteley, moving closer to the fire and

looking overcome by dread. 'Lots of 'em,' he went on in an undertone.
'I've seen enough of them in my time—beyond numbering, they've
been, the bad 'uns. I've seen many a saintly, righteous man, too, but
the sinful ones are past counting. Save us, Holy Mother, have mercy!
I remember once—thirty years ago, maybe more—I was driving a
merchant from Morshansk. He was a grand fellow, a striking-looking
man he was, that merchant, and he weren't short of money. He was a
good man, no harm to him. Well, we're a-going along like, and we
puts up at an inn for the night. Now, inns in the north ain't like those
in these parts. Their yards are roofed in, same as the cattle sheds and
threshing barns on big southern estates—only them barns would be
higher.

'Well, we put up there, and it's all right. My merchant has a room,
and I'm with the horses, and everything's proper like. Well, I says my
prayers before going to sleep, lads, and I goes out for a walk in the
yard. But the night's pitch black—not a blind thing can you see. I
walks up and down a bit till I'm near the wagons like, and I sees a
light a-twinkling. Now that's a bit rum, that is. The landlord and his
lady have long been abed, it seems, and there ain't no other guests,
barring me and the merchant. So what's that light doing? I don't like
the look of things. So I goes up to it, and—Lord have mercy on us,
Holy Mother save us! Right down on ground level I sees a little window with bars on it—in the house, that is. I get down on the ground
for a look, and a cold chill runs right through me.'

Kiryukha thrust a bundle of brushwood into the fire, trying to do
so quietly, and the old man waited for it to stop crackling and hissing
before going on.

'I look in there and I see a big cellar—all dark and gloomy. There's
a lamp a-burning on a barrel, and there's a dozen men in there in red
shirts with rolled-up sleeves, a-sharpening of long knives. "Oho!"
thinks I. "We've fallen in with a gang of highwaymen." So what's to
be done? I run to the merchant, I wake him quiet like. "Don't be
afeared, Mister Merchant," says I, "but we're in a bad way, we are.
We're in a robbers' den." His face changes. "What shall we do, Panteley?" he asks. "I've a lot of money with me—'tis for the orphans. As
for my soul," says he, "that's in the Lord's hands. I ain't afeared to die.
But," says he, "I am afeared of losing the orphan fund." Well, I'm
proper flummoxed. The gates are locked, there's no getting out by
horse or by foot. If there'd been a fence you could have climbed over,
but the yard has a roof to it. "Well, Mister Merchant," says I. "Never

you fear, you say your prayers. Happen the Lord won't harm them orphans. Stay here," says I, "and don't let on, and happen I'll hit on something in the meantime."

'So far so good. I says a prayer, and the good Lord enlightens me mind. I climb on me carriage and, quiet as could be so no one will hear, I start stripping the thatch from the eaves, I make a hole and out I crawl. Then, when I'm outside, I jump off the roof and down the road I run as fast as me legs'll carry me—run, run, run till I'm worn to a frazzle. Happen I do three miles in one breath, or more. Then, praise the Lord, I see a village. I rush to a hut, bang on the window. "Good people," says I, and I tells them the tale. "Don't you let 'em destroy a Christian soul." I wake them all up, the villagers gather and off we go together. Some take rope, some cudgels, some pitchforks. We break the inn gate down and straight to the cellar we go.

'By now them robbers have finished sharpening their knives, and they're just going to cut the merchant's throat. The peasants grab the lot of them, tie them up and take them to the authorities. The merchant's so pleased he gives them three hundred roubles and me five gold coins—and he writes my name down so he can remember me in his prayers. They do say a mighty lot of human bones was found in that cellar later. Aye, bones. They'd been a-robbing of people and then burying them to cover the traces, see? Aye, and later on the Morshansk executioners has the flogging of 'em.'

His story finished, Panteley surveyed his audience while they said nothing and looked at him. The water was boiling now, and Styopka was skimming off the froth.

'Is the lard ready?' whispered Kiryukha.

'In a minute.'

Styopka—fixing his eyes on old Panteley, as if fearing to miss the beginning of another story before he got back—ran to the wagons, but soon returned with a small wooden bowl and began rubbing pork fat in it.

'I went on another journey with a merchant,' continued Panteley in the same low voice, not blinking his eyes. 'Name of Peter Grigoryevich, as I now mind. A decent fellow he were, the merchant.

'We stay at an inn, same as before—him in a room, me with the horses. The landlord and his wife seem decent folks, kindly like, and their workers seem all right too. But I can't sleep, lads, there's something on me mind. A hunch it were, no more to be said. The gates are open and there's lots of folk about, but I'm kind of frightened, I don't feel right at all. Everyone has long been asleep, it's far into the night and it'll soon be time to get up, but I just lie alone there in me covered wagon, and I don't close me eyes no more than an owl do. And I can hear this tapping noise, lads: tap, tap, tap. Someone steals up to the wagon. I stick out me head for a look and there's a woman in nothing but a shift, barefoot.

'"What do you want, missus?" I ask and she's all of a dither, she looks like nothing on earth. "Get up, my good man!" says she. "It's trouble. The inn folks are up to no good, they want to do your merchant in. I heard it with me own ears—the landlord and his wife a-whispering together." Well, no wonder I'd had that feeling inside me. "And who might you be?" I asked. "Oh, I'm the cook," says she. So far so good. I get out of the carriage, go to the merchant, wake him up. "There's mischief afoot, Mister Merchant," says I, and so on and so forth. "There'll be time for sleep later, sir," says I. "But you get dressed now, before it's too late, and we'll make ourselves scarce while the going's good."

'Barely has he started dressing himself when—mercy on us!—the door opens, and blow me down if I don't see the landlord, his missus and three workmen come in. So they'd talked their workmen into joining in. "The merchant has a lot of money, and we'll go shares." Every one of the five holds a long knife—a knife apiece they had. The landlord locks the door. "Say your prayers, travellers," says he. "And if so be you start shouting," says he, "we shan't let you pray before you die." As if we could shout! We're a-choking with fear, we ain't up to shouting. The merchant bursts into tears. "Good Christian folk," says he, "you've decided to murder me because you've taken a fancy to my money. Well, so be it. I ain't the first, and I shan't be the last. Not a few of us merchants have had our throats cut in inns. But why kill my driver, friends? Why must he suffer for my money?" And he says it all pathetic like. "If we leave him alive, he'll be the first to bear witness against us," says the innkeeper. "We can just as well kill two as one—may as well hang for a sheep as a lamb," says he. "You say your prayers and that's that, it ain't no use talking."

'The merchant and I kneel down together, weeping like, and we start praying. He remembers his children, while I'm still young, I am, I want to live. We look at the icons and we pray—so pathetic like, it makes me cry even now. And the landlord's missus looks at us. "Don't bear a grudge against us in the other world, good people," says she. "And don't pray to God for us to be punished, for 'tis poverty as drove us to it." Well, we're a-praying and a-weeping away, and God hears us—takes pity on us, He do. Just when the innkeeper had the merchant by the beard—so he could cut his throat, see?—suddenly there's no end of a knock on the window from outside. We cower down and the innkeeper lets his hands fall. Someone bangs the window.

' "Mister Peter, are you there?" a voice shouts. "Get ready, it's time we left."

'The landlord and his missus see that someone's come for the merchant, they're afeared and they take to their heels. We hurry into the yard, hitch up the horses and make ourselves scarce.'

'But who was it banged the window?' asked Dymov.

'Oh, that. Some saint or angel, I reckon, for there weren't no one else. When we drove out of the yard there weren't no one in the street. 'Twas God's doing.'

Panteley told a few more yarns, 'long knives' figuring in all of them, and all having the same ring of fiction. Had he heard these tales from someone else, or had he made them up himself in the distant past, and then, beginning to lose his memory, confused fact and fiction till he could no longer tell one from the other? All things are possible. It is odd, though, that whenever he happened to tell a story, now and throughout the journey, he clearly favoured fantasy and never recounted his actual experiences. Yegorushka took it all at face value at the time, believing every word, but he wondered afterwards that one who had travelled the length and breadth of Russia in his time— who had seen and known so much, whose wife and children had been burnt to death—should so disparage his eventful life that when he sat by the camp-fire he either said nothing or spoke of what had never been.

Over the stew all were silent, thinking of what they had just heard. Life is frightening and marvellous, and so whatever fearful stories you may tell in Russia, and however you embellish them with highway-men's lairs, long knives and such wonders, they will always ring true to the listener, and only a profoundly literate person will look askance, and even he will not say anything. The cross by the road, the dark bales, the vast expanse around them, the fate of those round the camp-fire—all this was so marvellous and frightening in itself that the fantastic element in fiction and folk-tale paled and became indistinguishable from reality.

Everyone ate out of the pot, but Panteley sat apart eating his stew from a wooden bowl. His spoon was different from the others', being of cypress wood with a little cross on it. Looking at him, Yegorushka remembered the lamp glass and quietly asked Styopka why the old fellow sat by himself.

'He's a Dissenter,' whispered Styopka and Vasya, looking as if they had mentioned a weakness or a secret vice.

All were silent, thinking. After the frightening tales they did not feel like talking about everyday things.

Suddenly in the silence Vasya drew himself upright, fixed his lustreless eyes on one point and pricked up his ears.

'What is it?' Dymov asked.

'Someone's coming this way,' answered Vasya.

'Where do you see him?'

'There he is. A faint white shape.'

In the direction in which Vasya was looking nothing could be seen but darkness. All listened, but no steps were heard.

'Is he on the road?' asked Dymov.

'No, he's coming across country. He's coming this way.'

A minute passed in silence.

'Well, perhaps it's the merchant haunting the steppe, the one that's buried here,' said Dymov.

All cast a sidelong glance at the cross, but then they looked at each other and broke into a laugh, ashamed of their panic.

'Why should he haunt the place?' asked Panteley. 'The only ghosts are them that the earth don't accept. And the merchants were all right. They received a martyr's crown, them merchants did.'

But then hurrying footsteps were heard.

'He's carrying something,' said Vasya.

They could hear the grass rustle and the coarse weeds crackle under the walker's feet, but could see no one because of the fire's glare. At last the steps sounded close by and someone coughed. The flickering light seemed to yield, the veil fell from their eyes, and the carters suddenly saw before them a man.

Whether it was due to the flickering light, or because all were keen to make out the man's face, it turned out—oddly enough—that it was neither his face nor his clothes that struck everyone first, but his smile. It was an uncommonly good-natured, broad, gentle smile, as of a waking baby—infectious and tending to evoke an answering smile. When they had looked him over the stranger turned out to be a man of thirty, ugly and in no way remarkable. He was a southerner—tall, with a long nose, long arms and long legs. Everything about him seemed long except his neck—so short that it gave him a stooped look. He wore a clean white shirt with an embroidered collar, baggy white trousers and new riding boots, seeming quite a dandy by comparison with the carters. He was carrying a large white object, mysterious at first sight, and from behind his shoulder peeped out a gun barrel, also long.

Emerging from darkness into the circle of light, he stood stock-still and looked at the carters for half a minute as if calling on them to admire his smile. Then he went to the fire, grinned even more broadly and asked if a stranger might claim their hospitality, 'country fashion'.

'You're welcome indeed,' Panteley answered for everyone.

The stranger laid the object he was carrying near the fire—a dead bustard—and greeted them again.

All went up and examined the bustard.

'A fine big bird—how did you get it?' asked Dymov.

'Buckshot. Small shot's no use, you can't get near enough. Like to buy it, lads? It's yours for twenty copecks.'

'It ain't no use to us. 'Tis good enough roasted, but stewed—powerful tough it be, I reckon!'

'Oh, bother it. I could take it to the squire's lot on the estate. They'd give me half a rouble, but that's a way off—ten mile, it be.'

The stranger sat down, unslung his gun and put it by him. He seemed torpid and sleepy as he smiled and squinted in the light, evidently thinking agreeable thoughts. They gave him a spoon and he started eating.

'And who might you be?' asked Dymov.

Not hearing the question, the smiler neither answered nor even looked at Dymov. He probably could not taste the stew either, for he chewed lazily and rather automatically, his spoon sometimes chock full and sometimes quite empty as he raised it to his mouth. He was not drunk, but he did seem a trifle unhinged.

'I asked you who you were,' Dymov repeated.

'Me?' The stranger gave a start. 'I'm Constantine Zvonyk from Rovnoye, about three miles from here.'

To make it clear from the beginning that he was a cut above your average peasant, he hastened to add that he kept bees and pigs.

'Do you live with your father or in a place of your own?'

'Oh, I'm by myself now, set up on me own I have. I was married this month after St. Peter's Day. So now I'm a husband. 'Tis the eighteenth day since we was wed.'

'That's a fine thing,' said Panteley. 'No harm in having a wife. God has blessed you.'

'His young wife sleeps at home while he's a-wandering the steppes,' laughed Kiryukha. 'Strange doings!'

Constantine winced as though pinched in a sensitive place, laughed and flared up. 'Lord love us, she ain't at home,' he said, quickly taking the spoon from his mouth and surveying everyone with glad surprise. 'That she ain't. She's gone to her mother's for two days. Aye, off she's gone, and I'm a bachelor, like.'

Constantine dismissed the subject with a gesture and flexed his neck, wanting to go on thinking but hindered by the joy irradiating his face. He shifted his position, as if sitting was uncomfortable, laughed and then made another dismissive gesture. He was ashamed to betray his pleasant thoughts to strangers, yet felt an irresistible urge to share his happiness. 'She's gone to her mother's at Demidovo.' He blushed and moved his gun to another place. 'She'll be back tomorrow, she said she'd be back for dinner.'

'Do you miss her?' Dymov asked.

'Lord, yes—what do you think? I ain't been wed but a few days and she's already gone. See what I mean? And she's a little bundle of mischief, Lord love us. Aye, she's marvellous she is, marvellous, always a-laughing and a-singing, a proper handful she be. When I'm with her I don't know whether I'm on me head or me heels, and without her I feel as how I've lost something and I wander over the steppe like a fool. I've been at it since dinner—past praying for, I am.'

Constantine rubbed his eyes, looked at the fire and laughed.

'You must love her then,' said Panteley, but Constantine did not hear.

'She's marvellous, marvellous,' he repeated. 'She's such a good housewife, so clever, so intelligent—you couldn't find another woman like her in the whole county, not among us common folk you couldn't. She's gone away. But she misses me, I know. Aye, that she does, the naughty little thing. She said she'd be back by dinner tomorrow. But what a business it was.' Constantine almost shouted, suddenly pitching his voice higher and shifting his position. 'She loves me and misses me now, but she never did want to wed me, you know.'

'Have something to eat,' said Kiryukha.

'She wouldn't marry me,' Constantine went on, not hearing. 'Three years I spent arguing with her. I saw her at Kalachik fair, and I fell madly in love, I were downright desperate. I live at Rovnoye and she was at Demidovo nigh on twenty mile away and there weren't nothing I could do. I send matchmakers to her, but she says no, the naughty little creature. Well I try one thing and another. I send her ear-rings, cakes and twenty pound of honey, but it's still no. Can you believe it? But then again, when you come to think of it, I'm no match for her. She's young, beautiful and a proper little spitfire, but I'm old —I'll soon be thirty. And then I'm so handsome, ain't I—what with me fine beard the size of a matchstick and me face so smooth that it's one mass of pimples? What chance had I got with her? The only thing was, we are quite well off, but them Vakhramenkos live well too. They keep six oxen and two labourers.

'Well, I were in love with her, lads—proper crazy I was. Couldn't sleep, couldn't eat. God help us, I were that befuddled. I longed to see her, but she was at Demidovo. And do you know—I ain't lying, as God's my witness—I used to walk there about three times a week just to look at her. I stopped working, and I were in such a pother I even wanted to hire myself out as a labourer at Demidovo to be closer to her like. Sheer torture it was. My mother called in a village woman that could cast spells, and my father was ready to beat me a dozen times. Well, I put up with it for three years, and then I decided I'd go and be a cabbie in town, botheration take it! It weren't to be, I reckoned. At Easter I went to Demidovo for a last look at her.'

Constantine threw his head back and gave a peal of merry chuckles, as if he had just brought off a particularly cunning piece of deception. 'I see her with some lads near the stream,' he went on. 'And I feel proper angry. I call her to one side and I say all manner of things to her —for a full hour, maybe. And she falls in love with me! For three years she didn't love me, but she loved me for them words.'

'But what were them words?' Dymov asked.

'The words? I don't recall—how could I? At the time it all comes straight out like water from a gutter—blah, blah, blah, without me stopping to breathe. But I couldn't say one word of it now. So she weds me. And now she's gone to see her mother, the naughty lass, and here I am a-wandering the steppes without her. I can't stay at home, I can't abide to.'

Constantine awkwardly unwound his legs from under him, stretched out on the ground, propped his head on his fists, and then stood up

and sat down again. By now everyone could clearly see that here was
a man happy in love, poignantly happy. His smile, his eyes, his every
movement reflected overwhelming bliss. He fidgeted, not knowing
what posture to adopt or avoid, being drained of vitality through
excess of delectable thoughts. Having poured his heart out to strangers,
he settled down quietly at last, deep in thought as he gazed at the
fire.

Seeing a happy man, the others felt depressed, wanting to be happy
themselves, and fell to pondering. Dymov stood up and slowly
strolled about near the fire, his walk and the movement of his shoulder-
blades showing how weary and depressed he was. He stood still for a
while, looked at Constantine and sat down.

The camp-fire was dying down by now, no longer flickering, and
the patch of red had shrunk and dimmed. And the quicker the fire
burnt out the clearer the moonlight became. Now the road could be
seen in its full width—the bales of wool, the wagon shafts, the munching horses. On the other side was the hazy outline of the second cross.

Dymov propped his cheek on his hand and softly sang a mournful
ditty. Constantine smiled drowsily, and joined in with his reedy little
voice. They sang for less than a minute and fell silent. Yemelyan gave
a start, flexed his elbows and flicked his fingers. 'I say, lads, let's sing a
holy song,' he entreated them.

Tears came into his eyes and he pressed his hand to his heart, repeating his appeal to sing 'a holy song'. Constantine said he 'didn't know
any', and everyone else refused. Then Yemelyan started on his own.
He conducted with both hands, he tossed his head back and he opened
his mouth, but from his throat burst only a hoarse, voiceless breath.
He sang with his arms, head and eyes, and even with the swelling on
his cheek. He sang fervidly and with anguish, and the more he strained
his chest to extract a note, be it but a single one, the less sound did his
breath carry.

Overcome by depression like everyone else, Yegorushka went to
his wagon, climbed on the bales and lay down. He looked at the sky,
thinking of lucky Constantine and his wife. Why do people marry?
Why are there women in the world, the boy vaguely wondered,
thinking how nice it must be for a man to have a loving, cheerful,
beautiful woman constantly at his side. For some reason thoughts of
Countess Dranitsky came into his head. How agreeable it must be to
live with a woman like that! Perhaps he would have liked to marry
her himself, had the notion not been so embarrassing. He recalled her

eyebrows, the pupils of her eyes, her coach and the clock with the horseman. The quiet, warm night settled down over him, whispering something in his ear, and he felt as if that same beautiful woman was bending over him, looking at him, smiling, wanting to kiss him.

Nothing was left of the camp-fire but two little red eyes that dwindled and dwindled. The carters and Constantine sat round it—dark, still figures—and there seemed to be far more of them than before. The twin crosses were equally visible, and somewhere far away on the road a red light glowed—someone else cooking a meal, probably.

> 'Here's to good old Mother Russia,
> Finest nation in the world,'

Kiryukha suddenly sang out in a harsh voice, then choked and grew silent. The prairie echo caught his voice and carried it on so that the very spirit of stupidity seemed to be trundling over the steppe on heavy wheels.

'Time to go,' said Panteley. 'Up you get, mates.'

While they were hitching up Constantine was walking about by the wagons singing his wife's praises. 'Thanks for the hospitality, lads, and good-bye,' he shouted as the convoy moved off. 'I'll make for the other fire. It's all too much for me, it is.'

He quickly disappeared in the gloom, and could long be heard walking towards the glimmering light so that he could tell those other strangers of his happiness.

When the boy woke up next day it was early morning and the sun had not risen. The wagons had halted. Talking to Dymov and Kiryukha by the leading vehicle was a man on a Cossack pony—he wore a white peaked cap and a suit of cheap grey cloth. About a mile and a half ahead of the wagons were long, low white barns and cottages with tiled roofs. Neither yards nor trees were to be seen near them.

'What village is that?' Yegorushka asked the old man.

'Them farms are Armenian, young feller,' answered Panteley. ' 'Tis where the Armenians live—not a bad lot, they ain't.'

The man in grey finished talking to Dymov and Kiryukha, reined in his pony and looked at the farms.

' 'Tis a proper botheration,' sighed Panteley, also looking at the farms and shivering in the cool of the morning. 'He sent a man to the farm for some bit of paper, but he hasn't come back. He should have sent Styopka.'

'But who is he?' asked the boy.

'Varlamov.'

Varlamov! Yegorushka quickly jumped to his knees and looked at the white cap. It was hard to recognize the mysterious, elusive Varlamov, who was so much in demand, who was always 'knocking around', and who had far more money than Countess Dranitsky, in this short, grey, large-booted little man on the ugly nag who was talking to peasants at an hour when all decent people are abed.

'He's all right, a good sort he is,' said Panteley, looking at the farms. 'God grant him health, he's a fine gentleman, is Simon Varlamov. It's the likes of him as keeps the world a-humming, lad. Aye, that they do. It ain't cock-crow yet, and he's already up and about. Another man would be asleep, or he'd be at home gallivanting with his guests, but Varlamov's out on the steppe all day, knocking around like. Never misses a deal, he don't—and good for him, say I.'

Varlamov was staring fixedly at one of the farms, discussing something while his pony shifted impatiently from foot to foot.

'Hey, Mr. Varlamov!' shouted Panteley, taking off his hat. 'Let me send Styopka. Yemelyan, give a shout—send Styopka, tell 'em.'

But now at last a man on horseback was seen to leave the farm. Leaning heavily to one side and swinging his whip over his head, as if giving a rodeo performance and wanting to dazzle everyone with his horsemanship, he flew like a bird to the wagons.

'That must be one of his rangers,' said Panteley. 'A hundred of them he has, or more.'

Reaching the first wagon, the rider pulled up his horse, doffed his cap and gave a little book to Varlamov, who removed several papers from it and read them.

'But where's Ivanchuk's letter?' he shouted.

The horseman took the book back, looked at the papers and shrugged. He began saying something, probably in self-defence, and asked permission to go back to the farms. The pony suddenly gave a start as if Varlamov had become heavier, and Varlamov also gave a start.

'Clear out!' he shouted angrily, brandishing his whip at the rider. Then he turned his pony round and rode along the wagons at a walk, examining the papers in the book. When he reached the last wagon Yegorushka strained his eyes to get a good look. Varlamov was quite old. He had a small grey beard, and his simple, sunburnt, typically Russian face was red, wet with dew and covered with little blue veins.

He had exactly the same businesslike expression as Ivan Kuzmichov, and the same fanatical devotion to affairs. But what a difference you could feel between him and Kuzmichov! Besides wearing an air of businesslike reserve, Uncle Ivan always looked worried and afraid— of not finding Varlamov, of being late, of missing a bargain. But in Varlamov's face and figure there was nothing of your typical little man's dependent look. This man fixed the price himself. He didn't go round looking for people, and he depended on no one. Nondescript though his appearance might be, everything about him—even the way he held his whip—conveyed a sense of power and the habit of authority over the steppe.

He did not glance at the boy as he rode past. Only his pony deigned to notice Yegorushka, gazing at him with large, foolish eyes—and even the pony was not very interested. Panteley bowed to Varlamov, who noticed this but did not take his eyes off his papers and just said: 'Greetings, grandpa,' gargling the 'r's in his throat.

Varlamov's interchange with the horseman and the swish of his whip had evidently demoralized the whole party, for all looked grave. Quailing before the strong man's wrath, the horseman remained by the front wagon with his head bare, let his reins hang loose and said nothing, as if unable to believe that the day had begun so badly for him.

'He's a rough old boy,' muttered Panteley. 'Real hard. But he's all right—a good sort he is. He don't harm no one without reason. He's all right he is!'

After examining the papers, Varlamov thrust the book in his pocket. Seeming to understand his thoughts, the pony quivered and careered down the road without waiting for orders.

VII

On the following night the wagoners again halted to cook their meal, but on this occasion everything seemed tinged with melancholy from the start. It was sultry and they had all drunk a great deal, but without in the least quenching their thirst. The moon rose—intensely crimson and sullen, as if it were ailing. The stars were gloomy too, the mist was thicker, the distant prospect was hazier, and all nature seemed to wilt at some intimation of doom.

There was no more of the previous day's excitement and conversation round the camp-fire. All were depressed, all spoke listlessly and reluctantly. Panteley did nothing but sigh and complain of his feet, while occasionally invoking the topic of dying 'contumaciously'.

Dymov lay on his stomach, silently chewing a straw. He wore a fastidious expression as if the straw had a bad smell, and he looked ill-tempered and tired. Vasya complained that his jaw ached, and forecast bad weather. Yemelyan had stopped waving his arms, and sat still, looking grimly at the fire. Yegorushka was wilting too. The slow pace had tired him, and he had a headache from the day's heat.

When the stew was cooked Dymov began picking on his mates out of boredom. He glared spitefully at Yemelyan. 'Look at old Lumpy Jaws sprawling there! Always first to shove his spoon in, he is. Talk about greed! Can't wait to grab first place by the pot, can he? Thinks he's the lord of creation because he used to be a singer. We know your sort of choirboy, mister—there's tramps like you a-plenty singing for their suppers up and down the high road.'

Yemelyan returned the other's angry glare. 'Why pick on me?'

'To teach you not to dip in the pot before others. Who do you think you are?'

'You're a fool, that's all I can say,' wheezed Yemelyan.

Knowing from experience how such conversations usually ended, Panteley and Vasya intervened, urging Dymov to stop picking a quarrel.

'You—sing in a choir!' The irrepressible bully laughed derisively. 'Anyone can sing like that, rot you—sitting in the church porch a-chanting of your "Alms for Christ's sake!"'

Yemelyan said nothing. His silence exasperated Dymov, who looked at the ex-chorister with even greater hatred. 'I don't want to soil me hands, or I'd teach you not to be so stuck up.'

Yemelyan flared up. 'Why pick on me, you scum? What have I done to you?'

'What did you call me?' Dymov straightened up, his eyes blood-shot. 'What was that? Scum, eh? Very well—now you can go and look for that!'

He snatched the spoon from Yemelyan's hands and hurled it far to one side. Kiryukha, Vasya and Styopka jumped up and went to look for it, while Yemelyan fixed an imploring and questioning look on Panteley. His face suddenly shrinking, the former chorister frowned, blinked and wept like a baby.

Yegorushka, who had long hated Dymov, felt as if he had started to choke, and the flames of the fire scorched his face. He wanted to run quickly into the darkness by the wagons, but the bully's spiteful, bored eyes had a magnetic effect. Longing to say something exceedingly offensive, the boy took a step towards Dymov. 'You're the worst of the lot,' he panted. 'I can't stand you!'

That was when he should have run to the wagons, but he seemed rooted to the spot. 'You will burn in hell in the next world,' he continued. 'I'm going to tell Uncle Ivan about you. How dare you insult Yemelyan?'

'Now, ain't that a nice surprise, I must say!' Dymov laughed. 'A little swine, what ain't dry behind the ears, a-laying down the law! Want a clip on the ear-'ole?'

The boy felt as if there was no air to breathe. He suddenly shivered all over and stamped his feet, something that had never happened to him before.

'Hit him, hit him!' he yelled in a piercing voice. Tears spurted from his eyes, he felt ashamed and he ran staggering to the wagons. What impression his outburst produced he did not see. 'Mother, Mother!' he whispered, lying on the bale, weeping, jerking his arms and legs.

The men, the shadows round the camp-fire, the dark bales and the distant lightning flashing far away every minute—it all seemed so inhuman and terrifying now. He was horrified, wondering in his despair how and why he had landed in this unknown land in the company of these awful peasants. Where were his uncle, Father Christopher and Deniska? Why were they so long in coming? Could they have forgotten him? To be forgotten and abandoned to the whim of fate— the thought so chilled and scared him that he several times felt like jumping off the bale and running headlong back along the road without looking behind him. What stopped him was the memory of those grim, dark crosses that he was bound to meet on his way, and also the distant lightning flashes. Only when he whispered 'Mother, Mother!' did he feel a little better.

The carters must have been scared too. After the boy had run from the fire they said nothing for a while, and then spoke of something in hollow undertones, saying that 'it' was on its way, and that they must hurry up and get ready to escape it. They quickly finished supper, put out the fire and began hitching up the horses in silence. Their agitation and staccato speech showed that they foresaw some disaster.

Before they started off Dymov went up to Panteley. 'What's his name?' he asked quietly.

'Yegorushka,' answered Panteley.

Dymov put one foot on a wheel, seized the cord round a bale and hoisted himself. The boy saw his face and curly head—the face looked pale, weary and grave, but no longer spiteful. 'Hey, boy!' he said quietly. 'Go on, hit me!'

Yegorushka looked at him in amazement, and at that moment there was a flash of lightning.

'It's all right, hit me!' continued Dymov. Without waiting to see whether the boy would hit him or talk to him, he jumped down. 'I'm bored,' he said. Then, rolling from side to side and working his shoulder-blades, he slowly strolled down the wagon line.

'God, I'm bored,' he repeated in a tone half plaintive, half irritated. 'No offence, old son,' he said as he passed Yemelyan. 'It's cruel hard, our life.'

Lightning flashed on the right, and immediately flashed again far away, as if reflected in a mirror.

'Take this, boy,' shouted Panteley, handing up something large and dark from below.

'What is it?' asked Yegorushka.

'Some matting. Put it over you when it rains.'

The boy sat up and looked around. It had grown noticeably blacker in the distance, with the pale light now winking more than once a minute. The blackness was veering to the right as if pulled by its own weight.

'Will there be a storm, Grandad?' asked the boy.

'Oh, my poor feet, they're so cold,' intoned Panteley, not hearing him and stamping his feet.

On the left, as if a match had been struck on the sky, a pale phosphorescent stripe gleamed and faded. Very far away someone was heard walking up and down on an iron roof—barefoot, presumably, because the iron gave out a hollow rumble.

'Looks like a real old downpour,' shouted Kiryukha.

Far away, beyond the horizon on the right, flashed lightning so vivid that it lit up part of the steppe and the place where the clear sky met the black. An appalling cloud was moving up unhurriedly—a great hulk with large black shreds hanging on its rim. Similar shreds pressed against each other, looming on the horizon to right and left. The jagged, tattered-looking cloud had a rather drunken and disorderly air. There was a clearly enunciated clap of thunder. Yegorushka crossed himself, and quickly put on his overcoat.

'Real bored, I am.' Dymov's shout carried from the leading wagons, his tone showing that his bad temper was returning. 'Bored.'

There was a sudden squall of wind so violent that it nearly snatched the boy's bundle and matting off him. Whipping, tearing in all directions, the mat slapped the bale and Yegorushka's face. The wind careered whistling over the steppe, swerving chaotically and raising such a din in the grass that it drowned the thunder and creak of wagon wheels. It was blowing from the black thunderhead, bearing dust clouds, and the smell of rain and damp earth. The moon misted over, seeming dirtier, the stars grew dimmer still, dust clouds and their shadows were seen scurrying off somewhere back along the edge of the road. Eddying and drawing dust, dry grass and feathers from the ground, whirlwinds soared right into the upper heavens, it seemed. Uprooted plants must be flying around close by the blackest thunderhead, and how terrified they must feel! But dust clogged the eyes, blanking out everything except the lightning flashes.

Thinking the rain was just about to pour down, the boy knelt up and covered himself with his mat. From in front came a shout of 'Panteley', followed by some incomprehensible booming syllables.

'I can't hear!' loudly intoned Panteley in response, and the voice boomed out again.

An enraged clap of thunder rolled across the sky from right to left and then back again, dying away near the leading wagons.

'Holy, holy, holy, Lord God of Sabaoth,' whispered Yegorushka, crossing himself. 'Heaven and earth are full of thy glory.'

The sky's blackness gaped, breathing white fire, and at once there was another thunderclap. Barely had it died away when there was a flash of lightning so broad that the boy could see the whole road into the far distance, all the carters and even Kiryukha's waistcoat through the cracks in the matting. The black tatters on the left were already soaring aloft, and one of them—crude, clumsy, a paw with fingers—reached out towards the moon. Yegorushka decided to shut his eyes tightly, pay no attention and wait for it all to end.

The rain was long delayed for some reason, and the boy—hoping that the thunder cloud might pass over—peeped out from his mat. It was fearfully dark, and he could see neither Panteley nor the bale nor himself. He squinted towards where the moon had been, but it was pitch black there, as on the wagon. In the darkness the lightning flashes seemed whiter and more blinding, hurting the eyes.

He called Panteley's name, but there was no answer. Then, in the end, the wind gave a last rip at the mat and flew off. A low, steady throb was heard, and a large, cold drop fell on the boy's knee, while another crawled down his hand. Realizing that his knees were uncovered, he tried to rearrange the matting, but then came a pattering and a tapping of something on the road, and on the shafts and the bale. Rain. It seemed to have an understanding with the mat, for the two started some discussion—rapid, cheerful and exceedingly objectionable, like a couple of magpies.

Yegorushka knelt up—squatted, rather, on his boots. When the rain rapped the mat he leant forward to shield his suddenly soaked knees. He managed to cover them, but in less than a minute he felt an unpleasant penetrating wetness behind, on back and calves. He resumed his former position and stuck his knees out into the rain, wondering what to do and how to rearrange the mat that he could not see in the dark. But his arms were already wet, water was running down his sleeves and behind his collar, his shoulder-blades were cold. And so he decided to do nothing, but to sit still and wait for it all to end. 'Holy, holy, holy,' he whispered.

Suddenly, directly over his head, came an almighty deafening crash and the sky broke in two. He bent forwards—holding his breath, expecting the pieces to fall on his neck and back. He chanced to open his eyes, blinking half a dozen times as a penetrating, blinding light flared up, and he saw his fingers, his wet sleeves and the streams flowing off the mat, over the bale and down below on the earth. Then a new blow, no less mighty and awesome, resounded. No longer did the sky groan or rumble, but gave out crackles like the splitting of a dry tree.

The thunder's crash-bang beats were precisely enunciated as it rolled down the sky, staggered, and—somewhere by the leading wagons or far behind—tumbled over with a rancorous, staccato drumming.

The earlier lightning flashes had been awesome, but with thunder such as this they seemed downright menacing. The weird light penetrated your closed eyelids, percolating chillingly through your whole body. Was there a way to avoid seeing it? The boy decided to turn his face backwards. Carefully, as if afraid of being observed, he got on all fours, slid his palms over the wet bale and turned round.

The great drumming swooped over his head, collapsed under the wagon and exploded.

Again his eyes chanced to open and he saw a new danger. Behind the wagon stalked three giants with long pikes. The lightning flashed on the points of their pikes, distinctly lighting up their figures. These were people of vast dimensions with hidden faces, bowed heads and heavy footsteps. They seemed sad, despondent and lost in thought. Their aim in stalking the convoy may not have been to cause damage, but there was something horrible in their proximity.

The boy quickly turned forwards. 'Panteley! Grandad!' he shouted, shaking all over.

The sky answered him with a crash, bang, crash.

As he opened his eyes, to see whether the carters were there, the lightning flashed in two places, illuminating the road to the far horizon, the entire convoy and all the men. Rivulets streamed down the road, and bubbles danced. Panteley strode by his wagon, his high hat and shoulders covered with a small mat. His figure expressed neither fear nor alarm, as though he had been deafened by the thunder and blinded by the lightning.

'Grandad, see the giants!' the boy shouted at him, weeping.

But the old man heard nothing. Further ahead Yemelyan walked along, covered with a large mat from head to foot and triangular in shape. Vasya, who had nothing over him, stepped out in his usual clockwork style—lifting his feet high, not bending his knees. In the lightning the convoy seemed motionless, with the carters rooted to the spot and Vasya's raised leg frozen rigid in position.

Yegorushka called the old man again. Receiving no answer, he sat still, but he was no longer expecting it all to end. He was certain that the thunder would kill him that very instant, that he would open his eyes by accident and see those frightful giants. No longer did he cross himself, call the old man or think of his mother—he was simply numb with cold and the certainty that the storm would never end.

Suddenly voices were heard.

'Yegorushka, you asleep, or what?' shouted Panteley from below. 'Get down. Has he gone deaf, the silly lad?'

'Quite a storm!' It was a deep, unfamiliar voice, and the speaker cleared his throat as if he had tossed down a glassful of vodka.

The boy opened his eyes. Down near the wagon stood Panteley, triangle-shaped Yemelyan and the giants. The latter were now much shorter and turned out, when Yegorushka got a proper sight of them, to be ordinary peasants shouldering iron pitch-forks, not pikes. In the space between Panteley and the triangular Yemelyan shone the window of a low hut—the wagons must have halted in a village. Yegorushka threw off his mat, took his bundle and hurried down from the wagon. Now, what with people speaking near by and the lighted window, he no longer felt afraid, though the thunder crashed as loudly as ever and lightning scourged the whole sky.

'A decent storm—not bad at all, praise the Lord,' muttered Panteley. 'My feet have gone a bit soft in the rain, but no matter. Are you down, boy? Well, go in the hut. It's all right.'

'It must have struck somewhere, Lord save us,' wheezed Yemelyan. 'You from these parts?' he asked the giants.

'Nay, from Glinovo. From Glinovo we be. We work at the squire's place—name of Plater.'

'Threshers, are you?'

'We do different things. Just now we be getting in the wheat. But what lightning, eh? There ain't been a storm like this for many a moon.'

Yegorushka went into the hut, where he was greeted by a lean, hunchbacked old woman with a sharp chin. She held a tallow candle, screwing up her eyes and giving prolonged sighs.

'What a storm God has sent us!' she said. 'And our lads are spending the night on the steppe—what a time they'll have of it, poor souls. Now, take your clothes off, young sir—come on.'

Trembling with cold, shrinking fastidiously, the boy pulled off his wet overcoat, spread his hands and feet far apart and did not move for a long time. The slightest motion evoked a disagreeably damp, cold sensation. The sleeves and the back of his shirt were sopping, his trousers stuck to his legs, his head was dripping.

'Don't stand there splayed out like,' said the old woman. 'Come and sit down, lad.'

Straddling his legs, Yegorushka went to the table and sat on a bench near someone's head. The head moved, emitting a stream of air through the nose, made a chewing sound and subsided. From the head a mound covered with a sheepskin stretched along the bench—a sleeping peasant woman.

Sighing, the old woman went out and suddenly came back with a big water-melon and a small sweet melon. 'Help yourself, young man, I've nothing else for you.'

Yawning, she dug into a table drawer and took out a long, sharp knife much like those used by highwaymen to cut merchants' throats in inns. 'Help yourself, young sir.'

Trembling as if in fever, the boy ate a slice of sweet melon with black bread, and then a slice of water-melon, which made him even colder.

'Out on the steppe our lads are tonight,' sighed the old woman while he ate. ' 'Tis a proper botheration. I did ought to light a candle before the icon, but I don't know where Stepanida's put it. Help yourself, young man, do.' The old woman yawned, reached back with her right hand, and scratched her left shoulder. 'Two o'clock it must be,' she said. 'Time to get up soon. Our lads are outside for the night. Soaked to the skin they'll be, for sure.'

'I'm sleepy, Grannie,' said the boy.

'Then lie down, young man, do,' sighed the old woman, yawning. 'I was asleep meself, when—Lord God Almighty!—I hear someone a-knocking. I wake up and I see God's sent us a storm. I'd light a candle, dear, but I couldn't find one.'

Talking to herself, she pulled some rags off the bench, probably her bedding, took two sheepskins from a nail near the stove, and began making up a bed for the boy. ' 'Tis as stormy as ever,' she muttered. 'I'm afeared it might start a fire, you never can tell. The lads are out on the steppe all night. Lie down, young man, go to sleep. God bless you, my child. I won't clear away the melon—happen you'll get up and have a bite.'

The old soul's sighs and yawns, the measured breathing of the sleeping woman, the hut's dim light, the sound of rain through the window—it all made him sleepy. Shy of taking his clothes off in the old woman's presence, he removed only his boots, lay down and covered himself with the sheepskin.

A minute later Panteley's whisper was heard. 'Is the lad lying down?'

'Yes,' whispered the old woman. ' 'Tis a proper botheration. Bang, crash, bang—no end to it.'

'It'll soon be over,' wheezed Panteley, sitting down. 'It's quieter now. The lads have gone to different huts, and a couple have stayed with the horses. Aye, the lads. Have to do it, or else the horses will be stolen. Well, I'll stay a while, and then take my turn. Have to do it, or they'll be stolen.'

Panteley and the old woman sat side by side at Yegorushka's feet, talking in sibilant whispers punctuated by sighs and yawns. But the boy just could not get warm. He had a warm, heavy sheepskin over him, but his whole body shivered, his hands and legs were convulsed with cramps, his insides trembled. He undressed under the sheepskin, but it made no difference. The shivering became more and more pronounced.

Panteley left to take his turn with the horses and then came back

4

again, but Yegorushka still could not sleep, and was still shivering all over. His head and chest felt crushed and oppressed by—by what he did not know. Was it the old people whispering or the strong smell of the sheepskin? The melons had left a nasty metallic taste in his mouth, besides which he was being bitten by fleas. 'I'm cold, Grandad,' he said, not recognizing his own voice.

'Sleep, son, sleep,' sighed the old woman.

Titus approached the bed on his thin legs, waved his arms, and then grew as tall as the ceiling and turned into a windmill. Father Christopher—not as he had been in the britzka, but in full vestments and carrying his aspergillum, walked around the mill, sprinkling it with holy water and it stopped turning. Knowing he was delirious, the boy opened his eyes. He called to the old man. 'Water!'

No answer. Finding it unbearably close and uncomfortable lying there, Yegorushka stood up, dressed and went out of the hut. It was morning now and the sky was overcast, but the rain had stopped. Trembling, wrapping his wet overcoat round him, he walked up and down the muddy yard, trying to catch a sound amid the silence. Then his eyes lighted on a small shed with a half-open door made of thatch. He looked in, entered and sat in a dark corner on a heap of dry dung.

His head felt heavy, his mind was in a whirl and there was a dry, unpleasant sensation in his mouth owing to the metallic taste. He looked at his hat, straightened its peacock feather, and remembered going to buy it with his mother. Putting his hand in his pocket, he took out a lump of brown, sticky paste. How did that stuff get in there? He thought, he sniffed it. A smell of honey. Ah, yes—the Jewish cake. How sodden the poor thing was!

The boy looked at his overcoat—grey with big bone buttons, cut like a frock-coat. A new and expensive garment, it had not hung in the hall at home, but with his mother's dresses in the bedroom. He was only allowed to wear it on holidays. The sight of it moved him to pity—he recalled that he and the overcoat had both been abandoned to their fate, and would never go home again. And he sobbed so loudly that he nearly fell off the dung pile.

A big white dog, sopping wet and with woolly tufts like curling papers on its muzzle, came into the shed and stared quizzically at the boy. It was obviously wondering whether to bark or not, but decided that there was no need, cautiously approached the boy, ate the lump of paste and went out.

'Them's Varlamov's men,' someone shouted in the street.

Having cried his eyes out, the boy left the shed, skirted a puddle and made his way to the street, where some wagons stood immediately in front of the gates. Wet carters with muddy feet, listless and drowsy as autumn flies, drifted near by or sat on the shafts. Looking at them, Yegorushka thought what a boring, uncomfortable business it was, being a peasant. He went up to Panteley and sat down on the shaft beside him. 'I'm cold, Grandad.' He shivered and thrust his hands into his sleeves.

'Never mind, we'll be there soon,' yawned Panteley. 'You'll get warm, never fear.'

It was quite cool, and the convoy made an early start. Yegorushka lay on his bale, trembling with cold, though the sun soon came out and dried his clothes, the bale and the ground. Barely had he closed his eyes when he saw Titus and the windmill again. Nauseated, feeling heavy all over, he fought to dispel these images, but as soon as they disappeared the bullying Dymov would pounce on him—roaring, red-eyed, his fists raised, or would be heard lamenting how 'bored' he was. Varlamov rode past on his Cossack pony, and happy Constantine walked by with his smile and his bustard. How depressing, intolerable and tiresome they all were!

In the late afternoon the boy once raised his head to ask for a drink. The wagons had halted on a large bridge over a wide river. Down below the river was shrouded in smoke through which a steamer could be seen towing a barge. Ahead, beyond the river, was a huge vari-coloured mountain dotted with houses and churches. At its foot a railway engine was being shunted round some goods wagons.

Never had the boy seen steamers, railway trains or wide rivers before, but as he glanced at them now he was neither frightened nor surprised. Nor did his face even express any semblance of curiosity. Nauseated, he quickly lay down with his chest on the bale's edge, feeling ready to vomit. Panteley saw him, grunted and shook his head.

'Our little lad's poorly,' said he. ' 'Tis a chill on the stomach, I'll be bound. Aye, and that far from home like. 'Tis a bad business.'

VIII

The wagons had stopped at a large commercial inn not far from the harbour. Climbing down from the wagon, Yegorushka heard a familiar voice and someone gave him a hand. 'We arrived yesterday evening. We've been expecting you all day. We meant to catch you up yesterday, but it didn't work out and we took a different route. Hey, what a mess you've made of your coat! Your uncle *will* give you what for!'

Gazing at the speaker's mottled face, Yegorushka remembered it as Deniska's.

'Your uncle and Father Christopher are in their room at the inn having tea. Come on.'

He took the boy to a big two-storey building—dark, gloomy, resembling the almshouse at N. By way of a lobby, a dark staircase and a long, narrow corridor Yegorushka and Deniska came to a small room where Ivan Kuzmichov and Father Christopher indeed were seated at a tea table. Both old men showed surprise and joy at seeing the boy.

'Aha, young sir! Master Lomonosov in person!' intoned Father Christopher.

'So it's the gentleman of the family,' said Kuzmichov. 'Pleased to see you.'

Taking his overcoat off, the boy kissed his uncle's hand and Father Christopher's, and sat down at the table.

'Well, how was the journey, *puer bone*?' Father Christopher showered him with questions, pouring him tea and smiling his habitual radiant smile. 'Sick of it, I'll be bound? Never travel with a wagon train or by ox-cart, God forbid. You go on, on, on, Lord help us, you glance ahead and the steppe's just as long-windedly elongated as ever, no end or limit to it. It's not travel, it's a downright travesty of it. But why don't you drink your tea? Go on! Well, while you were trailing along with the wagons we fixed things up to a tee here, thank God. We've sold our wool to Cherepakhin at tip-top prices—done pretty well, we have.'

On first seeing his own people, the boy felt an irresistible urge to complain. Not listening to Father Christopher, he wondered where to start and what exactly to complain of. But Father Christopher's voice, seeming harsh and disagreeable, prevented him from concentrating and confused his thoughts. After sitting for less than five minutes, he got up from table, went to the sofa and lay down.

Father Christopher was amazed. 'Well, I never! What about your tea?'

Still wondering what to complain of, Yegorushka pressed his forehead against the back of his sofa and burst into sobs.

'Well, I never!' repeated Father Christopher, getting up and going over to him. 'What's the matter with you, boy? Why the tears?'

'I—I'm ill.'

'Ill, eh?' Father Christopher was rather put out. 'Now, that's quite wrong, old son. You mustn't fall ill on a journey. Oh dear me, what a thing to do, old son, eh?'

He placed his hand on the boy's head and touched his cheek.

'Yes, your head's hot. You must have caught a chill, or else you've eaten something. You must pray to God.'

'We might try quinine.' Kuzmichov was somewhat abashed.

'No, he should eat something nice and hot. How about a nice bowl of soup, boy?'

'No—I don't want any,' answered Yegorushka.

'Feeling shivery, eh?'

'I was, but now I feel hot. I ache all over.'

Kuzmichov went over, touched the boy's head, cleared his throat in perplexity, and went back to the table.

'Well, you'd better get undressed and go to sleep,' said Father Christopher. 'What you need is a good rest.'

He helped the boy undress, gave him a pillow, covered him with a quilt with Kuzmichov's topcoat over it, and then tiptoed off and sat at the table. Closing his eyes, Yegorushka immediately imagined that he was not in an inn room but on the high road by the camp-fire. Yemelyan swung his invisible baton while red-eyed Dymov lay on his stomach looking sarcastically at Yegorushka.

'Hit him, hit him!' the boy shouted.

'He's delirious,' said Father Christopher in an undertone.

Kuzmichov sighed. 'Oh, what a nuisance!'

'We ought to rub him with oil and vinegar. Let's hope to God he'll be better tomorrow.'

Trying to shake off his irksome fancies, Yegorushka opened his eyes and looked at the light. Father Christopher and Kuzmichov had finished their tea and were having a whispered discussion. The former smiled happily, obviously unable to forget that he had netted a good profit on his wool. It was less the actual profit that cheered him than the prospect of assembling all his large family on his return, and of giving a knowing wink and a mighty chuckle. First he would mislead them, claiming to have sold the wool below its value, but then he'd give his son-in-law Michael a fat wallet. 'There you are,' he'd say. 'That's how to do a deal.' But Kuzmichov did not seem pleased, retaining his old air of businesslike reserve and anxiety. 'If only I'd known Cherepakhin would pay that much!' He spoke in an under-tone. 'I wouldn't have sold Makarov that five tons at home, drat it. But who could have known that the price had gone up here?'

A white-shirted waiter cleared the samovar away, and lit the lamp before the icon in the corner. Father Christopher whispered something in his ear. He gave an enigmatic, conspiratorial look as if to say he understood, went out, came back a little later and placed a bowl under the sofa. Kuzmichov made up a bed on the floor, yawned several times, lazily said his prayers and lay down.

'I'm thinking of going to the cathedral tomorrow,' said Father Christopher. 'I know a sacristan there. I ought to go and see the Bishop after the service, but he's said to be ill.' He yawned and put out the lamp. Now only the icon lamp was burning. 'They say he doesn't see anyone.' Father Christopher was removing his robes. 'So I shall just leave without meeting him.'

When he took off his caftan he seemed just like Robinson Crusoe to Yegorushka. Crusoe mixed something in a dish, and went up to the boy. 'Asleep, are we, Master Lomonosov? Just sit up and I'll rub you with oil and vinegar. It'll do you good, but you must say a prayer.'

Yegorushka quickly raised himself and sat up. Father Christopher took the boy's shirt off and began rubbing his chest, cowering and breathing jerkily, as if it was he that was being tickled.

'In the name of the Father, the Son and the Holy Ghost,' he whis-pered. 'Now turn on to your face. That's the idea. You'll be well to-morrow, but don't let it happen again. Why, he's almost on fire! I suppose you were on the road in the storm.'

'Yes.'

'No wonder you're poorly. In the name of the Father, the Son and the Holy Ghost. No wonder at all.'

When the rubbing was finished Father Christopher put Yegorushka's shirt back on, covered him, made the sign of the cross over him, and went away. Then the boy saw him praying. The old man must know a lot of prayers because he stood whispering before the icon for quite a time. His devotions completed, he made the sign of the cross over the windows, the door, Yegorushka and Kuzmichov. Then he lay on a divan without a pillow, covering himself with his caftan. The cor-ridor clock struck ten. Remembering how much time was left before morning, the boy miserably pressed his forehead against the sofa back, no longer trying to shake off his hazy, irksome fancies. But morning came much sooner than he expected.

He seemed to have been lying there with his forehead against the sofa back for only a short time, but when he opened his eyes sunbeams were slanting to the floor from the room's two windows. Father Christopher and Kuzmichov had gone out, and the place had been tidied. It was bright, comfortable and redolent of Father Christopher, who always smelt of cypress and dried cornflowers—at home he made his holy-water sprinklers out of cornflowers, also decorating icon cases with them, and that was why he had become saturated with their scent. Looking at the pillow, the slanting sunbeams and his boots— now cleaned and standing side by side near the sofa—the boy laughed. He found it odd that he was not on the bale of wool, that all around him was dry, and that there was no thunder or lightning on the ceiling.

Jumping up, he began to dress. He felt wonderful. Nothing remained of yesterday's illness but a slight weakness of the legs and neck. The oil and vinegar must have done the trick. Remembering the steamer, the railway engine and the wide river that he had dimly glimpsed yesterday, he was in a hurry to dress so that he could run to the quayside and look at them. He washed, and the door catch suddenly clicked as he was putting on his red shirt. On the threshold appeared the top-hatted Father Christopher wearing a brown silk cassock over his canvas caftan and carrying his staff. Smiling and beaming—old men are always radiant when just returning from church—he placed a piece of communion bread and a parcel on the table and prayed to the icon.

'God has been merciful,' he added. 'Better, are we?'

'All right now.' The boy kissed his hand.

'Thank God. I'm just back from service. I went to see my friend the sacristan. He asked me in for breakfast, but I didn't go. I don't like calling on people too early in the morning, dash it.'

He took his cassock off, stroked his chest and unhurriedly undid the bundle. The boy saw a tin of unpressed caviare, a piece of smoked sturgeon and a French loaf.

'I bought these as I was passing the fishmonger's,' said Father Christopher. 'It's an ordinary weekday and no occasion for a treat, but there's a sick person back there, thinks I to meself, so it may be forgiven. And the caviare is good—real sturgeon's roe.'

The waiter in the white shirt brought a samovar and a tray of crockery.

'Have some.' Father Christopher spread caviare on a piece of bread and gave it to the boy. 'Eat now and enjoy yourself, and in fullness of time you will study. But mind you do so with attention and zeal, that good may come of it. What you need to learn by heart, you learn by heart. And when you have to describe a basic concept in your own words without touching on its outer form, then you do it in your own words. And try to master all subjects. Some know mathematics well, but they've never heard of Peter Mogila, and there's those as know about Peter Mogila but can't tell you about the moon. No, you study so you understand everything. Learn Latin, French, German—geography, of course, and history, theology, philosophy and mathematics. And when you've mastered everything—slowly, prayerfully and zealously—then you go and take up a profession. When you know everything things will be easier for you in every walk of life. Do but study and acquire grace, and God will show you your path in life—a doctor it might be, or a judge or an engineer.'

Father Christopher spread a little caviare on a small piece of bread and put it in his mouth. 'The Apostle Paul says: "Be not carried about with divers and strange doctrines." Of course if so be you study the black arts, blasphemy, conjuring up spirits from the other world like Saul, or such-like lore—which is no good to you nor to anyone else, either—then better not study at all. You must apprehend only that which God has blessed. Take good thought. The holy apostles spoke in all tongues, so you learn languages. Basil the Great studied mathematics and philosophy, so you study them too. St. Nestor wrote history, so you study and write history. Take example from the saints.'

Father Christopher sipped tea from his saucer, wiped his whiskers, flexed his neck. 'Good,' said he. 'I'm one of the old school. I've forgotten a lot, but even so my way of life is different from others'—there's no comparison. For instance, in company—at dinner, say, or at a meeting—one may pass a remark in Latin, or bring in history or philosophy. It gives other people pleasure and me too. Or, again, when the assizes come round and you have to administer the oath, the other priests are all a bit bashful like, but me—I'm completely at home with the judges, prosecutors and lawyers. You say something in the learned line, you have tea with them, you have a laugh, and you ask them things you don't know. And they like it. That's the way of it, old son. Learning is light and ignorance is darkness. So you study. It won't be easy, mind, for it doesn't come cheap nowadays, learning doesn't. Your mother's a widow on a pension. And, well, obviously——'

Father Christopher looked fearfully at the door. 'Your Uncle Ivan will help,' he went on in a whisper. 'He won't abandon you. He has no children of his own and he'll take care of you, never fear.' He looked grave and began whispering even more quietly. 'Now, boy, as God may preserve you, see you never forget your mother and your Uncle Ivan. The commandment bids us honour our mother, and Mr. Kuzmichov's your benefactor and guardian. If you go in for book-learning and then—God forbid!—get irked with folks and look down on them because they're stupider than you, then woe, woe unto you!'

Father Christopher raised his hand aloft. 'Woe, woe unto you!' he repeated in a reedy voice. Having warmed to his theme, he was really getting into his stride, as they say, and would have gone on till dinner-time. But the door opened, and in came Uncle Ivan, who hastily greeted them, sat down at table and began rapidly gulping tea.

'Well, I've settled all my business,' said he. 'We might have gone home today, but there's more bother with Yegorushka here. I must fix him up. My sister says her friend Nastasya Toskunov lives some-where round about, and she might put him up.'

He felt inside his wallet, removed a crumpled letter and read it. ' "Mrs. Nastasya Toskunov, at her own house in Little Nizhny Street." I must go and look her up at once. What a nuisance!'

Soon after breakfast Uncle Ivan and Yegorushka left the inn. 'A nuisance,' muttered Uncle. 'Here I am stuck with you, confound you. It's studying to be a gentleman for you and your mother, and nothing but trouble for me.'

When they crossed the yard the wagons and carters were not there, having all gone off to the quay early in the morning. In a far corner of the yard was the dark shape of the familiar britzka. Near it stood the bays, eating oats.

'Good-bye, carriage,' thought the boy.

First came a long climb up a broad avenue, and then they crossed a big market square, where Uncle Ivan asked a policeman the way to Little Nizhny Street. The policeman grinned. 'Ar! That be far away. Out towards the common, that be.'

They met several cabs on the way, but Uncle Ivan permitted himself such weaknesses as cab drives only on exceptional occasions and major holidays. He and the boy walked along paved streets for a long time, and then along unpaved streets with paved sidewalks until they finally reached streets lacking both amenities. When their legs and tongues had got them to Little Nizhny Street both were red in the face, and they took their hats off to wipe away the sweat.

'Tell me, please!' Uncle Ivan was addressing a little old man sitting on a bench by a gate. 'Where is Nastasya Toskunov's house hereabouts?'

'No Toskunovs round here,' the old man answered, after some thought. 'Perhaps it's the Timoshenkos you want?'

'No, Mrs. Toskunov.'

'Sorry, there ain't no such missus.'

Uncle Ivan shrugged his shoulders and trudged on.

'No need to go a-looking,' the old man shouted from behind. 'When I say ain't I mean ain't.'

Uncle Ivan spoke to an old woman who was standing on a corner selling sunflower seeds and pears from a tray. 'Tell me, my dear, where's Nastasya Toskunov's house hereabouts?'

The old woman looked at him in surprise. 'Why, does Nastasya live in a house of her own then?' she laughed. 'Lord, it be seven years since she married off her daughter and gave the house to the son-in-law. It's him lives there now.' And her eyes asked how they could be such imbeciles as not to know a simple thing like that.

'And where does she live now?' Kuzmichov asked.

'Lord love us!' The old woman threw up her arms in surprise. 'She moved into lodgings ever so long ago. Nigh on eight years it be. Ever since she made her house over to the son-in-law. What a thing to ask!'

She probably expected that Kuzmichov would be equally surprised, and would exclaim that it was 'out of the question'. But he asked very calmly where her lodgings were.

The fruit-seller rolled up her sleeves, and pointed with her bare arm. 'You walk on, on, on,' she shouted in a shrill, piercing voice. 'You'll pass a little red cottage, and then you'll see a little alley on your left. Go down the alley and it will be the third gate on the right.'

Kuzmichov and Yegorushka reached the little red cottage, turned left down the alley and headed for the third gate on the right. On both sides of this ancient grey gate stretched a grey fence with wide cracks. It had a heavy outward list on the right, threatening to collapse, while the left side was twisted back towards the yard. But the gate itself stood erect, apparently still debating whether it was more convenient to fall forwards or backwards. After Uncle Ivan had opened a small wicket-gate he and the boy saw a big yard overgrown with burdock and other coarse weeds. There was a small red-roofed cottage with green shutters a hundred paces from the gate, and in the middle of the yard stood a stout woman with her sleeves rolled up and her apron held out. She was scattering something on the ground, shouting 'Chick, chick, chick!' in a voice as shrill and piercing as the fruit-seller's.

Behind her sat a red dog with pointed ears. Seeing the visitors, it ran to the wicket-gate and struck up a high-pitched bark—red dogs are all tenors.

'Who do you want?' shouted the woman, shielding her eyes from the sun with a hand.

'Good morning,' Uncle Ivan shouted back, waving his stick to keep off the red dog. 'Tell me, please, does Mrs. Toskunov live here?'

'She does! What do you want with her?'

Kuzmichov and Yegorushka went up to her, and she gave them a suspicious look. 'What do you want with her?' she repeated.

'Perhaps *you* are Mrs. Toskunov?'

'All right then, I am.'

'Very pleased to meet you. Your old friend Olga Knyazev sends her respects, see? This is her little son. And perhaps you remember me—her brother Ivan. We all come from N., you see. You were born in our town and you were married there.'

Silence ensued, and the stout woman stared blankly at Kuzmichov, as if not believing or understanding. But then she flushed all over and flung up her hands. Oats fell from her apron, tears sprang from her eyes. 'Olga!' she shrieked, panting with excitement. 'My darling, my darling! Heavens, why am I standing here like an idiot? My pretty little angel!' She embraced the boy, wet his face with her tears and broke down completely.

'Heavens!' She wrung her hands. 'Olga's little boy! Now that *is* good news! And isn't he like his mother—her very image, he is. But why are you standing out in the yard? Do come inside.' Weeping, gasping, talking as she went, she hurried to the house, with the guests plodding after her. 'It's so untidy here.' She ushered the visitors into a stuffy parlour crammed with icons and pots of flowers. 'Oh, goodness me! Vasilisa, at least go and open the shutters. The little angel—now, isn't he just lovely! I had no idea dear Olga had such a dear little boy.'

When she had calmed down and got used to the visitors Kuzmichov asked to speak to her in private. The boy went into another room, containing a sewing-machine, a cage with a starling in the window, and just as many icons and flowers as the parlour. A little girl—sunburnt, chubby-cheeked like Titus, wearing a clean little cotton frock —was standing stock-still near the sewing-machine. She looked at Yegorushka unblinkingly, obviously feeling very awkward. After gazing at her in silence for a moment he asked what her name was.

The little girl moved her lips, looking as if she was going to cry. 'Atka,' she answered softly.

This meant 'Katka'.

'He'll live here, if you will be so kind,' Kuzmichov whispered in the parlour. 'And we'll pay you ten roubles a month. The boy isn't spoilt, he's a quiet lad.'

'I really don't know what to say, Mr. Kuzmichov,' sighed Nastasya plaintively. 'Ten roubles is good money, but I'm afraid of taking on someone else's child, see? He might fall ill or something.'

When they called the boy back into the parlour his Uncle Ivan had stood up and was saying good-bye, hat in hand. 'Very well then, let him stay with you now.' He turned to his nephew. 'Good-bye, Yegorushka, you're to stay here. Mind you behave yourself and do as Mrs. Toskunov says. Good-bye then. I'll come again tomorrow.'

And off he went.

Nastasya embraced the boy again, calling him a little angel and began tearfully laying the table. Three minutes later Yegorushka was sitting next to her, answering her endless questions and eating rich, hot cabbage stew.

In the evening he was back at the same table, resting his head on his hand as he listened to Nastasya. Now laughing, now crying, she talked of his mother's young days, her own marriage, her children. A cricket chirped in the stove and the lamp burner faintly buzzed. The mistress of the house spoke in a low voice, occasionally dropping her thimble in her excitement, whereupon her granddaughter Katka would crawl under the table after it, always staying down there a long time and probably scrutinizing Yegorushka's feet. He listened, he dozed, and he examined the old woman's face, her wart with hairs on it, the tear stains. And he felt sad, very sad. They made him a bed on a trunk, saying that if he was hungry in the night he should go into the corridor and take some of the chicken under a bowl on the window-sill.

Next morning Ivan Kuzmichov and Father Christopher came to say good-bye. Mrs. Toskunov was pleased to see them and was going to bring out the samovar, but Kuzmichov was in a great hurry and dismissed the idea with a gesture.

'We've no time for tea, sugar and the rest of it, we're just leaving.'

Before parting, all sat in silence for a minute. Nastasya gave a deep sigh, gazing with tearful eyes at the icons.

'Well, well,' began Ivan, getting up. 'So you'll be staying here.' The businesslike reserve suddenly vanished from his face. 'Now, mind you study.' He was a little flushed and smiled sadly. 'Don't forget your mother and obey Mrs. Toskunov. You study well, boy, and I'll stand by you.'

He took a purse from his pocket, turned his back to the boy, burrowed in the small change for a while, found a ten-copeck piece and gave it to him.

Father Christopher sighed and unhurriedly blessed Yegorushka. 'In the name of the Father, the Son and the Holy Ghost. Study, lad, work hard. Remember me in your prayers if I die. And here's ten copecks from me too.'

Yegorushka kissed his hand and burst into tears. Something inside him whispered that he would never see the old man again.

'I've already applied to the local high school,' Kuzmichov told Nastasya in a voice suggesting that there was a dead body laid out in the room. 'You must take him to the examination on the seventh of August. Well, good-bye and God bless you. Farewell, nephew.'

'You might have had a little tea,' groaned Nastasya.

Through the tears blinding his eyes the boy could not see Uncle Ivan and Father Christopher leave. He rushed to the window, but they were gone from the yard. The red hound had just barked, and was running back from the gate with an air of duty fulfilled. Not knowing why, the boy jumped up and rushed from the house, and as he ran out of the gate Kuzmichov and Father Christopher—the first swinging his stick with the curved handle and the second his staff—were just rounding the corner. Yegorushka felt that his entire stock of experience had vanished with them like smoke. He sank exhaustedly on a bench, greeting the advent of his new and unknown life with bitter tears.

What kind of life would it be?

AN AWKWARD BUSINESS

[Неприятность]

(1888)

AN AWKWARD BUSINESS

GREGORY OVCHINNIKOV was a country doctor of about thirty-five, haggard and nervous. He was known to his colleagues for his modest contributions to medical statistics and keen interest in 'social problems'. One morning he was doing his ward rounds in his hospital, followed as usual by his assistant Michael Smirnovsky—an elderly medical orderly with a fleshy face, plastered-down greasy hair and a single ear-ring.

Barely had the doctor begun his rounds when a trifling matter aroused his acute suspicions—his assistant's waistcoat was creased, and persistently rode up even though the man kept jerking and straightening it. His shirt too was crumpled and creased, and there was white fluff on his long black frock-coat, on his trousers, and even on his tie. The man had obviously slept in his clothes, and—to judge from his expression as he tugged his waistcoat and adjusted his tie—those clothes were too tight for him.

The doctor stared at him and grasped the situation. His assistant was not staggering, and he answered questions coherently, but his grim, blank face, his dim eyes, the shivering of his neck and hands, the disorder of his dress, and above all his intense efforts to control himself, together with his desire to conceal his condition—it all testified that he had just got up, had not slept properly and was still drunk, seriously drunk, on what he had taken the night before. He had an excruciating hangover, he was in great distress, and he was obviously very annoyed with himself.

The doctor, who had his own reasons for disliking the orderly, was strongly inclined to say: 'Drunk, I see.' He was suddenly disgusted by the waistcoat, the long frock-coat and the ear-ring in that meaty ear. But he repressed his rancour, and spoke gently and politely as always.

'Did Gerasim have his milk?'

'Yes, Doctor,' replied Smirnovsky, also softly.

While talking to his patient, Gerasim, the doctor glanced at the temperature chart, and felt another surge of hatred. He held his breath to stop himself speaking, but could not help asking in a rude, choking voice why the temperature had not been recorded.

'Oh, it was, Doctor,' said Smirnovsky softly. But on looking at the chart and satisfying himself that it indeed was not, he shrugged his shoulders in bewilderment.

'I don't understand, Doctor—it must be Sister's doing,' he muttered.

'It wasn't recorded last night either,' the doctor went on. 'All you ever do is get drunk, blast you! You're positively pie-eyed at this moment. Where *is* Sister?'

Sister Nadezhda Osipovna, the midwife, was not in the wards, though she was supposed to be on duty every morning when the dressings were changed. The doctor looked around him, and received the impression that the ward had not been tidied and was in an unholy mess, that none of the necessary routine had been carried out, and that everything was as bulging, crumpled and fluff-bedecked as the orderly's odious waistcoat. He felt prompted to tear off his white apron, rant, throw everything over, let it all go to hell, and leave. But he mastered himself and continued his rounds.

After Gerasim came a patient with a tissue inflammation of the entire right arm. He needed his dressing changed. The doctor sat by him on a stool and tackled the arm.

'They were celebrating last night—someone's name-day,' he thought, slowly removing the bandage. 'You just wait, I'll give you parties! What can I do about it, though? I can do nothing.'

He felt an abscess on the purple, swollen arm and called: 'Scalpel!'

Trying to show that he was steady on his feet and fit for work, Smirnovsky rushed off and quickly came back with a scalpel.

'Not this—a new one,' said the doctor.

The assistant walked mincingly to the box—which was on a chair—containing material for the dressings, and quickly rummaged about. He kept on whispering to the nurses, moving the box on the chair, rustling it, and he twice dropped something. The doctor sat waiting, and felt a violent irritation in his back from the whispering and rustling.

'How much longer?' he asked. 'You must have left them downstairs.'

The orderly ran up and handed over two scalpels, while committing the indiscretion of breathing in the doctor's direction.

'Not these!' snapped the doctor. 'I told you quite clearly to get me a new one. Oh, never mind, go and sleep it off—you reek like an alehouse. You're not fit to be trusted.'

'What other knives do you want?' asked the orderly irritably, slowly shrugging his shoulders. Annoyed with himself, and ashamed to have the patients and nurses staring at him, he forced a smile to conceal his embarrassment. 'What other knives do you want?' he repeated.

The doctor felt tears in his eyes and a trembling in his fingers. He made another effort to control himself. 'Go and sleep it off,' he brought out in a quavering voice. 'I don't want to talk to a drunk.'

'You can't tell me off for what I do off duty,' went on the orderly. 'Suppose I did have a drop—well, it don't mean anyone can order me about. I'm doing me job, ain't I? What more do you want? I'm doing me job.'

The doctor jumped to his feet, swung his arm without realizing what he was doing, and struck his assistant in the face with his full force. Why he did it he did not know, but he derived great pleasure from the punch landing smack on the man's face and from the fact that a dignified, God-fearing family man, a solid citizen with a high opinion of himself, had reeled, bounced like a ball and collapsed on a stool. He felt a wild urge to land a second punch, but the feeling of satisfaction vanished at the sight of the nurses' pale and troubled faces near that other hated face. With a gesture of despair he rushed out of the ward.

In the grounds he encountered the Sister on her way to the hospital —an unmarried woman of about twenty-seven with a sallow face and her hair loose. Her pink cotton dress was very tight in the skirt, which made her take tiny, rapid steps. She rustled her dress, jerking her shoulders in time with each step, and tossing her head as if humming a merry tune to herself.

'Aha, the Mermaid!' thought the doctor, recalling that the staff had given the Sister that nickname, and he savoured the prospect of taking the mincing, self-obsessed, fashion-conscious creature down a peg.

'Why are you never to be found?' he shouted as their paths crossed. 'Why aren't you at the hospital? The temperatures haven't been taken, the place is in a mess, my orderly is drunk, and you sleep till noon. You'd better find yourself another job—you're not working here any more.'

Reaching his lodgings, the doctor tore off his white apron and the piece of towelling with which it was belted, angrily hurled them both into a corner, and began pacing his study.

'Good grief, what awful people!' he said. 'They're no use, they're only a hindrance. I can't carry on, I really can't. I'm getting out.'

His heart was thumping, he was trembling all over, and on the brink of tears. To banish these sensations he consoled himself by considering how thoroughly justified he was, and what a good idea it had been to hit his assistant. The odious thing was, he reflected, that the fellow had not got his hospital job in the ordinary way, but through nepotism—his aunt worked for the Council Chairman as a children's nurse. And what a loathsome sight she was when she came in for treatment—this high-powered Auntie with her offhand airs and queue-jumping presumptions! The orderly was undisciplined and ignorant. What he did know he had no understanding of at all. He was drunken, insolent, unclean in his person. He took bribes from the patients and he sold the Council's medicines on the sly. Besides, it was common knowledge that he practised medicine himself on the quiet, treating young townsfolk for unmentionable complaints with special concoctions of his own. It would have been bad enough had he just been one more quack. But this was a quack militant, a quack with mutiny in his heart! He would cup and bleed out-patients without telling the doctor, and he would assist at operations with unwashed hands, digging about in the wounds with a perennially dirty probe—all of which served to demonstrate how profoundly and blatantly he scorned the doctor's medicine with all its lore and regulations.

When his fingers were steady the doctor sat at his desk and wrote a letter to the Chairman of the Council.

'Dear Leo Trofimovich,

'If, on receipt of this note, your Committee does not discharge the hospital orderly Smirnovsky, and if it denies me the right to choose my own assistants, I shall feel obliged—not without regret, I need hardly say—to request you to consider my employment as doctor at N. Hospital terminated, and to concern yourself with seeking my successor. My respects to Lyubov Fyodorovna and Yus.

'Faithfully,

G. OVCHINNIKOV'

Reading the letter through, the doctor found it too short and not formal enough. Besides, it was highly improper to send his regards to Lyubov Fyodorovna and Yus (nickname of the Chairman's younger son) in an official communication.

'Why the blazes bring in Yus?' wondered the doctor. He tore the letter up, and began planning another.

'Dear Sir,' he thought, sitting at his open window, and looking at the ducks and ducklings which hurried down the road, waddling and stumbling, and which must be on their way to the pond. One duckling picked a piece of offal from the ground, choked and gave a squeak of alarm. Another ran up to it, tore the thing out of its beak and started choking too. Far away, near the fence, in the lacy shadows cast on the grass by the young limes, Darya the cook was wandering about picking sorrel for a vegetable stew. Voices were heard. Zot the coachman, a bridle in his hand, and the dirty-aproned hospital odd-job-man Manuylo stood near the shed discussing something and laughing.

'They're on about me hitting the orderly,' thought the doctor. 'This scandal will be all over the county by tonight. Very well then. "Dear Sir, unless your Committee discharges——" '

The doctor was well aware that the Council would never prefer the orderly to him, and would rather dispense with every medical assistant in the county than deprive itself of so distinguished an individual as Doctor Ovchinnikov. Barely would the letter have arrived before Leo Trofimovich would undoubtedly be rolling up in his troika with his 'What crazy notion is this, old man?'

'My dear chap, what's it all about?' he would ask. 'May you be forgiven! Whatever's the idea? What's got into you? Where is the fellow? Bring the blackguard here! He must be fired! Chuck him out! I insist! That swine shan't be here tomorrow!'

Then he would dine with the doctor, and after dinner he would lie belly upwards on this same crimson sofa and snore with a newspaper over his face. After a good sleep he would have tea and drive the doctor over to spend the night at his house. The upshot would be that the orderly would keep his job and the doctor would not resign.

But this was not the result that the doctor secretly desired. He wanted the orderly's Auntie to triumph, he wanted the Council to accept his resignation without more ado—with satisfaction, even—and despite his eight years' conscientious service. He imagined leaving the hospital, where he had settled in nicely, and writing a letter to *The Physician*. He imagined his colleagues presenting him with an address of sympathy.

The Mermaid appeared on the road. With mincing gait and swishing dress she came up to the window.

'Will you see the patients yourself, Doctor?' she asked. 'Or do you want us to do it on our own?'

'You lost your temper,' said her eyes. 'And now that you've calmed down you're ashamed of yourself. But I'm too magnanimous to take any notice.'

'All right, I'll come,' said the doctor. He put on his apron again, belted it with the towelling and went to the hospital.

'I was wrong to run off after hitting him,' he thought on the way. 'It made me look embarrassed or frightened. I acted like a schoolboy. It was all wrong.'

He imagined the patients looking at him with discomfiture when he entered the ward, imagined himself feeling guilty. But when he went in they lay quietly in their beds, hardly paying him any attention. The tubercular Gerasim's face expressed total unconcern.

'He didn't do his job right, so you taught him what's what,' he seemed to be saying. 'That's the way to do things, old man.'

The doctor lanced two abscesses on the purple arm and bandaged it, then went to the women's wards and performed an operation on a peasant woman's eye, while the Mermaid followed him around, helping him as if nothing had happened and all was as it should be. His ward rounds done, he began receiving his out-patients. The window in the small surgery was wide open. You had only to sit on the sill and lean over a little to see young grass a foot or two below. There had been thunder and a heavy downpour on the previous evening, and so the grass was somewhat beaten down and glossy. The path running from just beyond the window to the gully looked washed clean, and the bits of broken dispensary jars and bottles strewn on both sides—they too had been washed clean, and sparkled in the sun, radiating dazzling beams. Farther on, beyond the path, young firs in sumptuous green robes crowded each other. Beyond them were birches with paper-white trunks, and through their foliage, as it gently quivered in the breeze, the infinite depths of the azure sky could be seen. As you looked out there were starlings hopping on the path, turning their foolish beaks towards your window and debating whether to take fright or not. Then, having decided on taking fright, they darted up to the tops of the birches, one after the other with happy chirps, as if making fun of the doctor for not knowing how to fly.

Through the heavy smell of iodoform the fresh fragrance of the spring day could be sensed. It was good to breathe.

'Anna Spiridonovna,' the doctor called.

A young peasant woman in a red dress entered the surgery and said a prayer before the icon.

'What's troubling you?' the doctor asked.

Glancing mistrustfully at the door through which she had come, and at the door to the dispensary, the woman approached the doctor.

'I don't have no children,' she whispered.

'Who else hasn't registered yet?' shouted the Mermaid from the dispensary. 'Report here!'

'What makes him such a swine is compelling me to hit someone for the first time in my life,' thought the doctor as he examined the woman. 'I was never involved in fisticuffs before.'

Anna Spiridonovna left. In came an old man with a venereal complaint, and then a peasant woman with three children who had scabies, and things began to hum. There was no sign of the orderly. Beyond the dispensary door the Mermaid merrily chirped, swishing her dress and clinking her jars. Now and then she came into the surgery to help with a minor operation, or to fetch a prescription—all with that same air of everything being as it should be.

'She's glad I hit the man,' thought the doctor, listening to her voice. 'Those two have always been at loggerheads, and she'll be overjoyed if we get rid of him. The nurses are glad too, I think. How revolting!'

When his surgery was at its busiest he began to feel that the Sister, the nurses, and the very patients, had deliberately assumed carefree, cheerful expressions. They seemed to realize that he was ashamed and hurt, but pretended not to out of delicacy. As for him, wishing to demonstrate that he was no whit disconcerted, he was shouting roughly.

'Hey, you there! Close that door, it's draughty.'

But ashamed and dejected he was, and after seeing forty-five patients he strolled slowly away from the hospital.

The Sister had already contrived to visit her lodgings. A gaudy crimson shawl round her shoulders, a cigarette between her teeth, and a flower in her flowing tresses, she was hurrying off, probably on a professional or private visit. Patients sat in the hospital porch, silently sunning themselves. Rowdy as ever, the starlings were hunting beetles.

Looking around him, the doctor reflected that among all these stable, serene lives only two stuck out like sore thumbs as obviously useless—the orderly's and his own. By now the orderly must have gone to bed to sleep it off, but was surely kept awake by knowing that he was in the wrong, had been maltreated, and had lost his job. His predicament was appalling. As for the doctor, having never struck anyone before, he felt as if he had lost his virginity. No longer did he blame his assistant, or seek to exculpate himself. He was merely perplexed. How had a decent man like himself, who had never even kicked a dog, come to strike that blow? Returning to his quarters, he lay on the study sofa with his face to the back.

'He's a bad man and a professional liability,' he thought. 'During his three years here I've reached the end of my tether. Still, what I did is inexcusable. I took advantage of my position. He's my subordinate, he was at fault and he was drunk to boot, whereas I'm his superior, I had right on my side and I was sober—which gave me the upper hand. Secondly, I struck him in front of people who look up to me, thus setting them a dreadful example.'

The doctor was called to dinner. After eating only a few spoonfuls of cabbage stew he left the table, lay on the sofa again and resumed his meditations.

'So what shall I do now? I must put things right with him as soon as possible. But how? As a practical man he probably thinks duelling stupid or doesn't recognize it. If I apologized to him in the same ward in front of the nurses and patients, that apology would only satisfy me, not him. Being a low type of person, he would put it down to cowardice, to fear of his complaining to the authorities. Besides, an apology would mean the end of hospital discipline. Should I offer him money? No, that would be immoral, and it would smack of bribery. Well, suppose we were to put the problem to our immediate superiors, the County Council, that is. They *could* reprimand or dismiss me, but they wouldn't. And, anyway, it wouldn't be quite the thing to involve the Council—which, incidentally, has no jurisdiction —in the hospital's domestic affairs.

Three hours after his meal the doctor was on his way to bathe in the pond, still thinking. 'Should I perhaps do what anyone else would do in the circumstances—let him sue me? Being unquestionably in the wrong, I shan't try to defend myself, and the judge will send me to gaol. Thus the injured party will receive satisfaction, and those who look up to me will see that I was in the wrong.'

The idea appealed to him. He was pleased, and felt that the problem had been solved in the fairest possible way.

'Well, that's fine!' he thought, wading into the water and watching shoals of golden crucians scurrying away from him. 'Let him sue. It will suit him all the better in that our professional relationship has been curtailed, and after this scandal one or other of us will have to leave the hospital anyway.'

In the evening the doctor ordered his trap, intending to drive over to the garrison commander's for bridge. When he had his hat and coat on, and stood in his study putting his gloves on ready to leave, the outer door opened creakingly, and someone quietly entered the hall.

'Who's there?' called the doctor.

A hollow voice answered. 'It's me, sir.'

The doctor's heart suddenly thumped. Embarrassment and a mysterious feeling of panic suddenly chilled him all over. Michael Smirnovsky, the orderly—it was he—coughed softly, and came timidly into the study.

'Please forgive me, Doctor,' he said in a hollow, guilty voice after a brief silence.

The doctor was taken aback, and did not know what to say. He realized that the man's reason for abasing himself and apologizing was neither Christian meekness, nor a wish to heap coals of fire on his ill-user, but simply self-interest. 'I'll make myself apologize, and with luck I won't get the sack and lose my livelihood.' What could be more insulting to human dignity?

'Forgive me,' repeated the man.

'Now then,' said the doctor, trying not to look at him, and still not knowing what to say. 'Very well, I assaulted you, and I, er, must be punished—must give you satisfaction, that is. You're not a duelling man. Nor am I, for that matter. I have given you offence and you, er, you can bring suit against me before the Justices of the Peace and I'll take my punishment. But we can't both stay on here. One of us—you or I—will have to go.'

('Oh God, I'm saying all the wrong things,' thought the doctor, aghast. 'How utterly stupid!')

'In other words, sue me. But we can't go on working together. It's you or me. You'd better start proceedings tomorrow.'

The orderly gazed sullenly at the doctor, and then his dark, dim eyes glinted with blatant contempt. He had always thought the doctor an unpractical, volatile, puerile creature, and he despised him now for being so nervous and talking so much fussy nonsense.

'Well, don't think I won't,' said he grimly and spitefully.

'Then go ahead.'

'You think I won't do it, don't you? Well, you're wrong! You have no right to raise your hand to me. You ought to be ashamed of yourself. Only drunken peasants hit people, and you're an educated man.'

Suddenly the doctor's hatred all boiled up inside him. 'You clear out of here!' he shouted in a voice unlike his own.

The orderly was reluctant to budge, as if having something else to say, but went into the hall and stood there, plunged in thought. Then, having apparently made up his mind to something, he marched resolutely out.

'How utterly stupid!' muttered the doctor after the other had gone. 'How stupid and trite it all is.'

His handling of the orderly had been infantile, he felt, and he was beginning to see that his notions about the lawsuit were all foolish, complicating the problem instead of solving it.

'How stupid!' he repeated as he sat in his carriage, and later while playing bridge at the garrison commander's. 'Am I really so uneducated, do I know so little of life, that I can't solve this simple problem? Oh, what shall I do?'

Next morning the doctor saw the orderly's wife getting into a carriage. 'She is off to Auntie's,' he thought. 'Well, let her go!'

The hospital was managing without an orderly, and though the Council should have been given notification, the doctor was still unable to frame a letter. It's tenor must now be: 'Kindly dismiss my orderly, though I am to blame, not he.' But to express the idea without it sounding foolish and ignominious—that was almost beyond any decent man.

Two or three days later the doctor was told that his assistant had gone and complained to Leo Trofimovich, the Chairman, who had not let him get a word out, but had stamped his feet and sent him packing.

'I know your sort!' he had shouted. 'Get out! I won't listen!'

From the Chairman the assistant had gone to the town hall, and had filed a complaint—neither mentioning the assault nor asking anything for himself—to the effect that the doctor had several times made disparaging comments about the Council and its Chairman in his presence, that the doctor's method of treating patients was incorrect, that he was neglectful in making his rounds of the district, and so on. Hearing of this, the doctor laughed and thought what a fool the man was. He felt ashamed and sorry for one who behaved so foolishly. The more stupid things a man does in his defence the more defenceless and feeble he must be.

Exactly one week later the doctor received a summons from the Justice of the Peace.

'Now this is idiocy run riot,' he thought as he signed the papers. 'This is the ultimate in sheer silliness.'

Driving over to the court-house on a calm, overcast morning, he no longer felt embarrassed, but was vexed and disgusted. He was furious with himself, with the orderly, with the whole business. 'I'll just tell the court that the whole lot of them can go to blazes,' he raged. ' "You're all jackasses, and you have no sense", I'll say.'

Driving up to the court-house, he saw three of his nurses and the Mermaid by the door. They had been called as witnesses. When he saw the nurses and that merry Sister—she was shifting from foot to foot in her excitement, and had even blushed with pleasure on seeing the protagonist of the impending trial—the incensed doctor wanted to pounce on them like a hawk and stun them with a 'Who said you could leave the hospital? Be so good as to return this instant.' But he took a hold on himself, tried to seem calm, and picked his way through the crowd of peasants to the court-house. The chamber was empty, and the judge's chain of office hung on the back of his armchair. Entering the clerk's cubicle, the doctor saw a thin-faced young man in a linen jacket with bulging pockets—the clerk—and the orderly, who sat at a table idly leafing through court records. The clerk stood up when the doctor came in. The orderly rose too, looking rather put out.

'Isn't Alexander Arkhipovich here yet?' the doctor asked uneasily.

'No, Doctor. He's at his house, sir,' the clerk answered.

The court-house was in one of the outbuildings of the judge's estate, and the judge himself lived in the manor house. Leaving the court-house, the doctor made his way slowly towards that residence, and found Alexander Arkhipovich in the dining-room, where a samovar was steaming. The judge wore neither coat nor waistcoat and had his shirt unbuttoned. He was standing by the table, holding a teapot in both hands and pouring tea as dark as coffee into a glass. Seeing his visitor, he quickly pulled up another glass and filled it.

'With or without sugar?' he asked by way of greeting.

A long time ago the judge had been a cavalryman. Now, through long service in elective office, he had attained high rank in the Civil Service, yet had never discarded his military uniform or his military habits. He had long whiskers like a police chief's, trousers with piping, and all his acts and words were military elegance personified. He spoke with his head thrown slightly back, larding his speech with your retired general's fruity bleats, flexing his shoulders and rolling his eyes.

When greeting someone or giving them a light he scraped his shoes, and when walking he clinked his spurs as carefully and delicately as if every jingle caused him exquisite pain. Having sat the doctor down to his tea, he stroked his broad chest and stomach and heaved a sigh.

'Hurrumph!' said he. 'Perhaps you'd like, m'yes, some vodka and a bite to eat, m'yes?'

'No thank you, I'm not hungry.'

Both felt that they were bound to discuss the hospital scandal, and both felt awkward. The doctor said nothing. With a graceful gesture the judge caught a gnat that had bitten his chest, scrutinized it keenly from all angles, and then let it go. Then he heaved a deep sigh and looked up at the doctor.

'Now then, why don't you get rid of him?' he asked succinctly.

The doctor sensed a note of sympathy in his voice, and suddenly pitied himself, jaded and crushed as he felt by the week's ructions. He rose from the table, frowned irritably and shrugged his shoulders, his expression suggesting that his patience had finally snapped.

'Get rid of him!' he said. 'Ye Gods, the mentality of you people! It really is remarkable! But how *can* I do that? You sit around here thinking I run my own hospital and can act as I please. The mentality of you people certainly is remarkable. Can I really sack an orderly whose aunt is nanny to our Chairman's children, and if our Chairman has a need for such toadies and blabbermouths as this Smirnovsky? What can I do if the Council doesn't care tuppence for us doctors, if it trips us up at every turn? I don't want their job, blast them, and that's flat—they can keep it!'

'There there, my dear chap. You're making too much of the thing, in a manner of speaking.'

'The Chairman tries his level best to prove we're all revolutionaries, he spies on us, he treats us as clerks. What right has he to visit the hospital when I'm away, and to question the nurses and patients? It's downright insulting. Then there's this pious freak of yours, this Simon Alekseyevich who does his own ploughing, rejects medicine because he's as strong as an ox—and eats as much!—vociferously calling us parasites to our faces and begrudging us our livelihood, blast him! I work day and night, I never take a holiday, I'm more necessary than all these prigs, bigots, reformers and buffoons put together! I've worked till I'm ill, and instead of any gratitude I'm told I'm a parasite. Thank you very, very much! Then again, everyone thinks himself entitled to poke his nose into other people's business, tell them how to do their job, order them about. Your pal Councillor Kamchatsky criticizes us doctors at the annual meeting for wasting potassium iodide, and advises us to be careful about using cocaine! What does he know about it, eh? What business is it of his? Why doesn't he teach you how to run your court?'

'But, but he's such a cad, old son—a bounder. You mustn't let him bother you.'

'He's a cad and a bounder, but it was you who elected this windbag to your Executive Committee, you who let him poke his nose into everything. All right, smile! These things are all trifles and pinpricks, think you. But so numerous are they that one's whole life now consists of them, as a mountain may consist of grains of sand—just you get that into your head! I can't carry on—I'm just about all in, Alexander Arkhipovich. Any more of this and I won't be punching faces, I'll be taking pot shots at people, believe you me! My nerves aren't made of steel, I tell you! I'm a human being like you——'

Tears came to the doctor's eyes, his voice shook. He turned away and looked through the window. Silence fell.

'Hurrumph, old fellow!' muttered the judge pensively. 'And then again, if one considers things coolly——'

He caught a gnat, squinted hard at it from all angles, squashed it and threw it in the slop-basin.

'——then, you see, there's no reason to dismiss him. Get rid of him and he'll be replaced by someone just like him, or even worse. You could run through a hundred of them and you wouldn't find one that was any good. They're all blackguards.' He stroked his armpits and slowly lit a cigarette. 'We must learn to put up with this evil. It's only among professional people and peasants—at the two poles of society, in other words—that one finds honest, sober, reliable workers nowadays, that's my opinion. A really decent doctor, a first-class teacher, a thoroughly honest ploughman or blacksmith—those you might, in a manner of speaking, find. But the in-betweeners, what you might call deserters from the peasantry who haven't acquired professional standing—they're the unreliable element. That's why it's so hard to find an honest, sober hospital orderly, clerk, farm bailiff and so on—exceedingly hard. I've been with the justice department since time immemorial, and I've never had one honest, sober clerk throughout my career, though I've booted them out by the sackful in my time. These people lack moral discipline, not to mention er, er, principles, in a manner of speaking——'

'What's all this in aid of?' wondered the doctor. 'What we're both saying is all beside the point.'

'Here's a trick my own clerk, Dyuzhinsky, played me only last Friday,' the judge continued. 'He got hold of some drunks—God knows who—and they spent all night boozing in my court-house. What do you say to that, now? I've nothing against drink. Let them guzzle themselves silly, confound them! But why bring strangers into my chambers? Just think—after all, would it take a second to steal a document, a promissory note or something, from the files? Well, believe it or not, after that orgy I had to spend two days checking all my files in case anything was missing. Now then, what will you do with this scallywag? Get rid of him? All right. And where's your guarantee that the next one won't be worse?'

'But how can he be got rid of?' the doctor asked. 'It's easy enough to talk, but how can I discharge him and take the bread out of his mouth when I know he's a family man with no resources. What would he and his family do?'

'I'm saying the wrong thing, damn it!' he thought, marvelling that he simply could not concentrate on any one definite idea or sentiment. 'That's because I'm shallow and illogical,' he reflected.

'The in-between man, as you call him, is unreliable,' he went on. 'We chase him out, we curse him, we slap his face, but shouldn't we try to see his point of view? He's neither peasant nor master, neither fish nor fowl. His past is grim and his present is a mere twenty-five roubles a month, a starving family and being ordered about, while his future is the same twenty-five roubles and the same inferior position even if he holds on for a hundred years. He has neither education nor property, he has no time to read and go to church, and he's deaf to us because we won't let him near us. And so he lives on from day to day till he dies without hoping for anything better, underfed, afraid of being turned out of his council flat, not knowing where to find a roof for his children. How can a man avoid getting drunk and stealing, how can he acquire principles in these conditions?

'Now we seem to be solving social problems,' he thought. 'And, my God, how clumsily! And what's the point of it all?'

Bells were heard as someone drove into the yard and bowled along to the court-house first, and then up to the porch of the big house.

'It's You-know-who,' said the judge, looking through the window. 'Well, you're for it!'

'Let's get it over quickly, please,' pleaded the doctor. 'Take my case out of turn if possible. I really can't spare the time.'

'Very well then. But I still don't know if the matter's within my jurisdiction, old man. After all, your relations with your assistant are, in a manner of speaking, official. Besides, you dotted him one when he was on official duty. I don't know for certain, actually, but now we can ask the Chairman.'

Hasty steps and heavy breathing were heard, and Leo Trofimovich, the Chairman, appeared in the doorway—a balding, white-haired old man with a long beard and red eyelids. 'Good day to you,' he panted. 'Phew, I say! Tell them to bring me some kvass, judge. This'll be the death of me.'

He sank into an armchair, but immediately sprang up, trotted over to the doctor, and glared at him furiously. 'Many, many thanks to you, Doctor.' He spoke in a shrill, high-pitched voice. 'You've done me no end of a good turn. Most grateful to you, I'm sure. I shan't forget you in a month of Sundays. But is this the way for friends to behave? Say what you like, but you haven't been all that considerate, have you? Why didn't you let me know? Do you take me for your enemy? For a stranger? Your enemy, am I? Did I ever refuse you anything, eh?'

Glaring and twiddling his fingers, the Chairman drank his kvass, quickly wiped his lips and continued.

'Thank you so very, very much! But why didn't you let me know? If you'd had any feelings for me at all you'd have driven over and spoken to me as a friend. "My dear Leo Trofimovich, the facts are this that and the other. What's happened is that et cetera et cetera." I'd have settled it all in two ticks, and there would have been no need for scandal. That imbecile seems to have gone clean off his rocker. He's touring the county muck-raking and gossiping with village women while you, shameful to relate, have stirred up one hell of a witch's brew, if you'll pardon my saying so, and have got this jackass to sue you. You should be downright ashamed of yourself. Everyone's asking me the rights and wrongs of it, and I—the Chairman!—don't know what you're up to. You have no use for me. Many, many thanks to you, Doctor.'

The Chairman bowed so low that he even turned purple. Then he went up to the window. 'Zhigalov, send Smirnovsky here,' he shouted. 'I want him this instant!' Then he came away from the window. 'It's a bad business, sir. Even my wife was upset, and you know how much she's on your side. You're all too clever by half, gentlemen. You're keen on logic, principles and such flapdoodle, but where does it get you? You just confuse the issue.'

'Well, you're keen on being illogical, and where does that get *you*?' the doctor asked.

'All right, I'll tell you. Where it gets me is this, that if I hadn't come here now you'd have disgraced both yourself and us. It's lucky for you I did come.'

The orderly entered and stood near the door. The Chairman stood sideways on to him, thrust his hands in his pockets and cleared his throat.

'Apologize to the doctor at once,' he said.

The doctor blushed and ran into another room.

'There, you see, the doctor doesn't want to accept your apology,' went on the Chairman. 'He wants you to show you're sorry in deeds, not words. Will you promise to do what he says and lead a sober life from this day onwards?'

'I will,' the orderly brought out in a deep, grim voice.

'Then watch your step, or heaven help you—you'll get the order of the boot double quick! If anything goes wrong you can expect no mercy. All right—off home with you.'

For the orderly, who had already accepted his misfortune, this turn of events was a delightful surprise. He even went pale with joy. He wanted to say something and put out his hand, but remained silent, smiled foolishly and went out.

'That's that,' said the Chairman. 'No need for a trial either.' He sighed with relief, surveyed the samovar and glasses with the air of one who has just brought off an extremely difficult and important *coup*, and wiped his hands.

'Blessed are the peacemakers,' said he. 'Pour me another glass, Alexander. Oh yes, and tell them to bring me a bite to eat first. And, well, some vodka——'

'I say, this just won't do!' Still flushed, the doctor came into the dining-room, wringing his hands. 'This, er—it's a farce, it's revolting. I can't stand it. Better have twenty trials than settle things in this cockeyed fashion. I can't stand it, I tell you!'

'What do you want then?' the Chairman snapped back. 'To get rid of him? Very well, I'll fire him.'

'No don't do that. I don't know what I do want, but this attitude to life, gentlemen—— God, this is sheer agony!'

The doctor started bustling nervously, looked for his hat, could not find it, and sank exhausted in an armchair. 'Disgusting,' he repeated.

'My dear fellow,' whispered the judge. 'To some extent I fail to understand you, in a manner of speaking. The incident was your fault, after all. Socking folks in the jaw at the end of the nineteenth century! Say what you like, but, in a manner of speaking, it isn't, er, quite the thing. The man's a blackguard, but you must admit you acted incautiously yourself.'

'Of course,' the Chairman agreed.

Vodka and hors-d'œuvre were served. On his way out the doctor mechanically drank a glass of vodka and ate a radish. As he drove back to hospital his thoughts were veiled in mist like grass on autumn mornings.

How could it be, he wondered, that after all the anguish, all the heart-searching, all the talk of the past week, everything had fizzled out in a finale so banal? How utterly stupid!

He was ashamed of involving strangers in his personal problem, ashamed of what he had said to these people, ashamed of the vodka that he had drunk from the habit of idle drinking and idle living, ashamed of his insensitive, shallow mind.

On returning to hospital, he at once started on his ward rounds. The orderly accompanied him, treading softly as a cat, answering questions gently. The orderly, the Mermaid, the nurses—all pretended that nothing had happened, that all was as it should be. The doctor too made every effort to appear unaffected. He gave orders, he fumed, he joked with the patients, while one idea kept stirring in his brain.

'The sheer, the crass stupidity of it all.'

THE BEAUTIES

[*Красавицы*]

(1888)

THE BEAUTIES

I

I REMEMBER driving with my grandfather from the village of Bolshaya Krepkaya, in the Don Region, to Rostov-on-Don when I was a high-school boy in the fifth or sixth form. It was a sultry August day, exhausting and depressing. Our eyes were practically gummed up, and our mouths were parched from the heat and the hot, dry wind that drove clouds of dust towards us. We did not feel like looking, speaking or thinking. When our dozing driver, a Ukrainian called Karpo, caught me on the cap with his whip while lashing at his horse, I neither protested nor uttered a sound, but just opened my eyes, half asleep as I was, and looked dispiritedly and mildly into the distance to see if a village was visible through the dust.

We stopped to feed the horse in the large Armenian settlement of Bakhchi-Salakh, at the house of a rich Armenian whom my grandfather knew. Never in my life have I seen anything more grotesque. Imagine a small, cropped head with thick, beetling eyebrows, a beaked nose, long white whiskers, and a wide mouth with a long cherry-wood chibouk sticking out of it. The small head has been clumsily tacked to a gaunt, hunched carcase arrayed in bizarre garb—a short red jacket and gaudy, sky-blue, baggy trousers. The creature walks about splaying its legs, shuffling its slippers, speaking with its pipe in its mouth, yet comporting itself with the dignity of your true Armenian—unsmiling, goggle-eyed, and trying to take as little notice of his visitors as possible.

The Armenian's dwelling was wind-free and dust-free inside, but it was just as disagreeable, stuffy and depressing as the prairie and the road. I remember sitting on a green chest in a corner, dusty and exhausted by the heat. The unpainted wooden walls, the furniture and the ochre-stained floorboards reeked of dry sun-baked wood. Wherever I looked there were flies, flies, flies. In low voices Grandfather and the Armenian discussed sheep, pasturage and grazing problems. I knew they would be a good hour getting the samovar going, and that Grandfather would spend at least another hour over his tea, after which he would sleep for two or three hours more. A quarter of my day would be spent waiting, and then there would be more heat, more dust, more jolting roads. Listening to the two mumbling voices, I felt as if I had long, long ago seen the Armenian, the cupboard full of crockery, the flies and the windows on which the hot sun beat, and that I should cease to see them only in the far distant future. I conceived a loathing for the steppe, the sun and the flies.

A Ukrainian woman wearing a shawl brought in a tray of tea things and then the samovar. The Armenian went slowly out into the lobby. 'Masha, Masha!' he shouted. 'Come and pour the tea! Where are you, Masha?'

Hurried footsteps were heard, and in came a girl of about sixteen wearing a simple cotton dress and a white shawl. Rinsing the crockery and pouring the tea, she stood with her back to me, and all I noticed was that she was slim-waisted and barefoot, and that her small heels were covered by long trousers.

The master of the house offered me tea. As I sat down at table I glanced at the face of the girl who was handing me my glass, and suddenly felt as if a fresh breeze had blown over my spirits and dispelled all the day's impressions, all the dreariness and dust. I saw the enchanting features of the loveliest face I have ever encountered either dreaming or waking. Here was a truly beautiful girl—and I took this in at first glance, like a lightning flash.

Though I am ready to swear that Masha—or 'Massya', as her father called her in his Armenian accent—was a real beauty, I cannot prove it. Clouds sometimes jostle each other at random on the horizon, and the hidden sun paints them and the sky every possible hue—crimson, orange, gold, lilac, muddy pink. One cloud resembles a monk, another a fish, a third a turbaned Turk. Embracing a third of the sky, the setting sun glitters on a church cross, and on the windows of the manor house. It is reflected in the river and the ponds, it quivers on the trees. Far, far away, against the sunset a flock of wild ducks flies off to its night's rest. The boy herding his cows, the surveyor driving along the mill dam in his chaise, the ladies and gentlemen who are out for a stroll—all gaze at the sunset, all find it awesomely beautiful. But wherein does that beauty lie? No one knows, no one can say.

I was not alone in finding the Armenian girl beautiful. My old grandfather, a man of eighty—tough, indifferent to women and the beauties of nature—gazed at her tenderly for a full minute.

'Is that your daughter, Avet Nazarovich?' he asked.

'Yes, she is,' the Armenian answered.

'A fine-looking young lady.'

An artist would have called the Armenian girl's beauty classic and severe. To contemplate such loveliness is to be imbued, heaven knows why, with the conviction that the regular features, that the hair, eyes, nose, mouth, neck and figure, together with all the motions of the young body, have been unerringly combined by nature in a harmonious whole without a single discordant note. You somehow fancy that the ideally beautiful woman must have a nose just like hers, straight but slightly aquiline, the same big, dark eyes, the same long lashes, the same languorous glance. The curly black hair and eyebrows seem ideally suited to the delicate white skin of the forehead and cheeks, just as green reeds and quiet streams go together. Her white neck and youthful bosom are not fully developed, but only a genius could sculpt them, you feel. As you gaze you gradually conceive a wish to say something exceedingly pleasant, sincere and beautiful to the girl—something as beautiful as herself.

At first I was offended and disconcerted by Masha taking no notice of me, but casting her eyes down all the time. It was as if some special aura, proud and happy, segregated her from me, and jealously screened her from my gaze.

'It must be because I'm covered with dust, because I'm sunburnt, because I'm only a boy,' I thought.

But then I gradually forgot myself and surrendered entirely to the sensation of beauty. I no longer remembered the dreary steppe and the dust, no longer heard the flies buzzing, no longer tasted my tea. All I was conscious of was the beautiful girl standing on the other side of the table.

My appreciation of her beauty was rather remarkable. It was not desire, not ecstasy, not pleasure that she aroused in me, but an oppressive, yet agreeable, melancholia—a sadness vague and hazy as a dream. I somehow felt sorry for myself, for my grandfather, for the Armenian —and even for the girl. I felt as if we had all four lost, irrecoverably, something vitally important. Grandfather too grew sad. He no longer spoke of sheep and grazing, but was silent, and glanced pensively at the girl.

After tea Grandfather took his nap, and I went out and sat on the porch. This house, like all the others at Bakhchi-Salakh, caught the full heat of the sun. There were no trees, no awnings, no shadows. Overgrown with goose-foot and wild mallow, the Armenian's big yard was lively and cheerful despite the intense heat. Threshing was in progress behind one of the low hurdles intersecting the large expanse at various points. Twelve horses, harnessed abreast and forming a single long radius, trotted round a pole fixed in the exact centre of the threshing area. Beside them walked a Ukrainian in a long waistcoat and broad, baggy trousers, cracking his whip and shouting as if to tease the animals and flaunt his power over them.

'Come on there, damn you. Aha! Come on, rot you! Afraid, are you?'

The horses—bay, grey and skewbald—had no idea why they were being forced to rotate in one spot and tread down wheat straw. They moved reluctantly, as though with difficulty, lashing their tails offendedly. The wind raised great clouds of golden chaff from under their hoofs and bore it far away across the hurdles. Women with rakes swarmed near the tall new ricks, and carts went to and fro. In a second yard beyond those ricks another dozen such horses trotted round their pole, while a similar Ukrainian cracked his whip and mocked them.

The steps on which I was sitting were hot. Owing to the heat glue was oozing here and there from the wood of the slender banisters and window-frames. In the streaks of shade beneath the steps and shutters tiny red beetles huddled together. The sun baked my head, chest and back, but I paid no attention to it, being conscious only of the rap of bare feet on the wooden floor of the lobby and the other rooms behind me. Having cleared away the tea, Masha ran down the steps, disturbing the air as she passed, and flew like a bird to a small, grimy outhouse—it must be the kitchen—whence proceeded the smell of roast mutton and the sound of angry Armenian voices. She disappeared through the dark doorway, where her place was taken by a bent, red-faced old Armenian woman wearing baggy green trousers, and angrily scolding someone. Then Masha suddenly reappeared in the doorway, flushed from the kitchen's heat, and carrying a big black loaf on her shoulder. Swaying gracefully under the bread's weight, she ran across the yard to the threshing floor, leapt a hurdle, plunged into a golden cloud of chaff, and vanished behind the carts. The Ukrainian in charge of the horses lowered his whip, stopped talking to them, and gazed silently towards the carts for a minute. Then, when the girl once more darted past the horses and jumped the hurdle, he followed her with his eyes, shouting at his horses in a highly aggrieved voice.

'Rot, you hell-hounds!'

After that I continually heard her bare feet, and saw her rushing round the place with a grave, preoccupied air. Now she ran down the steps, passing me in a gust of air, now to the kitchen, now to the threshing floor, now through the gate, and I could hardly turn my head fast enough to watch.

The more often I caught sight of this lovely creature the more melancholy I became. I felt sorry for myself, for her, and for the Ukrainian mournfully watching her as she ran through the chaff to the carts. Did I envy her beauty? Did I regret that the girl was not mine and never would be, that I was a stranger to her? Did I have an inkling that her rare beauty was accidental, superfluous, and—like everything else on earth—transitory? Was my grief that peculiar sensation which the contemplation of true beauty arouses in any human being? God only knows.

The three hours of waiting passed unnoticed. I felt that I had not had enough time to feast my eyes on Masha when Karpo rode off to the river, bathed the horse, and began to hitch it up. The wet animal snorted with pleasure and kicked his hoof against the shafts.

'Get back!' Karpo shouted.

Grandfather woke up, Masha opened the creaking gates, and we got into the carriage and drove out of the yard—in silence, as if angry with one another.

When Rostov and Nakhichevan appeared in the distance a couple of hours later, Karpo, who had said nothing all that time, looked round quickly.

'Splendid girl, the old Armenian's daughter,' said he, and whipped the horse.

II

On another occasion, after I had become a student, I was travelling south by rail. It was May. At a station—between Belgorod and Kharkov, I think—I got out of the carriage to stroll on the platform.

Evening shadows had already fallen on the station garden, on the platform and on the fields. The station building hid the sunset, but you could tell that the sun had not yet vanished completely by the topmost, delicately pink puffs of smoke from the engine.

While pacing the platform, I noticed that, of the other passengers who were taking an airing, the majority were strolling or standing near one of the second-class carriages, their attitude conveying the impression that someone of consequence must be sitting in it. Among these inquisitive persons I saw the artillery officer who was my travelling companion—an intelligent, cordial, likeable fellow, as is everybody with whom one strikes up a brief acquaintance on one's journeys.

I asked him what he was looking at.

He said nothing in reply, but just indicated a feminine figure with his eyes. It was a young girl of seventeen or eighteen in Russian national costume, bare-headed, with a lace shawl thrown carelessly over one shoulder. She was not a passenger, and I suppose she was the station-master's daughter or sister. She stood near a carriage window, talking to an elderly female passenger. Before I knew what was happening I was suddenly overwhelmed by the same sensation that I had once experienced in the Armenian village.

That the girl was strikingly beautiful neither I nor the others gazing at her could doubt.

Were one to describe her appearance item by item, as is common practice, then the only truly lovely feature was her thick, fair, undu-lating hair—loose on her shoulders and held back on her head by a dark ribbon. All her other features were either irregular or very ordinary. Her eyes were screwed up, either as a flirtatious mannerism or through short-sightedness, her nose was faintly *retroussé*, her mouth was small, her profile was feeble and insipid, her shoulders were narrow for her age. And yet the girl produced the impression of true loveli-ness. Gazing at her, I realized that a Russian face does not require strict regularity of feature to seem handsome. Indeed, had this young woman's up-tilted nose been replaced by another—regular and impeccably formed, like the Armenian girl's—I fancy her face would have lost all its charm.

Standing at the window, talking and shivering in the cool of the evening, the girl kept looking round at us. Now she placed her hands on her hips, now raised them to her head to pat her hair. She spoke, she laughed, she expressed surprise at one moment and horror at the next, and I don't recall a moment when her face and body were at rest. It was in these tiny, infinitely exquisite movements, in her smile, in the play of her expression, in her rapid glances at us that the whole mystery and magic of her beauty consisted—and also in the way this subtle grace of movement was combined with the fresh spontaneity and innocence that throbbed in her laughter and speech, together with the helplessness that so appeals to us in children, birds, fawns, young trees.

This was the beauty of a butterfly. It goes with waltzing, fluttering about the garden, laughing and merry-making. It does not go with serious thought, grief and repose. Had a gust of wind blown down the platform, had it started raining, then the fragile body would suddenly, it seemed, have faded, and the wayward loveliness would have been dispersed like pollen from a flower.

'Ah, well,' muttered the officer, sighing, as we went to our carriage after the second bell, but what his interjection meant I do not pretend to judge.

Perhaps he felt sad and did not want to leave the girl and the spring evening for the stuffy train. Or perhaps, like me, he was irrationally sorry for the lovely girl, for himself, for me, and for all the passengers as they drifted limply and reluctantly back to their compartments. We walked past a station window behind which a wan, whey-faced telegraphist, with upstanding red curls and high cheek-bones, sat at his apparatus.

'I'll bet the telegraph operator is in love with the pretty little miss,' sighed the officer. 'To live out in the wilds under the same roof as that ethereal creature and not fall in love—it's beyond the power of man. And what a misfortune, my dear chap, what a mockery to be round-shouldered, unkempt, dreary, respectable and intelligent, and to be in love with that pretty, silly little girl who never pays you a scrap of attention! Or, even worse: suppose the lovesick telegraphist is married, suppose his wife is as round-shouldered, unkempt and respectable as himself. What agony!'

A guard stood on the small open platform between our carriage and the next. Resting his elbows on the railing, he was gazing towards the girl, and his flabby, disagreeably beefy face, exhausted by sleepless nights and the train's jostling, expressed ecstasy combined with the most profound sorrow, as if he could see his own youth, his own happiness, his sobriety, his purity, his wife, his children reflected in the girl. He seemed to be repenting his sins, and to be conscious with every fibre of his being that the girl was not his, and that for him—prematurely aged, clumsy, fat-visaged—the happiness of an ordinary human being and train passenger was as far away as heaven.

The third bell rang, whistles sounded, the train trundled off. Past our window flashed another guard, the station-master, the garden, and then the lovely girl with her marvellous, childishly sly smile.

Putting my head out and looking back, I saw her watching the train as she walked along the platform past the window with the telegraph clerk, then patted her hair and ran into the garden. No longer did the station buildings hide the sunset. We were in open country, but the sun had already set and black puffs of smoke were settling over the green, velvety young corn. The spring air, the dark sky, the railway carriage—all seemed sad.

Our guard, that familiar figure, came in and began lighting the candles.

THE PARTY

[Именины]

(1888)

THE PARTY

I

AFTER the eight-course banquet and the interminable conversation Olga Mikhaylovna went out into the garden. It was her husband's name-day party, and she was utterly exhausted by the obligation to smile and talk incessantly, by the clatter of dishes, by the servants' stupidity, by the long intervals between courses, and by the corset that she had put on to hide her pregnancy from the guests. She wanted to get away from the house, sit in the shade, and relax by thinking of the child that she was to bear in about two months' time. Such thoughts habitually occurred to her whenever she turned left from the main avenue into a narrow path. Here, in the dense shade of plum and cherry trees, dry branches caught her neck and shoulders, and cobwebs brushed her face, while she would find herself imagining a small, vague-featured person of indefinite sex, and feeling as if it was not the cobwebs but this small person that was affectionately tickling her face and neck. When, at the path's end, a flimsy wattle fence appeared, and beyond it the pot-bellied hives with their earthenware roofs, and when the scent of hay and honey, accompanied by the brief buzz of bees, infused the still and stagnant air, this small person would take complete control of her. She would sit brooding on the bench near the hut of plaited osiers.

This time too she went as far as the bench, sat down, and began thinking. But instead of the small person it was the big persons she had just left that came to mind. She was greatly distressed that she, the hostess, had abandoned her guests, and she remembered her husband Peter and her Uncle Nicholas arguing about trial by jury, the press and women's education at luncheon. As usual her husband had argued to parade his conservative views to his guests, and above all so that he could disagree with her uncle, whom he disliked. But her uncle contradicted him and quibbled over every word to show the company that he, the uncle, still retained a young man's alertness and mental flexibility despite his fifty-nine years. By the end of the meal Olga herself could not resist embarking on a clumsy defence of higher education for women. It was not that it needed defending—simply that she wanted to annoy her husband, whom she believed to have been

unfair. The guests were bored by the argument, but they all thought
fit to make verbose interventions, though none of them cared a fig for
trial by jury or women's education.

Olga was sitting on the near side of the fence by the hut. The sun
was hidden behind clouds, the trees and the air were sombre, rain
seemed likely—and yet it was hot and sultry. Hay had been cut under
the trees on St. Peter's Eve, and still lay ungathered. Sad, with its
wilting flowers in a variety of hues, it gave off an irksome, cloying
smell. All was quiet, and bees buzzed monotonously beyond the
fence.

Then footsteps and voices were unexpectedly heard—someone was
coming down the path towards the hives.

'How stuffy it is!' It was a woman's voice. 'Will it rain or won't it,
what do you think?'

'It will, my precious, but not before dark—there will be a shower.'
The voice was male, languid and only too familiar.

If she quickly hid in the hut they would pass on without noticing
her, Olga calculated. Then she would not be compelled to talk and
force herself to smile. She picked her skirts up, bent down and went
inside, whereupon her face, neck and arms were plunged into an
atmosphere as stifling as steam. Had it not been for the stuffiness and a
choking smell, of rye bread, of dill and osiers, that took away her
breath, this would have been the perfect place, with its thatched roof
and dim light, to hide from her guests and think about the small
person. It was snug and quiet.

'What a lovely spot! Let's sit down, Peter.' It was the woman's
voice again.

Peeping through a crack between the reeds, Olga saw her husband
Peter and a guest, Lyubochka Sheller, a girl of seventeen who had just
left boarding-school. Peter—hat pushed to the back of his head,
relaxed and slothful from drinking too much at dinner—was strolling
near the fence and kicking the hay into a pile. Pink from the heat and
pretty as always, Lyubochka stood with her hands behind her back
watching the indolent motions of his big, handsome frame.

Knowing how attractive her husband was to women, Olga disliked
seeing him with them. There was nothing remarkable in his idly kicking some hay into a pile so as to sit on it with Lyubochka and gossip.
Nor was there anything remarkable in pretty Lyubochka gazing at him
so tenderly. Yet Olga felt annoyed with her husband, and both
frightened and pleased at the prospect of eavesdropping.

'Sit down, enchantress.' Peter sank on to the hay and stretched. 'That's right. Now, talk to me.'

'Oh yes! And as soon as I start talking you'll fall asleep.'

'Fall asleep? Allah forbid! Can one sleep with those pretty little eyes gazing at one?'

Her husband's words, his lolling about in a lady's presence with his hat on the back of his head—these things too were wholly unremarkable. He had been spoilt by women. Knowing that he attracted them, he would address them in the special tone generally thought to become him. He was treating Lyubochka just like any other woman, but that did not stop Olga feeling jealous.

'Tell me something,' said Lyubochka after a short pause. 'Do you really face prosecution?'

'Me? Yes, indeed. I've joined the criminal classes, my precious.'

'But what for?'

'No reason at all. It just happened—largely a matter of politics.' Peter yawned. 'It's Left versus Right. I'm a reactionary fuddy-duddy who dared to employ, in an official document, expressions derogatory to such Gladstonian paragons as our local Justice of the Peace Mr. Kuzma Vostryakov, not to mention Vladimir Vladimirov Esquire.

'In our society,' he continued with another yawn, 'you may disparage the sun, the moon and anything you please, but God help you and heaven preserve you if you lay a hand on a liberal! Your liberal's just like that foul puff-ball toadstool which covers you with clouds of dust if you accidentally touch it.'

'But what happened to you?'

'Nothing really—just a case of much ado about nothing. Some miserable little schoolmaster of clerical origin brought suit in Vostryakov's court against an innkeeper for slander and assault in a public place. Both teacher and innkeeper were drunk as lords by all accounts, and both behaved equally badly. Even if an offence was committed there were certainly faults on both sides. Vostryakov should have fined both for disturbing the peace and thrown the case out of court—and that would have been that. But such is not our way, oh dear me no! What counts with us is never the individual, never the facts, but the pigeonhole they go into. However scoundrelly a schoolmaster may be, he's automatically right just because he's a schoolmaster. And a publican is always wrong just because he's a money-grubbing publican. Vostryakov gave the publican a gaol sentence, and the man appealed to Sessions, which solemnly confirmed Vostryakov's findings.

Well, I expressed a dissenting judgement—got a bit heated, that's all.'

Peter spoke calmly, with casual irony, though he was in fact seriously worried about his impending trial. Olga remembered him returning from that ill-fated hearing and doing his utmost to hide his dejection and feeling of inadequacy from the household. As an intelligent man he could not help feeling that he had overstepped the mark in expressing dissent, and what a lot of dissemblance had been necessary to hide this feeling from himself and others! How many unnecessary discussions there had been, how much muttering and false laughter at things that were not funny at all! On learning that he was to stand trial he had suddenly felt fatigued and depressed, had begun sleeping badly, and had taken to standing by a window and drumming his fingers on the panes more often than was his wont. He was ashamed to confess his distress to his wife, and that riled her.

'I'm told you've been down Poltava way,' said Lyubochka.

'Yes, I got back the day before yesterday,' Peter answered.

'It must be awfully nice there.'

'Very nice indeed. I happened to arrive just in time for haymaking, and that's the most romantic season in the South, I can tell you. Now, this house and garden here are large, with no end of servants and commotion, and so you never see the mowing, it all goes unnoticed. But my place down south has forty acres of meadowland, all open to the view, and you can see the mowers from any window. They mow the meadows, they mow the garden. There are no visitors or ructions, so you can't help seeing, hearing and feeling haymaking. There's the scent of hay outdoors and indoors, and the clang of scythes from dawn to dusk. It's charming country, is the good old South. Drinking the water at the wells with their sweeps, and the ghastly vodka in those Jewish taverns, with the sound of the local fiddles and tambourines wafted on the calm evening air—do you know, I was taken by the enchanting thought of settling down on my southern farm and living out my life far from these appeal sessions, intellectual conversations, philosophizing women and interminable dinners.'

Peter was not lying. He had been dispirited and longed for a holiday, and had only gone to Poltava to escape his study, his servants, his friends and all reminders of his wounded vanity and blundering.

Lyubochka suddenly jumped up with a horrified gesture. 'Oo, a bee, a bee—it'll sting me!' she shrieked.

'Nonsense, it won't. What a little coward you are!'

'No, no, I can't bear it!' cried Lyubochka, looking back at the bee as she beat a hasty retreat.

Peter followed her, gazing at her with melancholy appreciation. As he looked he must have been thinking of his southern farm, of solitude, and—who knows—he may even have thought how warm and snug life on his farm would be if this child—young, pure, fresh, unspoilt by higher education, not pregnant—had been his wife.

When their voices and footsteps had died away Olga emerged from the hut and set off for the house. She was on the verge of tears, and by now she was terribly jealous. She understood Peter's fatigue, his sense of inadequacy, his embarrassment. And embarrassed people always do shun their intimates above all, unburdening themselves only to strangers. She also realized that Lyubochka was no danger to her—nor were any of the other women now having coffee in the house. But it was all so puzzling and frightening, and Olga felt that Peter only half belonged to her.

'He has no right, none whatever,' she muttered, trying to analyse her jealousy and her annoyance with her husband. 'I'm going to give him a piece of my mind this instant.'

She decided to find her husband at once and have it out with him. It was downright disgusting, the way he attracted strange women, seeking their admiration as if it were the elixir of life. It was unfair and dishonourable of him to bestow on others what rightly belonged to her, his wife, and to hide his heart and conscience from her only to reveal them to the first pretty face. What harm had she done him? What had she done wrong? And, finally, she was sick and tired of his subterfuges. He was always posturing, flirting, saying things he didn't mean, trying to seem other than what he was and should be. Why all the dissimulation? How ill it became any decent man! His affectations insulted both herself and those at whom they were directed, also showing disrespect for the material of his prevarications. Posing and giving himself airs on the bench, holding forth on the prerogatives of power at mealtimes just to annoy her uncle—well, really! Couldn't he see that it all showed he didn't give a rap for the court, for himself, or for anyone listening to him and watching him?

Emerging into the avenue, Olga tried to look as if she had been engaged on some domestic errand. There were gentlemen drinking liqueurs and eating soft fruit on the veranda. One of them, the examining magistrate—a stout, elderly man, a great clown and wit—must have been telling a *risqué* story because he suddenly clapped his hand over his fat lips when he saw his hostess and sat down goggle-eyed.

Olga did not care for the local officials. She disliked their clumsy, self-important wives, their tittle-tattle, their constant visiting and their flattery of her husband, whom they all hated. But now, as they sat drinking—having had plenty to eat and making no move to leave—she found their presence excruciatingly irksome, yet greeted the examining magistrate with a smile, wagging a threatening finger at him to avoid any suggestion of ungraciousness. She crossed the ballroom and drawing-room, smiling and looking as if she was off to issue some order and make some arrangements.

'I hope to God no one stops me,' she thought, but forced herself to pause in the drawing-room and listen for appearance' sake to a young man playing the piano. She stood for a minute, shouted 'Bravo, bravo, Monsieur Georges!', clapped her hands twice and went on.

She found her husband sitting at the desk in his study deep in thought and looking stern, preoccupied and guilty. This was not the Peter who had argued at dinner, and whom his guests knew, but a different man —exhausted, guilty, inadequate-feeling—whom only his wife knew. He must have come to the study for some cigarettes. Before him lay a full case, open, and one hand was still in the desk drawer—he had suddenly become immobile in the act of taking out the cigarettes.

Olga felt sorry for him. He was tired, out of sorts, and probably at odds with himself—that was as clear as daylight. She approached the desk without a word, shut the cigarette case and put it in his side pocket, trying to pretend that she had forgotten the argument at dinner and was not angry with him any more.

'What can I tell him?' she wondered. 'I'll say that dissimulation is a morass—the farther you get in the harder it is to get out. I'll tell him he's been carried away by the false role he's been playing and has gone too far. "You've insulted people who were devoted to you and never did you any harm. So go and tell them you're sorry, laugh at yourself, and you'll feel better. And if you want quiet and solitude let's go away together."'

Meeting his wife's eyes, Peter suddenly adopted the indifferent and mildly ironical expression that he had worn at dinner and in the garden. He yawned, stood up and looked at his watch.

'It's after five. Even if our guests take pity on us and leave at eleven we still have to get through another six hours. A cheerful prospect, I must say!'

Whistling some tune, he slowly left the room, his gait as magisterial as ever. His sedate tread was heard as he traversed the hall and drawing-room, uttered his proconsular laugh, and called a casual 'Bravo!' to the young pianist. His footsteps soon died away—he must have gone into the garden. It was no longer jealousy and annoyance, now, that obsessed Olga, but downright hatred of his walk, his hypocritical laugh, his voice. When she went to the window and looked into the garden Peter was strolling down the avenue. He had one hand in his pocket and was snapping the fingers of the other. With his head thrown slightly backwards he rolled portentously along, looking exceedingly satisfied with himself, his dinner, his digestion and his scenery.

Two little schoolboys appeared on the path—sons of a Mrs. Chizhevsky, an estate owner. They had just arrived with their tutor, a student in a white tunic and very narrow trousers. Coming up to Peter, they stopped, probably to wish him a happy name-day. He patted the children's cheeks, twisted his shoulders elegantly, and casually presented his hand to the student without looking at him. The student must have praised the weather, comparing it to St. Petersburg's, because Peter answered in a loud voice in the tone of one addressing a court bailiff or a witness rather than a guest.

'Eh? Cold in St. Petersburg, is it? Now, here, my dear fellow, we have a salubrious atmospheric mix, what? And fruits of the earth in abundance, eh?'

Placing one hand in his pocket and clicking the fingers of the other, he strode off. Olga continued to stare at the back of his neck in bewilderment until he vanished behind the hazel bushes. Where did this man of thirty-four acquire his pompous, person of consequence's walk? Whence the ponderously elegant tread? And whence the authoritative resonance in his voice, and all this 'eh?', 'what!', 'my dear fellow!' stuff?

To escape being bored and lonely at home in the first months of her marriage, Olga had (she recalled) attended court hearings in town—at which her husband sometimes presided in place of her godfather Count Alexis. In his judge's seat, in his uniform, wearing the chain on his chest, Peter was a different man, what with all the majestic gestures, the thunderous voice, the 'What, sirs?' the 'H'm, very wells', the off-hand tone. Ordinary human qualities, everything individual that Olga was used to seeing in him at home—it was all swamped in grandeur, and the man in the judge's seat was not her Peter but someone else: a Your Honour, as everyone called him. Conscious of being a power in the land, he found it impossible to sit still, but seized every opportunity to ring his bell, glare at the public and shout. And what of his short-sightedness and deafness? Suddenly myopic and hard of hearing, frowning his proconsular frown, he would require people to speak louder and approach the bench. Such difficulty did he have in dis-tinguishing faces and sounds from so sublime an eminence that, if Olga herself had come near him at such times, he would probably have shouted: 'Your name, madam?' He condescended to peasant wit-nesses, and he bellowed at the public in a voice that could be heard out in the street. As for his treatment of counsel, that was impossible. When a barrister came to speak Peter would sit half turned away, squinting at the ceiling and thereby indicating that the man was utterly superfluous here, and that he would neither acknowledge him nor listen to him. But if some poorly dressed local solicitor spoke, then Peter was all ears, surveying him with a look of withering scorn that said: 'Is this what the legal profession has come to?'

'Just what are you trying to say?' he would interpose.

If some rhetorically-minded barrister employed a word of foreign origin—'factitious' instead of 'fictitious', say—Peter would suddenly become agitated.

'Eh? What was that, sir? Factitious, eh? And just what is that supposed to mean?'

Then he would tell the man sententiously not to 'use words you don't understand'. His speech finished, the lawyer would retreat from the bench red-faced and bathed in sweat, while Peter lolled back in his seat, celebrating his triumph with a complacent grin. In his handling of lawyers he tended to ape Count Alexis. But when, for instance, the Count said, 'Will defence counsel kindly be silent?' the effect was paternally good-humoured and natural, whereas Peter made it sound forced and rather uncouth.

II

Applause broke out as the young pianist finished playing. Re-membering her guests, Olga hurried to the drawing-room and approached the piano.

'I did so much enjoy your playing. You do have a remarkable gift, but don't you think our piano needs tuning?'

At that moment the two schoolboys and the student entered the room.

'Heavens! Why, it's Mitya and Kolya!' Olga joyously drawled, going to meet them. 'How you *have* grown! I hardly recognized you! But where's your mother?'

'Many happy returns and all best wishes to our host,' said the student rather offhandedly. 'And Mrs. Chizhevsky also sends her best wishes, coupled with her apologies—she's not feeling very well.'

'Oh, how unkind of her! And I've been looking forward to seeing her all day! Now, when did you leave St. Petersburg? And how is the weather there?'

Not waiting for a reply, she looked fondly at the little boys. 'And aren't they big boys now! It's not so long since they used to visit us with their nanny, and now they're at high school! Old folk grow old and young folk grow up! Have you had dinner?'

'Oh, please don't trouble,' said the student.

'But you haven't, have you?'

'Please don't go to any trouble.'

'Well, you are hungry, aren't you?' Olga asked in a rude, harsh, impatient, irritated voice. The effect was unintended and immediately set her coughing, smiling and blushing. 'How they have grown!' she said softly.

'Please don't bother,' the student repeated.

He begged her not to bother, and the boys did not speak—obviously all three were hungry. Olga led them to the dining-room and told Vasily to set the table.

'How unkind of your mother!' She sat them down. 'She has quite forgotten me! It's downright cruel of her, and you must tell her so from me. And what are you studying?' she asked the student.

'Medicine.'

'Ah, I'm very partial to doctors, you know. I'm sorry my husband isn't one. What courage it must take to operate, say, or dissect corpses. Simply dreadful! Aren't you scared? I think I'd die of fright. You will take vodka of course?'

'Please don't bother.'

'But you must, must, must have a drink after your journey. I my-self sometimes drink, even though I am a woman. And Mitya and Kolya can have some Malaga—it's not a strong wine, don't worry. What fine young men they are, honestly—it's high time they were married, ha, ha, ha.'

Olga spoke without pausing, knowing from experience how much easier it is to talk than to listen when entertaining. So long as you talk there is no need to tax your brain, think of answers to questions and vary your facial expression. But she inadvertently raised some serious question, and the student began to hold forth, so that she had no choice but to listen. Knowing that she had been to university, the student adopted an air of earnestness when addressing her.

'And what is your subject?' she asked, forgetting that she had already put the question.

'Medicine.'

She remembered that she had neglected the ladies for some time.

'Really? You're to be a doctor then?' She stood up. 'How nice—I wish I'd studied medicine myself. Now, you have your meal, gentlemen, and then come out into the garden and I'll introduce you to the young ladies.'

She looked at her watch as she went out—it was five minutes to six. She was amazed that time should pass so slowly, and horrified that there were still six hours till midnight, when her guests would leave. How could she get through those six hours? What words was she to utter? How should she treat her husband?

There was not a soul in the drawing-room or on the veranda, all the guests having wandered off into the garden.

'I'll have to suggest a walk to the birch wood before tea, or else boating,' thought Olga as she hurried to the croquet lawn, whence talking and laughter proceeded. 'And we must get the old people playing bridge.'

The footman Gregory came towards her from the croquet lawn carrying some empty bottles, and she asked him where the ladies were.

'In the raspberry patch. The master's there too.'

An exasperated shout came from the croquet lawn. 'Oh, for heaven's sake! If I've told you once I've told you a thousand times—to know your Bulgarians you have to visit them, you can't go by the newspapers!'

Either because of this outburst, or for some other reason, Olga suddenly felt utterly weak all over, especially in the legs and shoulders. She had a sudden urge to stop speaking, listening and moving.

'When you serve tea or anything, Gregory, please don't come to me,' she said languidly and with some effort. 'Don't ask me anything, don't bother me with anything. You do it all yourself. And don't, please don't, make all that noise with your feet. This is all beyond me, because——'

She continued towards the croquet lawn without finishing what she was saying, but remembered the ladies on the way and turned to the raspberry patch. The sky, air and trees were still sombre, still threatening rain. It was hot and stuffy. Huge flocks of crows sailed, cawing, over the garden in anticipation of bad weather. The closer the paths were to the kitchen garden the more neglected, dark and narrow they became. On one of them—hidden in a thicket of wild pears, wood-sorrel, young oaks and hops—clouds of tiny black midges enveloped her. She covered her face with her hands, making an effort to imagine the small person, but through her mind flitted Gregory, Mitya, Kolya and the faces of the peasants who had come to offer their best wishes that morning.

Hearing footsteps, she opened her eyes to find her Uncle Nicholas approaching at speed.

He was out of breath. 'That you, my dear? I'm so glad, I want a word with you.'

He mopped his red, clean-shaven chin with a handkerchief, took an abrupt backward step, threw up his arms and opened his eyes wide. 'My dear, how long will this go on?' he spluttered. 'Are there no limits, that's what I'd like to know? I ignore the demoralizing effect of his die-hard views on our set, and the fact that he is a living insult to me and to all that is best and most sublime in every honest, thinking man. These things I pass over, but let him at least observe the proprieties! Well, really! He shouts, he snarls, he gives himself airs, he struts about as if he was Lord God Almighty, he won't let anyone else get a word in edgeways, dash it! And what of his lordly gestures, his peremptory laugh, his patronizing tone? And just who does he think he is, may I ask? You tell me that! He's his wife's shadow, a nobody, a petty landowner turned jack-in-office who had the luck to marry money. He's just one more bounder and popinjay! He's a sort of stage fuddy-duddy! I swear to God that he's either suffering from megalomania or else that demented old fogey Count Alexis is right in saying that children and young people mature very late nowadays, and go on playing cab-drivers and generals till they're forty.'

Olga agreed. 'All very true. And now do you mind if I go?'

'And where's it all going to end, eh?' he continued, blocking her path. 'Where will this hidebound, dyed-in-the-wool act lead? He's already being prosecuted, oh yes he is. And I'm delighted! That's where all the tumult and shouting have got him, into the dock! And not just locally either—in the High Court! Could anything be worse?

And then again, he has quarrelled with everyone. Today's his name-day, but just look who's missing! Neither Vostryakov, nor Yakhontov, nor Vladimirov, nor Shevud, nor the Count has come. Who could be more conservative than Count Alexis—but even he hasn't shown up. And he'll never come here again, you mark my words.'

'Oh dear, what has all this to do with me?' Olga asked.

'What has it to do with you? You're his wife, aren't you? You're intelligent, you've been to college, and it's in your power to make an honest citizen of him.'

'They don't teach you how to influence difficult people at college. I suppose I shall have to apologize to all of you for going to the univer-sity.' She spoke sharply. 'Look here, Uncle, if someone kept practising scales right in your ear over and over again all day, you wouldn't stay put, but run off. Well, I've been hearing the same thing day in day out all year long, and it really is time you all took pity on me.'

Her uncle looked very grave, glanced at her quizzically and curled his lip in an ironical smile. 'So that's how it is,' he crooned like an old crone. 'My apologies, madam.' He gave a ceremonious bow. 'If you have fallen under his influence yourself and changed your convictions, then you should have told me so before. I'm very sorry, madam!'

'Yes, I have changed my convictions,' she shouted. 'And you can put that in your pipe and smoke it!'

'I beg your pardon, madam.' Her uncle made a last formal bow from a rather sideways-on position, cringed low, clicked his heels and went his way.

'Imbecile,' thought Olga. 'I hope he's going home.'

She found the ladies and the young people among the raspberries in the kitchen garden. Some were eating the fruit, while others had had enough of it and were strolling through the strawberry beds or ferreting in the sugar peas. A little to one side of the raspberries, near a spreading apple tree comprehensively propped up with poles pulled out of an old fence, Peter was scything grass. His hair hung over his forehead, his tie had untied itself, his watch chain dangled from his fob. Each step that he took, each sweep of his scythe, showed skill and great resources of strength. Near him stood Lyubochka and the daughters of a neighbour, Colonel Bukreyev—Natalya and Valentina, or 'Nata and Vata', as everyone called them. These were anaemic, unhealthy, plump, fair-haired girls of sixteen or seventeen, wearing white dresses and strikingly similar in looks. Peter was teaching them to mow.

'It's all very simple,' said he. 'You only need to know how to hold the scythe. And you mustn't get excited and use too much force. This is the way. Now, how about having a go?'

He offered Lyubochka the scythe. 'Come on.'

Lyubochka clumsily picked up the scythe, suddenly blushed and burst out laughing.

'Don't be afraid, Lyubochka, don't be afraid,' Olga shouted loudly enough for all the ladies to hear her and know that she was among them. 'You must learn. If you marry a Tolstoyan he'll make you mow.'

Lyubochka picked up the scythe but burst out laughing again, which so enfeebled her that she dropped it. She felt embarrassed, but pleased to be treated as a grown-up. Then Nata—unsmiling, with no sign of nervousness, looking cool and solemn—picked the scythe up, swung it and got it tangled in the grass. Vata, also unsmiling, also cool and solemn like her sister, silently took the scythe and got it stuck in the ground. After this exploit the two sisters linked arms and went off to the raspberry patch without a word.

Playful as a schoolboy, Peter laughed at them, and this childlike, frolicsome, exceedingly good-natured mood suited him far better than any other. Olga loved him like that. But his boyishness did not usually last, and so it proved on this occasion. After fooling with the scythe he thought fit to introduce a serious note.

'You know, I feel healthier and more normal when I'm mowing,' said he. 'I think I'd go out of my mind if I was limited to a purely intellectual life. I don't think I was born for the cultivated life—I need to mow, plough, sow, break in horses.'

Peter and the ladies discussed the advantages of physical labour, culture, and the evils of money and property. Listening to her husband, Olga remembered her dowry for some reason, and thought that a time would surely come when he would blame her for being richer than he was. 'He's proud and conceited, and perhaps he'll hate me because I've done so much for him.'

She stopped by Colonel Bukreyev, who was eating raspberries while also taking part in the conversation.

'Do join us.' He made room for Olga and Peter. 'The ripest ones are here. And so, in Proudhon's view,' he went on, raising his voice, 'property is theft. But, frankly, I don't recognize Proudhon or consider him a philosopher. For me the French are no authority, confound them.'

'Now, I'm a bit weak on the Proudhons and the Buckles,' said Peter.

'For philosophy you must apply to my lady wife here. She has been to college, and Schopenhauer, Proudhon and Company she has thoroughly——'

Olga again felt dispirited. Again she set off through the garden, down the narrow path by the apple and pear trees, and again she had the air of one engaged on some vital errand. She came to the gardener's cottage. In the doorway sat his wife Barbara and her four small children, all with big, close-cropped heads. Barbara was pregnant too, and reckoned that her baby was due by Elijah's Day. After greeting her, Olga silently examined her and the children.

'Well, how do you feel?' she asked.

'Oh, all right.'

Silence followed, both women seeming to understand each other without words.

Olga thought for a moment. 'It's frightening, having a first baby. I keep thinking I won't get through it, that I'll die.'

'That's how I felt. But I'm alive, ain't I? There's worse worries.'

Pregnant for the fifth time and a woman of experience, Barbara treated her mistress somewhat condescendingly, addressing her in a lecturing tone, and Olga could not but recognize her authority. She would have liked to speak of the child, and of her fears and sensations, but was afraid to seem trivial and naïve. And so she said nothing, waiting for Barbara to speak.

'We're going indoors, dear,' called Peter from the raspberry patch.

Olga liked silently waiting and watching Barbara. She would have been willing to stand there without speaking till nightfall, pointless though it would be. But she had to go. Just as she left the cottage Lyubochka, Vata and Nata ran to meet her. The two sisters stopped a couple of yards short, as if rooted to the spot, but Lyubochka ran and flung herself on Olga's neck.

'Darling! Dearest! Treasure!' She kissed Olga's face and neck. 'Do let's have tea on the island.'

'Yes, yes, yes, the island!' chorused the unsmiling doubles Vata and Nata.

'But it's going to rain, dears.'

'It isn't, it isn't,' shouted Lyubochka with a tearful pout. 'Everyone wants to go, my dearest darling.'

Peter joined them. 'They've all decided to have tea on the island,' he said. 'You arrange it. We'll all go in the boats, and the samovars and other stuff can go by carriage with the servants.'

He fell in beside his wife and took her arm. Olga wanted to say something unpleasant and wounding, and even to mention her dowry perhaps—the more brusquely the better, she felt. But she thought for a moment and said:

'Why hasn't Count Alexis come? What a pity!'

'I'm only too glad he hasn't,' Peter lied. 'I'm sick of that pious freak. He gets on my nerves.'

'And yet before lunch you were dying to see him!'

III

Half an hour later the guests were all thronging on the bank near the stakes to which the boats were moored. There was a lot of talk and laughing, and so much unnecessary commotion that the seating arrangements went sadly awry, three boats being jam-packed while two stood empty. The keys for these boats were nowhere to be found, and there was a lot of rushing to and fro between river and house by people sent to look for them. Some said that Gregory had them, others that the steward had them, while a third faction was for fetching the blacksmith to break the padlocks. All spoke at once, interrupting and shouting each other down.

'In hell's name!' yelled Peter, impatiently pacing the bank. 'Those keys are supposed to be left on the window-sill in the hall. Who dared take them? The steward can get himself a boat of his own if he wants.'

In the end the keys were found. Then two oars turned out to be missing and chaos broke loose again. Bored with striding up and down, Peter jumped into a long, narrow skiff hollowed out of a poplar trunk, and pushed off with a lurch that nearly tumbled him into the water, whereupon the other boats followed one after the other amid loud laughter and shrieks from the young ladies.

The white, cloudy sky, the trees on the banks, the reeds and the boats with their passengers and oars—all were mirrored in the water. Under the boats, in that bottomless abyss far down below, was another sky with birds flying about. The bank belonging to the estate was high, steep and wooded, while the other sloped gently, with broad green water-meadows and gleaming inlets. When the boats had gone a hundred yards some cottages and a herd of cows came into sight from behind the melancholy weeping willows on the low bank. Songs, drunken cries and the strains of a concertina were heard.

Here and there on the river scurried the craft of fishermen who had come to place their nets for the night. In one boat tipsy amateur musicians played on home-made fiddles and a cello.

Olga sat at the tiller, smiling affably and chattering away to entertain her guests, while shooting sideways glances at her husband. He was standing up and sculling away in his skiff ahead of everyone else. The light, sharp-prowed vessel moved swiftly. To all the guests it was 'the old crock', but Peter for some reason called it *Penderakliya*. It had an air of lively cunning, seeming to resent the heavy Peter while awaiting a convenient moment to slip from under him. Looking at her husband, Olga was repelled by his good looks and attractiveness, by the back of his neck, by his posturing, by his familiar manner with the women. She hated all the women in the boat, feeling jealous of them, while constantly trembling with fear of Peter's wobbly craft capsizing and causing further disasters.

'Not so fast, Peter,' she shouted, her heart sinking with fear. 'Sit down, can't you? There's no need to prove how brave you are.'

She was also disconcerted by those in the boat with her. They were all ordinary folk—not bad sorts, fairly average—but now each seemed abnormal and evil. She saw nothing but falseness in any of them.

'Take that young man rowing over there,' she thought, '—the one with the auburn hair, the gold-rimmed spectacles and the handsome beard. He's a rich, smug, invariably lucky mother's darling universally regarded as an honest, independent-minded, progressive person. It's less than a year since he graduated and moved to the country, yet he's already talking of "us social workers". But in a year he'll be bored, too, and off he'll go to St. Petersburg like so many others, and he'll justify his flight by telling everyone how useless the local government organizations are, and how disappointed he has been. Meanwhile his young wife, who's in that other boat, can't take her eyes off him, believing him to be a pillar of the local council, though she'll be equally convinced, one year from now, that the whole thing is pointless. And take that stout, meticulously shaved gentleman in the straw hat with the broad ribbon—the one with the expensive cigar in his mouth. He's always on about it being "time we gave up pipe dreams and tackled a real job of work". He has Yorkshire pigs, Butlerov hives, a crop of rapeseed, pineapples, two dairies—one for butter, one for cheese—and Italian double-entry bookkeeping. But every summer he sells some of his woods for timber, and mortgages part of his land, so that he can spend the autumn with his mistress in the Crimea. And there's Uncle Nicholas, who's furious with Peter, yet won't go home for some reason.'

Glancing at the other boats, Olga could see nothing but cranks, bores, humbugs and morons. She remembered everyone she knew in the county, but couldn't recall a single person of whom she could say or think anything good. She found them all so crass—so insipid, dim, narrow, bogus and callous. They neither said what they meant nor did what they wanted. Suffocated by *ennui*, desperate, she wanted to wipe the smile off her face, spring up, shout 'I'm fed up with you all', and then jump out of the boat and swim ashore.

'I say, everyone, let's give Peter a tow,' someone shouted.

The others picked up the cry. 'Tow him, tow him! Take your husband in tow, Olga!'

Sitting at the tiller, Olga had to seize the right moment, nimbly grasping *Penderakliya* by the chain at its prow. As she leant over to reach for it Peter frowned and looked at her in alarm. 'I do hope you won't catch cold.'

'If you're so worried about me and the baby then why torment me?' Olga wondered.

Acknowledging defeat, but not wanting to be towed, Peter jumped from *Penderakliya* into the already overcrowded boat—jumped so clumsily that it keeled hard over and everyone screamed in terror.

'He did that jump to please the ladies,' thought Olga. 'He knows how dashing it looks.'

Her arms and legs began to shake—the result, she supposed, of dejection, vexation, forced smiling and the discomfort that she felt all over her body. To conceal her trembling from the guests she tried to talk louder, to laugh, and to keep moving. 'If I suddenly burst into tears I'll say I have toothache,' she thought.

Well, they finally beached the boats at the 'Isle of Good Hope', this being a peninsula formed by a sharp bend in the river and overgrown with a coppice of old birch trees, willows and poplars. Under the trees stood tables with steaming samovars on them. Vasily and Gregory, in tail-coats and white knitted gloves, were busy with the tea things. On the far bank, opposite 'Good Hope', were the carriages that had brought the provisions, and from them baskets and bundles of food were being ferried to the Isle in a skiff much like *Penderakliya*. The footmen, the coachmen, and even the peasant manning the skiff—all had the solemn, festive air seen only in children and servants.

While Olga made tea and poured the first glasses, the guests were busy with cordials and sweetmeats. There ensued the kind of tea-drinking chaos usual at picnics and so tiresome and exhausting for hostesses. Hardly had Gregory and Vasily had time to take the tea round when empty glasses were already being held out to Olga. One asked for it without sugar, another wanted it strong, a third wanted it weak, and a fourth was saying no more thank you. Olga had to remember all this and then shout, 'Were you the one without sugar, Ivan Petrovich?' or, 'I say, all of you, who wanted it weak?' But the person who had asked for it weak or without sugar had now forgotten which, being engrossed in agreeable conversation, and took the first glass that came to hand. A little way from the table drifted disconsolate ghostlike figures pretending to look for mushrooms in the grass or read the labels on boxes. These were the ones for whom there were not enough glasses.

'Have you had tea?' Olga would ask, and the person in question would tell her not to worry, adding that he would have some later, though it would have suited her better if the guests didn't have some later, but got a move on.

Some of them were absorbed in conversation and drank their tea slowly, holding on to their glasses for half an hour, while others—especially those who had drunk a great deal at dinner—stayed close to the table drinking glass after glass, so that Olga hardly had time to fill them. One young wag sipped his tea through a lump of sugar, and kept saying: 'I love to pamper myself, sinner that I am, with the Chinese herb.' From time to time he sighed deeply, asking for 'the favour of another tiny dish'. He drank a lot and crunched the sugar aloud, thinking this all very funny and original—and a superb take-off of a typical Russian merchant. That these trivialities were all agony to the hostess no one realized, and it would have been hard for them to do so because Olga was all affable smiles and idle chit-chat.

She was not feeling well. She was irritated by the crowd, by the laughter, by the questions, by the funny young man, by the footmen—at their wits' end and run off their feet—by the children hanging round near the table. She was irked by Vata looking like Nata, and Kolya like Mitya, so that you couldn't tell which had had tea and which hadn't. She sensed her strained smile of welcome turning sour, and she felt ready to burst into tears at any moment.

'I say, it's raining,' someone shouted.

Everyone looked at the sky.

'Yes, it's rain all right,' Peter affirmed, wiping his cheek.

The sky let fall only a few drops and it was not really raining, but the guests forsook their tea and made haste to leave. At first they all wanted to go back in the carriages, but then they changed their minds and made for the boats. On the pretext that she was behindhand with her supper arrangements Olga asked to be excused for leaving the company and going home by carriage.

The first thing she did in the carriage was to give her face a holiday from smiling, and she drove grim-visaged through the village, responding ungraciously to the bows of the peasants that she passed. Arriving home, she went to her bedroom by the back entrance and lay on her husband's bed.

'Merciful God, why this hellish drudgery?' she whispered. 'Why do they all mill around pretending to enjoy themselves? Why my hypocritical smiles? I don't understand at all.'

She heard footsteps and voices. Her guests had returned. 'I don't care,' she thought. 'I'll lie down a bit longer.'

But the maid came into the bedroom. 'Marya Grigoryevna's leaving, mum.'

Olga jumped up, tidied her hair and rushed out of the room. 'My dear, but this is unheard of!' she began in an insulted voice, going up to her guest. 'Why all the hurry?'

'I can't stay, darling, I really can't. I've been here too long already—my children are expecting me at home.'

'Well, I think you're most unkind! Why didn't you bring your children with you?'

'I'll bring them on an ordinary day, my dear, if you'll allow me, but today——'

'But of course!' Olga broke in. 'I'll be delighted! You have such nice children—do give them all a kiss from me. But I'm seriously offended! Where's the hurry, that's what I don't understand.'

'I can't stay, really. Good-bye, dearest, and do look after yourself. In your, er, condition, you know——'

They kissed. After seeing her to her carriage, Olga joined the ladies in the drawing-room where the lamps had been lit and the gentlemen were sitting down to cards.

IV

After supper, at a quarter past twelve, the guests began to leave while Olga stood in the porch and saw them off. 'Now, you really should take a shawl,' she said. 'It's getting rather cool. I do hope you won't catch cold.'

'Don't worry,' the guests answered, getting into their carriages. 'Well, good-bye. And remember we're expecting you. Don't disappoint us.'

'Whoa there!' The coachman held back the horses.

'Off we go, Denis! Good-bye, Olga.'

'Kiss the children for me.'

The carriage moved off and instantly vanished in the darkness. In the red circle cast on the drive by the lamp a new pair or trio of impatient horses would appear, their driver silhouetted with his arms thrust out in front of him. There were more kisses, more reproaches, and more requests to come again or take a shawl. Peter kept running out of the hall and helping the ladies into their carriages.

'Make straight for Yefremovshchina, my man,' he instructed a coachman. 'The Mankino route's shorter, but that road is worse—you could overturn as easily as anything. Good-bye, my precious. *Mille compliments* to your artistic friend.'

'Good-bye, Olga darling. Go inside or you'll catch cold—it's damp.'

'Whoa there! Play me up, would you?'

'Now, where did you get those horses?' Peter asked, and the coachman told him that they had 'bought them from Khaydarov in Lent'.

'Fine horses.' Peter slapped the trace-horse on the crupper. 'All right, off with you! Godspeed!'

Finally the last guest left. The red circle on the drive wavered, drifted off to one side, shrank, and vanished as Vasily took the lamp from the porch. After seeing their guests off on previous occasions Peter and Olga had usually danced up and down in the ballroom, face to face and clapping hands as they sang: 'They've gone, gone, gone!' But Olga did not feel like that now. She went to the bedroom, undressed and got into bed.

She felt that she would doze off at once and sleep soundly. There was a nagging ache in her legs and shoulders, and her head was clogged with talk. Once again she felt vaguely uncomfortable all over. Covering her head, she lay there for a few minutes, then peeped out from the blanket at the icon-lamp, listened to the silence and smiled.

'Good, good,' she whispered, curling her legs, which seemed to have been stretched by so much walking about. 'Sleep, sleep——'

Her legs would not stay still, her whole body felt uncomfortable and she turned over on her other side. A large fly flew about the room, buzzing and banging restlessly against the ceiling. She could also hear the careful tread of Gregory and Vasily as they cleared the tables in the ballroom. She sensed that she would never feel at ease or fall asleep until these noises stopped. Once more she turned over impatiently.

She heard her husband's voice in the drawing-room. A guest must be staying for the night because Peter was addressing someone in a loud voice. 'I'm not saying Count Alexis is a hypocrite, but he can't help seeming so because you people all try to see him as different from what he really is. People think he's original because he's a crank, kind-hearted because he's over-familiar, and conservative because he has no views at all. Let us even grant that he really is a hundred per cent copper-bottomed Tory. But what, actually, is conservatism?'

Enraged with Count Alexis, with his guests and with himself, Peter was really letting himself go. He abused the Count, he abused his guests, and he was so vexed with himself that he was ready to hold forth and blurt out absolutely anything. Having seen the guest to his room, he stalked up and down the drawing-room, then paced the dining-room, the corridor and his study, and then the drawing-room again before entering the bedroom. Olga lay on her back with the blanket only up to her waist—by now she was hot—and she was looking peevishly at the fly thumping into the ceiling.

'Is someone staying the night?' she asked.

'Yegorov.'

Peter undressed and lay on his bed. He lit a cigarette in silence, and he too started watching the fly. His gaze was grim and troubled. Olga examined his handsome profile for five minutes without speaking, somehow feeling that if he suddenly turned to her and said: 'I'm so miserable, darling,' she would burst into tears or laugh, and would feel better. The ache in her legs and the discomfort of her whole body were due to nervous tension, she thought.

'What are you thinking about, Peter?' she asked.

'Oh, nothing,' replied her husband.

'You've started having secrets from me lately. That's wrong.'

'What's wrong about it?' Peter answered drily, after a pause. 'We all have our own personal lives, so we're bound to have our own secrets.'

'Personal lives, own secrets—that's just words. Can't you see how much you're hurting me?' She sat up in bed. 'If you're worried, why hide it from me? And why do you think fit to confide in strange women rather than your own wife? Oh yes, I heard you by the bee-hives this afternoon, pouring your heart out to Lyubochka.'

'My congratulations, I'm glad you did hear it.' This meant: 'Leave me alone, and don't bother me when I'm thinking.'

Olga was outraged. The irritation, hatred and anger that had accumulated inside her during the day—it all seemed to boil over suddenly. She felt like speaking her mind to her husband at once, without waiting for the morning, she wanted to insult him and have her own back.

'It's all so odious, loathsome and vile, I tell you.' She was trying not to shout. 'I've hated you all day—now look what you've done!'

Peter sat up in bed.

'Oh, how utterly, utterly vile!' Olga added, shaking all over. 'And don't you congratulate me—better congratulate yourself! It's a down-right disgrace! You've become such a fraud that you're ashamed to be in the same room as your own wife. You're so bogus! I can see right through you, and I understand every single step you take.'

'Perhaps you could warn me when you're in a bad mood, Olga, so I can go and sleep in the study.'

With these words Peter took his pillow and left the room. This Olga had not foreseen. For a few minutes she gazed—silent, open-mouthed and quivering all over—at the door through which her husband had disappeared, and tried to understand what this meant. Was it one of those procedures employed during quarrels by deceitful persons when they are in the wrong? Or was it a deliberate insult to her self-respect? How should she take it? She remembered her cousin the army officer—a cheerful sort, who had often laughingly told her that, 'when my lady wife nags me of a night', he usually took a pillow and went whistling off to his study, leaving her looking very foolish. She was a rich, neurotic, silly woman whom he did not respect and barely tolerated.

Olga jumped out of bed feeling that she had only one recourse—to dress as fast as she could and leave home for ever. The house belonged to her, but so much the worse for Peter. Without thinking whether it was necessary or not, she rushed to the study to inform her husband of her decision—the thought 'how like a woman' flashed through her mind—and add some sarcastic parting shot.

Peter lay on the sofa, pretending to read a newspaper. There was a lighted candle on a chair near him, and his face was hidden behind the paper.

'Be so good as to tell me the meaning of this! I await your explanation.'

'Be so good as——.' Peter mimicked her voice, not showing his face. 'I've had enough of this, Olga, honestly. I'm tired and I'm not in the mood. We can have our quarrel tomorrow.'

'Oh, I see through your little game,' she went on. 'You hate me—oh yes, you do—because I'm better off than you. For that you will never forgive me, and you'll never be straightforward with me.' (The thought 'how like a woman' flashed through her mind again.) 'At this very moment you're laughing at me, I know. I'm quite certain you only married me for my money and those horrid horses. Oh, I'm so unhappy!'

Peter dropped his paper and sat up, dumbfounded by the unexpected insult. He smiled as helplessly as a baby, looked perplexedly at his wife, held out his hands to her, as if to ward off blows, and called her name as if pleading with her.

Expecting her to make some further outrageous remark, he shrank against the back of the sofa, his large frame looking as childishly helpless as his smile.

'My dear, how can you say such things?' he whispered.

Coming to her senses and suddenly realizing that she loved this man passionately, Olga remembered that he was her husband Peter, that she couldn't live one day without him, and that he loved her madly too. Bursting into loud sobs, not recognizable as hers, she clutched her head and ran back into the bedroom.

She collapsed on the bed, and the room echoed to curt, hysterical sobs that choked her and cramped her arms and legs. Remembering that they had a guest sleeping three or four rooms away, she buried her head under the pillow to stifle her sobs, but the pillow slipped to the floor and she almost fell off the bed herself as she bent down for it. She made to pull the blanket up to her face, but her hands would not obey her, tearing convulsively at everything they clutched.

She felt that all was lost, and that the lie she had told to wound her husband had shattered her life into fragments. Never would he forgive her, for the insult was not such as any vows or embraces could gainsay. How to convince her husband that she did not mean what she had said?

'It's all over—finished,' she shouted, not noticing that the pillow had slipped to the floor again. 'Oh, for heaven's sake——'

No doubt her cries had roused the guest and the servants by now, and tomorrow the whole county would know that she had had hysterics, and everyone would blame Peter. She strove to restrain herself, but her sobs grew louder every minute.

'For God's sake, for God's sake!' she shouted in a voice not her own and without knowing why.

She felt as if the bed had collapsed under her and her legs were tangled in the blanket. Peter came in wearing his dressing-gown and carrying a candle.

'Hush,' he said.

She raised herself on to her knees in bed, squinting in the candle-light. 'You must, must understand—', she said between sobs.

She wanted to tell him that she had been plagued by their visitors, by his lies and by her own lies, till everything was seething inside her, but all she could bring out was that he 'must, must understand'.

'Here, drink this.' He gave her some water. She obediently took the glass and began drinking, but the water splashed and spilt over her hands, breast and knees.

'I must look hideous,' she thought.

Silently Peter put her back in bed, covered her with the blanket, took his candle and went out.

'For God's sake!' she shouted again. 'Try to understand, Peter.'

Then, suddenly, something took a grip beneath her stomach and back so violently that it cut short her tears, and made her bite the pillow in agony, but the pain relented at once and she began sobbing again.

In came the maid and rearranged the blanket. 'Mistress—what's the matter, my dear?' she asked anxiously, but Peter, who was coming towards the bed, told the girl to clear out.

'You must, must understand,' kept on Olga.

'Please calm yourself, dear,' said he. 'I didn't want to hurt you. I wouldn't have left the room if I'd known it would affect you like that. I simply felt miserable. I tell you quite honestly——'

'But you must understand! You behaved so falsely, and so did I——'

'I do understand. There, there, that'll do. I understand,' he said tenderly as he sat down on the bed.

'You spoke in anger, it's understandable. I swear to God I love you more than anything on earth, and when I married you I never once thought about your being rich. I loved you infinitely, that's all. Believe me, I've never been short of money or known the value of it,

and so I can't appreciate the difference between your means and mine.
I've always felt as if we were equally well off. As for my dissembling
over trifles—well, that's true of course. Till now the pattern of my life
has been so frivolous that it's somehow been impossible to avoid
prevarication. I'm pretty depressed myself at the moment. Let's not go
on like this, for heaven's sake.'

Once more Olga felt a sharp pain and clutched her husband's sleeve.
'It hurts, oh how it does hurt!' she said rapidly.

'Damn and blast those guests!' Peter muttered, standing up. 'You
shouldn't have gone to the island this afternoon,' he shouted. 'Why
didn't I have the sense to stop you, God help me?'

He scratched his head irritably and left the room with a gesture that
dismissed the subject.

After that he kept coming back, sitting on her bed and talking at
length, now most tenderly, now angrily, but she barely heard. Her
sobs alternated with atrocious pangs, each more violent and prolonged
than the last. At first she held her breath when the pain came, biting
her pillow, but later she uttered hideous, piercing screams. Once,
seeing her husband near her, she remembered insulting him, and, without stopping to think whether it was a hallucination or the real Peter,
she seized his hand in both hers and began kissing it.

'We've both been dishonest,' she pleaded. 'You must, must understand. They've tortured me, driven me out of my mind——'

'We're not alone, dear,' Peter told her.

She raised her head and saw Barbara kneeling by the chest of
drawers and pulling out the lowest drawer. The top drawers were
already out. Having done this, she stood up, flushed by her exertions,
and began opening a small chest, looking cool and solemn.

'I can't unlock it, Marya,' she whispered. 'You do it, can't you?'

The maid Marya, who was digging a candle stub out of the candle-
stick with a pair of scissors so that she could fit a fresh one, went over
to Barbara and helped her open the chest.

'Nothing must be left shut,' whispered Barbara. 'Open this little
box too, my dear.' She turned to Peter. 'You should send to Father
Michael, sir, to open the gates in front of the altar—you must.'

'Do whatever you like.' Peter breathed unevenly. 'Only get the
doctor or midwife quickly, for God's sake. Has Vasily gone? Send
someone else as well. Send your husband.'

'I'm in labour,' Olga realized. 'But it won't be born alive, Barbara,'
she groaned.

'Now, 'twill be all right, mum,' whispered Barbara—to say 'it will' was beyond her, it seemed. ' 'Twill live, God willing. 'Twill live.'

When Olga came to after the next pain she was no longer sobbing or tossing about, but just moaning. She just could not help moaning even in the intervals between the pangs. The candles were still burning, but daylight was already thrusting through the shutters—it must be about five o'clock. A modest-looking woman in a white apron, whom Olga did not know, sat at a round table in the bedroom, her posture indicating that she had been there for some time. Olga guessed that she was the midwife.

'Will it be over soon?' she asked, detecting an odd, unfamiliar ring, never heard before, in her own voice. 'I must be dying in childbirth,' she thought.

Peter came cautiously into the bedroom wearing his day clothes, and stood by the window with his back to his wife. He raised the blind and looked out.

'What rain!' he said.

'What's the time?' Olga asked in order to hear the unfamiliar ring of her voice again.

'A quarter to six,' the midwife answered.

'But what if I really am dying?' wondered Olga, watching her husband's head and the window panes on which the rain was beating. 'How will he live without me? Who will he drink tea and have his meals with, talk to in the evenings, sleep with?'

He seemed like a little orphan child to her, and she felt sorry for him, wanting to say something nice, kind and soothing to him. She remembered his intending to buy some hounds in the spring, but she had stopped him because she thought hunting a cruel, dangerous sport.

'Peter, do buy those hounds,' she groaned.

He lowered the blind, went to the bed and made to say something, but just then Olga felt a pang and gave a hideous, piercing shriek.

She was numb with the pain and all the screaming and groaning. She could hear, see and occasionally speak, but she understood little, conscious only of being, or of being about to be, in pain. It was as if Peter's name-day had ended long, long ago—not yesterday, but something like a year earlier, as if her new life of agony had lasted longer than her childhood, boarding-school days, university course and married life combined, seeming likely to go on for ever and ever without end. She saw them bring the midwife her tea, and call her for lunch at midday, and later for dinner. She saw Peter acquire the habit of coming in, standing for some time by the window, and going out, and she saw that certain strange men, the maid and Barbara had also taken to coming in. All Barbara could do was to say ' 'twill this' and ' 'twill that', and she was annoyed when anyone closed the drawers in the chest of drawers. Olga watched the light change in the room and at the windows. Sometimes it was twilight, sometimes it was dim and misty, sometimes it was bright daylight, as at dinner time on the previous day, and then twilight again. Each of these changes seemed to last as long as her childhood, her schooldays, her university course.

In the evening two doctors—one bony, bald, with a broad red beard, another swarthy and Jewish-looking, wearing cheap spectacles —performed an operation on her. She was wholly indifferent to strange men touching her body, having lost all shame and will-power. Anyone could do what he liked to her. If, at this time, someone had attacked her with a knife, insulted Peter or deprived her of the right to the small person, she would not have said a word.

She was given chloroform for the operation. Later, when she came to, the pains were still there, still unbearable. It was night, and Olga remembered another such night—the stillness, the icon-lamp, the midwife sitting motionless by the bed, the drawers of the chest of drawers pulled out and Peter standing by the window. But that had been long, long ago.

V

'I'm not dead,' Olga reflected when the pain was over and she was once more aware of her surroundings.

A fine summer day peeped in through the two wide open bedroom windows. Outside in the garden sparrows and magpies kept up their incessant din.

The drawers of the chest of drawers were now shut, and her husband's bed had been made. There was no midwife, no Barbara, no maid in the bedroom, but only Peter standing stock-still by the window as before, and looking into the garden.

There was no baby's crying to be heard, there were no congratulations or rejoicing, and it was clear that the small person had not been born alive.

She called Peter's name and he looked round. Much time must have passed since the last guest's departure and her insults to her husband, for he had become noticeably thin and haggard.

'What is it?' He came over to the bed.

He looked away, his lips twitched and he smiled his helpless childlike smile.

'Is it all over?' she asked.

Peter wanted to answer, but his lips trembled and his mouth twisted like an old man's—like toothless Uncle Nicholas's.

'My darling.' He was wringing his hands, and great tears suddenly fell from his eyes. 'I don't need your property, dear, I don't need any court hearings, or'—he gulped—'dissenting judgements, or those guests, or your dowry. I don't need anything at all. Why did we have to lose our baby? Oh, what's the point of talking?'

With a gesture of despair he left the room.

But nothing mattered to Olga any more. Her head was hazy from the chloroform, she felt spiritually drained, and still numb with the apathy that had come over her while the two doctors had been performing the operation.

A NERVOUS BREAKDOWN

[Припадок]

(1888)

A NERVOUS BREAKDOWN

I

ONE evening a medical student, called Mayer, and Rybnikov—a pupil at the Moscow Institute of Painting, Sculpture and Architecture—went to see their friend Vasilyev, a law student, and suggested a joint expedition to S. Street. It was some time before Vasilyev would agree to go, but in the end he put his coat on and left with them.

He knew of 'fallen women' only by hearsay and from books, and never in his life had he been in their 'houses'. He knew that there are immoral women, forced to sell their honour for money under pressure of dire circumstances—environment, bad upbringing, poverty and so on. They know nothing of pure love, they have no children, no civil rights. Their mothers and sisters mourn them as dead, science treats them as an evil, and men address them slightingly. Yet, despite all this, they have not lost the semblance and image of God. They all acknowledge their sin, hoping to be saved, and means of salvation are lavishly available to them. Society does not forgive people their past, true—and yet St. Mary Magdalene is no lower than the other saints in the sight of God. When Vasilyev chanced to recognize a prostitute on the street by her dress or manner, or to see a picture of one in a comic paper, he always remembered a story that he had once read: a pure, self-sacrificing young man loves a fallen woman and offers to make her his wife, but she considers herself unworthy of such happiness and takes poison.

Vasilyev lived in one of the side streets off the Tver Boulevard. It was about eleven o'clock when he left home with his friends, it had just begun to snow for the first time that winter, and all nature was under the spell of the fresh snow. The air smelt of snow, snow crunched softly under the feet and everything—the ground, the roofs, the trees, the boulevard benches—was soft, white and fresh, so that the houses looked quite different from the day before. The street lamps shone more brightly, the air was clearer, the carriages' rumble was muffled. In the fresh, light, frosty air, a sensation akin to the feel of white, fluffy, newly fallen snow seemed to obtrude itself on one's consciousness.

The medical student began singing in a pleasing tenor:

'Against my will to these sad shores
An unknown force has drawn me.'

The art student chimed in:

'Behold the windmill, now in ruins——'

'Behold the windmill, now in ruins,'

repeated the medical student, raising his eyebrows and shaking his head sadly.

After pausing, rubbing his forehead and trying to remember the words, he sang out so loudly and professionally that passers-by looked round at him:

'Twas here that I did once encounter
A love as carefree as my own free self.'

The three men called at a restaurant, and each drank two glasses of vodka at the bar without taking off his overcoat. Before they gulped their second vodka Vasilyev noticed a piece of cork in his. He raised the glass to his eyes and peered into it for some time, squinting short-sightedly.

The medical student did not understand his expression. 'Hey, what are you staring at? No metaphysics, please. Vodka's for drinking, sturgeon's for eating, women are for consorting with, and snow is for walking on. Do behave like a proper human being for one evening.'

'I, er, I'm all for it,' laughed Vasilyev.

The vodka warmed his chest. He looked dotingly at his friends, admiring and envying them. How well poised these healthy, strong, cheerful fellows were, how well rounded and smooth their minds and spirits! They sing, they adore the stage, they sketch, they talk a great deal, they drink without having headaches next day, they are romantic and dissolute, tender and bold. They can work, protest indignantly, laugh for no reason, talk nonsense. They are ardent, decent, self-sacrificing, and no worse human beings than Vasilyev himself—so careful of his every step and word, so squeamish, so guarded, so ready to make mountains out of molehills. And so he felt the impulse to spend one evening like his friends, to let himself go, to fling caution to the winds. Was there vodka to be drunk? Then drink it he would, even if it meant a splitting headache next morning. Were there girls to be visited? Then he would visit them. He would laugh, play the fool, respond cheerily to contact with passers-by.

He came out of the restaurant laughing. He liked his friends, the one with his parade of artistic unconventionality and crumpled broad-brimmed hat, the other in his sealskin cap—a man of means, but with an air of academic Bohemianism about him. He liked the snow, the pale street lamps, the sharp black imprints made on the fresh snow by the feet of passers-by. He liked the air, and especially the limpid, tender, innocent, almost virginal atmosphere that nature displays only twice a year—when everything is covered with fresh snow, and on bright days or moonlit nights when the ice breaks up on the river in the spring.

He sang in an undertone:

> 'Against my will to these sad shores
> An unknown force has drawn me.'

For some reason he and his friends had this tune on the brain as they went along, all three of them rendering it unthinkingly, not in time with each other.

In ten minutes, Vasilyev imagined, he and his friends would knock on a door and creep along dark passages and dark rooms to the women. Taking advantage of the darkness he would strike a match, and suddenly illumine and behold a martyred face and guilty smile. The unknown woman, fair or dark, would surely have her hair down and wear a white nightgown. She would be scared of the light and terribly embarrassed.

'Heavens, what are you doing?' she would say. 'Put that light out.'

It was all very frightening, yet piquant and novel.

II

The friends turned off Trubny Square into Grachovka Road and quickly entered the side street which Vasilyev knew only by hearsay. He saw two rows of houses with brightly lit windows and wide open doors, and heard the merry strains of pianos and fiddles fluttering out of all the doors and mingling in a weird medley, as if an unseen orchestra was tuning up in the darkness above the roofs.

He was surprised. 'What a lot of houses!'

'That's nothing,' said the medical student. 'There are ten times as many in London. There are about a hundred thousand of these women there.'

The cabbies sat on their boxes as calmly and unconcernedly as in any other street. Pedestrians walked the pavements as in other streets. No one hurried, no one hid his face in his coat collar, no one shook his head reproachfully. This unconcern, that medley of pianos and fiddles, the bright windows, wide open doors—it all struck a garish, impudent, dashing, devil-may-care note. There was obviously just the same sort of bustle and high spirits, with people's faces and walk expressing just the same offhandedness, at slave markets in the old days.

'Let's begin at the beginning,' said the art student.

The friends entered a narrow passage lit by a lamp with a reflector. When they opened the door a man in a black frock-coat, with an unshaven, flunkeylike face and sleepy eyes, slowly arose from a yellow sofa. The place smelt like a laundry with a dash of vinegar. A door led from the hall into a brightly lit room. In this doorway the medical student and the artist stopped and craned their necks, both peering into the room at once.

'Buona sera, signori and gents.' The art student gave a theatrical bow. 'Rigoletto, Huguenotti, Traviata!'

'Havana, Cucaracha, Pistoletto!' added the medical student, pressing his hat to his breast and bowing low.

Vasilyev stood behind them, also desirous of giving a theatrical bow and saying something nonsensical, but he only smiled, feeling an embarrassment akin to shame, and impatiently awaiting further developments.

In the doorway appeared a small fair girl of seventeen or eighteen, crop-haired and wearing a short blue frock with a white metallic pendant on her breast. 'Don't stand in the doorway,' she said. 'Do take your coats off and come into the lounge.'

Still talking 'Italian', the medical student and the art student went into the lounge, followed by the irresolute Vasilyev.

'Take off your coats, gentlemen,' said a servant sternly. 'This won't do.'

Besides the blonde there was another girl in the lounge—very tall and stout, foreign-looking, with bare arms. She sat near the piano playing patience on her lap and paying no attention whatever to the guests.

'Where are the other young ladies?' asked the medical student.

'Having tea,' said the blonde. 'Stepan,' she shouted, 'go and tell the girls that some students have arrived.'

Soon afterwards a third girl came in wearing a bright red dress with blue stripes. Her face was heavily and unskilfully made up, her forehead was hidden by her hair, and there was a look of fear in her unblinking gaze. After entering she at once began singing some song in a powerful, crude contralto. After her a fourth girl appeared, and then a fifth.

Vasilyev found nothing novel or interesting in any of this, feeling as if he had seen it all several times before—the lounge, the piano, the mirror with its cheap gilt frame, the pendant, the dress with the blue stripes, the blank, indifferent faces. Of the darkness, the stillness, the secrecy, the guilty smile and all that he had expected and feared to meet here he saw no trace.

Everything was ordinary, prosaic, boring. Only one thing slightly piqued his curiosity—the dreadful and seemingly intentional bad taste evident in the cornices, in the inane pictures, the dresses and that pendant. There was something significant and noteworthy about this lack of taste.

'How cheap and silly it all is!' Vasilyev thought. 'This trumpery that I see before me—what is there in it all to tempt a normal man and make him commit the fearful sin of buying a human being for a rouble? I understand sinning for the sake of glamour, beauty, grace, passion, good taste, but this is different. What's worth sinning for here? But I must stop thinking.'

The fair woman addressed him. 'Hey, you with the beard, treat me to some porter.'

Vasilyev was suddenly embarrassed. 'With pleasure.' He bowed politely. 'But you must excuse me, madame—I er, shan't drink with you, I'm not a drinking man.'

Five minutes later the friends were on their way to another house.

'Now, why did you order porter?' the medical student raged. 'Think you're a millionaire? That's a complete waste of six roubles.'

'Why not give her the pleasure if she wanted it?' Vasilyev riposted.

'The pleasure wasn't hers, it was the Madame's. They tell the girls to ask the customers for a drink, because they're the ones who make the profit.'

'Behold the windmill, now in ruins,' sang the art student.

Arriving at another house, the friends stopped in the hall, not entering the lounge. As in the first house a figure wearing a frock-coat, with a sleepy flunkey's face, got up from the sofa in the hall. Looking at the fellow, his face and shabby frock-coat, Vasilyev thought: 'What an ordinary simple Russian must have suffered before landing up on the staff of this dump!' Where had he been before, what had he done? What future had he? Was he married? Where was his mother, and did she know he was employed here? From now on Vasilyev could not help paying particular attention to the servant in each house. In one of them—he thought it was the fourth—there was a frail, emaciated little flunkey with a watch-chain on his waistcoat. He was reading *The Leaflet*, and paid no attention to the visitors. Glancing at his face, Vasilyev somehow fancied that a man with a face like that was capable of robbery, murder and perjury. And his face was really interesting—the big forehead, the grey eyes, the squashed little nose, the small, pursed lips, and an expression simultaneously blank and insolent, like a young whippet's as it chases a hare. Vasilyev felt he would like to touch the man's hair to see if it was soft or coarse. It must be coarse like a dog's.

III

After two glasses of porter the art student suddenly became drunk and unnaturally animated.

'Let's go to another,' he commanded, flourishing his arms. 'I'll take you to the best of the lot.'

After bringing his friends to 'the best of the lot', he evinced an urgent desire to dance a quadrille. The medical student muttered something about their having to pay the band a rouble, but agreed to join him. They started dancing.

It was just as nasty in the best house as in the worst. Mirrors, pictures, coiffures, dresses—all looked just the same as before. Scrutinizing the appointments and costumes, Vasilyev realized that this was by no means lack of taste, but something worthy to be called the taste—the style, even—of S. Street. A quality to be found nowhere else on earth, it had the integrity of its own ugliness, and—far from being accidental—it was the outcome of a lengthy evolution. After visiting eight brothels he was no longer surprised at the colour of the dresses, the long trains, the gaudy ribbons, the sailor suits or the thick, mauvish rouge on the cheeks. He realized that it was all as it should be—had even one of the women been dressed like a human being, had but a single decent engraving hung on any of the walls, then the general tone of the entire street would have suffered.

'How clumsily they market themselves,' he thought. 'Can't they see that vice is seductive only when it's attractive and hidden—when it's packaged as virtue? Modest black dresses, pale faces, sad smiles and darkness would be far more potent than this tawdry glitter. The imbeciles! If they can't see it for themselves, couldn't their clients have taught them or something?'

A young lady in a Polish dress trimmed with white fur came and sat by him. 'Attractive dark man, why aren't you dancing?' she asked. 'Why do you look so bored?'

'Because I *am* bored.'

'Then give me some claret and you won't be bored any more.'

Vasilyev made no answer.

'What time do you go to bed?' he asked after a pause.

'About half past five.'

'And when do you get up?'

'Sometimes two o'clock, sometimes three.'

'And what do you do when you get up?'

'We have coffee, and we have our dinner at about half past six.'

'And what do you eat?'

'Nothing special. Soup or cabbage stew. Beefsteak, dessert. Madame looks after the girls very well. But why ask all these questions?'

'Er, for something to say'.

There was a great deal that Vasilyev wanted to discuss with the girl. Where had she been born? Were her parents still alive, and did they know that she was here? How had she come to enter this house? Was she happy and contented? Or sad and oppressed by gloomy thoughts? And had she any hope of escaping from her present predicament? He felt a strong urge to discover these things, but where to begin and how to frame a question so as not to seem indiscreet—that was quite beyond him.

'How old are you?' he asked after a long pause for thought.

'Eighty,' joked the girl, laughing as she watched the art student, who was waving his arms and legs about.

Then something made her suddenly burst out laughing, and she brought out a long, obscene sentence in full hearing of everyone. Vasilyev was aghast, and, not knowing how to look, gave a strained smile. He was the only one to smile, and all the others—his friends, the band and the women—did not even glance at his companion, and seemed not to have heard her.

'Get me some claret,' she repeated.

Repelled by her white fur trimming and her voice, Vasilyev left her. He felt stifled and hot, and his heart began pounding with slow, powerful hammer-like thuds.

'Let's go.' He pulled the art student's sleeve.

'Just a moment—let me finish.'

While the art student and the medical student were completing their quadrille Vasilyev scrutinized the band so as to avoid looking at the women. At the piano was a venerable, bespectacled old man resembling Marshal Bazaine. The violinist was a young man dressed in the latest fashion and sporting a fair beard. Far from looking haggard, his face seemed intelligent, clever, youthful, fresh. He was fastidiously and tastefully dressed, and played with feeling. Problem: how did he and that respectable-looking, venerable old man get here, and why weren't they ashamed to be in this place? What did they think of when they looked at the women?

Had the pianist and the fiddler been ragged, starving, saturnine, drunken with haggard or stupid faces, their presence might have been understandable. As it was, Vasilyev understood nothing. He remembered the story about the fallen woman that he had once read, but that image of humanity with the guilty smile had nothing in common with the present scene, he found. He was not watching fallen women now, he felt, but another, utterly peculiar, alien, incomprehensible world. Had he seen this world previously, on the stage, had he read of it in a book, he would never have believed in it.

The woman with the white fur trimmings gave another loud guffaw and uttered an obnoxious phrase in a loud voice. Overcome by revulsion, he blushed and went out.

'Wait, we're coming too,' the art student shouted after him.

IV

'My partner and I had a conversation as we were dancing,' said the medical student when all three had come out into the street. 'We spoke of her first love affair. Her knight in shining armour was some Smolensk bookkeeper with a wife and five children. She was seventeen —living with her father and mother, who sold soap and candles.'

'How did he win her heart?' asked Vasilyev.

'Bought her fifty roubles' worth of underclothes, damn it.'

Yet the medical student had contrived to worm out his young woman's love story, which is more than I could, thought Vasilyev.

'Well, I'm going home,' he said.

'Why?'

'Because I don't know how to behave here. Besides, I'm bored and disgusted. Where's the fun in it? If only they were human beings—but they're savages and animals. I'm going, do what you like.'

'Ah Gregory, my dear old Greg!' wheedled the art student, putting his arm round Vasilyev. 'Let's visit just one more, and then to hell with them. Come on, Gregorius!'

They persuaded Vasilyev and led him up a staircase. The carpet, the gilt banisters, the porter who opened the door, the vestibule panelling —all had the S. Street touch, but in perfected and imposing form.

'I really must go home,' said Vasilyev as he took his coat off.

'Now, now, my dear chap.' The art student kissed him on the neck. 'Don't be naughty, Greg, old son—be a pal. We came together, so we'll leave together. What a chump you are, really.'

'I can wait in the street—this place disgusts me, honestly.'

'Now, now, Gregory! If it's disgusting you can observe it. Just observe it—see?'

'One must take the objective view,' said the medical student sententiously.

Vasilyev went into the lounge and sat down. There were several other visitors there besides him and his friends: two infantry officers, a baldish, white-haired gentleman in gold-rimmed spectacles, two beardless youths from the College of Surveyors and a very drunk man who looked like an actor. The girls were all busy with these guests, and paid no attention to Vasilyev. Only one of them, dressed as Aida, gave him a sidelong glance and smiled.

'A dark stranger has arrived,' she yawned.

Vasilyev's heart pounded and his face burned. He was ashamed to face the other visitors—a loathsome, agonizing sensation. It was agony to realize that he, a decent, warm-hearted man, which was how he had always thought of himself, hated the women and felt only revulsion for them. The women, the band, the staff—he was sorry for none of them.

'That's because I don't try to understand them,' he thought. 'They all resemble animals more than people, yet they are human, of course, they do have souls. One must understand them before judging them.'

'Don't leave, Gregory, wait for us,' shouted the art student, and disappeared.

Soon the medical student too had disappeared.

'Yes, I must try to understand them, one mustn't be like this,' continued Vasilyev's train of thought.

He began staring intensely at each woman's face, looking for a guilty smile. But either he failed to read their expressions, or else not one of them did feel guilty, for on each face he detected only a crass look of banal, humdrum boredom and complacency. Stupid eyes, stupid smiles, harsh, stupid voices, immodest movements—that was all. In the past they had evidently all had their affair with the bookkeeper and the fifty roubles' worth of underclothes, and the only bright spots in their present existence were the coffee, the three-course meals, the wine, the quadrilles and sleeping till two in the afternoon.

Not finding a single guilty smile, Vasilyev tried to see if there was anyone who looked intelligent, and his attention was caught by one pale, rather sleepy, exhausted face—that of a dark woman, no longer young, in a dress covered with spangles. She sat in an armchair, looking at the floor, plunged in thought. Vasilyev paced up and down the room and sat by her side as if by accident.

'I must start with some commonplace, and then gradually become serious,' he thought.

'What a nice dress you have.' He touched the gilt fringe on her shawl.

'Oh, do I?' said the brunette listlessly.

'Where do you come from?'

'Eh? From a long way off—Chernigov.'

'That's a nice area. It's nice there.'

'Absence makes the heart grow fonder.'

'A pity I'm no good at nature descriptions,' thought Vasilyev. One might be able to move her with descriptions of the Chernigov scenery. No doubt she was fond of it if she was born there.

'Don't you get bored here,' he asked.

'Of course I do.'

'Why don't you leave then, if you're bored?'

'Where should I go? Want me to beg for my living?'

'Begging would be easier than living here.'

'How do you know? Have you tried it?'

'Yes I have—when I couldn't pay my tuition fees. And it would be obvious even if I hadn't. At least a beggar's a free man, but you're a slave.'

The dark girl stretched and sleepily watched a waiter who was bringing glasses and soda-water on a tray.

'Get me some porter.' She yawned again.

'Porter, eh?' thought Vasilyev. 'But what if your brother or mother walked in here now? What would you say? And what would they say? They'd give you porter, I'll be bound!'

Suddenly the sound of weeping was heard, and from the adjoining room—to which the waiter had taken the soda-water—swiftly emerged a red-faced, angry-eyed fair-haired man, followed by the tall, plump Madame.

'Who said you could slap girls' faces?' she screeched. 'We have classier guests than you, and they don't make trouble, you rotten fraud!'

Such a din arose that Vasilyev was frightened and turned pale. In the next room someone was sobbing the heartfelt sobs of the grievously ill-used. Now he realized that the people in this place were genuine human beings who were ill-treated, who suffered, who wept, and who called for help like people anywhere else. His deep loathing and abhorrence gave way to a sensation of acute pity and of anger against the transgressor. He rushed into the room from which the sobs proceeded, and discerned a martyred, tear-stained face between rows of bottles on a marble table top. Holding out his hands towards the face, he took a step towards the table—only to recoil at once, aghast. The weeping girl was drunk.

His heart sank as he made his way through the noisy crowd gathered round the man, and he felt childishly scared, fancying that the denizens of this weird, mysterious world wanted to chase him, beat him and shower him with obscenities. He snatched his coat from the hook and rushed headlong downstairs.

V

Huddling against the fence, he stood near the house and waited for his companions to emerge. The strains of pianos and fiddles—cheerful, reckless, insolent, mournful—blended into a sort of chaotic medley that again sounded as if an unseen orchestra was tuning up in the darkness above the roof. If you looked up into this darkness the black background was spangled with moving white dots—falling snow. As the snowflakes came into the light they floated round lazily in the air like feathers, and descended still more languidly to the ground. A host of them whirled round Vasilyev, clinging to his beard, his eyelashes, his eyebrows. Cabmen, horses, pedestrians—all were white.

'How can snow fall in this street?' Vasilyev wondered. 'Damn these blasted brothels!'

His legs were buckling with fatigue from running all the way downstairs, he was panting as if he was climbing a hill, and he could hear his heart pounding. He was consumed by a desire to escape from the street quickly and go home, but even stronger was his desire to wait for his companions and vent his ill humour on them.

There was much about the houses that he did not understand, and the doomed women's mentality was still a closed book to him, but it was evident that things were far worse than he could have imagined. If that guilty woman—the one who had poisoned herself in the story— was to be called 'fallen', then it was hard to find a suitable name for all those now dancing to the musical pandemonium and mouthing their long, obscene sentences. They were not so much doomed as damned.

'There is vice here,' he thought. 'But there is neither the sense of guilt nor the hope of salvation. They are bought and sold, they flounder in strong drink and other abominations, they're as silly as sheep, they're casual and insensitive. God, God, God!'

He also saw that everything covered by the terms *human dignity*, *individuality* and *God's semblance and image* was defiled, becoming—in drunkards' parlance—'utterly smashed', and that the street and the stupid women were not the only factors responsible.

A group of students passed him—white with snow, cheerfully chattering and laughing. One, tall and slim, stopped and looked at Vasilyev's face.

'It's one of our lot,' said the drunken voice. 'Been overdoing it, old boy? Ah well, my dear fellow, never mind, you have a good time. Push the boat out! Don't be downhearted, old son!'

He took Vasilyev by the shoulders, placed his cold, wet moustache against his cheek, then slipped and staggered. 'Hold on! Don't fall!' he shouted, throwing up both arms, and rushed to catch up his companions with a laugh.

Through the hubbub the art student's voice was heard. 'How dare you hit a woman? I won't have it, blast you! Rotten swine!'

The medical student appeared in the doorway, glanced about him, and spotted Vasilyev. 'So there you are,' he said in a worried voice. 'I say, one should never go out with Yegor, honestly. I just can't make him out. He's made a scene! Hey, Yegor, are you there?' he shouted into the doorway.

'I won't let you hit a woman!' It was the art student's piercing voice, carried from aloft.

Then something awkward and lumbering rolled downstairs. It was the art student flying head over heels, evidently being thrown out.

He picked himself up from the ground, shook his hat and brandished his fist upwards with a look of outraged spite. 'Bastards! Swindlers! Bloodsuckers!' he yelled. 'I won't have any beating! To beat a weak, drunken woman! Oh, you——'

'Yegor! Come, Yegor!' the medical student implored him. 'I swear I'll never go out with you again—my word, I won't.'

The art student gradually calmed down and the friends set off for home.

The medical student started singing.

> 'Against my will to these sad shores
> An unknown force has drawn me.'

A little later the artist chimed in:

> 'Behold the windmill, now in ruins.

What snow, heaven help us! But why did you leave, Gregory? You're a lily-livered coward, and that's a fact.'

Vasilyev walked behind his friends and examined their backs.

'We can't have it both ways,' he reflected. 'Either we only imagine that prostitution is an evil and we exaggerate it. Or else, if prostitution really is as great an evil as is commonly supposed, then my dear old pals are slave-owners, rapists and murderers just as much as the inhabitants of Syria and Cairo caricatured in *The Meadow*. There they are singing, roaring with laughter, and reasoning so sagely. But haven't they just been exploiting hunger, ignorance and stupidity? They—well, I was a witness to it. Where's their humanity, their medicine, their painting? The learning, the art, the lofty sentiments of these assassins remind me of the piece of bacon in the story. Two robbers cut a beggar's throat in a wood, begin sharing his clothes between them, and find a piece of bacon in a bag. "Very nice—let's eat it," says the one. "Are you mad?" asks the other, aghast. "Have you forgotten today's a Wednesday—a fast-day?" So they didn't eat it. First they cut a man's throat, and then they come out of the wood thinking what good Christians they are! These two are the same—buying women and then strutting about thinking what great artists and scholars they are.'

'Listen, you!' he said abruptly and furiously. 'Why do you come here? Can't you see the horror of it? Well, can't you? Medicine teaches you that every one of these women dies before her time from tuberculosis or some other cause. And the arts tell us that she's morally dead long before that. Every one of them dies from entertaining an average of five hundred men in her life. So each one's murdered by five hundred men. And you're two out of the five hundred! Now, if you each visit this or similar places two hundred and fifty times, in the course of your lives, it follows that you'll be jointly responsible for murdering one woman. Can't you see it? And isn't it appalling? To conspire with one, two, three, five others to kill one foolish, hungry woman! My God, if that isn't horrible what is?'

The art student frowned. 'I knew it would end like this. We should never have brought this blithering idiot along. You think your head's full of grand ideas and notions, don't you? Hell knows what they are, but ideas they are not. You look at me with loathing and disgust, but in my view you'd be better occupied building another twenty brothels than going round with that look on your face. There's more immorality in your eyes than there is in the whole street. Come on, Volodya, and to hell with him. He's no more than a blithering idiot.'

'We human beings do kill each other,' said the medical student. 'It is immoral, of course, but talking about it won't help. Good-bye.'

On Trubny Square the friends said good night and parted. Left to himself, Vasilyev quickly strode off down the boulevard. He was scared of the dark, scared of the snow falling on the ground in large flakes and apparently wanting to envelop the entire globe. He was scared, too, of the lamplight dimly glinting through the clouds of snow. An unaccountable, craven fear took possession of him. Though occasional passers-by came his way, he fearfully kept his distance, feeling as if women and only women were coming at him and staring at him from all sides.

'It's starting,' he thought. 'I'm having a breakdown.'

VI

At home he lay on his bed, shivering all over. 'They're alive, alive— ye Gods, alive!' he said.

He gave his imagination free rein, fancying himself now as the brother of a fallen woman, now as her father, now as the woman herself with her painted cheeks—and it all appalled him.

For some reason he felt he must solve the problem immediately at all costs, and that it was his personal problem, no one else's. He strained every sinew, fought back his despair, sat on his bed, clutched his head in his hands, and began wondering how to save all the women he had seen that day. As an educated man he was familiar with the procedure for solving all manner of problems, and, agitated though he was, he followed that routine rigorously. He called to mind the history of the problem and its literature, pacing his room between three and four o'clock in the morning as he tried to remember all the modern techniques of rescuing women. He had many good friends and acquaintances with lodgings in St. Petersburg—at Falzstein's, Galyashkin's, Nechayev's and Yechkin's. Among them were a good few honourable and self-sacrificing men, some of whom had tried to rescue women.

'These few attempts can all be divided into three groups,' thought Vasilyev. 'One lot have ransomed a woman from her brothel, rented her a room and bought her a sewing-machine, and she has become a seamstress. The rescuer has, willingly or reluctantly, made her his mistress, and has then disappeared after graduating and consigning her to some other decent fellow as though she were an object. But fallen the fallen woman has remained. Others, having redeemed one, and having likewise taken a separate room for her—and also bought her the regulation sewing-machine—have further brought to bear homilies, writing lessons and books. As long as this has remained an interesting novelty to the woman, she has stayed and done her sewing. But then she has become bored and begun to entertain men without the knowledge of the homily-deliverers. Or else she has run off back to the place where she can sleep till three in the afternoon, drink coffee and have plenty to eat. A third group, the most ardent and selfless of all, have taken a bold and resolute step. They have married the girl. And when this brazen, crushed, spoilt or stupid animal has become a wife, the mistress of a home and then a mother, her life and outlook have been so transformed that it has been hard to recognize the one-time fallen woman in the wife and mother. Yes, marriage is the best means, and perhaps the only one.'

'But it's impossible,' said Vasilyev aloud, sinking on to his bed. 'I'm the last person to get married. For that one needs to be a saint, incapable of feeling hatred and revulsion. But let's suppose that the medical student, the art student and I all overcame our scruples and each married one—suppose they all got married. What would the result be? The result would be that while they're getting married here in Moscow your Smolensk bookkeeper will be debauching another batch, and this other lot will come rushing here to fill the vacancies along with girls from Saratov, Nizhny Novgorod and Warsaw. And what about London's hundred thousand whores—not to mention those of Hamburg?'

The oil had burnt down in his lamp, and it had begun to smoke, but Vasilyev did not notice. He began pacing to and fro again, still brooding. He was now posing the problem differently: what must be done to remove the demand for fallen women? This presupposed that men —their purchasers and murderers—must appreciate the immorality of their slave-owning role and recoil from it in horror. The men it was who needed saving.

'Obviously the scientific and artistic approaches lead nowhere,' thought Vasilyev. 'Missionary work is the only answer.'

He imagined himself standing on the street corner on the next evening, and asking every passer-by where he was going and why. Why? 'Have you no fear of God?'

He would address the apathetic cabmen. 'Why are you waiting here? Where are your feelings of indignation and outrage? You believe in God, don't you? You know that it's a sin, that people will go to hell for it, so why don't you speak up? They're strangers to you, true, but they too have fathers and brothers just like you, don't they?'

A friend of Vasilyev's had once described him as a gifted man. There are literary, theatrical and artistic talents, but his special flair was for human beings. He was keenly and splendidly sensitive to pain in all its forms. As a good actor reflects others' movements and voices, so could Vasilyev echo another's hurt in his soul. Seeing tears, he wept. In the presence of the sick he himself became ill and groaned. Witnessing an act of violence, he would feel as if he personally were the victim, take fright childishly and run off in panic for help. Others' pain irritated him, stimulated him, aroused him to ecstasy, and so on. Whether the friend was right I do not know, but Vasilyev's reaction to having, as it seemed, solved his problem was akin to inspiration. He wept, he laughed, he spoke aloud the words that he would say on the next day, feeling the keenest affection for those who would hearken to him and stand by him on the street corner to preach. He sat down to write letters, swore vows to himself.

His reaction also resembled inspiration in proving short-lived, for he soon tired. The whores of London, Hamburg and Warsaw bore down on him with their collective weight as mountains press on the earth, and he quailed, disconcerted by their sheer bulk. He remembered that he had no talent for speaking, that he was craven and cowardly, that apathetic persons would hardly wish to hear and understand him —a law student in his third year, a quaking nonentity—that true evangelism involved deeds as well as pious words.

When it was light, and carriages were beginning to rumble in the street, Vasilyev lay quite still on his sofa, staring into space. No longer was he brooding on women, men or evangelism, his entire attention being focused on the spiritual anguish that tormented him. It was a dull, abstract, undefined hurt akin to misery, despair and terror in the ultimate degree. He could indicate its location—in his chest, beneath his heart—but there was nothing to which he could compare it. He had suffered acute toothache, pleurisy and neuralgia in his time, but all that was nothing to this spiritual agony. With pain like this life seemed utterly repugnant. His academic thesis, an admirable composition already completed, the people he was fond of, the rescue of fallen women, together with all that had evoked his sympathy or indifference on the previous day—it exasperated him now, as he recalled it, no less than the carriages' clatter, the scurrying of the servants in his lodging house, the daylight. Had anyone now performed some great deed of mercy in his presence, or an outrageous act of violence, he would have been equally repelled by both. Among all the notions idly drifting through his head there were only two that did not irk him: one, that it was within his power to kill himself any moment, and the other that his sufferings would last no more than three days. This he knew from experience.

After lying down for a while he stood up, wringing his hands, and paced the room in a square, along the walls—not from corner to corner as usual. He glanced at himself in the mirror. His face was pale and cadaverous, his temples were hollow, his eyes bigger, darker and less mobile, as if they belonged to someone else, and they expressed intolerable mental anguish.

At midday the art student knocked on the door. 'Are you in, Gregory?'

Receiving no answer, he stood for a minute, pondered and answered himself in southern dialect. 'He bain't here. Danged if he haven't gone off to that there mooniversity, drat 'im!'

He went away. Lying down on his bed, his head under the pillow, Vasilyev began crying in his agony, and the more profusely the tears flowed the more terrible his spiritual anguish became. When it grew dark he remembered the excruciating night that faced him, and was overwhelmed by sheer despair. He dressed quickly, ran from his room, leaving the door wide open, and drifted without aim or reason into the street. Without thinking where he was going, he set off rapidly down Sadovy Street.

Snow was falling as heavily as yesterday, but it was thawing. Thrusting his hands into his sleeves, shuddering, scared of the clatter, the tram-bells and the pedestrians, he walked down Sadovy Street to Sukharev Tower and the Red Gate, and then turned into Basmanny Street. He went into a tavern and gulped a large vodka, but felt no better for it. Reaching Razgulyay, he turned right and strode down side streets where he had never been in his life. He reached the old bridge where the Yauza murmurs and from which you can see the long rows of lights in the windows of the Red Barracks. Wanting to relieve his mental anguish with some new sensation or different pain, but not knowing how to achieve this, he unbuttoned his overcoat and frock-coat, weeping and trembling, and bared his chest to the sleet and the wind. But that did not alleviate his sufferings either. Then he bent over the railings on the bridge, gazed down at the black, turbulent Yauza, and was prompted to throw himself in head first, not because he recoiled from life, or wanted to commit suicide, but to replace one pain with another, if only by smashing himself up. But the black water, the darkness, the deserted snowy banks—they were all so frightening. He shuddered and went on. He went past the Red Barracks, and then came back again, went down into a copse and came back out of it on to the bridge again.

'No, I'll go home. Home,' he thought. 'It will be easier there.'

He set off and, on arriving home, tore off his wet overcoat and cap, and began pacing along the walls, continuing to do so without stopping until morning came.

VII

When the art student and the medical student came to see him next morning he was lurching about the room groaning with pain, his shirt torn and his hands bitten.

'For God's sake!' he sobbed on seeing his friends. 'Take me where you like, do what you want, but in pity's name hurry up and save me. I shall kill myself.'

The art student was taken aback and turned pale, while the medical student—though also near to tears—felt that the medical profession should be cool and composed in all emergencies, and he remarked coldly that Vasilyev was having a nervous breakdown. 'But it's all right—we'll go to the doctor's at once.'

'Anything you like, but for God's sake hurry!'

'Don't get so excited. Try and control yourself.'

The art student and the medical student put Vasilyev's coat on with trembling hands, and took him into the street.

'Michael Sergeyevich has wanted to meet you for ages,' said the medical student on the way. 'He's a charming fellow, very good at his job. He only graduated in 1882, but he has an enormous practice already. He's very matey with students.'

'Hurry, hurry!' said Vasilyev.

Michael Sergeyevich, a stout, fair-haired doctor, received the friends with frigid courtesy and dignity, smiling on only one side of his face. 'Mayer and your art student friend have told me of your illness. I'm glad to be of service. Now, sit down, pray.'

He sat Vasilyev in a big armchair near the table and moved a box of cigarettes towards him. 'Now then,' he began, smoothing the knees of his trousers. 'Let's get to work. How old are you?'

The doctor asked the questions and the medical student answered them. He asked about Vasilyev's father. Had he had any particular illnesses? Did he drink to excess, was he remarkable for cruelty or any other aberrations? He asked the same questions about his grandfather, mother, sisters and brothers. On learning that his mother had a fine voice, and had sometimes performed on the stage, he evinced sudden signs of animation.

'Excuse me,' he said, 'but was the stage a positive obsession with your mother, do you recall?'

Twenty minutes passed. The doctor kept stroking his knees while saying the same thing over and over again, and Vasilyev found this boring.

'So far as I understand your questions, Doctor,' he said, 'you wish to know if my illness is hereditary or not. It is not.'

The doctor proceeded to ask whether Vasilyev had had any secret vices as a boy. Had there been any head injuries, fads, vagaries, obsessive proclivities? Half the questions commonly asked by painstaking doctors may safely be left unanswered without risk to health, but Michael Sergeyevich, the medical student and the art student all wore expressions suggesting that, should Vasilyev fail to answer a single one, then all was lost. On receiving the replies the doctor jotted them down on paper for some reason, and on learning that Vasilyev had taken a degree in natural science and was now studying law, he cogitated deeply.

'He wrote a first-rate dissertation last year,' said the medical student.

'I'm sorry, but don't interrupt me—you're stopping me concentrating.' The doctor smiled on one side of his face. 'Yes, of course, that too plays a role in the evolution of the case. Intense intellectual work, exhaustion—. Ah, yes indeed.' He addressed Vasilyev. 'And do you drink vodka?'

'Very seldom.'

Another twenty minutes passed. Speaking in an undertone, the medical student began stating his view on the immediate cause of the attack, explaining that he and the art student had accompanied Vasilyev to S. Street two days earlier.

The offhand, neutral, nonchalant tone in which his friends and the doctor alluded to the women, and to that wretched street, struck Vasilyev as most peculiar.

'Tell me one thing, Doctor,' he said, making an effort not to speak rudely. 'Is prostitution an evil or isn't it?'

'No one denies that, my dear fellow, no one at all,' said the doctor, his expression suggesting that he had long ago found answers to all such questions.

'Are you a psychiatrist?' Vasilyev asked rudely.

'Yes sir, I am.'

'Perhaps all of you are right, you may be.' Vasilyev stood up and paced the room. 'But I find it most remarkable. For me to have studied in two faculties rates as a heroic exploit. My authorship of a thesis which will be neglected and forgotten in three years' time—that's a reason for lauding me to the skies. But my inability to allude to fallen women as casually as I might to these chairs—that is a reason for taking me to a doctor, for calling me insane, and for being sorry for me!'

Vasilyev somehow felt immense pity for himself, for his companions, for all the people he had seen two days earlier, and for the doctor. He burst into tears and collapsed in the armchair.

His friends looked enquiringly at the doctor. With an air of fully comprehending the tears and despair, and of feeling himself a specialist in that line, he went up to Vasilyev, silently gave him some drops to drink, and then, when he had calmed down, got him undressed, and began investigating the sensitivity of his skin, his knee reflexes and so on.

Vasilyev began to feel easier. When he left the doctor's he felt ashamed of himself, he was no longer exasperated by the carriages' clatter, and the weight beneath his heart was growing lighter and lighter as if it was melting away. He was carrying two prescriptions— the one for bromide, the other for morphia.

He had taken all that stuff before!

He stood in the street and thought for a while, then said good-bye to his friends and sauntered languidly off towards the university.

THE COBBLER AND THE DEVIL

[*Сапожник и нечистая сила*]

(1888)

THE COBBLER AND THE DEVIL

It was Christmas Eve. Marya had long been snoring on the stove, and the paraffin in the little lamp had burnt out, but Theodore Nilov still sat over his work. He would have stopped long ago and gone out into the street, but a customer from Kolokolny Road, who had ordered some new vamps for his boots a fortnight ago, had come in on the previous day, sworn at him and told him to finish the work at once without fail, before morning service.

'It's a rotten life,' grumbled Theodore as he worked. 'Some folks have been asleep for ages, others are enjoying themselves, while I'm just a dogsbody cobbling away for every Tom, Dick or Harry.'

To stop himself falling asleep he kept taking a bottle from under the table and drinking, flexing his neck after each swallow. 'Pray tell me this,' he said in a loud voice. 'Why can my customers enjoy themselves while I'm forced to work for them. What sense is there in it? Is it because they have money and I'm a beggar?'

He hated all his customers, especially the one who lived in Kolokolny Road. This was a personage of lugubrious aspect—long-haired, sallow, with big blue-tinted spectacles and a hoarse voice. He had an unpronounceable German surname. What his calling might be, what he did, was a complete mystery. When Theodore had gone to take his measurements a fortnight ago, he had been sitting on the floor pounding away at a mortar. Before the cobbler could say good day the contents of the mortar suddenly flashed and blazed up with a bright red flame, there was a stench of sulphur and burnt feathers, and the room was filled with dense pink smoke that made Theodore sneeze five times.

'No God-fearing man would meddle with the likes of that,' he reflected on returning home.

When the bottle was empty he put the boots on the table and pondered. Leaning his heavy head on his fist, he began thinking of his poverty, and of his gloomy, cheerless life. Then he thought of the rich with their big houses, their carriages, their hundred-rouble notes. How nice it would be if the houses of the bloody rich fell apart, if their horses died, if their fur coats and sable caps wore threadbare. How splendid if the rich gradually became beggars with nothing to eat,

while the poor cobbler turned into a rich man who went round bullying poor cobblers on Christmas Eve.

Thus brooding, he suddenly remembered his work and opened his
eyes. 'What a business!' he thought, looking at the boots. 'The job was
finished long ago, and here I sit. I must take them to the gentleman.'

He wrapped his work in a red handkerchief, put his coat on and
went into the street. Fine, hard snow was falling and pricked his face
like needles. It was cold, slippery and dark, the gas lamps were dim,
and there was such a smell of paraffin in the street for some reason that
he spluttered and coughed. Rich men drove up and down the road,
each with a ham and a bottle of vodka in his hand. From the carriages
and sledges rich young ladies peeped at Theodore, putting out their
tongues and shouting.

'A beggar! A beggar! Ha ha ha!'

Students, officers, merchants and generals walked behind him, all
jeering. 'Boozy bootmaker! Godless welt-stitcher! Pauper! But his
soles go marching on, ha ha ha!'

It was all most offensive, but he said nothing and only spat in disgust.
Then he met Kuzma Lebyodkin, a master bootmaker from Warsaw.
'I married a rich woman,' Kuzma told him. 'And I have apprentices
working for me. But you're a pauper and have nothing to eat.'

Theodore could not resist running after him. He chased him until he
found himself in Kolokolny Road, where his customer lived in a top-
floor flat in the fourth house from the corner. To reach him you had
to cross a long, dark courtyard, and then climb a very high slippery
staircase that vibrated under your feet. When the cobbler entered, the
customer was sitting on the floor pounding something in a mortar,
just as he had been a fortnight earlier.

'I've brought your boots, sir,' said Theodore sullenly.

The other stood up without speaking and made to try the boots on.
Wishing to help him, Theodore went down on one knee and pulled
one of his old boots off, but immediately sprang up, aghast, and backed
away to the door. In place of a foot the creature had a hoof like a
horse's!

'Dear me!' thought the cobbler. 'What a business!'

The best thing would have been to cross himself, drop everything
and run downstairs. But he immediately reflected that this was his
first, and would probably be his last, encounter with the Devil, and
that it would be foolish not to take advantage of his good offices.

Pulling himself together, he decided to chance his luck, and clasped his hands behind his back to stop himself making the sign of the cross.

'Folks say there's nothing more diabolical and evil on this earth than the Devil,' he remarked with a respectful cough. 'But to my way of thinking, your Reverence, the Prince of Darkness must be highly educated like. The Devil has hoofs and a tail, saving your presence, but he's a sight more brainy than many a scholar.'

'Thank you for those kind words,' said the customer, flattered. 'Thank you, cobbler. What do you desire?'

Losing no time, the cobbler began complaining of his lot, and started with having envied the rich since childhood. He had always resented folk not living alike in big houses, with fine horses. Why, he wondered, was he poor? How was he worse than Kuzma Lebyodkin from Warsaw who owned his own house, whose wife wore a hat? He had the same sort of nose, hands, feet, head and back as the rich, so why was he forced to work while others enjoyed themselves? Why was he married to Marya, not to a lady smelling of scent? He had often seen beautiful young ladies in the houses of rich customers, but they had taken no notice of him, except for laughing sometimes and whispering to each other.

'What a red nose that cobbler has!'

True, Marya was a good, kind, hard-working woman, but she was uneducated, wasn't she? She had a heavy hand, she hit hard, and you only had to speak of politics or something brainy in her presence for her to chip in with the most arrant nonsense.

'So what are your wishes?' broke in his customer.

'Well, seeing as how you're so kind, Mr. Devil, sir, I'd like your Reverence to make me rich.'

'Certainly. But you must give me your soul in return, you know. Before the cocks crow, go and sign this paper assigning your soul to me.'

'Now see here, your Reverence,' said Theodore politely. 'When you ordered the vamps done I didn't take money in advance. You must carry out the order first and ask for payment afterwards.'

'Oh, all right,' agreed the customer.

Bright flame suddenly flared in the mortar, followed by a gust of dense pink smoke and the smell of burnt feathers and sulphur. When the smoke had dispersed Theodore rubbed his eyes and saw that he was no longer Theodore the shoemaker but quite a different person— one who wore a waistcoat with a watch-chain, and new trousers—and that he was sitting in an armchair at a big table. Two footmen were serving him dishes with low bows and a 'Good appetite, sir'.

What wealth! The footmen served a large slice of roast mutton and a dish of cucumbers. Then they brought roast goose in a pan followed shortly afterwards by roast pork and horse-radish sauce. And how classy it was, all this—this was real politics for you! He ate, gulping a large tumbler of excellent vodka before every course like any general or count. After the pork, buckwheat gruel with goose fat was served, and then an omelette with bacon fat and fried liver, all of which he ate and thoroughly enjoyed. And what else? They also served onion pie and steamed turnips with kvass.

'I wonder the gentry don't burst with meals like this,' he thought.

Finally a large pot of honey was served, and after the meal the Devil appeared wearing his blue spectacles. 'Was dinner satisfactory, Mr. Cobbler?' he asked with a low bow.

But Theodore could not get a word out, for he was nearly bursting after his meal. He had the disagreeable, stuffed sensation that comes from overeating, and tried to distract himself by scrutinizing the boot on his left foot.

'I never charged less than seven-and-a-half roubles for boots like that,' he thought, and asked which cobbler had made it.

'Kuzma Lebyodkin,' answered a footman.

'Tell that imbecile to come here!'

Soon Kuzma Lebyodkin from Warsaw appeared.

'What are your orders, sir?' He stopped by the door in a respectful attitude.

'Hold your tongue!' cried Theodore, stamping his foot. 'Don't answer me back! Know your place, cobbler, and your station in life! Oaf! You don't know how to make boots! I'll smash your face in! Why did you come here?'

'For my money, sir.'

'What money? Be off with you! Come back on Saturday. Clout him one, my man!'

Then he immediately remembered what a life his own customers had led him, and he felt sick at heart. To amuse himself he took a fat wallet from his pocket and started counting his money. There was a lot of it, but he wanted even more. The Devil in the blue spectacles brought him another, fatter wallet, but he wanted more still, and the more he counted the more discontented he grew.

In the evening the Devil brought him a tall, full-bosomed lady in a red dress, explaining that she was his new wife. He spent the whole evening kissing her and eating gingerbreads, and at night he lay on a soft feather bed, tossing from side to side. But he just couldn't get to sleep, and he felt as if all was not well.

'We have lots of money,' he told his wife. 'But it might attract burglars. You'd better take a candle and have a look.'

He couldn't sleep all night, and kept getting up to see if his trunk was all right. In the morning he had to go to matins. Now, rich and poor receive equal honours in church. When Theodore had been poor he had prayed 'Lord forgive me, sinner that I am,' in church. He said the same prayer now that he was rich, so where was the difference? And when the rich Theodore died he wouldn't be buried in gold and diamonds, but in black earth like the poorest beggar. He would burn in the same fire as cobblers. All this he resented. And then again, he still felt weighed down by the meal, and his mind was not on worship, but was assailed by worries about his money chest, about burglars, and about his doomed and bartered soul.

He came out of church in a bad temper. To banish evil thoughts he followed his usual procedure of singing at the top of his voice, but barely had he begun when a policeman ran up and saluted.

'Gents mustn't sing in the street, squire. You ain't no cobbler!'

Theodore leant against a fence and began wondering how to amuse himself.

'Don't lean too hard on the fence, guv'nor, or you'll dirty your fur coat,' a doorkeeper shouted.

Theodore went into a shop, bought their best concertina, and walked down the street playing it. But everyone pointed at him and laughed.

'Cor, look at his lordship!' jeered the cabmen. 'He's carrying on like a cobbler.'

'We can't have the nobs disturbing the peace,' said a policeman. 'You'll be going to the ale-house next!'

'Alms for the love of Christ!' wailed beggars, surrounding Theodore on all sides. 'Give us something, mister.'

Beggars had never paid him any attention when he had been a cobbler, but now they wouldn't leave him alone.

At home he was greeted by his new wife, the lady. She wore a green blouse and a red skirt. He wanted a bit of a cuddle, and had raised his hand to give her a good clout on the back when she spoke angrily.

'Yokel! Bumpkin! You don't know how to treat a lady. Kiss my hand if you love me. Fisticuffs I do not permit.'

'What a bloody life!' thought Theodore. 'What an existence! It's all don't sing, don't play the concertina, don't have fun with your woman. Pshaw!'

No sooner had he sat down to tea with his lady than the Devil appeared in his blue spectacles. 'Now, Mr. Cobbler,' said he, 'I've kept my part of the bargain, so sign the paper and come with me. Now you know what being rich means, so that's enough of that!'

He dragged him off to hell, straight to the furnace, and demons flew up, shouting, from all sides.

'Idiot! Blockhead! Jackass!'

There was a fearful smell of paraffin in hell, it was fit to choke you.

But suddenly it all vanished. Theodore opened his eyes and saw his table, the boots and the tin lamp. The lamp glass was black, stinking smoke belched from the dimly glowing wick as from a chimney. The blue-spectacled customer stood near it.

'Idiot! Blockhead! Jackass!' he was yelling. 'I'll teach you a lesson, you rogue! You took my order a fortnight ago, and the boots still aren't ready! Expect me to traipse round here for them half a dozen times a day? Blackguard! Swine!'

Theodore tossed his head and tackled the boots while the customer cursed and threatened him for a time. When he at last calmed down Theodore sullenly enquired what his occupation was.

'Making Bengal lights and rockets—I'm a manufacturer of fireworks.'

Church bells rang for matins. Theodore handed over the boots, received his money and went to church.

Carriages and sledges with bearskin aprons careered up and down the street, while merchants, ladies and officers walked the pavement, together with humbler folk. But no longer did Theodore envy anyone, or rail against his fate. Rich and poor were equally badly off, he now felt. Some could drive in carriages, others could sing at the top of their voices and play concertinas, but one and the same grave awaited all alike. Nor was there anything in life to make it worth giving the Devil even a tiny scrap of your soul.

THE BET

[Пари]

(1889)

THE BET

I

ONE dark autumn night an elderly banker was pacing up and down his study and recalling the party that he had given on an autumn evening fifteen years earlier. It had been attended by a good few clever people, and fascinating discussions had taken place, one of the topics being capital punishment. The guests, including numerous academics and journalists, had been largely opposed to it, considering the death penalty out of date, immoral and unsuitable for Christian states. Several of them felt that it should be replaced everywhere by life imprisonment.

'I disagree,' said their host the banker. 'I've never sampled the death penalty or life imprisonment myself. Still, to judge *a priori*, I find capital punishment more moral and humane than imprisonment. Execution kills you at once, whereas life imprisonment does it slowly. Now, which executioner is more humane? He who kills you in a few minutes, or he who drags the life out of you over a period of several years?'

A guest remarked that both were equally immoral. 'Both have the same object—the taking of life. The state isn't God, and it has no right to take what it can't restore if it wishes.'

Among the guests was a young lawyer of about twenty-five. 'The death sentence and the life sentence are equally immoral,' said he when his opinion was canvassed. 'But, if I had to choose between them, I'd certainly choose the second. Any kind of life is better than no life at all.'

A lively argument had ensued. The banker, younger and more excitable in those days, had suddenly got carried away and struck the table with his fist. 'It's not true!' he shouted at the young man. 'I bet you two million you wouldn't last five years in solitary confinement.'

'I'll take you on if you mean it,' was the reply. 'And I won't just do a five-year stretch, I'll do fifteen.'

'Fifteen? Done!' cried the banker. 'Gentlemen, I put up two million.'

'Accepted! You stake your millions and I stake my freedom,' said the young man.

And so the outrageous, futile wager was made. The banker, then a spoilt and frivolous person, with more millions than he could count, was delighted, and he made fun of the lawyer over supper. 'Think better of it while there's still time,' said he. 'Two million is nothing to me, young man, but you risk losing three or four of the best years of your life, I say three or four because you won't hang on longer. And don't forget, my unfortunate friend, that confinement is far harder when it's voluntary than when it's compulsory. The thought that you can go free at any moment will poison your whole existence in prison. I'm sorry for you.'

Pacing to and fro, the banker now recalled all this. 'What was the good of that wager?' he wondered. 'What's the use of the man losing fifteen years of his life? Or of my throwing away two million? Does it prove that the death penalty is better or worse than life imprisonment? Certainly not! Stuff and nonsense! On my part it was a spoilt man's whim, and on his side it was simply greed for money.'

Then he recalled the sequel to that evening. It had been decided that the young man should serve his term under the strictest supervision in one of the lodges in the banker's garden. For fifteen years he was to be forbidden to cross the threshold, to see human beings, to hear the human voice, to receive letters and newspapers. He was allowed a musical instrument, and books to read. He could write letters, drink wine, smoke. It was stipulated that his communications with the outside world could not be in spoken form, but must take place through a little window built specially for the purpose. Anything he needed—books, music, wine and so on—he could receive by sending a note, and in any quantity he liked, but only through the window. The contract covered all the details and minutiae that would make his confinement strictly solitary, and compel him to serve precisely fifteen years from twelve o'clock on the fourteenth of November 1870 until twelve o'clock on the fourteenth of November 1885. The slightest attempt to break the conditions, even two minutes before the end, absolved the banker from all obligation to pay the two million.

So far as could be judged from the prisoner's brief notes, he suffered greatly from loneliness and depression in his first year of incarceration. The sound of his piano could be heard continually, day and night, from the lodge. He refused strong drink and tobacco. Wine stimulates desires, wrote he, and desires are a prisoner's worst enemy. Besides, is there anything drearier than drinking good wine and seeing nobody? And tobacco spoilt the air of his room. The books that he had sent during the first year were mostly light reading—novels with a complex love plot, thrillers, fantasies, comedies and so on.

In the second year there was no more music from the lodge, and the prisoner's notes demanded only literary classics. In the fifth year music was heard again, and the captive asked for wine. Those who watched him through the window said that he spent all that year just eating, drinking and lying on his bed, often yawning and talking angrily to himself. He read no books. Sometimes he would sit and write at night. He would spend hours writing, but would tear up everything he had written by dawn. More than once he was heard weeping.

In the second half of the sixth year the captive eagerly embraced the study of languages, philosophy and history. So zealously did he tackle these subjects that the banker could hardly keep up with his book orders—in four years some six hundred volumes were procured at his demand. During the period of this obsession the banker incidentally received the following letter from the prisoner.

'My dearest Gaoler,
'I write these lines in six languages. Show them to those who know about these things. Let them read them. If they can't find any mistakes I beg you to have a shot fired in the garden—it will show me that my efforts have not been wasted. The geniuses of all ages and countries speak different languages, but the same flame burns in them all. Oh, did you but know what a transcendental happiness my soul now experiences from my ability to understand them!'

The captive's wish was granted—the banker had two shots fired in the garden.

After the tenth year the lawyer sat stock-still at the table, reading only the Gospels. The banker marvelled that one who had mastered six hundred obscure tomes in four years should spend some twelve months reading a single slim, easily comprehensible volume. Theology and histories of religion followed the Gospels.

In the last two years of his imprisonment the captive read an enormous amount quite indiscriminately. Now it was the natural sciences, now he wanted Byron or Shakespeare. There were notes in which he would simultaneously demand a work on chemistry, a medical textbook, a novel and a philosophical or theological treatise. His reading suggested someone swimming in the sea surrounded by the wreckage of his ship, and trying to save his life by eagerly grasping first one spar and then another.

II

'He regains his freedom at twelve o'clock tomorrow,' thought the old banker as he remembered all this. 'And I should pay him two million by agreement. But if I do pay up I'm done for—I'll be utterly ruined.'

Fifteen years earlier he had had more millions than he could count, but now he feared to ask which were greater, his assets or his debts. Gambling on the stock exchange, wild speculation, the impetuosity that he had never managed to curb, even in old age—these things had gradually brought his fortunes low, and the proud, fearless, self-confident millionaire had become just another run-of-the-mill banker trembling at every rise and fall in his holdings.

'Damn this bet!' muttered the old man, clutching his head in despair. 'Why couldn't the fellow die? He's only forty now. He'll take my last penny, he'll marry, he'll enjoy life, he'll gamble on the Exchange, while I look on enviously, like a pauper, and hear him saying the same thing day in day out: "I owe you all my happiness in life, so let me help you." No, it's too much! My only refuge from bankruptcy and disgrace is that man's death.'

Three o'clock struck and the banker cocked an ear. Everyone in the house was asleep, and nothing was heard but the wind rustling the frozen trees outside. Trying not to make a noise, he took from his fireproof safe the key of the door that had not been opened for fifteen years, put his overcoat on, and went out.

It was dark and cold outside, and rain was falling. A keen, damp wind swooped howling round the whole garden, giving the trees no rest. Straining his eyes, the banker could not see the ground, the white statues, the lodge or the trees. He approached the area of the lodge, and twice called his watchman, but there was no answer. The man was obviously sheltering from the weather, and was asleep somewhere in the kitchen or the greenhouse.

'If I have the courage to carry out my intention the main suspicion will fall on the watchman,' the old man thought.

He found the steps to the lodge and the door by feeling in the dark, entered the hall, groped his way into a small passage, and lit a match. There was no one there—just a bedstead without bedding on it, and the dark hulk of a cast-iron stove in the corner. The seals on the door leading to the captive's room were intact. When the match went out the old man peered through the small window, trembling with excitement.

In the prisoner's room a candle dimly burned. He was sitting near the table, and all that could be seen of him were his back, the hair on his head and his hands. On the table, on two armchairs, and on the carpet near the table, lay open books.

Five minutes passed without the prisoner once stirring—fifteen years of confinement had taught him to sit still. The banker tapped the window with a finger, but the captive made no answering movement. Then the banker cautiously broke the seals on the door, and put the key in the keyhole. The rusty lock grated and the door creaked. The banker expected to hear an immediate shout of surprise and footsteps, but three minutes passed and it was as quiet as ever in there. He decided to enter.

At the table a man unlike ordinary men sat motionless. He was all skin and bones, he had long tresses like a woman's, and a shaggy beard. The complexion was sallow with an earthy tinge, the cheeks were hollow, the back was long and narrow, and the hand propping the shaggy head was so thin and emaciated that it was painful to look at. His hair was already streaked with silver, and no one looking at his worn, old-man's face would have believed that he was only forty. He was asleep, and on the table in front of his bowed head lay a sheet of paper with something written on it in small letters.

'How pathetic!' thought the banker. 'He's asleep, and is probably dreaming of his millions. All I have to do is to take this semi-corpse, throw it on the bed, smother it a bit with a pillow, and the keenest investigation will find no signs of death by violence. But let us first read what he has written.'

Taking the page from the table, the banker read as follows.

'At twelve o'clock tomorrow I regain my freedom and the right to associate with others. But I think fit, before I leave this room for the sunlight, to address a few words to you. With a clear conscience, and as God is my witness, I declare that I despise freedom, life, health and all that your books call the blessings of this world.

'I have spent fifteen years intently studying life on earth. True, I have not set eyes on the earth or its peoples, but in your books I have drunk fragrant wine, sung songs, hunted stags and wild boars in the forests, loved women. Created by the magic of your inspired poets, beautiful girls, ethereal as clouds, have visited me at night, and whispered in my ears magical tales that have made my head reel. In your books I have climbed the peaks of Elbrus and Mont Blanc, whence I have watched the sun rising in the morning, and flooding the sky, the ocean and the mountain peaks with crimson gold in the evening. From there I have watched lightnings flash and cleave the storm-clouds above me. I have seen green forests, fields, rivers, lakes, cities. I have heard the singing of the sirens and the strains of shepherds' pipes. I have touched the wings of beautiful devils who flew to me to converse of God. In your books I have plunged into the bottomless pit, performed miracles, murdered, burnt towns, preached new religions, conquered whole kingdoms.

'Your books have given me wisdom. All that man's tireless brain has created over the centuries has been compressed into a small nodule inside my head. I know I'm cleverer than you all.

'I despise your books, I despise all the blessings and the wisdom of this world. Everything is worthless, fleeting, ghostly, illusory as a mirage. Proud, wise and handsome though you be, death will wipe you from the face of the earth along with the mice burrowing under the floor. Your posterity, your history, your deathless geniuses—all will freeze or burn along with the terrestrial globe.

'You have lost your senses and are on the wrong path. You take lies for truth, and ugliness for beauty. You would be surprised if apple and orange trees somehow sprouted with frogs and lizards instead of fruit, or if roses smelt like a sweating horse. No less surprised am I at you who have exchanged heaven for earth. I do not want to understand you.

'To give you a practical demonstration of my contempt for what you live by, I hereby renounce the two million that I once yearned for as one might for paradise, but which I now scorn. To disqualify myself from receiving it I shall leave here five hours before the time fixed, thus breaking the contract.'

After reading this the banker laid the paper on the table, kissed the strange man on the head and left the lodge in tears. At no other time—not even after losing heavily on the stock exchange—had he felt such contempt for himself. Returning to his house, he went to bed, but excitement and tears kept him awake for hours.

Next morning the watchmen ran up, white-faced, and told the banker that they had seen the man from the lodge climb out of his window into the garden, go to the gate and vanish. The banker went over at once with his servants and made sure that the captive had indeed fled. To forestall unnecessary argument he took the document of renunciation from the table, went back to the house and locked it in his fireproof safe.

STORY NOT INCLUDED BY CHEKHOV
IN HIS *COLLECTED WORKS*

LIGHTS

[*Огни*]

(1888)

LIGHTS

OUTSIDE the hut a dog was barking nervously. The engineer, who was called Ananyev, his student assistant (a Baron Von Stenberg) and I went out to see who had caused it to bark. As a visitor I could have stayed inside, but I confess my head was somewhat fuddled with wine, and I was glad of a breath of fresh air.

'No one about,' said Ananyev, when we were outside. 'So why pretend, Azorka? Stupid dog!'

There was not a soul to be seen. Timidly, wagging his tail, the stupid black watchdog Azorka came towards us, probably wanting to apologize for his pointless barking. The engineer bent down and touched him between the ears.

'Why bark for nothing, you silly creature?' he asked in the tone that easygoing people employ with children and dogs. 'Had a bad dream, eh? I commend him to your attention, Doctor,' he went on, addressing me. 'A remarkably neurotic specimen. He can't stand being on his own, believe it or not. He has terrible dreams—excruciating nightmares—and if you shout at him he goes into hysterics or something.'

'Yes, he's a delicate hound,' the student confirmed.

Azorka must have known that we were discussing him, for he lifted his muzzle and whimpered piteously. 'Yes,' he seemed to say. 'My sufferings are sometimes past endurance, so pray excuse me.'

It was an August night, with stars, but dark. Never having been in surroundings as peculiar as those I had now stumbled upon, I found the starry night dull, inhospitable and gloomier than it actually was. I was on a railway line under construction. The high, half-completed embankment, the heaps of sand, clay and rubble, the huts, the pits, the wheelbarrows dotted here and there, the low mounds above the dugouts where the navvies lived—rendered monochrome by the darkness, all this clutter somehow gave the earth a weird, bizarre configuration redolent of primeval chaos. So little order was there in what met my eyes, and so hideously rutted was the monstrous scene, that human silhouettes and graceful telegraph poles looked rather out of place. These things spoilt the general impression, seeming to belong to another world. It was quiet, except for the telegraph wires droning their mournful chant high above our heads.

We climbed the embankment and looked down. A hundred yards

away, where ruts, pits and heaps merged with nocturnal gloom, a dim light flickered. Beyond that shone a second light, and then a third, after which two red eyes glowed side by side about another hundred yards on—the windows of some hut, probably—and a long row of such lights, growing ever dimmer and closer to each other, followed the line to the very horizon, before wheeling left in a crescent and vanishing in the distant gloom. The lights were motionless. There seemed to be something in common between them, the night's still-ness and the telegraph wires' disconsolate chant. Under the embank-ment, it seemed, lay buried some vital secret known only to the lights, the night and the wires.

'God, how marvellous!' Ananyev sighed. 'That great expanse, all that splendour—it's almost too much! And what of our embankment? That's no embankment, man, it's a regular Mont Blanc. It's costing millions.'

Exulting in the lights and the embankment that was costing millions, a little tipsy from the wine that he had drunk, and in sentimental mood, the engineer clapped young Von Stenberg on the shoulder.

'Found food for thought, have you, Michael?' he continued whim-sically. 'I bet you're glad to see the work of your own hands, aren't you? Last year it was all bare steppe just here, there wasn't even a whiff of humanity. But see now—the place has come alive, it's being civilized. And, ye Gods, how wonderful it all is! We're building a railway, you and I, and after us—in a century or two, say—good people will be building factories, schools and hospitals here, and things will start moving, eh?'

The student stood quite still, his hands in his pockets, his eyes fixed on the lights. He did not hear Ananyev, for his mind was elsewhere, and he was obviously in no mood for talking or listening. After a long silence he turned to me.

'Know what those endless lights remind me of?' he asked quietly. 'They suggest something long extinct that lived thousands of years ago—an Amalekite or Philistine encampment, that kind of thing. It's as if some Old Testament tribe had pitched camp, and was waiting for dawn to do battle with a Saul or a David. All we need to complete the illusion is trumpets blaring and sentries calling to each other in Ethiopian or something.'

'Perhaps,' the engineer agreed.

As if on cue, a gust of wind blew down the line with a noise like the clash of weapons. Silence followed. What the engineer and the student were thinking I don't know, but I felt I really could see a long departed scene before me. I even heard sentries talking in an unknown tongue. My imagination hastened to picture tents, outlandish folk, their raiment, their martial gear.

'Yes,' muttered the student pensively. 'Philistines and Amalekites did once live on this earth. They waged their wars, they played their part, but now they're gone without trace. It will be the same with us too. We're building our railway now, we stand here, we air our thoughts. But in a couple of thousand years this embankment, and all those men asleep after a hard day's work—they'll have vanished into thin air. It's truly appalling.'

'You mustn't think such things,' the engineer solemnly insisted.

'Why not?'

'Because—. Those are thoughts for life's end, not for its beginning. You're too young for them.'

'But why?' the young man asked him again.

'These ideas about transience and futility, about life being pointless and death inevitable, about the shadows of the grave and all that—take it from me, old chap, all these lofty notions are perfectly acceptable and natural in old age, when they're the outcome of prolonged spiritual travail, have been earned by suffering, and represent a genuine intellectual asset. But for a young brain, scarcely launched on independent life, they're sheer disaster!

'Sheer disaster!' repeated Ananyev with a dismissive gesture. 'At your age it's a sight better to have no head on your shoulders at all than to think along those lines. Or so I think. I'm perfectly serious, Baron, and I've meant to discuss it with you for some time because I spotted your addiction to these pernicious notions the very first day we met.'

'But, good God, why pernicious?' The young man smiled, his voice and face showing that he replied only out of ordinary courtesy, and that the engineer's argument interested him not at all.

I could hardly keep my eyes open, longing for us to say good night and go to bed as soon as our walk was over, but it was some time before my wish was granted. When we had returned to the hut the engineer put the empty bottles under the bed, took two full ones out of a wicker hamper, opened them, and sat down at his desk with the obvious intention of going on drinking, talking and working. Taking an occasional sip from his glass, he pencilled jottings on some plans while continuing to impress upon the young man that his attitude was mistaken. Von Stenberg sat beside him checking accounts and saying nothing. Like me, he did not feel like talking or listening. To avoid interrupting their work, I sat away from the table on the engineer's crooked-legged camp bed. I expected them to suggest that I went to bed at any moment, and I was bored. It was past midnight.

Having nothing to do, I watched my new friends. I had never seen Ananyev or the young man before, for the night that I am describing was the occasion of our first meeting. Late that evening I had been riding back from a fair to the house of a landowner where I was staying, had taken the wrong turning in the dark and lost my way. Wandering around near the railway line, and seeing the dark night grow darker, I had recalled the tales of those 'barefoot navvies' who waylay passers-by on foot and on horseback. Feeling scared, I had knocked at the first hut I came to, where Ananyev and the student had made me welcome. As happens when strangers meet by accident, we had quickly hit it off together, and struck up a friendship. Over tea followed by wine we had come to feel as if we had known each other for years. Within an hour or so I knew who they were, and how their destiny had brought them from the capital into the distant steppe, while they knew who I was, what my job was, and how my mind worked.

Nicholas Ananyev, the engineer, was thickset and broad-shouldered, looking as if, like Othello, he was already 'declined into the vale of years', and was putting on weight. He was of exactly the age known as 'the prime of life' to marriage-brokers—neither young nor old, in other words, fond of a square meal, a drink, a talk about the good old days, given to puffing slightly when he walked, to snoring loudly when he slept, and to displaying in his manner towards those around him the calm, imperturbable benevolence acquired by decent men when they stumble into senior rank and start putting on weight. Though his head and beard were still far from grey, he was already—without meaning to, somehow, and all unconsciously—patronizing young men as 'my dear chap', and feeling entitled to lecture them good-humouredly about their general attitude. His movements and voice were calm, level, confident—those of one well aware of being a successful self-made man, of possessing a definite job, a secure livelihood and a fixed outlook.

'I'm well-fed, healthy and content,' his sunburnt face, stubby nose and muscular neck seemed to say. 'And in good time you young fellows will also be well-fed, healthy and content.'

He wore a cotton shirt with the collar cut slantwise, and wide linen trousers stuck into large riding boots. From certain details—his coloured worsted belt, for instance, his embroidered collar, the patch on his elbow—I could tell that he was married and, in all probability, dearly loved by his wife.

Baron Michael Von Stenberg, a student at the Transport Institute, was a young man of twenty-three or twenty-four. Only his fair hair and sparse beard, and perhaps a certain crudity and leanness of the facial features, hinted at a Baltic baronial ancestry. Everything else— his Christian name, his religion, his ideas, his manner, his facial expression—were purely Russian. Sunburnt, dressed—like Ananyev—in an open-necked cotton shirt and high boots, somewhat stooping, and much in need of a hair-cut, he resembled neither a student nor a baron, but an ordinary Russian apprentice. His words and gestures were few, he drank his wine reluctantly, without gusto, and he checked his accounts automatically, seeming to have his mind on something else. His movements and voice were calm and smooth too, but with a calm entirely different from the engineer's. His sunburnt, slightly ironical, pensive face, a somewhat distrustful look in his eyes, and his whole figure expressed spiritual sloth and mental sluggishness. He looked as if he did not in the least care whether or not he had a light burning in front of him, whether his wine was palatable or not, whether the accounts that he was checking did or did not balance.

The message conveyed by his calm, intelligent face was this. 'So far I see no merit in a definite job, a secure livelihood or a fixed outlook. That's all rubbish. I used to live in St. Petersburg. Now I'm stuck in this hut. In autumn I shall go back to St. Petersburg. I shall return here in the spring. What good will come of it I don't know. Nor does anyone else, and so there's no point in discussing it.'

He listened to the engineer without interest, condescendingly indifferent like senior cadets when their kindly old corporal sounds off about something. None of the engineer's remarks were new to the young man, apparently, and he would have said something cleverer and more original himself, if he could have been bothered to speak. Meanwhile Ananyev had the bit between his teeth. Having dropped his relaxed, jocular tone, he was speaking earnestly, and with a passion wholly incompatible with his calm expression. He was obviously keen on abstract problems. But, fond of them though he was, he lacked aptitude and practice in handling them. So strongly was this

unfamiliarity reflected in his words that I could not catch his drift
at first.

'I wholeheartedly loathe those ideas,' he said. 'I was infected by
them myself in youth, I'm still not entirely rid of them. And I tell you
this—they did me nothing but harm, perhaps because I'm stupid and
they were the wrong nourishment for my brain. Now, there's no
mystery about this. The pointlessness of life, the futility and transience
of the visible world, Solomon's vanity of vanities—these concepts have
constituted, they still do constitute, the ultimate zenith, in the realm
of thought. When the thinker reaches that stage the machine stops.
There's nowhere else to go. The culminating point of a normal
brain's activity has been reached, and that's all very right and proper.
But it's at this apogee that we begin our thinking, worse luck. Our
starting point is what ordinary people end with. In the first flush of
our brain's independent activity we climb to the ultimate, the very
topmost rung, ignoring the lower stages.'

'And what's wrong with that?' the young man asked.

'Can't you see it's unnatural?' shouted Ananyev, looking at him with
something like anger. 'If we've found a way to climb to the top rung
without using the lower ones, then the whole long ladder—the whole
of life with its colours, sounds and thoughts, in other words—loses all
meaning for us. How evil and absurd such thinking is at your age you
can see from every stage of your rational independent life. Let's say
you sit down this minute to read Darwin, Shakespeare or someone.
Hardly have you finished one page before the poison begins to work.
Your own long life, with Shakespeare and Darwin thrown in, seems
just so much fatuous tomfoolery because you know you're going to
die. You know Shakespeare and Darwin have died too, and without
their ideas saving either themselves or the world or you. You also
know that, if life is so utterly pointless, then all your knowledge,
poetry and fine thoughts are just idle playthings, the futile toys of
grown-up children. And so you stop reading at the second page. Now,
suppose someone comes to you and asks what you, as an intelligent
man, think about war, say. Is it desirable, is it morally justified, or
isn't it? In reply to this awesome question you'll only shrug your
shoulders and limit yourself to some truism, because you, with your
slant on things, don't care a rap whether hundreds of thousands of
people die a violent or a natural death. In either event the outcome's
exactly the same—ashes and oblivion. We're building this railway, you
and I. But why, one wonders, should we rack our brains, tax our

ingenuity, rise above routine, take care of our men, steal or not steal, when we know the railway will be dust and ashes in a couple of thousand years? And so on and so forth.

'This lamentable frame of mind rules out all progress, you must agree, together with all science, all art and even thought itself. We think ourselves cleverer than the rabble, and cleverer than Shakespeare, but in fact our reasoning is nullified because we don't feel like descending to the lower rungs, because we have nowhere higher to climb, and so our brain just sticks at freezing point without going up or down.

'I was in bondage to such notions for about six years, and all that time I swear to God I never read a single decent book. I neither grew one whit more intelligent nor raised my moral stature by an iota. What a calamity! Furthermore, not content with being poisoned ourselves, we also poison the lives of those around us. If we turned our backs on life in our pessimism and withdrew to the catacombs, or hurried up and died, it would be all right, but we submit to the universal law, don't we? We live, we feel, we love women, we bring up children, we build railways.'

'Our ideas are neither one thing nor the other,' said the young man reluctantly.

'Oh, honestly. Do chuck it, for heaven's sake! You haven't even smelt life yet. When you've lived as long as I have, young fellow, you'll know what's what. That way of thinking isn't as harmless as you think. In practice, when you come up against other people, it leads to horror and folly. I've found myself in predicaments I wouldn't wish on my worst enemy.'

'Such as?' I asked.

'Such as?' repeated Ananyev. He thought for a moment and smiled. 'Such as the following incident, for instance. Or, rather, it's not so much an incident as a regular drama complete with plot and dénouement. A most splendid lesson—a fine lesson indeed!'

He poured us wine, gave himself some, emptied his glass, stroked his broad chest and continued, addressing himself to me more than to the student.

This took place one summer in the late 1870s, soon after the War, when I had just completed my studies. I was going to the Caucasus, and on my way there I put up in the seaside town of N. for five days. It's the town where I was born and grew up, I must explain. And so there's nothing odd in my thinking it exceedingly comfortable, congenial and attractive, though people from St. Petersburg or Moscow find life as boring and uncomfortable there as in Chukhloma, Kashira or anywhere like that. I walked miserably past the high school where I had been a pupil, and took a melancholy stroll in the town park that I knew so well, sadly trying to take a closer look at people whom I still remembered, though I hadn't seen them for years.

It was all rather depressing.

Amongst other things I drove out to the so-called Quarantine one evening—a small, scraggy bit of copse that had once been a real quarantine station during some long-forgotten plague outbreak, but was now the site of holiday cottages. It was about three miles' drive from town on a good, soft surface. As you drove along you could see the blue sea on your left and the unending, melancholy steppe on your right. A man can breathe there and look about him freely. The copse itself is right above the sea. Dismissing my cab, I passed through the familiar gate, and at once turned down the avenue leading to a small stone summer-house, a favourite haunt of my childhood. Resting on clumsy columns, and combining the picturesque atmosphere of an old tomb with an uncouth, rough-hewn air, this cumbrous circular building was to me the town's most romantic spot. It stood on the very cliff edge with a good view of the sea.

I sat on a bench, leant over the railing and looked down. From the summer-house a path ran down the steep, almost sheer cliff, past lumps of clay and burdock clumps. Far below, where it ended at the sandy beach, low waves lazily foamed, purring gently. The sea was as majestic, as vast and as forbidding as it had been seven years earlier when I had left the high school and my home town for St. Petersburg. There was a dark plume of smoke in the distance—a passing steamer— but apart from this barely visible and unmoving streak, and terns flitting over the water, nothing animated the monotonous vista of sea and sky. To right and left of the summer-house stretched irregular clay cliffs.

You know, when a man of melancholy disposition is on his own by the sea, or contemplates any scenery that impresses him with its grandeur, his sadness is always combined with a conviction that he'll live and die in obscurity, and his automatic reaction is to reach for a pencil and hasten to write his name in the first place that comes handy. That's probably why all lonely, secluded spots like my summer-house are always covered with pencil scrawls and knife carvings. I remember, as if it were today, looking at the railings and reading: 'Ivan Korolkov was here, 16 May 1876.' Alongside Korolkov some local philosopher had signed his name, and added:

> 'He stood on that deserted strand,
> His mind obsessed with concepts grand.'

The handwriting was dreamlike, and limp as wet silk. A certain Kross—a trivial little man, probably—had felt his own insignificance so acutely that he had let fly with his penknife, inscribing his name in deep letters nearly two inches high. Mechanically taking a pencil from my pocket, I too signed my name on a column. But all this is beside the point, actually. I'm sorry, I don't know how to keep a story short.

I felt sad and a little bored. The boredom, the quiet, the waves' purring, gradually brought on that very train of thought of which we were just speaking. At that time, the end of the seventies, it was coming into vogue with the public, after which, at the beginning of the eighties, it gradually spread from the public into literature, science and politics. Though no more than twenty-six years old at the time, I was already well aware that existence lacked all meaning and purpose, that everything was a sham and an illusion, that the life of convicts in Sakhalin was essentially and ultimately no different from life in Nice, that the difference between the brain of a Kant and that of a fly had no real significance, that no one in this world was either right or wrong, that everything was stuff and nonsense, and could go to hell. I lived as if I was conferring a favour on the unknown force that forced me to live. It was as if I was telling it: 'Look, you, I don't care a damn about life, but I go on living all the same.' My thoughts all followed a single definite pattern, but with every possible variation, in which I resembled the artful gourmet who could make a hundred tasty dishes from nothing but potatoes. I was one-sided, no doubt, and even rather narrow, but at the time I felt that my intellectual horizon had neither beginning nor end, and that my thinking was as boundless as the sea. Well, judging from my own case, the line of thought under discussion has an addictive, narcotic element, like tobacco or morphia, at its core. It becomes a habit, a craving. You exploit every moment of solitude, seize every chance to gloat over the pointlessness of existence and the darkness of the grave. While I sat in the summer-house, some long-nosed Greek children proceeded decorously down the avenue, and I took the opportunity to reflect along the following lines as I looked round at them.

'Why are these children born, I wonder, what do they live for? Is there any sense in their existence? They'll grow up not knowing why, they'll live in this God-forsaken dump for no good reason, and they'll die.'

I actually felt annoyed with those children for walking so decorously and conversing in their dignified fashion, as if they indeed did set a high value on their colourless little lives and knew what they were living for. Then I remember three female figures appearing far away at the end of the avenue, young ladies of some sort. One in a pink dress and two in white, they walked side by side and arm in arm, talking and laughing.

'It would be nice to distract oneself with a woman for a couple of days,' I thought as I watched them.

I incidentally remembered that it was three weeks since my last visit to my St. Petersburg lady friend, and I reflected that a brief romance would come in very handy at the moment. The girl in white in the middle seemed younger and better-looking than her friends. To judge from her manner and laughter she was in the top form of the girls' high school.

'She'll learn music and deportment,' I meditated, looking somewhat lecherously at her bosom. 'Then she'll marry some greasy little Greek, Lord love us! She'll lead a grey, stupid, futile life, she'll bear a litter of children without knowing why, and she'll die. An absurd life!'

As a rule I was pretty good, I may say, at combining flights of lofty fancy with the lowliest of prose. Thoughts of the darkness of the grave did not prevent me paying due tribute to bosoms and legs, just as our dear Baron's high-flown ideas don't in the least prevent him from driving over to conduct amorous forays in Vukolovka of a Saturday. To be perfectly honest with you, my relations with women have been highly invidious for as long as I can recall. Remembering that high-school girl at this moment, I blush to think of my attitude, but my conscience was completely clear at the time. The son of respectable parents, a Christian, a university man, not naturally vicious or stupid, I never felt the faintest compunction when I paid women what the Germans call *Blutgeld*, or when I pursued schoolgirls with offensive glances.

The trouble is, youth has its rights, and our philosophy has no objection in principle to those rights, be they good or be they ob-

jectionable. You can't know that life is pointless and death inevitable
without being highly indifferent to the struggle against your own
nature, and to the concept of sin. Struggle or not, you're going to die
and rot anyway. And in the second place, good sirs, our philosophy
induces even very young men to adopt the so-called 'rational approach'.
Our reason dominates our heart, overwhelmingly so. Spontaneous
feeling and inspiration are smothered in pernickety analysis. Now, to
adopt the rational approach is to be cold-blooded, and—let's face it—
cold-blooded people know nothing about chastity, a virtue that's
confined to the warm-hearted, to the impulsive, to those capable of
love. Thirdly, by denying life all meaning, our philosophy scouts the
validity of the individual personality. If I deny the individuality of
some Natalya or other, then I must obviously be entirely indifferent to
whether I give her offence or not. One day you insult her dignity as a
human being and pay her *Blutgeld*, and by the next day you've already
forgotten her.

So there I sat in the summer-house looking at the girls, when another
female figure appeared in the avenue. Her fair head was uncovered,
and she wore a white knitted shawl over her shoulders. After walking
along the avenue she entered the summer-house and gripped the
railings, looking listlessly down at the distant sea. She paid me no
attention when she came in—it was as if she had not noticed me. I
looked her over—not from top to toe, as one looks at a man, but the
other way round—and found her young, not more than twenty-five,
nice-looking, with a good figure, probably married, and a respectable
woman. She was dressed casually, but fashionably and tastefully, as
middle-class married women do dress in N. as a rule.

'That one would do,' I thought, looking at her shapely waist and
arms. 'Not bad at all. She must be the wife of some local medico or
schoolmaster.'

But to have an affair with her, to make her the heroine of a typical
tourist's lightning romance, in other words—that would not be easy,
it might barely be possible. Or so I felt as I gazed at her face. Her
look, her whole expression seemed to say that she was fed up with
the sea, the distant smoke and the sky, that she was sick and tired of
looking at them. Obviously weary, bored and a prey to cheerless
thoughts, she did not even have the air of preoccupation and affected
nonchalance that almost all women adopt on sensing the presence of
a strange man.

The fair girl gave me a bored glance, and sat on the bench deep in

8

thought. I could tell from her face that she took no interest in me, that I and my metropolitan countenance did not arouse even ordinary curiosity in her. But I decided to talk to her all the same.

'Madam,' said I, 'may I ask at what time the public conveyances go to town from here?'

'At ten or eleven, I think.'

I thanked her. She glanced at me once or twice, and then a quizzical look suddenly flickered on her impassive face, followed by something like surprise. I hurriedly adopted an indifferent expression, and assumed the proper pose—she had taken the bait! But she suddenly shot to her feet as if stung, smiled gently and quickly looked me over.

'I say, your name isn't Ananyev by any chance?' she asked nervously.

I replied that it was.

'You don't recognize me then?'

Somewhat disconcerted, I stared at her, and did recognize her, not—would you believe it?—by her face or figure but by her gentle, weary smile. It was Natalya Stepanovna, also known as Kitty, the girl I had been head over heels in love with seven or eight years earlier when I was still wearing my schoolboy's uniform.

> 'But these are tales of ancient times
> Long-buried myths, ancestral legends.'

I remember her as a thin little schoolgirl of fifteen or sixteen, when she was a sort of schoolboy's ideal created specially by nature for platonic love. And what a delightful little creature she had been! The pale, fragile, dainty little thing, she looked as if one breath would send her flying like thistledown to the very skies. Her face was gentle and puzzled, her hands were small, her long, soft hair reached down to her belt, she was wasp-waisted. Altogether she was a creature ethereal and transparent as moonlight—a boy's idea of perfection, in sum.

I loved her, ah, how I loved her! Couldn't sleep at night, wrote poetry. In the evenings she'd sit on a park bench and we boys would crowd around, gazing reverently. In response to all our compliments, posturings and sighs, she would nervously hunch her shoulders together in the damp of the evening, narrow her eyes and smile gently, looking terribly like a pretty little kitten. As we gazed at her, we each longed to fondle and stroke her like a cat, which is how she got the name of Kitty.

She had changed a great deal in the seven or eight years since our last meeting. She had matured and grown more buxom, she no longer bore the faintest resemblance to a soft, fluffy kitten. It was not so much that her features had faded and grown older as that they had somehow lost their sparkle and become more austere. Her hair seemed shorter, she was taller, her shoulders were almost twice as broad, and above all her face already wore the expression of motherliness and resignation characteristic of respectable women of her age, though I had never seen her look like that before, of course. All that remained of her former schoolgirlish sexless quality, in fact, was her gentle smile.

We started talking, and she was immensely pleased to learn that I was now a qualified engineer. 'How marvellous!' She gazed happily into my eyes. 'What a splendid thing! And what wonderful boys you all are! Not one failure in all your year, everyone's turned out well. One's an engineer, another's a doctor, a third's a teacher, and yet another's a famous singer in St. Petersburg, they say. Well done, all of you! Now, isn't it wonderful?'

Her eyes shone with unfeigned joy and good will as she took pride in me like an elder sister or former schoolmistress. Looking at her lovely face, I thought how nice it would be to become her lover that very day.

I asked whether she remembered my once bringing her a bunch of flowers and a note in the park. 'You read the note, and looked quite flabbergasted.'

'No, I'd forgotten.' She laughed. 'But I do remember you wanting to challenge Florens to a duel over me.'

'Now, that I'd forgotten, can you believe it?'

'Yes, it's all over and done with.' Kitty sighed. 'Once I was your idol, but now it's my turn to look up to all of you.'

From further discussion I learnt that she had married a couple of years after leaving school—a local man, half-Greek and half-Russian, who worked for a bank or an insurance company, and was also in the grain business. He had a rather elaborate surname—Popoulakis, Skarandopoulos or something. I've forgotten what, damn it. Of herself she spoke seldom and reluctantly, the sole topic of conversation being me. She asked about my institute, my colleagues, St. Petersburg, my plans. Everything I said afforded her the most active delight.

'Now, isn't that splendid!' she would exclaim.

We climbed down to the shore and strolled on the sands. Then, when the damp evening breeze blew off the sea, we went back up the cliff. The talk was all about me, and about the past. We continued strolling until the sunset's reflection began to fade from the cottage windows.

'Come in and have tea,' Kitty suggested. 'The samovar must have been on the table for ages.

'I'm all alone at home,' she added, as her cottage appeared through the leaves of the acacias. 'My husband's always in town. He only comes back at night, and not always then. I'm bored to death, I confess.'

I followed her, admiring her back and shoulders, and glad that she was married, since married women are better material for a brief affair than young girls. I was glad, too, that the husband was out. And yet my instincts also told me that there was no romance in the offing.

We went indoors. The rooms were small and low-ceilinged with the appointments typical of summer cottages, for your holiday-making Russian likes awkward, cumbrous, dingy furniture that he has no room for, but thinks too good to throw away. One or two small details showed that she and her husband lived pretty well, though, and must get through five or six thousand roubles a year. In what she called the dining-room there was, I remember, a round table which had six legs for some reason. On it were a samovar and cups, and on its edge lay an open book, a pencil and an exercise book. Glancing at the book, I recognized Malinin and Burenin's *Arithmetic Problems*. It was open, as I now remember, at 'The Rules of Proportion'.

'Who are you coaching?' I asked.

'No one. It's just something I've been doing. Being bored and at a loose end, I think of the old days and do the sums.'

'Have you any children?'

'I had a baby boy, but he only lived a week.'

We started drinking tea. Delighting in me, Kitty repeated how splendid it was for me to be an engineer, and how pleased she was by my success. The more she said, and the more sincerely she smiled, the stronger grew my conviction that there was nothing doing. Already a connoisseur of love affairs, I could gauge my chances of success or failure accurately. You can bank on succeeding if you're pursuing a foolish woman, one who craves adventure and excitement like yourself, or some insinuating creature with whom you have nothing in common. But if you meet a sensible, serious woman who looks fatigued, submissive and kind, who is genuinely pleased to see you, who above all respects you, then you can kiss your chances good-bye. To succeed in such cases requires more than one day.

Now, Kitty looked even more attractive in the evening light than by day. I was more and more drawn to her, and she seemed to like me. The situation, too, had eminently romantic possibilities—the husband out, no servants in evidence, and everything so quiet. Low as I rated my prospects, I nevertheless decided to launch the attack on the off chance. The first thing was to adopt a familiar tone, converting her exalted solemnity into something more light-hearted.

'Let's change the subject,' I began. 'Let's talk about something amusing. But first permit me to call you Kitty for old time's sake.'

She gave her permission.

'I'd like to ask you something,' I went on. 'What on earth has bitten the fair sex around here? What's going on, Kitty? They always used to be so moral and virtuous—but now! Upon my word! Whoever you ask about you're told things to make you simply despair of human nature. One young woman elopes with an officer. Another seduces a schoolboy and goes off with him. A third woman, married, leaves her husband for an actor, a fourth takes up with an officer. And so on and so forth, it's a positive epidemic! This way there soon won't be one girl or young wife left in town.'

I spoke in a vulgar, playful tone. Had her response been to laugh I would have gone on in the following style. 'Now, you mind some officer or actor doesn't carry you off, Kitty dear!'

She would have lowered her eyes. 'Who'd want to run away with someone like me. There are younger and prettier girls.'

'Oh, get away with you, my dear,' I'd have said. 'I for one would be delighted.'

And so it would have gone on, all in that style, and in the end I'd have pulled the thing off. But she gave no answering laugh. On the contrary, she looked grave.

'Those stories are all true.' She sighed. 'My cousin Sonya left her husband for an actor. It's quite wrong of course. Everyone must endure his lot in life, but I don't condemn them or blame them. Circumstances can be too strong for people.'

'Just so. But what circumstances could produce such a regular epidemic?'

She raised her eyebrows. 'It's easy enough to see. Our local middle-class girls and women have absolutely nothing to do. Not all of them can go away to college, become teachers—lead, in fact, purposeful intellectual lives like men. They can only marry. But where are they supposed to find husbands? You boys leave school, go away to university, and never return to your home town. You marry in St. Petersburg or Moscow, while the girls are left behind here. So who do you want them to marry? Now, since there are no decent educated men they marry any old husband—commission agents, Levantine gentlemen whose skills are limited to drinking and horseplay at the local club. The girls marry anyone, pretty well at random. What sort of life do you expect after that? A cultivated, well-bred woman living with a curmudgeonly oaf of a husband—you can see what happens. She meets a professional man—an officer, actor or doctor—and, well, she falls in love with him, the situation becomes intolerable, and she leaves her husband. You can't condemn her.'

'Then why marry at all?'

'Why indeed?' She sighed. 'But don't all girls think any husband better than none at all? It's a poor, a very poor sort of life here for the most part, Nicholas. Married or single, a woman feels she can't breathe round here. People laugh at Sonya for leaving home, and with an actor too, but if they could know her true feelings they wouldn't laugh.'

Once again Azorka barked outside the door. He snarled viciously at someone, then gave an anguished howl and crashed heavily into the hut wall. Frowning sympathetically, Ananyev broke off his tale, went out and could be heard comforting the dog outside the door for a couple of minutes.

'Good dog! Poor old fellow!'

'Friend Nicholas does like his little chat,' laughed Von Stenberg. 'He's a good sort,' he added after a pause.

Returning to the hut, the engineer filled our glasses, smiled, stroked his chest and continued.

So my assault failed. But since there was nothing I could do about it I put impure thoughts aside for a more favourable occasion, resigned myself to my failure, and 'wrote the thing off', as the phrase goes. Indeed, I too gradually succumbed to a calm, sentimental mood, lulled by Kitty's voice, by the evening air and the quiet. I remember sitting in an armchair by the wide-open window, looking at the trees and the darkening sky. The outlines of the acacias and limes were just as they had been eight years ago. There was the tinkling of a cheap piano in the far distance, as in my boyhood, and the locals had kept their habit of strolling up and down the avenues. But they were different people. It was no longer I and my friends and the objects of my adoration who promenaded the avenues, but schoolboys and young ladies whom I did not know, and I felt sad. When my questions about acquaintances had received the answer 'dead' five times from Kitty, my melancholy turned into the sensation that one has at some worthy's funeral service. Sitting by the window, watching people promenading, and listening to the tinkling piano, I witnessed with my own eyes, for the first time in my life, the eagerness with which one generation hastens to supplant another and the momentous significance that even seven or eight years have in a man's life.

Kitty put a bottle of Santorin wine on the table. I had a drink, felt a bit sentimental, and embarked on some long story. She listened, still admiring me and my cleverness. Time passed. By now the sky was so dark that the silhouettes of the acacias and limes had merged, the locals had stopped promenading, the piano-playing had stopped too, and the only sound was the sea's even murmur.

Young men are all the same. Show one of them some affection, make a fuss of him, give him wine, let him feel he's attractive, and he'll put his legs under the table, forget it's time to leave, and talk, talk, talk. His hosts can't keep their eyes open, and it's already past their bedtime, but still he sits and talks. I was just the same. At one point I chanced to glance at the clock. It was half past ten, and I began to say good-bye.

'Have one for the road,' said Kitty.

I had one, embarked on another long rigmarole, forgot it was time to leave and sat down. But then came the sound of men's voices, footsteps and the clink of spurs as some people passed beneath the windows and stopped by the door.

Kitty listened. 'My husband must be back.'

The door clicked, voices were heard in the hall, and I saw two men go past the door to the dining-room. One was a stout, thick-set, dark-haired man with a hooked nose, wearing a straw hat, and the other a young officer in a white tunic. Both cast a casual glance at Kitty and me as they passed the door, and I fancied that both were drunk.

A minute later a loud voice, with a marked nasal twang, was heard. 'She must have been lying then. And you believed her! Now, in the first place it didn't happen at the big club but at the little one——'

'Thou art angry, Jupiter. Therefore thou art wrong.' It was another voice, obviously that of the officer, who was laughing and coughing. 'I say, can I stay the night? Be honest with me, would I be a nuisance?'

'What a question! You not only can, you must. Will you have beer or wine?'

They were sitting two rooms away from us, talking loudly and evidently taking no interest in either Kitty or her visitor. But a perceptible change came over her on her husband's return. First she blushed, then her face took on a timid, guilty expression. She was rather ill at ease, and I fancied she was ashamed to let me see her husband and wanted me to leave.

I began saying good-bye, and she saw me to the front door. I well remember her sad, gentle smile and the meek, tender look in her eyes as she shook my hand.

'We'll probably never meet again,' she said. 'Ah well, may God grant you every happiness. And thank you.'

There were no sighs, no fine phrases. As she said good-bye she was holding a candle, and bright patches danced over her face and neck as if chasing her sad smile. I imagined the former Kitty, the one you felt you wanted to stroke like a cat, while I stared intently at her as she now was, for some reason recalling what she had said—'Everyone must endure his lot in life'—and I felt deeply disturbed. Happy and uninvolved though I was, I instinctively guessed, and my conscience whispered, that I was face to face with a good, well-meaning and loving but tortured human creature.

I bowed and made for the gate. It was now dark. In the south night falls early and rapidly in July, and by ten o'clock you can't see an inch before your nose. I lit a couple of dozen matches while groping my way to the gate.

'Cab!' I shouted once I was clear of the gate, but not a peep nor a whisper did I hear.

'Cab!' I repeated. 'Hey, any cabs about?'

But there were no cabs or other vehicles for hire, there was only the silence of the tomb. All I could hear was the murmur of the drowsy sea, and my heart beating from the Santorin wine. I raised my eyes to the sky, but not a star could be seen. It was dark and gloomy—obviously the sky was overcast. For some reason I shrugged my shoulders, smiled stupidly and again called, rather more hesitantly, for a cab, only to be answered by a muffled echo of my own voice.

A three-mile walk across country in darkness was a disagreeable prospect, and before making up my mind to it I spent some time pondering and shouting for a cab. Then I shrugged my shoulders and strolled languidly back to the copse with no definite aim. It was fearfully dark. Here and there between the trees glowed dull red cottage windows. Roused by my footsteps, and frightened by the matches with which I was lighting my way to the summer-house, a crow was flying from tree to tree, making the foliage rustle. I was annoyed and ashamed, and the crow seemed to sense this, for there was a jeering note in its cawing. I was annoyed at having to walk, and ashamed to have gossiped so childishly to Kitty.

I made my way to the summer-house, felt for the seat and sat down. Far below me, beyond the dense blackness, the sea softly and angrily grumbled. I remember feeling like a blind man, for I could see neither sea nor sky, nor even the summer-house in which I sat. The thoughts fermenting in my wine-befuddled head, the unseen power murmuring so monotonously somewhere down below—these were the only things left in the whole wide world, I felt. Later, when I dozed off, I felt as if it was not the sea but my own thoughts that were murmuring. It was as if the entire world consisted of me alone. Having thus reduced the universe to the dimensions of myself, I forgot the cabs, the town and Kitty, and yielded to my favourite mood—one of terrible isolation, when it seems as if, in the whole of creation, dark and formless, only you exist. This proud, satanic sensation is something that only a Russian can feel—he whose thoughts and emotions are as broad, as boundless and as austere as his plains, forests and snows. Were I a painter I would make a point of portraying the facial expression of a Russian sitting motionless with his legs tucked under him and his head in his hands as he yields to this emotion. It is accompanied by thoughts about the pointlessness of life, about death and the darkness of the grave. The thoughts aren't worth a brass farthing, but the facial expression must be fine.

While I sat dozing, not venturing to stand up—I was warm and at peace—certain sounds suddenly detached themselves from the background of the sea's monotonous murmur, and distracted my attention from myself. Someone was rapidly approaching along the path. Reaching the summer-house, the unknown stopped, and there was a sound like a little girl sobbing.

'God, God, when will it all end?' asked a voice like a weeping child's.

To judge by the voice and the weeping it was a girl of between ten and twelve. She came hesitantly into the summer-house, sat down and began half-praying, half-lamenting.

'Merciful heavens!' she said tearfully, drawling out the words. 'This is past all endurance. It would try anyone's patience. I suffer in silence, but I do need something to live for, you must see that. Oh, my God, my God!'

There was more in the same style. I wanted to see the child and speak to her. So as not to frighten her I gave a loud sigh, coughed, and then cautiously struck a match. The bright light flashed in the darkness and illuminated the weeper. It was Kitty.

'Wonders will never cease,' sighed Von Stenberg. 'Black night, murmuring sea, weeping heroine, hero with feeling of cosmic isolation! Good grief, man! All that's lacking is Circassians with daggers.'

'This isn't a tale I'm telling you, it really happened.'

'What if it did? It's all pointless, and as old as the hills.'

'Don't be so quick to find fault. Let me finish.' Ananyev made a gesture of annoyance. 'Don't interrupt, I beg you. I'm talking to the doctor, not you.

'Well then.' He addressed himself to me, casting sidelong glances at the young man, who had bent over his abacus and seemed delighted to have baited him a little.

Well then (he went on), Kitty was not surprised or frightened to see me. It was as if she had known beforehand that she would find me in the summer-house. She was gasping and trembling all over, as if in fever. From what I could see, lighting match after match, her tear-stained face had lost its former intelligent, submissive, weary expression and changed into something that I still utterly fail to interpret. It conveyed nothing—neither pain, alarm nor anguish—of what was expressed in the words and tears. And it was probably because I failed to interpret it that, as I have to admit, I took her expression to be meaningless and the result of intoxication.

'I can't go on,' she muttered in her weeping little girl's voice. 'I can't cope, Nicholas, I'm sorry, I can't live like this. I'll go to my mother's in town. Take me there, for God's sake.'

When confronted by tears I could neither speak nor remain silent. I was flustered, and muttered some nonsense to console her.

'Yes, yes, I'll go to my mother's,' said Kitty resolutely, standing up and convulsively clutching my arm, her hands and sleeves being wet with tears. 'I'm sorry, Nicholas, but I'm going. I just can't bear any more.'

'But there are no cabs. How will you get there?'

'Don't worry, I'll walk. It's not far. It's just that I can't——'

I was disconcerted, but not profoundly moved. Her tears, her trembling, the blank look in her eyes—all suggested some trivial

French or Ukrainian melodrama where every cheap and empty dram
of woe is drenched in gallons of tears. I didn't understand her, was
aware of not doing so, and I should have said nothing. Yet, for some
reason—probably to prevent my silence being interpreted as stupidity
—I thought fit to urge her not to go to her mother's, but to stay at
home. When people cry they like their tears to go unobserved, but
I lit match after match, and went on striking till the box was empty.
Why I needed this ungracious illumination I still have no idea, but it's
true that the emotionally frigid are often awkward and downright
stupid.

In the end she took my arm and we left. We passed through the
gate, turned right and strolled slowly down the soft, dusty road. It was
dark, but after my eyes had gradually grown used to it I began to
discern the silhouettes of the gaunt old oaks and limes bordering the
road. Soon, on our right, dimly loomed a black streak of jagged,
precipitous cliff, traversed here and there by deep chines and gullies.
Near them nestled low bushes like seated human figures. The atmosphere was eerie. I squinted suspiciously at the cliff, and by now the
sea's murmur and the silence of the countryside were alarming my
imagination. Kitty did not speak. She was still trembling, and before
we had gone a few hundred yards she was exhausted by the walk and
out of breath. I too remained silent.

Less than a mile from the Quarantine is an abandoned four-storey
building with a very tall chimney. Once a steam flour-mill, it stands in
isolation near the cliff, and is visible from far away over sea and land
in daytime. The fact that it was abandoned, had no one living in it,
and possessed an echo that exactly repeated the footsteps and voices
of passers-by—all this gave it an air of mystery. Picture me in the dark
night, arm in arm with a woman who is running away from her
husband, beside this long, tall hulk that echoes all my steps and gazes
unmovingly at me with a hundred black windows. Under the circumstances any normal young man would have succumbed to romantic
urges. But not I.

'This is all very impressive,' I thought, looking at the dark windows.
'But a time will come when, of that building, of Kitty and her grief,
and of me and my thoughts, not one grain of dust will remain. All is
emptiness and vanity.'

When we reached the flour-mill she suddenly stopped and took her
arm out of mine. 'I know you're puzzled by all this, Nicholas.' She
had stopped talking like a little girl and was speaking in her normal

voice. 'But I'm terribly unhappy—how unhappy you can have no idea. No one could. I'm not discussing it because it's not the sort of thing you *can* discuss. Ah me, what a life, what——'

Kitty broke off, clenched her teeth and groaned as if making every effort not to scream with pain.

'What a life,' she repeated with horror in the lilting, southern, slightly Ukrainian accent that gives animated speech a singing cadence, especially a woman's. 'What a life! God, God, God, what does it mean?'

As if trying to solve the riddle of her existence, she shrugged her shoulders in bewilderment, shook her head and flung up her arms. She spoke in her sing-song voice, she moved gracefully and beautifully, and she reminded me of a certain well-known Ukrainian actress.

'God, I feel buried alive!' She was wringing her hands. 'If only I could have one minute of the sort of happiness other people enjoy! Heavens, I've sunk to running away from my husband at night in a strange man's company, like a loose woman! What good can come of that?'

As I admired her movements and voice, I suddenly found myself delighted at her being on bad terms with her husband. The idea of its being 'nice to have an affair with her' popped up—a callous notion that became fixed in my brain, haunting me all the way, and tickling my fancy more and more.

About a mile from the flour-mill we had to take a left turn past the cemetery to the town. At the corner of the cemetery is a stone windmill with the miller's small hut beside it. We passed the mill and hut, turned left and reached the cemetery gates. Here she stopped.

'I'm going back,' she said. 'You carry on, and God bless you, but I'm going back. I'm not afraid.'

'But that's ridiculous!' I was aghast. 'If you're leaving, then you'd better leave.'

'I shouldn't have been so hasty. It was all over a trifle. You and your talk reminded me of the past and put all sorts of ideas in my mind. I felt sad and wanted to cry, and my husband was rude to me in front of that officer. I lost my temper. But what's the point of my going to town to my mother's? Will it make me any happier? I must go back home.' Kitty laughed. 'Oh, all right, let's go on then. It makes no difference.'

I remembered the inscription on the cemetery gate: 'For the hour is coming, in the which all that are in the graves shall hear his voice.'

I was well aware that a time would come sooner or later when Kitty and I, her husband, and the officer in the white tunic would all lie under the dark trees beyond a wall. I knew that an unhappy, humiliated fellow-creature was walking by my side. Of all that I was clearly aware, but at the same time I was troubled by the disagreeable and unnerving fear that Kitty would turn back, and that I would lose the chance of telling her what was on my mind. At no other time have thoughts so loftily poetical been so interwoven in my brain with the lowest and most bestial prose. A dreadful business!

Not far from the cemetery we found a cab, and took it to the High Street, where Kitty's mother lived, then dismissed the driver and set off down the pavement. Kitty said nothing, while I looked at her, angry with myself. 'Why don't you start? Now's the time.' About twenty yards from my hotel she stopped near a lamp and burst into tears.

'I'll never forget your kindness, Nicholas.' She was laughing and crying at the same time, while gazing into my face with shiny, tearful eyes. 'What a fine man you are! And what splendid fellows you all are—honest, generous, sincere, clever! Isn't it marvellous!'

She saw me as an intellectual, as a thoroughly progressive man. Besides the ecstatic delight aroused in her by my person, her tear-stained, laughing face also expressed regret that she so rarely met such men, and that God had not granted her the happiness of being the wife of one. 'Isn't it marvellous?' she muttered.

The childlike joy in her expression, the tears, the gentle smile, the soft hair straying under her shawl, the shawl itself—thrown carelessly over her head—in the lamplight they reminded me of the Kitty whom I had wanted to stroke like a cat in the old days.

I could not help stroking her hair, shoulders, arms. 'Well, what is it you want, my dear?' I mumbled. 'Shall we go to the ends of the earth together? I'll take you away from this dump, I'll give you happiness. I love you. Shall we go, my darling? Well, shall we?'

Her face expressed bewilderment. She stepped back from the lamp and stared at me dumbfounded with huge eyes. I clutched her arm and began showering her face, neck and shoulders with kisses while I continued making promises and vows. Oaths and promises are practically a physiological necessity in love affairs. They are indispensable. Sometimes you know that you're lying, and that the promises aren't necessary, yet swear and promise you do. Meanwhile the astounded Kitty kept backing away and looking at me round-eyed.

'Stop, stop!' she muttered, pushing me off with her hands.

I clasped her tightly to me, but she suddenly burst into hysterical tears, and her face took on the blank, expressionless look that I had noticed when lighting matches in the summer-house. Without asking her consent, preventing her from speaking, I forcibly dragged her into my hotel. She seemed stunned and would not walk, but I took her by the arm and almost carried her. As we went upstairs, I remember, someone wearing a cap with a red band gave me a surprised look and bowed to her.

Ananyev blushed and stopped talking. He paced silently round the table, irritably scratched the back of his head, and several times hunched his shoulders and shoulder-blades convulsively, feeling a chill run down his large back. He was shamed and crushed by his memories, and he was struggling with himself.

'A bad business.' He drank a glass of wine and shook his head. 'At every introductory lecture on gynaecology medical students are said to be given this advice. "Before undressing and examining a sick woman, remember that you too have a mother, a sister, a fiancée." This advice wouldn't come amiss to anyone, medical student or not, who has any dealings with women. Oh, how well I understand it now that I have a wife and daughter myself—my God, I do! But you may as well hear the rest of it.'

Having become my mistress, Kitty viewed the matter differently from me. Above all, she loved me passionately and profoundly. What was an ordinary flirtation to me—to her it was the transformation of her whole life. I remember thinking she must have gone out of her mind. Happy for the first time in her life, looking five years younger, with an inspired, ecstatic expression, so happy that she did not know what to do with herself, she laughed and cried by turns, never ceasing to voice her dreams about us going to the Caucasus on the next day and then to St. Petersburg in the autumn, and about how we would live afterwards.

'Now, don't worry about my husband,' she said reassuringly. 'He's bound to give me a divorce. All the town knows he's sleeping with the elder Kostovich girl. We'll get a divorce and marry.'

When women are in love they become acclimatized, adapting themselves to people quickly, like cats. She had only been in the hotel room with me for an hour and a half, but she already felt at home there, and was treating my things as her own. She packed my case, told me off for not hanging my expensive new coat on a hook instead of tossing it on a chair like an old rag, and so on.

I looked at her, I listened, and I felt weary and irritated. I was rather put out to think that a decent, respectable, unhappy woman had, in some three or four hours, so readily yielded to the first man she had met. I disliked this in my own capacity as a respectable man, if you take my meaning. And then I was somewhat repelled by women of her type being shallow, superficial and too keen on having a good time, and by them even equating so essentially trivial a phenomenon as love for a man with their happiness, their suffering and the transformation of their whole existence. Besides, now that I had had what I wanted I was annoyed at my own foolishness in becoming entangled with a woman whom, like it or not, I should be compelled to deceive. May I add that, disorganized though my life was, I could not bear telling lies?

I remember her sitting at my feet, putting her head on my lap and looking at me, her eyes shining with love. 'Do you love me, Nicholas?' she asked. 'Very, very much?'

She laughed for sheer happiness. I found this sentimental, mawkish and stupid, being in a mood to make 'intellectual depth', as I called it, my main target in life.

'You'd better go home,' I told her. 'Otherwise your relatives are sure to miss you and start looking for you all over town. It's awkward, too, that it will be practically dawn when you get to your mother's.'

She agreed, and as we parted we arranged to meet at noon next day in the park, and to go on to Pyatigorsk on the day after. I went into the street to see her to the house, and I remember how tenderly and sincerely I caressed her on the way. There was a moment when her unconditional trust suddenly moved me to pity greater than I could endure, and I almost decided that I would indeed take her to Pyatigorsk. Remembering, however, that I had only six hundred roubles in my suitcase, and that it would be much harder to break things off in the autumn than now, I hastened to suppress my pity.

We came to the house where her mother lived, and I pulled the bell. When footsteps were heard behind the door Kitty suddenly looked grave, glanced up at the sky, quickly made the sign of the cross over me several times as if over a child, and then seized my hand, pressing it to her lips.

'Till tomorrow.' She vanished into the house.

I crossed to the opposite pavement and looked at the house from there. The windows were dark at first, but then one of them revealed the faint, bluish flare of a candle being lit. The light grew, emitting rays, and I saw it move from room to room accompanied by shadows. 'They weren't expecting her,' I thought.

Returning to my hotel room, I undressed, drank some Santorin, ate some fresh unpressed caviare that I had bought at the market that day, slowly went to bed and slept the tourist's deep, untroubled sleep.

Next morning I woke with a headache. I was in a bad mood, and something was bothering me. 'What's the matter,' I wondered, trying to explain my unease. 'What's the trouble?'

I ascribed my disquiet to a fear that Kitty might turn up at any moment and stop me leaving, and that I should have to dissimulate and tell lies. I quickly dressed, packed and left the hotel, telling the porter to bring my luggage to the station by seven that evening. I spent the whole day with a doctor friend, and left town in the evening. As you see, the profundity of my meditations did not prevent me from treacherously and meanly making myself scarce.

All the time I was with my friend, and later, when driving to the station, I was painfully ill at ease. I put it down to fear of Kitty meeting me and making a scene. At the station I deliberately sat in the cloak-room till the second bell rang, and on the way to my carriage I felt weighed down, felt as if I was dressed from head to foot in stolen articles. How impatiently and fearfully I awaited the third bell!

But then it rang, bringing my deliverance, and the train started. We passed the prison and the barracks, and came into open country, but the feeling of uneasiness persisted, to my great surprise, and I still felt like a thief obsessed with the urge to flee. Odd, wasn't it? To distract and calm myself I looked out of the window. The train was running along the coast. The sea was smooth, mirroring the serene turquoise sky, almost half of which was tinged with the delicate gold-crimson hue of the sunset. Black fishing boats and rafts dotted the surface here and there. Clean and spruce as a new toy, the town stood on a high cliff, and was already becoming shrouded in the evening mist. The churches' gilded domes, the windows, the greenery—all reflected the setting sun, burning and melting like molten gold. The scent of the fields blended with the delicate damp smell blowing in from the sea.

The train ran swiftly on. Passengers and conductors laughed, every-one was merry and light-hearted, but my mysterious unease kept growing and growing. I looked at the light mist veiling the town, imagining that somewhere in it, near the churches and houses, a woman was rushing here and there with a blank, expressionless look, searching for me and groaning 'Oh God, God!' in a little girl's voice, or in a sing-song cadence like a Ukrainian actress. I remembered her grave mien and large, troubled eyes when she had made the sign of the cross over me on the previous day as if I belonged to her, and I instinctively glanced at the hand that she had kissed.

'Surely I'm not in love?' I wondered, scratching my hand.

Only with nightfall, when the other passengers were asleep and I was left alone with my conscience, did I begin to see what I had been unable to grasp earlier. In the twilight of the carriage Kitty's image haunted me, and I now clearly recognized that I had committed a crime as bad as murder. My conscience tortured me. To suppress this intolerable sensation I told myself that all was emptiness and vanity, that Kitty and I would die and decay, that her grief was nothing compared to death, and so forth—and also that there was no such thing as free will in the last resort, and therefore I was not to blame. But all these considerations only irritated me, and were rapidly brushed aside by other thoughts. There was an aching sensation in the hand kissed by Kitty. I kept lying down and getting up again, I drank vodka at the stations, I forced myself to eat sandwiches, and once again took to arguing that life was meaningless. But it did no good at all. A strange and, if you like, comic ferment was working in my mind. The most heterogeneous thoughts towered up untidily on top of each other, mingling and impeding one another, while I, the thinker, bowed my head forward, understood nothing, and was simply unable to find my bearings in this clutter of notions relevant and irrelevant. It transpired that I, the great thinker, had not even mastered the elements of thinking, and that I was no more capable of deploying my own intellect than of repairing a watch. I was intently concentrating my brain for the first time in my life, and this seemed such an abnormality that I thought I was going mad. A man whose brain is active only sporadically, and at times of pressure, is often subject to delusions of insanity.

I suffered like this for a night, a day and another night. Once I had realized how little my meditations helped me, I saw the light and knew at last what kind of a creature I was. I realized that my notions weren't worth a brass farthing, and that before meeting Kitty I had never even begun thinking—had even lacked any conception of what serious thought meant. Now, having suffered so much, I realized that I possessed neither convictions nor a definite moral code, neither heart nor reason. My entire intellectual and moral resources consisted of specialized knowledge, fragments, useless memories, other people's ideas—and nothing more. My mental processes were as unsophisticated, crude and primitive as a Yakut's. If I disliked lying, stealing, murdering, while on the whole avoiding egregiously gross errors, this was not through my convictions—I had none—but only because I was bound hand and foot by nursery tales and copy-book ethics that had become part of my flesh and blood, and had guided me through life without my being aware of it, even though I considered them absurd.

I realized that I was neither a thinker nor a philosopher but simply a dilettante. God had given me a strong, healthy Russian brain and the rudiments of talent. Now, imagine this brain in its twenty-sixth year—untrained, not in the least stale, uncluttered by any kind of luggage, and just lightly besprinkled with a little information in the engineering line. The young brain instinctively craves activity and is on the look-out for it, when it is suddenly and quite arbitrarily assailed from without by this lovely, juicy concept—the pointlessness of life and the darkness of the grave. The brain ravenously gulps this in, assigns it all the available space, and begins playing all sorts of cat-and-mouse games with it. The brain is innocent of systematic erudition, but no matter. It handles wide-ranging speculation on the basis of its own innate resources—typical self-taught-man stuff. Not a month passes without the brain's proprietor cooking up a hundred tasty dishes consisting exclusively of potatoes, and fancying himself a thinker.

Your generation has carried this amateurism, this toying with serious thinking, into science, literature, politics, and into every other field that it has not been too lazy to enter. Together with the dilettante approach it has also introduced emotional sterility, boredom, one-sidedness. My impression is that it has already contrived to teach the masses a new and unprecedented attitude to serious ideas.

It was through misfortune that I came to comprehend and assess my own aberrations and all-round ignorance. And my sanity, I now feel, dates only from the time when I started learning the alphabet—when my conscience drove me back to N., and when, without making any bones about it, I told Kitty how sorry I was, asked her to forgive me, as a child might, and mingled my tears with hers.

After briefly describing his last meeting with Kitty, Ananyev fell silent.

'Ah well,' the student brought out through closed teeth when Ananyev had finished. 'Such things do happen in this world.'

His face still expressed intellectual inertia, and Ananyev's story had obviously not touched him at all. Only when, after a brief pause, the engineer once more began deploying his ideas, and repeating his earlier sentiments—only then did the student frown irritably, get up from table and go to his bed. He made the bed and began undressing.

'You look as if you think you'd actually converted someone,' he said exasperatedly.

'Me—convert anyone?' asked the engineer. 'My dear fellow, do I make any such claim? May God forgive you! There's no possibility of converting you, for conversion can only come through personal experience and suffering.'

'And then your way of arguing is so grotesque,' grumbled the student as he put his nightshirt on. 'The thoughts that you so strongly dislike as fatal to the young—they're perfectly normal for the old, as you yourself admit. It's as if it were a matter of grey hairs! But why should the old enjoy this privilege? On what principle? If these thoughts indeed are poisonous, then they're equally poisonous for everyone.'

'Oh no, my dear fellow, don't say such things,' remarked the engineer with a sly wink. 'Don't, please. In the first place old men aren't dilettantes. Their pessimism doesn't reach them from outside, nor yet by accident, but from the depths of their own minds, and only after they have studied the Hegels, the Kants and so on, only after they've suffered a lot, and made no end of mistakes—in fact, only after they've climbed the entire ladder from bottom to top. Their pessimism has both personal experience and sound philosophical training behind it. Secondly, the pessimism of these elderly philosophers isn't just a lot of mumbo-jumbo, as it is with you and me—it comes from the pain and suffering of the whole world. Theirs has a Christian foundation because it springs from love of man, and from thoughts about humanity totally lacking the egoism of your typical amateur. You despise life because its meaning and purpose are hidden from you in particular, and you fear only your own death. But the true philosopher suffers because the truth is hidden from all men, and his fears are for humanity at large. For instance, there's a government forestry officer living not far from here, an Ivan Aleksandrovich—a nice old boy who was once some sort of teacher, and used to do a bit of writing. Just what he's been the devil only knows, but he's a jolly brainy sort of chap and a dab hand at philosophy. He used to read a lot, and now he reads all the time. Well, I came across him not long ago on the Gruzovo sector at a time when they were laying sleepers and rails. It was easy work, but to old Ivan, who was a non-specialist, it seemed almost like magic.

'To lay a sleeper and fix the rail to it your skilled workman needs less than a minute. Well, the men were in good form, working smartly and quickly. There was one old reprobate in particular who had the knack of catching the nail just right and driving it home with a single blow of the hammer. Now, the handle of that hammer was nearly seven foot long, and each nail was a foot long! Old Ivan looked at the workers for a long time and was enchanted by them.

' "What a pity that these splendid men will die," he said to me with tears in his eyes. Now, such pessimism I do understand.'

'All that proves nothing and explains nothing.' The young man pulled his sheet over him. 'It's all a lot of hot air. Nobody knows anything, and words can prove nothing.'

He looked out from under the sheet and raised his head. 'One is very naïve if one believes in human thought and logic, and attaches overriding significance to humanity.' He spoke rapidly, with an irritated frown. 'You can prove and disprove any proposition you like in words, and men will soon perfect verbal acrobatics to the point where they will demonstrate that twice two is seven by the laws of mathematics. I like listening and reading, but I can't manage acts of faith, with due respect, and I don't want to. I shall believe only in God. As for you, you can go on talking till the cows come home, and seduce another five hundred Kitties, but I'll only believe you when I've gone off my head. Good night.'

The young man hid his head under the sheet and turned his face to the wall to show that he did not want to hear or say any more. With this the argument ended.

Before retiring I went out of the barracks with the engineer and saw the lights again.

'We have wearied you with our chatter.' Ananyev yawned and looked at the sky. 'Ah well, never mind, old man. One's only satisfaction in this boring dump is drinking and talking about things. What an embankment, ye Gods!' he said delightedly, when we came up to it. 'It's a regular Mount Ararat.'

'These lights remind the Baron of the Amalekites, but to me they're like human thoughts,' he said after a short pause. 'Each individual's thoughts are similarly chaotic and disordered, you know, and yet they do march towards some destination in single file through darkness. They illuminate nothing, they do not make the night clear, and they vanish somewhere far beyond the bounds of old age. However, enough of this idle talk! It's time for bed.'

When we got back to the hut the engineer was insistent in offering me his own bed to sleep on. 'Do take it,' he implored me, pressing both his hands to his heart. 'I beg you to. Don't worry about me. I can sleep anywhere—and, besides, I'm staying up for a while. You'll be doing me a favour.'

I accepted, undressed and lay down, while he sat at the table and took up his drawings.

'The likes of us don't have time to sleep, old man,' he said in an undertone after I had got into bed and shut my eyes. 'A man with a wife and a couple of kids is too busy for it. It's feed and clothe them now, and save money for their future. And I've two of them—a son and a daughter. The son has a jolly little face. He's not six yet, but he's remarkably able, I can tell you. I have their photographs somewhere. Oh, my children, my children!'

He rummaged in his papers, found the pictures and began looking at them. I fell asleep.

I was woken by Azorka's barking and loud voices. Von Stenberg—in underclothes, barefoot and unkempt—was standing in the doorway talking loudly to someone. Dawn was breaking, and its mournful, dark blue light peeped through the door, the windows and the cracks in the walls, faintly illuminating my bed, the table with the papers and Ananyev. Stretched on the floor on his cloak, puffing out his beefy, hairy chest, with a leather cushion under his head, he was asleep, snoring so loudly that I felt heartily sorry for the young man who had to share the room with him every night.

'Why on earth should we take delivery?' shouted Von Stenberg. 'It's nothing to do with us. Go and see the other engineer, Mr. Chalisov. Who sent these boilers?'

'Nikitin,' a deep voice gruffly answered.

'Then go and see Chalisov. This has nothing to do with us. What the hell are you hanging around for? Be on your way.'

'Sir, we've already been to Mr. Chalisov,' said the bass voice even more gruffly. 'We was looking for the gentleman up and down the line all day yesterday, and 'twas in his hut we was told he'd gone to the Dymkovo sector, sir. Be so kind as to take delivery—we can't lug them up and down the line for ever. It's been cart them here and cart them there, there ain't no end to it.'

'What is it?' asked Ananyev in a hoarse voice as he woke and quickly raised his head.

'They've brought some boilers from Nikitin,' said the young man. 'They want us to take them, but what concern is it of ours?'

'Tell them to go to hell!'

'Do us a favour, guv'nor, and sort it out for us. The horses ain't had nothing to eat for two days, and the boss is real peeved, for sure. We can't cart them back again! The railway ordered boilers, so they should take delivery.'

'Can't you see it's no concern of ours, you oaf? Go and see Chalisov.'

'What's this? Who's there?' repeated Ananyev hoarsely. 'Oh, damn and blast them!' He got up and went to the door. 'What's up?'

I dressed and went out of the hut two minutes later. Ananyev and the student, both in their underclothes, both barefoot, were forcefully and impatiently making their explanations to a peasant who stood before them with his hat off, holding a whip, and who obviously did not understand them. Both had the air of men preoccupied with everyday trivialities.

'What do I want with your boilers?' Ananyev shouted. 'Want me to wear them on my head? If you couldn't find Chalisov, then find his assistant and leave us in peace.'

Seeing me, Von Stenberg probably remembered the previous night's conversation, for the careworn look vanished from his sleepy face, being replaced by his expression of mental inertia. He waved the peasant away, and went off to one side deep in thought.

The morning was overcast. Along the line, where the lights had shone at night, were swarming navvies who had just woken up. Voices were heard, and the creak of wheelbarrows. The day's work had begun. One little horse, in a rope harness, was already trudging off to the embankment, stretching its neck for all it was worth, and pulling a cartload of sand.

I began saying good-bye. Much had been said that night, but I had no neat solutions to take away with me. As for all the talk, nothing of it remained on memory's filter in the morning but the lights and Kitty's image. Getting on my horse, I cast a last glance at Von Stenberg and Ananyev, at the hysterical dog with its dull, tipsy-looking eyes, at the navvies glimpsed through the morning mist, at the embankment, at the little horse straining its neck.

'Nothing in this world makes sense,' thought I.

When I had struck the horse and cantered down the line, and when, a little later, I could see nothing before me but the endless, lugubrious plain and the cold, overcast sky, I remembered the questions that had been aired that night. And, while I pondered, the sun-parched plain, the huge sky, the dark oak wood looming far ahead, the misty horizons —all seemed to say that 'No, indeed, nothing in this world makes sense.'

The sun began to rise.

APPENDIXES

APPENDIX I

THE STEPPE

1. Composition
2. Text
3. Variants

1. COMPOSITION

Among the impulses that led to the composition of *The Steppe* the most immediate was an invitation conveyed to Chekhov, in December 1887 and through the intermediary of the celebrated short-story writer V. G. Korolenko, from the no less celebrated literary critic and thinker N. K. Mikhaylovsky in his capacity as editorial adviser to the St. Petersburg literary monthly *Severny vestnik* [*The Northern Herald*]. Chekhov was asked to contribute a long story [*bolshuyu povest*] to the journal. The invitation had great significance for him, since he had not previously had a work published in any of the 'Thick Journals' (serious literary reviews, usually monthlies), of which *Severny vestnik* was one, and in one or other of which almost all the most important works of nineteenth-century Russian literature made their first appearance. The publication of *The Steppe* accordingly represents *the* major landmark in Chekhov's literary career, as is also noted in the Preface.

Principally known, before 1888, as a prolific author of short stories and sketches—uneven in quality, gradually improving over the years and already including some minor masterpieces—Chekhov had been under pressure to take his art more seriously for nearly two years. The promptings began when the distinguished elderly littérateur D. V. Grigorovich, whom Chekhov did not then know personally, unexpectedly wrote to him on 25 March 1886, entreating him at some length not to continue frittering away his energies on material unworthy of his evident potential. More recently other figures from the literary world—including the newspaper proprietor A. S. Suvorin (soon to become Chekhov's closest friend), the poet and editor A. N. Pleshcheyev, the editor V. V. Bilibin—had taken to making similar representations. Hence the self-consciousness betrayed by Chekhov when alluding, in his correspondence, to this work marking, in effect, his début as a serious writer. Hence, too, the many references to his own lack of experience, and to his diffidence, in penning this, his first 'large-scale' work.

As Chekhov also notes in his correspondence, the material of *The Steppe* is taken from his own boyhood memories. The action develops in the country-side near Taganrog, his native town, where he had been born in 1860, and where he had been accustomed, as a boy, to traverse the prairies by horse- or ox-cart on summer holiday journeys to his grandfather's. A more immediate inspiration was the six-week journey to this same region, including Taganrog and Novocherkassk, that Chekhov had undertaken as a man of twenty-seven in April and May 1887, less than a year before writing the story.

As we learn from Chekhov's correspondence, he conceived *The Steppe*, at the time of writing, as the first part of a longer work that he intended to complete if the story should be successful. And it indeed was to prove successful, provoking numerous reviews and critical assessments—largely, though by no means universally, favourable. Yet Chekhov never did embark on the projected sequel.

Work on *The Steppe* began on 1 January 1888 (or a few days earlier), the story being completed within a few weeks, on 2 February. During the period of composition, and that immediately following, Chekhov alluded to the work's evolution in over twenty letters, the following being the most instructive of the passages concerned.

'To avoid growing stale I'm going south at the end of March—to the Don Region, Voronezh County and so on, where I shall welcome the spring and refresh my fading memories. This will be a stimulus to my work, I think.' *(Letter to A. S. Suvorin, 10 Feb. 1887.)*

'I smell the steppe and hear the birds sing. I see my old friends the hawks flying over the steppe. The little burial mounds, the water-towers, the buildings are all so familiar and memorable. . . . Ukrainian peasants, oxen, hawks, white cottages, the southern streams, the branches of the Donetsk Railway with their single telegraph wire, landowners' and tenant farmers' daughters, russet hounds, green foliage—it all flashes past like a dream.' *(Letter to his family, 7 Apr. 1887.)*

'Tell the good Pleshcheyev I've embarked on a trifle for *Severny vestnik*. . . . I don't know when I'll finish. The thought of writing for a Thick Journal, and of people taking my trifle too seriously—it jogs my elbow as the devil jogged the monk's. I'm writing a steppe story.' *(Letter to I. A. Leontyev [Shcheglov], 1 Jan. 1888.)*

'On your kind advice I've begun a sort of longish short story [*malenkuyu povestushku*] for *Severny vestnik*. To start with I set myself to describe the steppes, the steppelanders and my own experience of them. It's a good subject, the writing is great fun. However, through lack of practice in writing at length, and through fear of saying too much, I unfortunately tend to get carried away. Every page comes out as compact as a very short story, while the scenes pile up—jostling, getting in each other's way, and thus wrecking the general impression. The result? Not a canvas with all its details fused into a single whole like the stars in the sky, but a précis, a dry catalogue of impressions. A writer —you, for instance—will understand me, but the reader will be bored and put off. (*Letter to V. G. Korolenko, 9 Jan. 1888.*)

'I'm tackling a big job. For my début in a Thick Journal I've taken the steppe, which hasn't been described for ages. I depict the plain, the mauve horizons, sheep drovers, Jews, priests, storms at night, inns, wagon-trains, steppe birds et cetera. Each separate chapter is a self-contained story, and the chapters are all intimately linked like the figures in the quadrille. I'm trying to give them a common smell and a common tone, and having a single character running through all the chapters may help me to pull it off. I feel I've got a lot of it under control, and there are passages that smell of hay, but the general effect is somehow weird and wildly eccentric. . . . The pages are squashed together as if they'd been put in a press. Impressions jostle, pile up, elbow each other out. The scenes . . . are jammed up against each other, following in continuous sequence, and are therefore tiring. The result is less a panorama than a dry, detailed catalogue of impressions rather like a précis. Instead of an artistically integrated picture of the steppe I offer the reader a sort of *Steppe Encyclopedia*. My first pancake a dumpling! But I'm not downhearted. Let's hope that even an encyclopedia will have its uses. It may open my contemporaries' eyes and show them what rich deposits of beauty still remain unmined, and how much scope a Russian artist still has. If my longish short story should remind my colleagues of the steppe, which they have forgotten, if only one of the motifs so curtly adumbrated should give some little poet food for thought, then that will be my reward. That *you* will understand it, that, for its sake, you will forgive me my unintentional transgressions I well know. And err unintentionally I do, for it turns out that *I am not capable* of writing anything large-scale yet.' (*Letter to D. V. Grigorovich, 12 Jan. 1888.*)

'It's fun to work on, but I fear that inexperience of writing on this scale causes me to strike the wrong note from time to time. I grow weary, I leave things unsaid, and I'm not serious enough. There are many passages that won't be understood either by critics or by the public—both will find them trivial and beneath notice. But I delightedly anticipate that these same passages will be understood and appreciated by two or three literary gourmets—which is good enough for me. I'm not satisfied with the story on the whole, for it seems clumsy, boring and too specialized. To the modern reader a subject like the steppe, its natural features and its peoples, seems narrow and trivial. (*Letter to Ya. P. Polonsky, 18 Jan. 1888.*)

'I'm writing a story for a Thick Journal. It describes the steppe—a romantic subject, and if I can keep up the tone of the beginning I'll produce one or two "special effects". Writing a longer work is very boring, and much harder than small-scale stuff. When you read it you'll see what a mass of difficulties has confronted my inexperienced brain. *(Letter to A. N. Plescheyev, 19 Jan. 1888.)*

'I'm scared, I'm afraid *The Steppe* will turn out trivial. I'm writing it slowly, as gourmets eat snipe—passionately, judiciously and deliberately. I'm straining every nerve, I'm puffing and blowing, but quite frankly I'm displeased with it on the whole, even if there are a few "purple passages" here and there. I'm still not used to writing longer works, I'm too lazy. Small-scale work has spoilt me.' *(Letter to A. N. Plescheyev, 23 Jan. 1888.)*

'I've wasted a lot of juice, energy and phosphorus on *The Steppe*. I've struggled, strained and forced myself, and I'm hideously exhausted. I don't know if it comes off or not, but in any case it's my masterpiece, I can't do better.' *(Letter to A. Lazarev-Gruzinsky, 1 Feb. 1888.)*

'There have been no stories like this in the Thick Journals for many a moon. The effect is original, but I shall get into hot water over it, as I did over *Ivanov* [Chekhov's play *Ivanov*, first staged in 1887]. It will cause a lot of talk.' *(Letter to M. V. Kiseleva, 3 Feb. 1888.)*

'I wanted to write two or three signatures, but wrote no less than five [one signature, or Printer's Sheet, being equivalent to about sixteen pages of print]. I'm exhausted, I've suffered agonies . . . and I feel I haven't half botched things. . . .

'*The Steppe*'s plot is trivial. If it succeeds at all I'm going to make it the basis for a whopping great saga and continue it. In it you'll see more than one noteworthy character meriting further development.

'While writing I could smell the summer and the steppe near me. I'd like to go there!' *(Letter to A. N. Pleshcheyev, 3 Feb. 1888.)*

'I realize that Gogol will turn in his grave, being Russian literature's King of the Steppe. I've well-meaningly trespassed on his preserves, but I haven't half botched things. Three-quarters of the story doesn't come off. . . .

'I convey a nine-year-old boy through all the eight chapters—a boy who, should he later turn up in St. Petersburg or Moscow, is bound to end up badly. If the story enjoys the slightest success I shall continue it, I have deliberately left it with an unfinished impression. As you'll see, it's like the first part of a longer work.' *(Letter to D. V. Grigorovich, 5 Feb. 1888.)*

'As for Yegorushka, I shall continue his story, but not now. Silly old Father Christopher is now dead. Countess Dranitsky . . . has fallen on evil days.

Varlamov is still "knocking" around .You write that you liked the idea of Dymov. Life creates mischief-makers like him not to be religious dissenters or tramps, nor yet to lead a settled existence, but expressly for revolution. There will never be a Russian revolution, and Dymov will end up taking to the bottle, or else in gaol. He's a superfluous man.

'Once, in 1877, I contracted peritonitis . . . while travelling, and spent an agonizing night at Moses' inn. The Hebrew gentleman [*zhidok*] spent the whole night applying mustard plasters and compresses.' *(Letter to A. N. Pleshcheyev, 9 Feb. 1888.)*

'The main character is called Yegorushka, and the action takes place in the south, not far from Taganrog.' *(Letter to G. M. Chekhov, 9 Feb. 1888.)*

2. TEXT

The present translation is made from the text in *Works*, 1974–82, *Sochineniya*, vol. vii, itself based on that of Chekhov's *Collected Works* (1901), vol. iv, as corrected in certain minor details.

There are six previous recensions:

(*a*) the text published in the magazine *Severny vestnik* [*The Northern Herald*] of March 1888;

(*b*) the text published in *Stories* (St. Petersburg, 1888), a selection of Chekhov's work lightly revised by the author in March–April 1888, with further minor emendations in four later editions of the same publication.

3. VARIANTS

The earliest recension involved changes so slight that the most significant is from 'M., a sizeable town in S. County' to 'N., a sizeable town in Z. County' (page 15).

Only when revising the text for his *Collected Works* did Chekhov embark on emendations of substance, consisting largely of cuts extensive enough to remove some ninety lines of the story as first published. The passages concerned are largely descriptions of the hero's dreams and reflections in Chapters One to Four; they also include part of the scene in the village shop in Chapter Five.

The following are the chief among passages excised at this stage:

. . . *like some wizard of the steppes* (p. 21). Yegorushka was entirely obsessed by the whirling mill sails, the intense heat and the tedium of the steppe. He froze to the spot as if petrified with cold. His mind went blank, he ceased to anticipate anything, and he did his utmost not to look at the mill.

... *more suffocating, hot and stagnant than ever* (p. 25). The song, as he continued listening to it, seemed to give him a constricting sensation akin to nausea in his chest, and he felt his brain becoming petrified, as previously by the turning mill sails.

... *started playing with the jet of water again* (p. 25). He stuck a finger in the outlet to the pipe, and the water obediently ceased to flow, gurgle and play in the sunlight. He took his finger out and the water spurted, lisping and gurgling, from the pipe just as if it had never been interrupted. Then he let it flow for a while before blocking the outlet again. There was no interest in this activity, but it so absorbed him that his face assumed a look of businesslike reserve, and ten minutes passed without his noticing.

Watching him out of sight, Yegorushka (p. 26) sat on the ground and entirely yielded to the disagreeable sensation of nausea evoked by the heat and the song. He *clasped his knees* ...

... *dragging the brown grass and sedge behind it, while Yegorushka* (p. 26), nauseated, and feeling as if a piece of hot iron had been placed against the back of his neck, *hurtled after the retreating perspective* ...

'... *why he not give it me? Why he burn it* (p. 39)?'
Moses' monotonous voice gradually turned into a gurgle. No longer understanding a word, Yegorushka gazed without moving at Titus, who had materialized from somewhere and was standing in front of him puffing out his plump cheeks. Three snipe squeaked as they flew to the sedge. Titus blew out his cheeks, became distended, and vanished. Far, far away swept the windmill sails, looking like a distant man swinging his arms. The mill now had a contemptuous expression like Solomon's, and its shiny sails wore a mocking grin.

... *you hear her anguished, hopeless cry for a bard, a poet of her own* (p. 43).
Influenced by the night, Yegorushka grew sad. This was not the weather for travelling to school, thought he, but for going home to supper and bed. He imagined himself driving home—not in the bumpy britzka, but in the carriage belonging to that Countess whom he had recently met. The carriage is soft, snug and roomy, and above all it has space to rest your elbows and put your head. He sits dozing by the Countess, and then puts his arms and head on her lap—nice and comfortable, that. He gradually falls asleep while the sprung, softly rustling carriage careers, swaying, down the dusty road with incredible speed. Before dropping off the boy raises his head, looks out into the moonlit night, listens to the insects' chatter, and puts his head back on the loving, lovely lady's lap. What a marvellous way to travel! Moses' inn, the windmill, the hillock with its stream—all have long been left behind. And look, there is the

familiar poplar on the hill. Barely has it flashed past when the brickyards come into view with their clouds of black smoke, together with the cemetery where Grandmother sleeps, the forges and the gaol. Here, at last, is his home.

'Whoa there!'

His mother and Lyudmila the cook run out of the house. Mother delightedly greets him.

'Who's the lady?' she whispers.

The boy answers that this is the Countess, the one with that clock with the gold horseman in her drawing-room. In gratitude for his return home he throws his arms round the Countess's neck, kissing her eyes, forehead, temples.

'I hope he wasn't naughty on the way,' his mother said.

'No,' answered the Countess. 'He was asleep all the time.'

After talking for a while Countess Dranitsky says good-bye and is about to leave, but Mother stops her getting into her carriage.

'Please do stay the night.'

The Countess agrees, and off runs Lyudmila to make up a bed on the drawing-room sofa. Yegorushka goes to his nursery, flops into bed without undressing and sleeps, sleeps, sleeps. His only sensation is of something sharp digging into his right thigh—the Jewish honey cake in his pocket. The boy is sleeping heartily and smiling delightedly when loud, harsh voices suddenly resound just above his ear.

'I'm going to Bondarenko's, I am (p. 58).'

The shopkeeper was offended, but neither his face nor his words betrayed this as he began silently and unhurriedly pouring the oats back from the sack to the bin. The alarmed customer embarked on a plaintive apology. Meanwhile Yegorushka had long emptied his glass. He wanted some more tea. But, not venturing to pour it from the teapot himself, he walked up and down the shop expectantly, and read the labels on boxes. Then, seeing that the shopkeeper had started refilling the sack with oats he shouted 'good-bye' and went out.

APPENDIX II

AN AWKWARD BUSINESS

1. Composition
2. Text
3. Variants

1. COMPOSITION

The first reference to the story occurs in a letter of Chekhov's to Ya. P. Polonsky of 22 February 1888: 'I have begun a short story for *Novoye vremya* [*New Time*].' But it was not until 23 May that the finished article was dispatched to the newspaper's proprietor A. S. Suvorin, being then entitled *A Trivial Matter*.

2. TEXT

The present translation is made from the text in *Works*, 1974–82, *Sochineniya*, vol. vii, itself based on that of Chekhov's *Collected Works* (1901), vol. v.

There are two previous recensions:

(*a*) that published in the newspaper *Novoye vremya* [*New Time*] of 3 and 7 June 1888 with a different title: *Zhiteyskaya meloch* [*A Trivial Matter*];

(*b*) that published with the present title in *Gloomy People* (St. Petersburg, 1890), a selection of Chekhov's stories.

3. VARIANTS

At the second stage of revision, that leading to the final version, Chekhov made only minor changes. They are not noted here. But at the first stage of revision, when preparing the story for *Gloomy People*, he made extensive cuts. The following are the most significant.

'*I can do nothing* (p. 100). I can't get rid of the orderly since he's a protégé of the Council Chairman. But never mind, so much the better. If I can't get rid of him I'll leave myself. I'll just tell them to go to hell and leave.'

. . . his embarrassment.

'*What other knives do you want?*' *he repeated* (p. 101).

The purple arm jerked in the doctor's hands and began swelling. When it had become grossly distended, red undulations began to course over it, and the *doctor felt tears in his eyes . . .*

. . . with all its lore and regulations (p. 102). In fact, were one to count and sum up all his transgressions, the resultant figure would be one that any doctor who loved his profession would have been glad to sock on the jaw.

. . . all with that same air of everything being as it should be (p. 105). The starlings had come back to the path, and were fighting over a May-bug. From time to time a warm, gentle breeze blew into the surgery, rustling the papers and toying with the doctor's towel.

. . . he strolled slowly away from the hospital (p. 107). He was usually famished after seeing his patients. But now, instead of being agreeably hungry, he felt heavy and replete, as if he had swallowed a large piece of cold lead.

. . . to drive over to the garrison commander's for bridge (p. 107). He felt that the further he went from the hospital the more easily and objectively he could review his position. And he was now faced with a new and exceedingly ticklish problem: how would he put his idea for a trial to the orderly, and what must he say or do to make the man understand him?

'*You're not a duelling man* (p. 107).' The panting, trembling doctor spoke more loudly than necessary, and in a screeching voice unlike his own, while reflecting that he was saying all the wrong things. '*Nor am I, for that matter . . .*'

. . . and stood there, plunged in thought (p. 108). By now he was quite sure that he had lost his job, and that further attempts to effect a reconciliation would be unavailing. And so he stood in the hall wondering what injury he could do to the hated doctor as a farewell present.

'*Well, let her go* (p. 108)*!*'

His nerves had been frayed by the previous day, and by his sleepless night, and so he did not even notice that the orderly failed to doff his hat on meeting him.

'I can't help what happens,' he thought. 'Oh, to hell with them all! I'll give it all up. I'll let them go to hell, and I'll leave.'

But where was he to go? When a habitually contented person suddenly becomes dissatisfied with himself and those around him, when he doesn't know how to shake off this grave dissatisfaction, when he finds fault both with himself and with the world at large, then his chief consolation is to indulge the impossible day-dreams of infancy. The doctor liked the idea of making a long, long journey—to the Caucasian shore of the Black Sea, say, of buying a little land there, and of tilling it with his own hands. He wouldn't meet other people nor they him. It would also be good to bury himself for life in a monastery cell. As he was a university man, and would therefore be something of a rarity in a monastery, they would be glad to grant him various privileges. They would not force him to attend matins and evensong, they would not made him work or fast, and so on. He would sit all day and night in a little tower with a single small window, listen to the doleful bell-ringing and write a history of medicine in Russia.

He was furious with himself, with the orderly, with the whole business (p. 109), which was taking such an idiotic turn. And since *he* felt foolish and ridiculous he consequently found the whole of existence foolish and ridiculous.

APPENDIX III

THE BEAUTIES

1. Composition
2. Text
3. Variants

1. COMPOSITION

The Beauties was written in mid-September 1888. On the eleventh of that month Chekhov informed his brother Alexander that he had begun work, and four days later he told A. N. Pleshcheyev that: 'I did find a wretched little subject, but I've already launched it, sending it off in the form of a short sketch to *Novoye vremya* [*New Time*], where I'm up to my ears in debt.'

The story is partly based on Chekhov's own memories of his childhood and youth in southern European Russia, which included travelling through an Armenian village, Bolshiye Saly, in the area at the age of seventeen. The links with Chekhov's childhood are further emphasized in a letter written to him by his cousin G. M. Chekhov on 11 October 1888. 'Thank you for *The Beauties*, which reminded me of our common grandfather, and of the coachman Karpo who used to visit us with Grandad. . . . In the Armenian that you visited with the grandfather [in the story] I at once seemed to recognize Nazar Minaich Nazarov, that forceful and headstrong character, and I remembered him coming into our father's shop of an evening' (*Works*, 1974–82, *Sochineniya*, vol. vii, p. 652).

2. TEXT

The present translation is made from the text in *Works*, 1974–82, *Sochineniya*, vol. vii, itself based on that of Chekhov's *Collected Works* (1901), vol. iii.

There are two previous recensions:

(*a*) that published in the newspaper *Novoye vremya* [*New Time*] of 21 September 1888;

(*b*) that published, together with other writers' work, in a symposium entitled *Incidentally* [*Mezhdu prochim*] (Moscow, 1894).

3. VARIANTS

At the second stage of revision, that leading to the *Collected Works* text, Chekhov made only minor corrections. At the earlier stage, that resulting in the *Incidentally* text, he had made a considerable number of cuts and alterations, the following being the most significant.

I conceived a loathing for the steppe, the sun and the flies (p. 120), and I was amazed that men as lively as grandfather and the Armenian could put up with this tedium and feel at ease with it.

. . . but was silent, and glanced pensively at the girl (p. 121). Our silence did not seem awkward because our host said nothing either. He knew that his daughter was supremely beautiful. In response to our silence he made an awkward grunting noise.

'She is very beautiful and unusual, but we'll pretend not to notice it,' his face seemed to say.

'*Rot, you hell-hounds* (p. 122)*!*'
The Armenian went outside, splaying his legs. On his way down the steps he passed me, spoke his daughter's name in a sort of guttural, sneezing voice without taking his chibouk from his mouth: 'Mshaa-tchaa!' When the girl ran up to him he spoke rapidly and angrily, probably in rebuke. She listened silently, with lowered eyes, then ran to the kitchen, and back to the threshing floor again. Once more, I noticed, the Ukrainian stopped shouting and cracking his whip to follow her with his eyes.

'*Get back!*' *Karpo shouted* (p. 123), while I was looking round for the Armenian girl, distressed to think that I should soon see her no more. *Grandfather woke up.*
'Mash-ya!' shouted the Armenian. 'Mshaa-tchaa.'
Masha opened the creaking gates, and we got into the carriage and drove out of the yard. A hot wind blew, raising dust along the road. It was hot and boring, but none of this dispelled my sadness. We drove *in silence, as if angry* . . .

. . . dispersed like pollen from a flower (p. 125). All the passengers were gazing at the beautiful creature in silence, except that I remember a lady speaking to someone behind me.

'I don't see anything special about her, Sasha. She's quite nice-looking, that's all.'
'Then you simply don't understand, my dear,' a man's voice answered.

APPENDIX IV

THE PARTY

1. Composition
2. Text
3. Variants

1. COMPOSITION

Chekhov wrote *The Party* in response to an invitation from A. N. Pleshcheyev, the literary editor of *Severny vestnik* [*The Northern Herald*], beginning work on 10 September 1888. 'I'm gradually getting on with it, but there's a note of anger in it, due to my own incensed condition' *(letter to A. N. Pleshcheyev, 15 September 1888)*. The story was completed on, or just before, 30 September. 'It has turned out longish (about 13,000 words), and rather depressing, but true to life and—believe it or not—with a "message" [*s "napravleniyem"*]' *(letter to the same, 30 Sept. 1888)*. '[The story] is sloppily and carelessly written, but I've no time to revise it' *(letter to A. S. Suvorin, 2 Oct. 1888)*. 'The beginning and the end are readable, but the middle is like chewed string' *(letter to Ye. M. Lintvaryova, 9 Oct. 1888)*. Chekhov wrote to Pleshcheyev particularly requesting that not a single line of *The Party* should be edited out, also remarking that he feared cuts imposed by the official literary censorship: he expected that his description of 'Peter' as Acting Chairman of the Appeal Court would be expunged as derogatory to the legal establishment, 'since all court chairmen are like that nowadays' *(letter to A. N. Pleshcheyev, 10 or 11 Oct. 1888)*. But this fear proved groundless, for the censor passed the story *in toto*, and it was Chekhov himself who was eventually to make extensive cuts (see Variants, below).

In answer to a complaint from A. S. Suvorin that *The Party*, as published in *Severny vestnik*, lacked polish, Chekhov—who, incidentally, had not been given the opportunity to correct his proofs—replied as follows on 27 October. 'I realize that I've made a complete hash of my characters, and wasted good material. Quite honestly, I'd gladly have spent six months on *The Party*. . . . I'd have been more than delighted to present a sensitive and succinct account of my hero's *entire* character, I'd have described his frame of mind while his wife was in labour, his trial, the foul after-taste left by his acquittal. I'd have described the midwife and the doctor having tea in the middle of the night, and I'd have described the rain. . . . I began the story on 10 September with the

thought that I must finish it by 5 October at the latest, and that if I took any
longer I'd be letting them down and wouldn't be paid. I wrote the beginning
calmly and without forcing myself, but in the middle I began losing heart and
worrying that it would be too long. . . . For some reason my beginnings
always are promising, as if I'd started a novel, but the middle is all bunched up
and tentative, while the end is something of a firework display, as in a "little
story" ' *(letter to A. S. Suvorin, 27 Oct. 1888;* reference is to the very short,
pithy, comic stories of which Chekhov had published scores during the preceding few years).

In his correspondence of the period Chekhov repeatedly reacts to a demand
commonly made on Russian imaginative writers by their reviewers and
critics, that their works should contain a bias, tendency or slant (all terms of
praise in this context) of a political or general philosophical nature—in other
words, that they should not merely describe life, but also purvey instruction
on how it should be lived. In his attitude towards this assumption Chekhov
was ambivalent. On the one hand he resented it: the more dominant reaction.
But he was also inclined to voice the counter-claim that his work did after all
contain 'messages' such as Russian critics expected to find on the pages of any
serious writer. The following passages from his correspondence include reflections on this topic inspired by *The Party*, together with other comments of
note bearing on the story.

'I fear those who read between my lines looking for messages, and are
determined to see me as a liberal or a conservative. I am not a liberal. I am not a
conservative. I am not an advocate of moderate reform. I am not a monk. Nor
am I committed to non-commitment. I should like to be a free artist, that's all,
and I'm only sorry God hasn't granted me the necessary strength. I hate violence and lies in all their manifestations. . . . It's not only in merchants' houses
and gaols that humbug, imbecility and capriciousness are rife. I see them in
learning, in literature, and among young people. My Holy of Holies is the
human body, health, intelligence, talent, inspiration and the most absolute
freedom—freedom from violence and falsehood, wherever these two ingredients
may be found. That is the programme I should follow, were I a great artist.'
(Letter to A. N. Pleshcheyev, 4 Oct. 1888.)

'Can it really be that no message [*napravleniye*] is detectable in my last story
[*The Party*]? You once told me that my stories lacked the element of protest,
that they were equally devoid of sympathies and antipathies. But what of *The
Party*? Isn't it one long protest against falsehood? And isn't that a message?
(Letter to A. N. Pleshcheyev, 8 Oct. 1888.)

'The middle of the story is grey and monotonous. I wrote it lazily and carelessly. Accustomed as I am to "little stories", consisting only of a beginning

and an end, I get bored and start marking time when I feel I'm writing the middle. You do well to voice your suspicion that I fear to be thought a liberal. It prompts me to examine my own insides. I think I could rather be accused of gluttony, drunkenness, frivolity, emotional atrophy, or of any crime in the calendar, than of wishing to seem to be, or of wishing not to seem to be, anything. I have never tried to hide my views. If my heroine Olga, a liberal and a former college student, is sympathetic to me, I don't hide the fact in the story —as is, I imagine, abundantly clear. Nor do I conceal my respect for our local government institutions, which I like, and for trial by jury. But can't you see that the true and false elements in my characters are what I try to balance—not conservatism and liberalism, which aren't the point at issue in my view? *(Letter to A. N. Pleshcheyev, 9 Oct. 1888.)*

2. TEXT

The present translation is made from the text in *Works*, 1974–82, *Sochineniya*, vol. vii, itself based on that of Chekhov's *Collected Works* (1901), vol. iv.

There are two previous recensions:

(*a*) that published in the magazine *Severny vestnik* [*The Northern Herald*] of November 1888;

(*b*) that brought out in pamphlet form by the publishing house 'Posrednik' (Moscow, 1893).

3. VARIANTS

When revising the story, as published in *Severny vestnik* in 1888, for its second recension (that brought out by 'Posrednik' in 1893), Chekhov made extensive cuts. When preparing the text for its third and final recension, that incorporated in his *Collected Works* of 1901, he made further cuts, but these were far less extensive than those implemented at the earlier stage.

The longest and most significant of these excised passages are given below, cuts implemented in 1901 being distinguished from those of 1893 by a vertical line in the relevant margins. The general effect of these revisions was to tone the story down by removing much of the more abrasive and satirical material. Chekhov also expunged one minor character, the bee-keeper Zakhar, together with material that had been criticized as excessively Tolstoyan in its manner: for instance, Olga's suddenly conceived dislike for the back of her husband's neck. This and other excisions were made partly in response to comments elicited by Chekhov from his editor Pleshcheyev.

Though the removal of this material has undoubtedly improved the story as a work of art, the passages in question nevertheless form a valuable comment on Chekhov's thought and attitudes, and they contain some of the most significant among the many variants to his work.

It was snug and quiet (p. 130). Amid all the rubbish that Zakhar [the bee-keeper who does not figure in the final version] slept on at night was a bowl containing remnants of gruel and a spoon. Next to it was a big, shiny black loaf. Squeamishly avoiding Zakhar's trappings, and fearing to soil her expensive dress, Olga did not sit down, but stood stooping. On the roof joists hung bundles of last year's dill, thyme and camomile that the old bee-keeper treasured for some reason. One of these, dry and prickly, caught in Olga's hair and slid down her back to the floor, while another—softer, with the sharp, aromatic scent of thyme—scratched her face and the back of her neck.

'. . . *just because he's a money-grubbing publican* (p. 131). To acquit an innkeeper when a schoolteacher takes him to court—ye Gods, what could be less liberal? Well, *Vostryakov gave the publican a gaol sentence*, of course, and our liberal appeal sessions solemnly confirmed his findings. Now, I sat on that appeal court. A court of law is neither an ale-house nor a room to be let furnished. Nor is it a proper place for demonstrations and for classes in liberal posturing. *I expressed a dissenting judgement*, which really did put the cat among the pigeons! Displeasure was caused.'

In the crack close to Olga's eyeballs a single ant crawled from left to right, followed by a second and then a third.

'So how will the trial end?' Lyubochka asked.

'Oh, it will come to nothing. I'll probably be acquitted, or at most reprimanded. It's a pure formality. Such things are a shot in the arm to the likes of me'.

Peter spoke calmly . . .

. . . *had suddenly felt fatigued and depressed* (p. 132). He had stopped conversing, grumbling and laughing. He *had begun sleeping badly*, he complained of boredom, and he stood by the window, *drumming his fingers on the panes more often than was his wont*. Olga had the impression that some degree of falseness had entered her relations with her husband at this point. He was ashamed to confess how depressed he was, and she was annoyed at his failure to make that admission. When she raised the subject of the appeal sessions or the impending trial he had tried to brazen it out with her—as he was now doing with Lyubochka.

'*I'm told you've been down Poltava way . . .*'

'. . . *and the clang of scythes from dawn to dusk* (p. 132). Now, the wail of a scythe, especially when it's being whetted, is dearer to my heart than any novels. *It's charming country, is the good old South.*'

At this point Peter raised himself on one knee, and laid his hand on his heart to add weight to his words, but a single ant had got up on its hind legs and blanked out his nose and lips. The waggling of the ant's feelers seemed to make Peter's face twitch convulsively.

'A lovely land, with its huge villages four or five miles long. What purity, what hues, what scenery! White cottages drowning chimney-deep in green foliage, beautiful women and children looking at passers-by over fences. What a people! *Drinking the water at the wells . . .*'

'*. . . philosophizing women and interminable dinners* (p. 132)?'
Peter was now speaking his own peculiar, picturesque language, with the sincerity that always accompanied his words when he cast off all affectations and became a nice, genuine person. He *was not lying . . .*

. . . reminders of his wounded vanity and blundering (p. 132).
The ant lowered itself and crawled off, and Olga saw her husband's face. It was smiling sadly, and it was as sincere, simple and relaxed as when he was asleep or alone in his room. But she was hurt, vexed and frightened that he should employ romantic language and voice his complaints to a little girl whom he didn't know, rather than to herself. He felt the need to unbosom himself to a stranger, obviously, but what did this need signify?

. . . emerged from the hut and set off for the house (p. 133). She was ready to weep with resentment, vexation and fear. She was jealous without adequate cause, which meant that each individual symptom of her jealousy was easily explicable, and therefore not alarming, but that all the symptoms in combination were incomprehensible and sinister, boding some kind of danger. *She understood Peter's fatigue . . .*

. . . his gait as magisterial as ever (p. 135). Olga flared up, quickly examined the walls, as if seeking witnesses to the offence done to her, and started nervously pacing the room. She was already regretting having spared this strong, excessively smug, arrogant person and not having come straight out with her opinion of him.

. . . satisfied with himself, his dinner, his digestion and his scenery (p. 135). During these bouts of hatred for some smug, stubborn awkward customer it's always the back of the neck that somehow seems the ugliest part of the body. And it was the back of his neck in particular—lordly, elegantly barbered and glistening—that Olga loathed about her husband. Never, she felt, had she noticed the back of that neck before.

. . . all this 'eh?', 'what!', 'my dear fellow!' stuff (p. 135)? Whence his majestic air and excessive poise?
'Oh yes,' thought Olga. 'He can strut and pose after getting three hundred thousand roubles by marrying me, not to mention the land. But I don't see him doing much strutting if it wasn't for me—him and that mortgaged Koshovka estate!'

Yet she was immediately scared by the unworthy thought of money that had flashed through her brain—unexpected, unsought, originating God knows where.

'I'm reacting like a typical woman,' she thought, only to banish the thought. 'His affected pose, his affected tone, every step and every word—it's all part of the role he's acting. He struts in that particular way, and not in any other, because he knows people are watching him, and that it suits him. It's all conceit, triviality and bogusness run riot. But, good grief, look at the audience he has for his dissembling, acting and posturing! Half of them are insignificant morons, and the other half are unhappy.'

And yet there had been a time, not more than a year ago, when the magisterial gait, the affected pose and the authoritative resonance of his voice had been attractive and had passed as true coin. When Peter had fallen in love with Olga and courted her, she had sensed something fresh, young and high-spirited in him. When visiting her Moscow flat, and meeting no one but students—both men and women—there, he had behaved exactly as he had at dinner today. Uninhibited by anyone in the room, he had come out with the most extreme conservative ideas, repudiating trial by jury, rural local government, the statute on urban local government. He had abused barristers, he had made jokes about feminism. In Olga's circle, where the very air seemed stale and stagnant from everyone thinking exactly alike, where everyone said the same thing over and over again day in day out, where all bowed down to the same shibboleths, such bravado could not but succeed. When the young, intelligent university graduate Peter impugned the jury system, say, or jeered at women going to college, when he flung a newspaper aside with a 'How can you read this nonsense?', and when he undertook to prove that this or that darling demigod of their circle was a charlatan and a nonentity, the general effect was wild, fresh, spontaneous, bold and even piquant. Just as those liberal notions suited the thin, often hungry, poorly dressed and timid students and college girls, so too did his conservatism become him—well-built, tall, well-fed, always fashionably dressed and as smart as a new pin. The liberal-minded Olga had originally told her women friends that she had nothing in common with 'that handsome baker'. But after falling in love with him and becoming engaged, she had taken some pride in calling him 'my monster' or 'my Savonarola'.

After getting married, however, she soon saw that all she had previously accepted as Peter's views and convictions was assumed and extraneous. He was clever, educated, honest, handsome, witty and devoid of malice, but he turned out to resemble that Moscow set exactly, in that he kept saying the same thing over and over again day in day out. Could the words employed by him to express his conservative ideas have been logged and counted, an exceedingly modest and impoverished vocabulary would have emerged. Just as the Moscow set chattered day in day out about 'science', 'the common people' and 'right-thinking persons', but did nothing whatever for science, the people or thought, so too

Peter chattered away about the evil of liberal institutions, while serenely playing his part in local elections, taking a lively interest in local gossip, intriguing and differing little from those solid burghers who hold no brief for trial by jury, the press and women's education.

... *made it sound forced and rather uncouth* (p. 136).

Observing her husband in court, Olga could not help remembering her Moscow friends—those charming people who, while reading some intensely boring and obscure book for hours on end, pretend to understand and enjoy it without being bored. These same people would never make a remark without looking round with an air of mystery at the door or the servants, and if they saw anyone who thought, spoke and dressed differently from themselves, they would look him up and down with devastating scorn. Through fear of seeming mediocrities all her Moscow friends tried to act a part. Peter too was acting a part.

What an unpleasant recollection!

'... *but don't you think our piano needs tuning* (p. 136)?'

'It does a bit,' said the young man, playing an octave.

'A remarkable gift!' repeated Olga, trying to think of something else to say.

'Yes, but he doesn't have a job,' sighed the young man's sister. 'And he never plays at home, you know.'

'Tut, tut!' Olga shook her head reproachfully. 'You should be ashamed of yourself, Monsieur Georges. Though actually,'—she sighed—'all gifted people are like that.'

'They are a bit,' agreed the young man, and again played an octave.

... *adopted an air of earnestness when addressing her* (p. 138).

'And he's just the same as the rest of them,' thought Olga, looking at his small mouth and little golden moustache. 'He too will take a degree, get a job, marry. He'll be surrounded by boredom, lies, starvation, illness, chaos. He'll have lots of his own and other people's mistakes on his conscience, his wife will become pregnant, and he'll carry on regardless, talking all sorts of nonsense. He'll strike poses and scrutinize every step he takes in case it's not liberal or conservative enough, and in case it might be unbecoming for him to tread in that particular way rather than in any other.

The footman Gregory came towards her from the croquet lawn, carrying some empty (p. 138) *soda syphons.* He paused.

'Where do you wish tea served, madam?'

'Let me think,' said Olga. 'Oh, actually, my head's going round, you'd better decide. But please make sure there's no delay with the samovars.'

Through the birch and lime trunks the figures of the examining magistrate and other gentlemen flitted past on the croquet lawn. No ladies were to be seen. She *asked him where the ladies were* . . .

'*They don't teach you how to influence difficult people at college* (p. 140).'
Olga felt intolerably dejected. The delighted panache with which her uncle was running down a man he disliked behind his back—it made her lose all patience.
'*I suppose I shall have* . . .'

'. . . *put that in your pipe and smoke it* (p. 140)*!* I'm a conservative, I don't believe in higher education for women, or in your courts or any of the rest of it. Yes, you can put that in your pipe and smoke it!'

'. . . *Schopenhauer, Proudhon and Company she has thoroughly* (p. 142) ——'
Whether it was that the Colonel detected mockery in Peter's voice, or whether he noticed Olga flare up and look angrily at her husband, he thought fit to speak like a defence counsel.
'Now, can one really call Olga a proper college girl? Oh, come off it, do! I've no doubt she turned up in her carriage a couple of times *à la grande dame*, listened patronizingly for a bit, and then went off on some visit. That wasn't going to college, it was just the fashion, the done thing.

. . . *seeming to understand each other without words* (p. 142). Olga remembered the feminine complaint that she had realized she was suffering from that afternoon. She felt no pain, but there was a sort of discomfort spread over her whole body.
'Does it matter?' she asked, after explaining the nature of the complaint.
'God only know, missus. Maybe it don't.'

'. . . *that the seating arrangements went sadly awry* (p. 143).' The magistrate had brought a bottle of red wine for the trip, and Colonel Bukreyev was trying to take it off him. Both were fooling around and roaring with laughter till the tears came, but were pretending to laugh at their own tomfoolery and not from pleasure. Three boats were *jam-packed while two stood empty* . . .

'. . . *the whole thing is pointless* (p. 144).' And there was another rower—bearded, earnest, perpetually frowning. He spoke little, he never smiled, and he spent all his time brooding and brooding. He wore an embroidered smock *à la* Colonel Polubotok [a Ukrainian Cossack leader, who died in 1623], and dreamed of liberating the Ukraine from the Russian yoke. Anyone indifferent to his embroidery and day-dreams he treated as a hidebound vulgarian.

. . . mistress in the Crimea (p. 144). He has looted and pillaged the land inherited from his father. There is no more timber, there are no old gardens, and the place is exhausted and half mortgaged. And over there is an elderly man, not yet grey-haired, in a cloak and a hat that has turned rust-coloured, with a faded yellow face. He is still exactly the same as she remembers him from her childhood—even his bald patch has not increased in size. He always speaks at length, monotonously and in a manner designed to emphasize his status as an educated person. For some reason he calls himself a Man of the Sixties—each town and county has one of these faded personages who claim a monopoly over that decade. At dinner, at tea, on a walk, in a carriage or a boat, he's for ever holding forth about ideas, women's emancipation, progress, sinister influences, science and literature. He ardently declaims verses in which the words 'dawn', 'sunset', 'torch' and 'rumble' frequently occur. He lays down the law about newspapers and journals, publishers and editors, praising some, accusing others of treachery and dubbing yet others 'base'. In his capacity as a Man of the Sixties he pines for the glorious past and condemns the present. In Peter he sees a dangerous reactionary, and he worships Olga as a liberal who has been to college. His language is ornate and recondite. For instance, he calls the future 'that which lies ahead'. Young people are 'the forces of youth', or 'the rising generation', while peasants are 'our good countryfolk', and so on. He never really says anything unpleasant, and he is always sincere, probably, but whenever he opens his mouth and gives tongue in his sepulchral tenor on the subject of emancipation or ideals, his whole being somehow smells like a derelict old cellar. Then there's Peter's liberal Uncle Nicholas, so bored with doing nothing and so glad when he runs across some wretched conservative. And how he does pounce on his victim like a vicious little fighting cock! With what relish he does let fly!

Glancing at the other boats . . .

'*I don't understand at all* (p. 147).'
She was exhausted and sleepy. But then, suddenly, the small person presented himself spontaneously and unbidden to her imagination. He laughingly tried to chase after her thoughts, he threw them into confusion, and then, when she closed her eyes, he lay on the pillow next to her face and began breathing on her cheeks.

When the small person was born he would (she thought) summon the large person.

'You've always lived a lie,' he would say. 'All right then. Go off to your appeal court or your Lyubochkas, and carry on lying. I don't need you any more. I already have an existence that fills my life. It's my own, and it belongs to me.'

'That existence is as much mine as yours,' Peter would say. 'And you have no right to dispose of it.'

She was suddenly amused to think that Peter also had a right to the small person. And because he had such rights she was no longer angry with him.

'All right then, you great lout,' I'll say. 'You come over here too, I was only joking.'

. . . the gentlemen were sitting down to cards (p. 147). Some ladies were crowding round the piano, others were strolling about the ballroom. They spoke of forfeits, of dancing and singing. Near the door from the drawing-room to the ballroom stood the young wife of a local councillor, unable to take her eyes off her husband who was sitting by the fireplace next to Peter discussing local government problems. Her languid, tender gaze and happy smile evoked a disagreeable sensation in Olga. She wanted to say something unpleasant to this happy woman and poison her happiness a little.

'So you can't take your eyes off your husband.' She smilingly approached the happy wife. 'It's rotten luck on us young wives, though. Actually, you know, if one considers things seriously, our husbands aren't worth a hundredth part of the tenderness that we lavish on them. After all, there are some authors who write in a smooth, soft, velvety style, but if you lift up a bit of the velvet you see a large, self-satisfied poisonous snake. That's what our husbands are like. They speak smoothly, they have fine feelings, they behave charmingly. But whatever virtues they bedeck themselves with, my dear, they can't hide the falseness and despotic ways that they have inherited from their daddies and grandpapas. You can trim a lap-dog to look like a lion, but a lap-dog it remains. Don't you agree?'

The councillor's wife, whose mind was entirely on love, did not understand. She gave a vague smile and looked at her husband in alarm—could Olga be hinting at future infidelity, or something like that?

'I'm malicious and stupid,' thought Olga. 'Anyway, don't listen to me, darling,' she said. 'As you know, I'm thought eccentric, and eccentrics are always saying the wrong thing.'

'*. . . off with you! Godspeed* (p. 148)*!*'

The hour of departure did not pass without surprises. For instance, it turned out that the schoolboys and the student with the little golden moustache had arrived on foot—a fact that they revealed only when everyone had left and all the horses and carriages had already been assigned. On hearing this, Peter took his wife to one side.

'Where can I find transport for them?' he asked in an accusing whisper. 'Think I keep a stud farm? Our horses are all over the place, as you know, and even those used for hauling water are out on the job. What the hell can I give them?'

'Well, they can't walk all that way at night,' said Olga rudely.

'Have the racing droshky hitched up for them,' said Peter without thinking, but then realized that there would be no room for them in that.

'Vasily!' he shouted. 'Trot along to the steward's and tell him to let them have his britzka till the morning. And wake up Andrian. He can drive the Chizhevsky boys.'

A minute later Peter had forgotten sending Vasily off.

'Vasily!' he was shouting. 'Where on earth's Vasily? Where have they all got to? Utter imbeciles!'

'Your mother really is unkind,' said Olga as the student and the little Chizhevskys were getting into the britzka. 'You mind you tell her so. It's very, very, very unkind of her! She has quite forgotten me.'

His gaze was grim and troubled (p. 149). He evidently feared to concentrate on the thoughts that occurred, as if to spite him, whenever he went to bed or was left on his own. He tried to banish them, but they dominated his will, and his face gradually relaxed, assuming a guilty, fatigued expression. His cigarette had gone out, and the ash was scattered over his nightshirt.

How should she take it (p. 150)? If a husband picks up a pillow and leaves the bedroom, does that not mean that, at the time in question, he does not love his wife, that he's laughing at her, that he despises her anger and words?

. . . her legs were tangled in the blanket (p. 152). Some horses ran through the bedroom one after the other, and the ants that she had seen in the hut began crawling. Ants, horses, icon-lamp, and the fly banging against the ceiling—all gave a childishly helpless smile. From all sides an imploring voice was heard: 'How could you say such a thing, Olga?'

. . . and she began sobbing again (p. 152). The horses ran past again, and again the ants crawled. The unsmiling doubles Nata and Vata stood and watched Peter sharpen his scythe, their faces pale and cold. 'What's he doing, mowing in the bedroom?' wondered Olga, and shouted: 'Go away, go away!'

. . . told the girl to clear out (p. 152). The maid went out, and Olga realized that the scythe-sharpening Peter had been a hallucination, and that the Peter now sitting down on his bed was the real one.

With a gesture of despair he left the room (p. 156). A little later he came in again, took something from the table and went out through the other door without a glance at his wife.

'Are you leaving, Doctor?' he asked from behind the door in a loud voice, and in the tone that he used with court bailiffs and witnesses. 'Finished one job and off to tackle another, eh? Ah well—the cobbler must stick to his last. We all have to work.'

He must have given the doctor some money because the man diffidently remarked that: 'You shouldn't have bothered.'

'But of course. The labourer is worthy of his hire. Most grateful to you, Doctor. And remember us miserable sinners another time, please.'

His speech was condescendingly casual, neither his voice, nor his tone, nor his sedate, heavy tread betraying the fact that the man had been in tears a moment ago! After seeing the doctor off he quickly crossed the bedroom on the way to his study. As he passed his wife he cast her a guilty and imploring glance.

'I can't help dissembling,' he seemed to say. 'I haven't the strength to stop myself. Help me.'

APPENDIX V

A NERVOUS BREAKDOWN

1. Composition
2. Text
3. Variants

1. COMPOSITION

This story about prostitution must presumably have been partly inspired (though we have no explicit documentary link) by Chekhov's experience of Moscow 'night life'. It is by no means clear precisely how much weight we should attach to his own perhaps whimsical boast, made in a letter of 13 November 1886 to A. N. Pleshcheyev, that he had been 'a great specialist on "tarts" [*devki*] in the old days.' But we do know that he frequently visited Moscow's Salon de Variété in his student years (1879–84), and that he described this notorious haunt of prostitutes in early journalistic articles. We also know of a visit paid by Chekhov, in 1884, as a last-year medical student or newly qualified doctor, together with two young colleagues, to a brothel in the comparably notorious Sobolev Street, which appears as the 'S. Street' of *A Nervous Breakdown*. The expedition was undertaken 'for research purposes', according to one of Chekhov's fellow-investigators. 'We had set ourselves the task of discovering directly from the white slaves in person how they had "come to such a pass". . . . To share our impressions and the results of the enquiry we called at a tavern near Sukharev Tower, drank tea and produced our notes' (P. Zelenin, cited in Gitovich, p. 99).

A more immediate impulse for *A Nervous Breakdown* came from the death of the short-story writer Vsevolod Garshin, who committed suicide on 24 March 1888 by throwing himself down the well of a staircase. The death of this popular and sensitive author, whose works treat the problem of suffering and of man's helplessness in seeking to alleviate it, came as profoundly distressing news to Chekhov (who was five years younger than Garshin) and to the literary world as a whole. Chekhov therefore readily accepted the suggestion that he should contribute a story to one or other of two projected literary symposia that were to be published in memory of Garshin. To K. S. Barantsevich, one of the sponsors, he wrote as follows on 30 March 1888. 'Your idea merits sympathy and respect, if only because such projects incidentally help to cement our literary fraternity together, for though our writers are not very numerous they do live all over the place and work in isolation from each other. The greater the solidarity and mutual support the sooner we shall learn to respect and value each other.' Chekhov added that he would send a contribution to Barantsevich's publication 'without fail', but then withdrew, transferring his allegiance to the rival collection that (as it later turned out) was to be edited by A. N. Pleshcheyev.

Far from cementing solidarity and mutual support the commemoration of Garshin had, in practice, led to a minor clash within the literary fraternity—between Barantsevich and Pleshcheyev. As for Chekhov, he much regretted the disagreement, and the dissipation of effort involved in publishing 'two volumes hallowed by one and the same aim, but with one [Barantsevich's] appearing three months before the other. They're bound to hamper each other considerably' (*letter to A. N. Pleshcheyev, 4 Apr. 1888*).

Five months rolled by without any contribution to Pleshcheyev's publication arriving from Chekhov, and Pleshcheyev accordingly wrote to him on 13 September begging him to hurry up. On the fifteenth of the month Chekhov replied that he was indeed anxious to send his contribution, since he dearly loved such people as Garshin. 'But I have absolutely no subjects in the least suitable. . . . Well, actually, I do have one: a young fellow of the Garshin type, a cut above average, decent and profoundly sensitive, finds himself in a brothel for the first time in his life. Since serious things must be seriously described I intend to call a spade a spade. Perhaps I'll manage to . . . produce the sense of oppression that I would wish, and perhaps it will turn out all right and suit the book. But can you, my dear fellow, guarantee that the censorship or your editorial office won't cut out what I consider vital material? . . . If you'll guarantee that *not one word* will be expunged I'll write the story in two evenings.'

Though Pleshcheyev was indeed able to offer the sought-for assurance about censorship, the story was far slower in taking shape than Chekhov had predicted. On 3 November he informed Pleshcheyev that he had made a start, and that one quarter had now been written; and he asked for a week in which to finish it. 'I describe Sobolev Street and its brothels—but cautiously, not stirring up the dirt or employing strong expressions. On 10 November Chekhov wrote to Pleshcheyev that he was now finishing the story. 'I'll finish it tomorrow or the day after. . . . While writing I keep trying to cultivate modesty and discretion—to the point of boredom. So sensitive is the subject, I feel, that the merest molehill may seem a mountain. I think the story will contrast sharply with the general level of the collection. It's sad, depressing and serious.'

On 11 November Chekhov wrote informing A. S. Suvorin that he had just finished the story. 'It's a load off my mind. . . . I discuss prostitution a great deal, but without coming to any conclusions. Why does your newspaper [the St. Petersburg daily *Novoye vremya*] never have anything about this subject? It is such an appalling evil, you know. Our Sobolev Street is simply a slave market.'

A Nervous Breakdown was at last despatched on 13 November, and Chekhov wrote to Pleshcheyev that he feared the finished article might prove unacceptable. 'The story is quite unsuitable for an almanac and for family reading, being inelegant and redolent of damp drain-pipes. But at least my conscience is clear. First, I've kept my promise. And, secondly, I've paid the late Garshin the tribute that I wished, and was able, to offer. As a medical man I feel I've described mental pain correctly, and in conformity with all the canons of psychiatry.' It is at this point that Chekhov volunteers the comment quoted above: about having been a great specialist on 'tarts' [*devki*] in the old days.

Other references to *A Nervous Breakdown* in Chekhov's correspondence include the following, in a letter to Ye. M. Lintvaryova of 23 November 1888. 'The story is long and not particularly stupid. It will be read with some benefit and create some degree of sensation. I treat an old and exceedingly ticklish problem—and fail to solve it, of course.' In a letter of 11 November 1888, to A. S. Suvorin, Chekhov hints at the traits that his hero Vasilyev has in common with Garshin: concern for the sufferings of others and his own distress at being unable to relieve those sufferings. 'In this story I've expressed my own view, which no one wants to hear, about such rare spirits as Garshin.'

A Nervous Breakdown did indeed arouse considerable interest, largely favourable, among reviewers and readers. Among the numerous recorded reactions the most amusing, perhaps, is that of the eminent novelist Leo Tolstoy, who said that, before embarking on his sufferings, Chekhov's hero ought to have 'partaken of' the brothels' wares (I. L. Leontyev [Shcheglov], cited in *Works*, 1974–82, *Sochineniya*, vol. vii, p. 664).

2. TEXT

The present translation is made from the text in *Works*, 1974–82, *Sochineniya*, vol. vii, itself based on that of Chekhov's *Collected Works* (1901), vol. v.

There are two previous recensions:

(*a*) that published in *In Memory of V. M. Garshin* (St. Petersburg, 1888), a symposium by various authors;

(*b*) that published in *Gloomy People* (St. Petersburg, 1890), a selection of Chekhov's stories.

3. VARIANTS

When preparing the Garshin symposium text for that published in *Gloomy People*, Chekhov made a few minor alterations, including the removal of the following:

'. . . *have fathers and brothers just like you, don't they* (p. 174)?'

Wild joy, and happiness at having finally solved his problem, overwhelmed Vasilyev.

When preparing his *Collected Works* text, Chekhov revised the story more extensively, largely by making further cuts. The following are the most important of the passages excised or changed at this stage:

. . . *stupid women were not the only factors responsible* (p. 170). And new, gloomy thoughts, such as had never occurred to him before, began tormenting him.

'*My God, if that isn't horrible what is* (p. 172)?'

'It's horrible indeed,' the medical student agreed. 'Of course we're in the wrong. But you're forgetting social conditions, my friend. Marriage is out of the question, so there's no point in discussing it.'

'Oh, that's enough double-talk about marriage! You avoid love on a non-commercial basis because it imposes obligations. That's downright nauseating and disgraceful!'

'. . . *artistic approach leads nowhere*,' *thought Vasilyev* (p. 174). 'However exalted science and the arts might seem, they still remain the work of human hands—flesh of our flesh, blood of our blood. They suffer from the same sickness as we, and it is in them above all that our occupation is reflected. Can you really say that literature and painting don't exploit the naked body and venal love? Or that science doesn't teach us to look on fallen women simply as trading stock that has to be junked when necessary? In moral questions missionary *work is the only answer* . . .'

. . . *had accompanied Vasilyev to S. Street two days earlier* (p. 178).

'They've forgotten why they brought me here,' thought Vasilyev. 'I'm sure I'd feel better at home than here. I'm leaving.'

. . . *burst into tears and collapsed in the armchair* (p. 178). One pain distracted him from the other, and he felt better. The people that he had seen two days ago were vividly glimpsed in his imagination.

'They're alive, alive!' He clutched his head in despair. 'If I break this lamp you'll be sorry. But those aren't lamps, are they? They're living people!'

. . . *got him undressed, and began* (p. 178) measuring *the sensitivity of his skin* with something like a geometric compass.

Rage with the doctor, pity for himself, his tears—all these things really did make Vasilyev feel better. *When he left the doctor's* . . .

APPENDIX VI

THE COBBLER AND THE DEVIL

1. Composition
2. Text
3. Variants

1. COMPOSITION

The story was written in response to a telegram from S. N. Khudekov, editor of the newspaper *Peterburgskaya gazeta* [*The St. Petersburg Gazette*], offering Chekhov 100 roubles for a story of 200 lines for the paper's Christmas Day (1888) number. The author's own references to the story are all disparaging. On 17 December he wrote to A. S. Suvorin expressing an intention of 'scribbling some sort of mawkish rubbish' for Khudekov. On 19 December he mentioned, again to Suvorin, his intention of writing on a theme so 'pathetic' that he was ashamed of it. 'I'd refuse, but I don't want to lose the hundred roubles.' He began work on 20 December, and within two days the story had already been sent to the newspaper.

Chekhov remained dissatisfied with *The Cobbler and the Devil*, telling Suvorin that he was 'ashamed of it' (23 December). To Suvorin's reproaches that Chekhov had sent the story to *Peterburgskaya gazeta*—instead of to Suvorin's own newspaper, *Novoye vremya*—Chekhov replied: 'Not for all the tea in China would I give you something I think so thoroughly rotten, otherwise I'd adorn your paper every week and be a rich man . . . I really must spare one newspaper, and I must also preserve my own reputation as a contributor to *Novoye vremya*. As for *Peterburgskaya gazeta*, that will swallow anything.'

That Chekhov later modified his extreme antagonism to *The Cobbler and the Devil* we may infer from his decision to include it in his *Collected Works* of 1901 —albeit in considerably revised form, so that some of the defects which he sensed in 1888 have presumably been removed from the canonical version.

On its first appearance the story had a mixed reception from Chekhov's associates, one of the more judicious assessments being that of his friend and former editor N. A. Leykin: 'Though the story is Tolstoyan in spirit rather that Chekhovian, it's still very charming' (N. A. Leykin, cited in *Works*, 1974–82, *Sochineniya*, vol. vii, p. 665).

2. TEXT

The present translation is made from the text in *Works*, 1974–82, *Sochineniya*, vol. vii, itself based on that of Chekhov's *Collected Works* (1899), vol. i.

There is one previous recension: that published in the newspaper *Peterburgskaya gazeta* [*The St. Petersburg Gazette*] of 25 December 1888.

3. VARIANTS

Chekhov substantially revised the story when preparing it for his *Collected Works*. He rewrote the scene in which the cobbler signs his contract with the Devil, also introducing the brief episode set in hell, and removing two scenes in which the temporarily rich cobbler misbehaves. The longer and more important of these variants are as follows:

. . . *he's a sight more brainy than* (p. 185) what's written in books. Students and doctors spend ten years at their studies, and no good comes of it. But the Devil has only to spit once to create such a great fog that you can't see anything.'
'*Thank you for those kind words . . .*'

. . . *he asked with a low bow* (p. 186).
'It tasted good while I was eating,' puffed Theodore. 'But once I'd had enough I stopped enjoying it.'
He raised his left foot and began scrutinizing the boot.
'It's a Hamburg article, welted,' he said, snapping a finger on it. '*I never charged less than . . .* '

'*Clout him one, my man* (p. 186)*!*'
Theodore amused himself making fun of Lebyodkin until the man had tears in his eyes. Theodore felt sorry for him, remembering what a life his own customers had led him, and he felt both conscience-stricken and bored. To lull his conscience and *amuse himself, he took . . .*

. . . *the more discontented he grew* (p. 186).
'You should send Marya ten roubles,' the Devil advised.
Theodore thought, scratched the back of his head, and decided to send only three. He grudged the money. Never, when he had been poor, had he grudged it as he did now.
'This money's nothing but trouble,' he muttered, as he locked it in a chest. 'There's no pleasure from it, just a lot of worry. Not having money's a nuisance, but so is having it. It doesn't make sense.'

He couldn't sleep all night, and (p. 187) as morning came on he put on a dress shirt, studs, a frock-coat, a fur coat and galoshes, and went to church. In church he worshipped and kept looking about him to see if the neighbours had noticed his fur coat. But not a soul paid attention to his clothes. *Now, rich and poor receive . . .*

'*. . . so sign the paper* (p. 188).'
'Not likely! Why should I?'
'What do you mean?' asked the astonished Devil. 'You're a big noise now, you have lots of money and you're married to a lady.'
'That's all very well.' Theodore scratched himself. 'But none of it's any good, old man. It's all worry and no fun. Why don't you offer me something breath-takingly enjoyable. And stop me thinking about things while you're about it?'
'Ah, so you're trying to wriggle out, old son.' The Devil frowned. 'It looks as if you've decided to cheat. But it's dangerous to jest with me, friend. I'll force you to sign, dear boy.'
'Go on then, force me. You just try!'
'Indeed I will,' shouted the Devil, slamming down his fist on the table. 'Thought you'd trifle with me, eh? Oaf! Ass! I'll drag you off myself.'
'Then take that, O Unclean Spirit.' And Theodore crossed himself.
But suddenly it all vanished . . .

Church bells rang for matins (p. 188). After letting the customer out Theodore went over to the stove to wake Marya, and ten minutes later both were slowly making their way to church and gasping from the intense cold.
'Oh, you great lump!' said Theodore, and clouted Marya on the back twice. The woman laughed and he clicked his tongue to express his pleasure.
Carriages and sledges . . .

. . . sing at the top of their voices (p. 188), stagger round drunk and land a clout on their women's broad backs. He looked around him, but there was nothing more to tempt him, and nothing in the streets to make it *worth giving the Devil . . .*

APPENDIX VII

THE BET

1. Composition
2. Text
3. Variants

1. COMPOSITION

After finishing *The Cobbler and the Devil* on 22 December 1888, Chekhov immediately sat down to write *The Bet* in order to pacify his close friend A. S. Suvorin, proprietor of the newspaper *Novoye vremya* [*New Time*]—who, as we remember from Appendix VI (p. 267, above), had taken offence at Chekhov's willingness to contribute the earlier story to the rival *Peterburgskaya gazeta*. On 19 December Chekhov had written to Suvorin promising him a 'folk tale' [*skazka*] for the New Year, and four days later he reported having begun work on the previous evening. On the twenty-eighth of the month he informed Suvorin that the story was finished, and that he was sending it off. As first published the story bore the title mentioned in Chekhov's letter, above: *Skazka* [*A Folk Tale*]. It then consisted of three chapters, whereas the canonical version has only two, the third chapter having simply been jettisoned *in toto* when Chekhov revised the text for his *Collected Works*; see further under Variants, below.

2. TEXT

The present translation is made from the text in *Works*, 1974–82, *Sochineniya*, vol. vii, itself based on that of Chekhov's *Collected Works* (1901), vol. iv.

There is one previous recension: that published in the newspaper *Novoye vremya* [*New Time*] of 1 January 1889 under the title *Skazka* [*A Folk Tale*].

3. VARIANTS

When preparing the *Novoye vremya* text for his *Collected Works* Chekhov changed the title from *A Folk Tale* to *The Bet*; made numerous minor changes in the text of Chapters One and Two; scrapped his original Chapter Three entirely. In that rejected chapter the former voluntary prisoner—described as

renouncing two million roubles at the end of Chapter Two—is shown returning a year later to ask for his money, or some of it, from the horrified and
almost bankrupt banker. This dénouement disconcerted some of the story's
first readers, since it not only seemed to turn the story's apparent moral (the
vanity of earthly goods) on its head, but to do so inelegantly and obscurely.
On 17 June 1903, nearly fifteen years after first writing *The Bet*, Chekhov
referred to it in a letter to a Dr. A. N. Popova. She had written to him in the
hope of settling an argument with another reader who had a different recollection of the story's ending from her own, and one evidently based on the
Novoye vremya version of 1889. 'In *Novoye vremya* of the 1880s [Chekhov
replied] I did indeed have the story published with the ending that was described to you. Later on, when I read it in proof, I took a strong dislike to that
ending—I forget the details now. I found it exceedingly frigid and obscure, and
so I abandoned it. I threw it out, adding two or three lines to replace it, and the
result is what—you now find—gives a diametrically opposite sense. I realize
now, of course, that I should not have published the story in the book [vol. iv
(1901) of his *Collected Works*], but why I did so and how it came about I don't
remember—it was so long ago.' Incidentally, Chekhov's memory betrayed
him over the 'two or three' substitute lines that he recalled putting in place of
the rejected Chapter Three, since he had simply expunged that chapter without making any substitution at all.

The four passages immediately following constitute the most important
among the numerous minor variants contained in the *Novoye vremya* text of
Chapters One and Two. These are followed by the whole of the rejected
Chapter Three.

. . . *the prisoner's notes demanded only* (p. 193) Shakespeare and Byron, but in
the third year, having probably tired of this particular field, he began ordering
works on Roman law and political economy. In the fourth year he again
asked for Byron and Shakespeare, together with Homer, Voltaire and Goethe.
In the fifth year . . .

. . . *eagerly grasping first one spar and then another* (p. 193). The last book that
he read was Cervantes's *Don Quixote*, and the one before that was Count
Tolstoy's *What I Believe*.

. . . *the dark hulk of a cast-iron stove in the corner* (p. 194), and on the slumping
shelf, amid boxes and books in old bindings, lay a stuffed eagle—broken and
with one wing sticking up.

He was sitting near the table (p. 195) in the posture of one reading a fascinating
but indecipherable manuscript.

The next variant consists of the rejected Chapter Three *in toto*:

III

A year passed and the banker was giving another party. It was attended by a good few clever people, and fascinating discussions took place, among the topics being the purpose of existence and the function of humanity. They spoke about the rich young man [in the Gospels], about self-perfection, about love as preached in the Gospels, about the vanity of vanities and so on. The guests, consisting for the most part of very wealthy men, almost all disparaged riches.

'Among those regarded as saints or geniuses, rich men are as rare as comets in the sky,' said one guest. 'It follows that wealth is not an essential prerequisite for the refinement of the human breed—or, more briefly, that it is quite superfluous. And anything superfluous is only a hindrance.'

'Of course,' agreed a second guest. 'And that's why the loftiest expression of human perfectibility—albeit a crude one, no more subtle manifestation having yet been invented—is monastic asceticism: that is, the complete renunciation of life for the sake of ideals. You can't serve ideals and the stock exchange at the same time.'

'I don't see why not,' a third guest interrupted irritably. 'To me the renunciation of life is wholly incompatible with the attainment of supreme perfection. Now, let's just get this straight. To reject a painting means rejecting the artist. To reject women, precious metals, wine and a good climate is to reject God, because God created all those things. But ascetics are supposed to be serving God, aren't they?'

'Quite true,' said an elderly millionaire, a rival of the banker's on the stock exchange. 'Besides which, ascetics only exist in people's imaginations. There aren't any on this earth. True, there are instances of old men renouncing women, of those who have too much of everything giving up money, and of disillusioned people turning their backs on fame. But I've been living on this earth for sixty-six years, and not once have I seen a strong, healthy, intelligent person who would turn his back on a million roubles, say.'

'Such people do exist,' said their host the banker.

'Have you ever seen one?'

'Happily, yes.'

'Impossible,' said the dubious millionaire.

'But I assure you. I know a poor man just like that, one who gave up two million on principle.'

'You've been taken in,' laughed the millionaire. 'I repeat, there are no such people, and I'm so sure of it I'm ready to bet anything—a million if you like.'

'Well, I bet three million,' shouted the banker.

'Done. Gentlemen, I accept the three million wager.'

The banker's head spun. So confident was he of victory that he was already regretting not having staked five million, a sum that would have sufficed to restore his fortunes on the exchange.

'Shake hands on it!' shouted the millionaire. 'Now, when will you show me your proofs?'

'This instant,' said the banker triumphantly.

He was about to go to his study to fetch the renunciation document from his fire-proof safe, but a footman came in and told him that 'a gentleman' wished to see him.

Excusing himself to his guests, the banker left the room. Barely had he reached the hall when he was pounced upon by a respectably dressed man, strikingly pale and with tears in his eyes, who clutched his sleeve.

'Pray excuse me,' said the newcomer in quavering tones.

'What can I do for you? And who are you?' asked the banker.

'I am that selfsame imbecile who wasted fifteen years of his life and renounced his two million.'

'But what can I do for you?' repeated the banker, turning pale.

'Oh, how wrong I was! No one should dare to judge life unless he knows it, and has the strength to enjoy its blessings. The sun shines so brightly! Women are so enchantingly beautiful! Wine tastes so good! Trees are magnificent things. Books are only a feeble shadow of reality, and it's this shadow that has robbed me.' The lawyer went down on his knees. 'My dear man, I don't ask you for the two million, for I have no right to it. But do give me one or two hundred thousand, I beg you. Otherwise I'll kill myself.'

'Very well,' said the banker in a hollow voice. 'Tomorrow you shall have what you want.'

He hurried back to his guests in a state of exaltation. He felt a burning desire to proclaim aloud to all and sundry there and then that he, the banker, deeply despised his millions, the stock exchange, freedom, the love of women, health and men's words, and that he voluntarily renounced life, would give all he had to the poor on the morrow, and intended to abjure the world. But on entering his banqueting hall he remembered that his debts exceeded his assets, that he no longer had the strength to love women and drink wine, for which reason his renunciation would seem to lack validity. Remembering this, he sank exhausted into an armchair.

'You win,' said he. 'I am ruined.'

APPENDIX VIII

LIGHTS

1. COMPOSITION

The composition of *Lights* was spread over two to three months, the story being completed on 23 April 1888. To contemporaries the town of 'N.', which forms the scene of the action, was immediately recognizable as Chekhov's home town Taganrog. Besides the area known as 'the Quarantine' (both in the story and in real life, and also called 'the Yelizaveta Park'), contemporaries claimed to recognize, in *Lights*, Taganrog's 'Petrovsky Street' and 'Hotel Europa' (in Chekhov's 'High Street' and in his unnamed hotel), together with some of the local inhabitants and their way of life; for instance, references to Taganrog's sizeable Greek population are not uncommon in the story; see further, A. B. Tarakhovsky, as cited in *Works*, 1974–82, *Sochineniya*, vol. vii, p. 646.

References in Chekhov's correspondence reflect his intense dissatisfaction with *Lights* both during and after the period of its composition. They also allude to extensive draft versions that were rejected and have not survived. Among the rejected passages was some sort of final 'show-down' between Ananyev and Kitty, eventually abandoned by Chekhov as 'an unimportant detail that held up the story' (*letter to A. S. Suvorin, 30 May 1888*).

Chekhov had begun work in February 1888. 'I've hardly done anything since *The Steppe*. I did start a gloomy short story [*Lights*] . . . wrote about three thousand words, not all that badly, but then put it aside till March' (*letter to Ya. P. Polonsky, 22 Feb. 1888*). Chekhov next alludes to *Lights*, in a letter of late March 1888 to A. N. Pleshcheyev, as a 'sort of longish story' (*povestushka*) which he is writing for *Severny vestnik*, but which is only 'limping along'. As the journal's literary editor, Pleshcheyev urged Chekhov to press on, but his progress was slow. 'I should have finished it long ago, but—alas!—I feel I'll hardly be done by May. To my sorrow it isn't taking shape properly—doesn't satisfy me, in other words, and I've decided not to send it to you until I've got it taped. Today I read everything I had written, made a fair copy, thought it over, and decided to start all over again. . . . It's as boring as the doldrums. I've shortened it, polished it, done a little sleight-of-hand on it, and I'm so sick of the wretched business that I've sworn to finish it by May, come what may, or else scrap the bloody thing (*letter to A. N. Pleshcheyev, 9 April 1888*). The story was turning out very boring, Chekhov wrote to V. G. Korolenko on the same day. 'I play all sorts of tricks, I shorten it, I polish it, but boring it remains. I'll be publicly disgraced!'

Other comments on work in progress from Chekhov's correspondence are:

'I've recast the *entire* framework, leaving only the foundation intact, since I disliked the thing *as a whole*, not its details. . . . It won't be much good, in fact, and the critics will only turn up their noses. This isn't false modesty. Its merits are brevity and an occasional touch of originality.' (*Letter to A. N. Pleshcheyev, 17 April 1888.*)

'I'm finishing an exceedingly tedious story. I decided to put in a bit of philosophy, but the result is a load of old codswallop. Reading over what I've written I salivate and feel nausea. It's ghastly. Anyway, to hell with it!' (*Letter to I. L. Leontyev [Shcheglov], 18 April 1888.*)

After dispatching *Lights* to *Severny vestnik* at the end of April, Chekhov continued to express dissatisfaction with the story: 'I'm rather ashamed of it. It's a bore, and there's so much sickly philosophical clap-trap.' (*Letter to I. L. Leontyev [Shcheglov], 3 May 1888.*)

The reactions of contemporary readers, critics and reviewers were extremely varied, many virtues being discovered in *Lights* despite a general tendency to share the author's own view that it was unsuccessful. That he maintained this low opinion until the end of his life we infer from his decision to exclude *Lights* from his *Collected Works* as published by A. F. Marks from 1899 onwards. *Lights* thus became the only one among Chekhov's 'Thick Journal' stories to be deliberately excluded by the author from his *Collected Works*; but see also *The Oxford Chekhov*, vol. ix, pp. ix–x, for comments on *All Friends Together*.

Low though Chekhov's opinion of *Lights* may have been, he was at least prepared to defend one aspect of the story: his alleged failure to offer, on its pages, any cut-and-dried author's solution to the problems faced by his characters. Complaints to this effect reached him from two close friends, I. L. Leontyev [Shcheglov] and A. S. Suvorin.

The former wrote, in a letter of 29 May 1888, that the ending ('Nothing in this world makes sense') was too abrupt. 'That's just what the writer's job is: to make sense of things, especially of his hero's inner world, but you don't make his psychology clear.' To this Chekhov replied as follows. 'I shall permit myself to disagree with you about the ending of *Lights*. It's not the psychologist's job to simulate understanding of what is incomprehensible to him. Furthermore, it's not his job to pretend he understands things that no one understands. So let's avoid all confidence tricks and state outright that nothing in this world makes sense. The only people who know and understand everything are idiots and charlatans' (*letter to I. L. Leontyev [Shcheglov], 9 June 1888*).

As for Suvorin's criticism, that has not survived, but it is evident from Chekhov's reply that his supposed failure to deal adequately with the problem of pessimism was the point at issue. 'You write that neither the discussion of pessimism nor my heroine's experiences shift or solve the problem of pessimism to the slightest extent. In my view it's not the writer's job to solve such problems as God, pessimism and so on. The writer's job is only to show who, how, in what context, spoke or thought about God and pessimism. The artist must not be the judge of his characters and of what they say: merely a dispassionate observer. . . . It's time that writers . . . realized that nothing in this world makes sense, as Socrates and Voltaire acknowledged in their day. . . . If the artist, in whom the rabble believes, ventures to declare that he understands nothing of what he sees, then that fact alone will form a substantial theoretical contribution and a great step forward' (*letter to A. S. Suvorin, 30 May 1888*).

2. TEXT

The present translation is made from the text in *Works*, 1974–82, *Sochineniya*, vol. vii, itself based on that published in the magazine *Severny vestnik* [*The Northern Herald*] of June 1888.

There are no other recensions.

3. VARIANTS

Though Chekhov rejected and rewrote drafts of the story (see Composition, above), none of the variants has survived.

NOTES

THE following notes, which have been kept as brief as possible, are designed to explain references in the text which might be obscure to English-speaking readers and to point out certain difficulties that have occurred in the translation.

Page

15 'a school of the type intended for gentlemen's sons.' In the context this phrase effectively translates the original *gimnaziya*. These 'high schools', as the word is elsewhere rendered, were maintained by the State, set exacting standards, and though originally intended for sons of the gentry (*dvoryan-stvo*), were not exclusive to them. Chekhov, himself a shopkeeper's son, had graduated from the *gimnaziya* at Taganrog in south Russia in 1879.

15 'a minor official.' Literally, 'a Collegiate Secretary': Class Ten in the Table of Ranks instituted for the civil service by Peter the Great in 1722.

16 'the day of Our Lady of Kazan.' According to tradition the Kazan Icon of the Virgin had been miraculously discovered in the ground at Kazan in 1579 by a ten-year-old girl. This event was celebrated annually, on 8 July, from 1595 onwards.

17 'Lomonosov.' M. V. Lomonosov (1711–65) was the son of a fisherman in the north Russian port of Archangel. He ran away to Moscow at the age of seventeen, and became famous as a scientist, educationist, poet and grammarian.

22 'on the saint's day of our most pious Sovereign Alexander the First of Blessed Memory.' Reference is to the Emperor Alexander I (1777–1825), who succeeded to the Russian throne in 1801, his saint's day being 30 August.

24 'And the Cherubims.' Ezekiel 10:19.

31 'the Two-Headed Eagle.' The emblem of Imperial Russia.

31 'the Molokan's farm.' The Molokans were members of a religious sect that arose in about 1765, and are sometimes said to derive their name from a habit of drinking milk (*moloko*) during Lent.

33 'an official application form.' In order to possess legal validity official applications of certain types had to be transcribed on *gerbovaya bumaga*: special paper bearing the Imperial Russian crest and sold at a price that constituted a form of taxation on the given transaction.

34 'Chernigov.' Large town in the Ukraine, about 80 miles north of Kiev.

45 'giants with seven-league boots.' Literally, 'broad-striding people like Ilya Muromets and Solovey the Brigand': two heroes from Russian folk myth.

47 'Slavyanoserbsk.' Small town in the Donbass, about 100 miles north of Taganrog.

Page

47 'St. Georgie-Porgie.' Reference is to St. George, the patron saint of England, martyred in Palestine, probably in the third or fourth century A.D. The name 'Yegor' (of which 'Yegorushka' is a derivative) is an alternative form to Russian 'Georgy' (George); the speaker here employs other variants: 'Yegory' and the comically eccentric form 'Yegorgy'.

47 'Tim in Kursk County.' Tim is a small town, about 400 miles south of Moscow, near the administrative centre of Kursk in central European Russia.

48 'St Barbara.' Martyred under Mamiminus Thrax (235–8) according to legend; the patron saint of pyrotechnicians.

50 'Lugansk.' Large town in the Ukraine, about 100 miles north of Taganrog.

50 'Donets.' River in the Ukraine and the south of European Russia, a tributary of the Don.

57 'Vyazma.' Large town about 160 miles west of Moscow.

59 'Nizhny Novgorod.' Large town, about 250 miles east of Moscow, now called Gorky.

61 'Oryol.' Large town, about 200 miles south of Moscow.

64 'Morshansk.' Small town, about 240 miles south-east of Moscow.

68 'a Dissenter.' That is, an adherent of the 'Old Belief'—the ritual of the Russian Orthodox Church as practised before the reforms of the Patriarch Nikon in the mid-seventeenth century.

70 'St Peter's Day.' 29 June.

90 'Peter Mogila.' A leading seventeenth-century cleric and educationist (1596–1647), who became Metropolitan of Kiev in 1632.

90 'Be not carried about . . .' Hebrews 13: 9.

90 'Basil the Great.' Leading fourth-century churchman (329–79).

90 'St. Nestor.' Ancient Russian historian and chronicler whose exact dates are unknown but who was probably a monk at the Monastery of the Caves, Kiev, in the late eleventh century.

103 *'The Physician.'* *Vrach:* a monthly medical newspaper, published in St. Petersburg from 1880 onwards.

109 'had attained high rank.' Literally, 'held the rank of Actual State Councillor'. This was Class Four in the Table of Ranks instituted for the civil service by Peter the Great in 1722.

114 'Blessed are the peacemakers.' Matthew 5: 9.

119 'Don Region . . . Rostov-on-Don.' Rostov-on-Don, a large town on the River Don, about 13 miles from its mouth in the Sea of Azov.

123 'Nakhichevan.' Nakhichevan-on-Don was a small town, an Armenian colony founded in 1780 near Rostov-on-Don, with which it is now merged.

123 'Belgorod.' Town about 40 miles north-east of Kharkov.

123 'Kharkov.' Large city in the Ukraine.

Page

124 'Russian national costume.' 'This [for women] usually consisted of a white, puff-sleeved embroidered blouse, worn with a full gathered skirt on a yoke ... and a white pinafore. With it went several rows of multicoloured beribboned beads and a red, or other bright-coloured, kerchief.' (Birkett and Struve, *Anton Chekhov* ..., p. 136.)

125 'The second bell.' Passengers on Russian railways were warned of a train's departure by a succession of three rings. 'The first (single) ring took place a quarter of an hour before departure, the second (double) ring gave five minutes' warning, and on the third (triple) peal the train pulled out.' (Hingley, *Russian Writers* ..., p. 40.)

132 'Poltava.' Town in the Ukraine, about 70 miles south-west of Kharkov.

141 'If you marry a Tolstoyan he'll make you mow.' The novelist and thinker L. N. Tolstoy (1828–1910) was a proselytizing simple-lifer.

141 'the Proudhons and the Buckles.' Reference is to the French Socialist thinker Pierre Joseph Proudhon (1809–65); and to Henry Thomas Buckle (1821–62), the English social historian and author of *History of Civilization* (1857–61), which enjoyed a great vogue in Russia.

142 'Schopenhauer.' The German philosopher Arthur Schopenhauer (1788–1860).

142 'Elijah's Day.' 20 June.

144 'Butlerov hives.' The invention of A. M. Butlerov (1828–86), an eminent Russian chemist whose other interests included agriculture, tea-growing in the Caucasus and spiritualism.

159 'Moscow Institute of Painting, Sculpture and Architecture.' In north-west Moscow.

159 'the Tver Boulevard.' In north-west Moscow.

160 'Against my will to these sad shores ...' The Prince's aria from the opera *The Mermaid* (first performed 1856) by A. S. Dargomyzhsky (1813–69), itself based on the dramatic poem *The Mermaid* (1832) by A. S. Pushkin (1799–1837).

161 'Trubny Square ... Grachovka Road.' In the north of central Moscow.

164 '*The Leaflet.*' Reference is to *Moskovsky listok* [*The Moscow Leaflet*], a political and literary weekly (1881–1918).

166 'Marshal Bazaine.' François Achille Bazaine (1811–88), French army commander in the Franco-Prussian War, who was court-martialled for dereliction of duty in 1873.

166 'Smolensk.' Large town, about 240 miles west of Moscow.

167 'Aida.' Heroine of Verdi's opera *Aida*, set in ancient Egypt and first produced in Russia in 1875 at St. Petersburg.

171 '*The Meadow.*' *Niva*, a weekly illustrated magazine for family reading (St. Petersburg, 1870–1918).

Page

171 '... today's a Wednesday.' For members of the Russian Orthodox Church the Wednesday and Friday of each week were fast-days.

174 'Saratov.' Town on the Volga, about 500 miles south-east of Moscow.

176 'Sadovy Street ... Sukharev Tower ... Red Gate ... Basmanny Street ... Razgulyay.' Vasilyev's walk began in the north of central Moscow (at a point about two miles north of the Kremlin), taking him about five miles in an easterly direction before he turned southwards towards the River Yauza (a tributary of the Moscow River) and the Red Barracks. The whole distance, there and back, must have been at least fifteen miles.

196 'Elbrus.' The highest mountain (18,470 ft.) in the main Caucasian range.

204 'declined into the vale of years.' Shakespeare, *Othello*, III. iii.

205 'Baltic baronial ancestry.' In the Baltic lands, as incorporated in Russia by Peter the Great in the early eighteenth century, the social élite consisted of Germans, some of whom had the title baron. Such Baltic Germans, or 'Baltic barons'—russified except in respect of their surnames and a reputation for stern efficiency—were prominent in Imperial Russia's civil and military hierarchies.

207 'soon after the War.' Reference is to the Russo-Turkish War of 1877-8.

208 'Chukhloma.' Small town, about 275 miles north-east of Moscow.

208 'Kashira.' Town, about 70 miles south of Moscow.

209 'He stood on that deserted strand ...' The opening lines of Pushkin's poem *The Bronze Horseman*, written in 1833.

209 'Sakhalin.' The large island and penal colony (which Chekhov was to visit in 1890) in the Russian Far East between the Sea of Okhotsk and the Sea of Japan.

212 'But these are tales of ancient times ...' The couplet comes from Canto One of Pushkin's poem *Ruslan and Lyudmila* (1820).

214 'Malinin and Burenin.' Reference is to *Sobraniye arifmeticheskich zadach dlya gimnazy* [*Collected Arithmetic Problems for High Schools*] by A. Malinin and K. Burenin (Moscow, 1866), p. 126.

217 'Santorin wine.' The Greek island of Santorin, also known as Thera, is the southernmost island in the Cyclades. 'Its excellent red and white grapes, the island's chief product, are made into strong wine exported principally to Odessa.' (Brokgauz and Efron, *Entsiklopedichesky slovar*, vol. 56, St. Petersburg, 1900), p. 366.

220 'Circassians.' Inhabitants of an area in the northern Caucasus.

222 'For the hour is coming ...' John 5: 28.

225 'Pyatigorsk.' Town and health resort in the northern Caucasus.

228 'a Yakut's.' The Yakuts, a Turkic-speaking people living over a large area in eastern Siberia, have been subject to Russia since the seventeenth century.

230 'Mount Ararat.' The highest point (17,000 ft.) in Armenia.

SELECT BIBLIOGRAPHY

I. BIBLIOGRAPHIES IN ENGLISH

Two useful, but now somewhat dated, bibliographies, published by the New York Public Library and containing in all nearly five hundred items, give a comprehensive picture of the literature relating to Chekhov published in English—translations of his writings, biographical and critical studies, memoirs, essays, articles etc. They are:

> *Chekhov in English: a List of Works by and about him.* Compiled by Anna Heifetz. Ed. and with a Foreword by Avrahm Yarmolinsky (New York, 1949) and
>
> *The Chekhov Centennial Chekhov in English: a Selective List of Works by and about him, 1949-60.* Compiled by Rissa Yachnin (New York, 1960).

Bibliographies in English will also be found in the books by David Magarshack *(Chekhov: a Life)*, Ernest J. Simmons and Ronald Hingley mentioned in Section III, below. Magarshack provides a bibliographic index of Chekhov's writings in alphabetical order of their English titles, Simmons includes a list of bibliographies in Russian. Hingley (1950) gives a list of Chekhov's translated stories in chronological order, while Hingley (1976) has an appendix on 'Chekhov in English', and another which discusses the 'Shape of Chekhov's Work' as a whole.

II. TRANSLATIONS INTO ENGLISH OF THE STORIES IN THIS VOLUME

(Where the titles of translated stories differ from those in the present volume, the title adopted here is given in square brackets if the difference is so great as to make it difficult to identify the story.)

(a) TR. BY CONSTANCE GARNETT

The Party, and Other Stories (New York, 1917).
  Includes: *The Party.*

The Bishop, and Other Stories (London, 1919).
  Includes: *The Steppe.*

The Schoolmistress, and Other Stories (London, 1920).
  Includes: *A Nervous Breakdown, The Bet, The Beauties, The Shoemaker and the Devil.*

Love, and Other Stories (London, 1922).
Includes: *Lights.*

(b) BY OTHER TRANSLATORS

Russian Silhouettes: More Stories of Russian Life. Tr. Marian Fell (London, 1915).
Includes: *Two Beautiful Girls* [*The Beauties*].

The Steppe, and Other Stories. Tr. Adeline Lister Kaye (London, 1915).
Includes: *The Steppe.*

The Bet, and Other Stories. Tr. S. Koteliansky and J. M. Murry (Dublin, 1915).
Includes: *The Bet.*

The Grasshopper, and Other Stories. Tr. with Introduction by A. E. Chamot
(London, 1926).
Includes: *The Wager* [*The Bet*].

The Second Bet [Chapter Three of *The Bet*], tr. Janka Karsavina, *The Golden
Book Magazine* (New York, 1931), vol. 14, pp. 15–17.

Tchekhov's Plays and Stories. Tr. S. S. Koteliansky. Introduction by David
Magarshack (London, 1937).
Includes: *A Fairy Tale* [Chapter Three of *The Bet*].

The Woman in the Case, and Other Stories. Tr. April Fitzlyon and Kyril Zino-
vieff. Introduction by Andrew G. Colin (London, 1953).
Includes: *An Unpleasant Incident* [*An Awkward Business*].

The Unknown Chekhov: Stories and Other Writings. Tr. with Introduction by
Avrahm Yarmolinsky (London, 1959).
Includes: *An Unpleasantness* [*An Awkward Business*].

Anton Chekhov: Selected Stories. Tr. with Introduction by Jessie Coulson
(London, 1963).
Includes: *The Beauties.*

Ward Six, and Other Stories. Tr. Ann Dunnigan. Afterword by Rufus W.
Matthewson.
Includes: *The Name-Day Party* [*The Party*].

III. BIOGRAPHICAL AND CRITICAL STUDIES

Leon Shestov, *Anton Tchekhov and Other Essays* (Dublin and London, 1916).
William Gerhardi, *Anton Chekhov: a Critical Study* (London, 1923).
Oliver Elton, *Chekhov* (The Taylorian Lecture, 1929; Oxford, 1929).

Nina Andronikova Toumanova, *Anton Chekhov: the Voice of Twilight Russia* (London, 1937).

W. H. Bruford, *Chekhov and his Russia: a Sociological Study* (London, 1948).

Ronald Hingley, *Chekhov: a Biographical and Critical Study* (London, 1950).

Irene Nemirovsky, *A Life of Chekhov.* Tr. from the French by Erik de Mauny (London, 1950).

David Magarshack, *Chekhov: a Life* (London, 1952).

David Magarshack, *Chekhov the Dramatist* (London, 1952).

Vladimir Yermilov [Ermilov], *Anton Pavlovich Chekhov, 1860–1904.* Tr. Ivy Litvinov (Moscow, 1956; London, 1957).

W. H. Bruford, *Anton Chekhov* (London, 1957).

T. Eekman, ed., *Anton Chekhov, 1860–1960* (Leiden, 1960).

Beatrice Saunders, *Tchehov the Man* (London, 1960).

Ernest J. Simmons, *Chekhov: a Biography* (Boston, Toronto, 1962; London, 1963).

Maurice Valency, *The Breaking String: the Plays of Anton Chekhov* (New York, 1966).

Thomas Winner, *Chekhov and his Prose* (New York, 1966).

Robert Louis Jackson, ed., *Chekhov: a Collection of Critical Essays* (Englewood Cliffs, N.J., 1967).

Nils Åke Nilsson, *Studies in Čechov's Narrative Technique:* The Steppe *and* The Bishop (Stockholm, 1968).

Karl D. Kramer, *The Chameleon and the Dream: the Image of Reality in Čexov's Stories* (The Hague, 1970).

J. L. Styan, *Chekhov in Performance: a Commentary on the Major Plays* (Cambridge, 1971).

Siegfried Melchinger, *Anton Chekhov.* Tr. by Edith Tarcov (New York, 1972).

Virginia Llewellyn Smith, *Anton Chekhov and the Lady with the Dog.* Foreword by Ronald Hingley (London, 1973).

Harvey Pitcher, *The Chekhov Play: a New Interpretation* (London, 1973).

Sophie Laffitte, *Chekhov, 1860–1904.* Tr. from the French by Moura Budberg and Gordon Latta (London, 1974).

Donald Rayfield, *Chekhov: the Evolution of his Art* (London, 1975).

Caryl Brahms, *Reflections in a Lake: a Study of Chekhov's Four Greatest Plays* (London, 1976).

Ronald Hingley, *A New Life of Anton Chekhov* (London, 1976).

Beverly Hahn, *Chekhov: a Study of the Major Stories and Plays* (Cambridge, 1977).

Paul Debreczeny and Thomas Eekman, ed., *Chekhov's Art of Writing: a Collection of Critical Essays* (Columbus, Ohio, 1977).

Kornei Chukovsky, *Chekhov the Man*. Tr. Pauline Rose (London, n.d.).

IV. LETTERS AND MEMOIR MATERIAL, ETC.

Letters of Anton Tchehov to his Family and Friends. Tr. Constance Garnett (London, 1920).

The Note-books of Anton Tchekhov together with Reminiscences of Tchekhov by Maxim Gorky. Tr. S. S. Koteliansky and Leonard Woolf (Richmond, Surrey, 1921).

Letters on the Short Story, the Drama and other Literary Topics. By Anton Chekhov. Selected and ed. Louis S. Friedland (New York, 1924).

Konstantin Stanislavsky, *My Life in Art*. Tr. J. J. Robbins (London, 1924; New York, 1956).

The Life and Letters of Anton Tchekhov. Tr. and ed. S. S. Koteliansky and Philip Tomlinson (London, 1925).

The Letters of Anton Pavlovitch Tchehov to Olga Leonardovna Knipper. Tr. Constance Garnett (London, 1926).

Anton Tchekhov: Literary and Theatrical Reminiscences. Tr. and ed. S. S. Koteliansky (London, 1927).

Vladimir Nemirovitch-Dantchenko, *My Life in the Russian Theatre*. Tr. John Cournos (London, 1937).

The Personal Papers of Anton Chekhov. Introduction by Matthew Josephson (New York, 1948).

Lydia Avilov, *Chekhov in my Life: a Love Story*. Tr. with an Introduction by David Magarshack (London, 1950).

Konstantin Stanislavsky, *Stanislavsky on the Art of the Stage*. Tr. with an introductory essay on Stanislavsky's 'System' by David Magarshack (London, 1950).

The Selected Letters of Anton Chekhov. Ed. Lillian Hellman, tr. Sidonie Lederer (New York, 1955).

Letters of Anton Chekhov. Tr. Michael Henry Heim in collaboration with Simon Karlinsky. Selection, Commentary and Introduction by Simon Karlinsky (New York, 1973).

Letters of Anton Chekhov. Selected and edited by Avrahm Yarmolinsky (New York, 1973).

V. OTHER WORKS USED IN THE PREPARATION OF THIS VOLUME

P. Semyonov (compiler), *Geografichesko-istorichesky slovar Rossiskoy imperii* (St. Petersburg, 1862–85).

F. A. Brokgauz and I. A. Efron, *Entsiklopedichesky slovar* (St. Petersburg, 1900).

Vsya Moskva na 1911 god (Moscow, 1911) [gazetteer].

Karl Baedeker, *Russia with Teheran, Port Arthur and Peking: Handbook for Travellers* (Leipzig, 1914).

Polnoye sobraniye sochineny i pisem A. P. Chekhova, ed. S. D. Balukhaty, V. P. Potyomkin, N. S. Tikhonov, A. M. Yegolin, 20 vols. (Moscow, 1944–51).

G. A. Birkett and Gleb Struve, ed., *Anton Chekhov: Selected Short Stories* (Oxford, 1951).

N. I. Gitovich, *Letopis zhizni i tvorchestva A. P. Chekhova* (Moscow, 1955).

Literaturnoye nasledstvo: Chekhov, ed. V. V. Vinogradov and others (Moscow, 1960).

A. P. Chekhov, *Polnoye sobraniye sochineny i pisem v tridtsati tomakh* (Moscow, from 1974; to be completed in 1982).

Ronald Hingley, *Russian Writers and Society in the Nineteenth Century*, 2nd, revised, edition (London, 1977).